A RED HERRING *Without* MUSTARD

"Alan Bradley's third Flavia de Luce mystery, *A Red Herring Without Mustard*, exceeds in every way, if that's even possible, his first two. Flavia uses her trademark cunning by scheming to get even with her older sisters, who lie in wait to torment her. She saves a Gypsy's life, befriends Porcelain, the Gypsy's granddaughter, solves a puzzling and bizarre murder involving an ancient nonconformist cult, collects clues the police have missed, and fearlessly ventures into danger. She is always feisty, always smart. I adore her. And while it is wonderful to read her as an adult, I wish I'd had Flavia as a role model while growing up. It's cool to be smart. It's cool to be Flavia! And it's great to be among her legion of fans."

—LOUISE PENNY, bestselling author
of *The Brutal Telling*

"As satisfying as the mystery is, the multiple-award-winning Bradley offers more. . . . Beautifully written, with fully fleshed characters . . . [Bradley] secures his position as a confident, talented writer and storyteller."

—*The Globe and Mail*

"Outstanding . . . In this marvelous blend of whimsy and mystery, Flavia manages to operate successfully in the adult world of crimes and passions while dodging the childhood pitfalls set by her sisters."

—*Publishers Weekly* (starred review)

The WEED That STRINGS the HANGMAN'S BAG

"Harriet the Spy by way of Agatha Christie, with a dash of Lemony Snicket and the Addams Family. Who could resist?"

—*The Globe and Mail*

"Flavia is incisive, cutting and hilarious . . . one of the most remarkable creations in recent literature."

—*USA Today*

"Bradley takes everything you expect and subverts it, delivering a smart, irreverent, unsappy mystery."

—*Entertainment Weekly*

"The real delight here is her droll voice and the eccentric cast. . . . Utterly beguiling."

—*People* (four stars)

"Flavia is a strikingly enjoyable heroine. . . . *The Weed That Strings the Hangman's Bag* offers a surfeit of pleasures, an old-fashioned puzzler of red herrings, left turns and sharp twists. It should easily please Bradley's fans, and newcomers will find themselves happily falling for Flavia's exploits."

—*Winnipeg Free Press*

The SWEETNESS *at the* BOTTOM *of the* PIE

BY ALAN BRADLEY

The Sweetness at the Bottom of the Pie

The Weed That Strings the Hangman's Bag

A Red Herring Without Mustard

I Am Half-Sick of Shadows

Speaking from Among the Bones

SPEAKING
FROM AMONG
the BONES

...

SPEAKING

FROM AMONG

the BONES

A *Flavia de Luce Novel*

ALAN BRADLEY

• • •

DOUBLEDAY CANADA

Doubleday Canada and colophon are registered trademarks

Library and Archives Canada Cataloguing in Publication
Bradley, Alan, 1938–
Speaking from among the bones : a novel / Alan Bradley.
Issued also in electronic format.
ISBN 978-0-385-66812-5
I. Title.
PS8603.R3315S64 2013   C813'.6   C2012-906538-2

This book is a work of fiction. Names, characters, places and incidents are
products of the author's imagination or are used fictitiously. Any resemblance
to actual events or locales or persons, living or dead, is entirely coincidental.

Text design by Diane Hobbing
Cover design: Joe Montgomery
Cover art: Ben Perini
Printed and bound in the USA

Published in Canada by Doubleday Canada,
a division of Random House of Canada Limited

Visit Random House of Canada Limited's website: www.randomhouse.ca

10 9 8 7 6 5 4 3 2 1

For Shirley

Now from yon black and fun'ral yew,
That bathes the charnel-house with dew,
Methinks I hear a voice begin;
(Ye ravens, cease your croaking din;
Ye tolling clocks, no time resound
O'er the long lake and midnight ground)
It sends a peal of hollow groans,
Thus speaking from among the bones.

THOMAS PARNELL
A Night-Piece on Death (1721)

SPEAKING
FROM AMONG
the BONES

...

· O N E ·

BLOOD DRIPPED FROM THE neck of the severed head and fell in a drizzle of red raindrops, clotting into a ruby pool upon the black and white tiles. The face wore a grimace of surprise, as if the man had died in the middle of a scream. His teeth, each clearly divided from its neighbor by a black line, were bared in a horrible, silent scream.

I couldn't take my eyes off the thing.

The woman who proudly held the gaping head at arm's length by its curly blue-black hair was wearing a scarlet dress—almost, but not quite, the color of the dead man's blood.

To one side, a servant with downcast eyes held the platter upon which she had carried the head into the room. Seated on a wooden throne, a matron in a saffron dress leaned forward in square-jawed pleasure, her hands clenched into fists on the arms of her chair as she took a good look at the grisly trophy. Her name was Herodias, and she was the wife of the king.

The younger woman, the one clutching the head, was—at least, according to the historian Flavius Josephus—named Salome. She was the stepdaughter of the king, whose name was Herod, and Herodias was her mother.

The detached head, of course, belonged to John the Baptist.

I remembered hearing the whole sordid story not more than a month ago when Father read aloud the Second Lesson from the back of the great carved wooden eagle which served as the lectern at St. Tancred's.

On that winter morning I had gazed up, transfixed, just as I was gazing now, at the stained-glass window in which this fascinating scene was depicted.

Later, during his sermon, the vicar had explained that in Old Testament times, our blood was thought to contain our lives.

Of course!

Blood!

Why hadn't I thought of it before?

"Feely," I said, tugging at her sleeve, "I have to go home."

My sister ignored me. She peered closely at the music book as, in the dusky shadows of the fading light, her fingers flew like white birds over the keys of the organ.

Mendelssohn's *Wie gross ist des Allmächt'gen Güte*.

"'How great are the works of the Almighty,'" she told me it meant.

Easter was now less than a week away and Feely was trying to whip the piece into shape for her official debut as organist of St. Tancred's. The flighty Mr. Collicutt, who had held the post only since last summer, had vanished suddenly from our village without explanation and Feely had been asked to step into his shoes.

St. Tancred's went through organists like a python goes through white mice. Years ago, there had been Mr. Taggart, then Mr. Denning. It was now Mr. Collicutt's kick at the cat.

"Feely," I said. "It's important. There's something I have to do."

Feely jabbed one of the ivory coupling buttons with her thumb and the organ gave out a roar. I loved this part of the piece: the point where it leaps in an instant from sounding like a quiet sea at sunset to the snarl of a jungle animal.

When it comes to organ music, loud is good—at least to my way of thinking.

I tucked my knees up under my chin and huddled back into the corner of the choir stall. It was obvious that Feely was going to slog her way through to the end come hell or high water, and I would simply have to wait it out.

I looked at my surroundings but there wasn't much to see. In the feeble glow of the single bulb above the music rack, Feely and I might as well have been castaways on a tiny raft of light in a sea of darkness.

By twisting my neck and tilting my head back like a hanged man, I could just make out the head of Saint Tancred, which was carved in English oak at the end of a hammer beam in the roof of the nave. In the weird evening light, he had the look of a man with his nose pressed flat against a window, peering in from the cold to a cozy room with a cheery fire burning on the hearth.

I gave him a respectful bob of my head, even though I knew he couldn't see me since his bones were moldering away in the crypt below. But better safe than sorry.

Above my head, on the far side of the chancel, John

the Baptist and his murderers had now faded out almost completely. Twilight came quickly in these cloudy days of March and, viewed from inside the church, the windows of St. Tancred's could change from a rich tapestry of glorious colors to a muddy blackness in less time than it would take you to rattle off one of the longer psalms.

To tell the truth, I'd have rather been at home in my chemical laboratory than sitting here in the near-darkness of a drafty old church, but Father had insisted.

Even though Feely was six years older than me, Father refused to let her go alone to the church for her almost nightly rehearsals and choir practices.

"A lot of strangers likely to be about these days," he said, referring to the team of archaeologists who would soon be arriving in Bishop's Lacey to dig up the bones of our patron saint.

How I was to defend Feely against the attacks of these savage scholars, Father had not bothered to mention, but I knew there was more to it than that.

In the recent past there had been a number of murders in Bishop's Lacey: fascinating murders in which I had rendered my assistance to Inspector Hewitt of the Hinley Constabulary.

In my mind, I ticked off the victims on my fingers: Horace Bonepenny, Rupert Porson, Brookie Harewood, Phyllis Wyvern. . . .

One more corpse and I'd have a full hand.

Each of them had come to a sticky end in our village, and I knew that Father was uneasy.

"It isn't right, Ophelia," he said, "for a girl who's—for a girl your age to be rattling about alone in an old church at night."

"There's nobody there but the dead." Feely had laughed, perhaps a little too gaily. "And they don't bother me. Not nearly so much as the living."

Behind Father's back, my other sister, Daffy, had licked her wrist and wetted down her hair on both sides of an imaginary part in the middle of her head, like a cat washing its face. She was poking fun at Ned Cropper, the potboy at the Thirteen Drakes, who had the most awful crush on Feely and sometimes followed her about like a bad smell.

Feely had scratched her ear to indicate she had understood Daffy's miming. It was one of those silent signals that fly among sisters like semaphore messages from ship to ship, indecipherable to anyone who doesn't know the code. Even if Father *had* seen the gesture, he would not have understood its meaning. Father's codebook was in a far different language from ours.

"Still," Father had said, "if you're coming or going after dark, you are to take Flavia with you. It won't hurt her to learn a few hymns."

Learn a few hymns indeed! Just a couple of months ago when I was confined to bed during the Christmas holidays, Mrs. Mullet, in giggling whispers and hushed pledges of secrecy, had taught me a couple of new ones. I never tired of bellowing:

"Hark the herald angels sing,
Beecham's Pills are just the thing.
Peace on earth and mercy mild,
Two for a man and one for a child!"

Either that or:

"We Three Kings of Leicester Square,
Selling ladies' underwear,
So fantastic, no elastic,
Only tuppence a pair."

—until Feely flung a copy of *Hymns Ancient and Modern* at my head. One thing I have learned about organists is that they have absolutely no sense of humor.

"Feely," I said, "I'm freezing."

I shivered and buttoned up my cardigan. It was bitterly cold in the church at night. The choir had left an hour ago, and without their warm bodies round me, shoulder to shoulder like singing sardines, it seemed even colder still.

But Feely was submerged in Mendelssohn. I might as well have been talking to the moon.

Suddenly the organ gave out a fluttering gasp, as if it had choked on something, and the music gargled to a stop.

"Oh, fiddle," Feely said. It was as close to swearing as she ever came—at least in church. My sister was a pious fraud.

She stood up on the pedals and waddled her way off the organ bench, making a harsh mooing of bass notes.

"Now what?" she said, rolling up her eyes as if an answer were expected from Above. "This stupid thing has been misbehaving for weeks. It must be the damp weather."

"I think it died," I told her. "You probably broke it."

"Hand me the torch," she said after a long moment. "We'll have a look."

We?

Whenever Feely was frightened out of her wits, "*I*" became "*we*" as quick as a flash. Since the organ at St. Tancred's was listed by the Royal College of Organists as a historic instrument, any damage to the dear old thing would probably be considered an act of national vandalism.

I knew that Feely was already dreading having to break the bad news to the vicar.

"Lead on, O Guilty One," I said. "How do we get at the guts?"

"This way," Feely answered, quickly sliding open a concealed panel in the carved woodwork beside the organ console. I hadn't even time to see how the trick was done.

Switching on the torch, she ducked through the narrow opening and vanished into the darkness. I took a deep breath and followed.

We were in a musty Aladdin's cave, hemmed in on all sides by stalagmites. In the sweep of the torch's beam, organ pipes towered above us: pipes of wood, pipes of metal, pipes of all sizes. Some were as small as pencils, some like drain spouts, and others as large as telephone posts. Not so much a cave, I decided, as a forest of giant flutes.

"What are those?" I asked, pointing to a row of tall, conical pipes which reminded me of pygmy blowguns.

"The Gemshorn stop," Feely said. "They're supposed to sound like an ancient flute made from a ram's horn."

"And these?"

"The Rohrflöte."

"Because it roars?"

Feely rolled her eyes. "*Rohrflöte* means 'chimney flute' in German. The pipes are shaped like chimneys."

And sure enough, they were. They wouldn't have been out of place among the chimney pots of Buckshaw.

Something hissed suddenly and gurgled in the shadows and I threw my arm round Feely's waist.

"What's that?" I whispered.

"The wind chest," she said, aiming the torch at the far corner.

Sure enough, in the shadows, a huge leather trunklike thing was slowly exhaling with various bronchial wheezings and hissings.

"Super!" I said. "It's like a giant's accordion."

"Stop saying 'super,'" Feely said. "You know Father doesn't like it."

I ignored her and, threading my way among some of the smaller pipes, hauled myself up onto the top of the wind chest, which gave out a remarkably realistic rude noise and sank a little more.

I sneezed—once—twice—three times—in the cloud of dust I had stirred up.

"Flavia! Come down at once! You're going to rip that old leather!"

I got to my feet and stood up to my full height of four foot ten and a quarter inches. I'm quite tall for my age, which is almost twelve.

"Yaroo!" I shouted, waggling my arms to keep my balance. "I'm the King of the Castle!"

"Flavia! Come down this instant or I'm telling Father!"

"Look, Feely," I said. "There's an old tombstone up here."

"I know. It's to add weight to the wind chest. Now get down here. And be careful."

I brushed away the dust with my hands. "*Hezekiah*

Whytefleet," I read aloud. "1679 to 1778. Phew! Ninety-nine. I wonder who he was?"

"I'm switching off the torch now. You'll be alone in the dark."

"All right," I said. "I'm coming. No need to get owly."

As I shifted my weight from foot to foot, the wind chest rocked and subsided a little more, so that I felt as if I were standing on the deck of a swamped ship.

Something fluttered just to the right of Feely's face and she froze.

"Probably just a bat," I said.

Feely gave a shriek, dropped the torch, and vanished.

Bats were high on the list of things that turned my sister's brains to suet pudding.

A further fluttering, as if the thing were confirming its presence.

Picking my way gingerly down from my perch, I retrieved the torch and dragged it along the rank of pipes like a stick on a picket fence.

A furious leathery flapping echoed in the chamber.

"It's all right, Feely," I called out. "It *is* a bat, and it's stuck in a pipe."

I popped out through the hatch into the chancel. Feely was standing there in an angled beam of moonlight, as white as an alabaster statue, her arms wrapped round herself.

"Maybe we can smoke it out," I said. "Got a cigarette?"

I was being facetious, of course. Feely was death on smoking.

"Maybe we can coax it out," I suggested helpfully. "What do bats eat?"

"Insects," Feely said blankly, as if she were struggling

awake from a paralyzing dream. "So that's no use. What are we going to do?"

"Which pipe is it in?" I asked. "Did you happen to notice?"

"The sixteen-foot diapason," she said shakily. "The D."

"I have an idea!" I said. "Why don't you play Bach's Toccata and Fugue in D Minor? Full throttle. That ought to fix the little sod."

"You're disgusting," Feely said. "I'll tell Mr. Haskins about the bat tomorrow."

Mr. Haskins was the sexton at St. Tancred's, who was expected to deal with everything from grave-digging to brass-polishing.

"How do you suppose it got into the church? The bat, I mean."

We were walking home between the hedgerows. Scrappy clouds scudded across the moon and a raw crosswind blew and tugged at our coats.

"I don't know and I don't want to talk about bats," Feely said.

Actually, I was just making conversation. I knew that bats didn't come in through open doors. There were enough of the things hanging in the attics at Buckshaw for me to know that they generally got in through broken windows or were dragged in, injured, by cats. Since St. Tancred's didn't have a cat, the answer seemed obvious.

"Why are they opening his tomb?" I asked, changing the subject. Feely would know I was referring to the saint.

"Saint Tancred? Because it's the quincentennial of his death."

"The what?"

SPEAKING FROM AMONG *the* BONES

"Quincentennial. It means five hundred years."

I let out a whistle. "Saint Tancred's been dead five hundred years? That's five times longer than old Hezekiah Whytefleet lived."

Feely said nothing.

"That means he died in 1451," I said, making a quick mental subtraction. "What do you suppose he's going to look like when they dig him up?"

"Who knows?" Feely said. "Some saints remain forever uncorrupted. Their complexions are still as soft and peachy as a baby's bottom, and they have a smell of flowers about them. 'The odor of sanctity,' it's called."

When she felt like it, my sister could be downright chatty.

"Supercolossal!" I said. "I hope I get a good squint at him when they drag him out of his box."

"Forget about Saint Tancred," Feely said. "You won't be allowed anywhere near him."

"It's like eatin' cooked 'eat," Mrs. Mullet said. What she meant, of course, was "eating cooked heat."

I stared doubtfully at the bowl of squash and parsnip soup as she put it on the table in front of me. Black peppercorns floated in the stuff like pellets of used birdshot.

"Looks almost good enough to eat," I remarked pleasantly.

Sticking a finger into *The Mysteries of Udolpho* to mark her place, Daffy shot me one of her paralyzing looks.

"Ungrateful little wretch," she muttered.

"Daphne . . ." Father said.

"Well, she is," Daffy went on. "Mrs. Mullet's soup is nothing to joke about."

Feely quickly clapped a napkin to her lips to stifle a smile, and I saw another of those silent messages wing its way between my sisters.

"Ophelia . . ." Father said. He had not missed it, either.

"Oh, it's nothin', Colonel de Luce," Mrs. Mullet said. "Miss Flavia 'as to 'ave 'er little joke. Me an' 'er 'as an understandin'. She means no 'arm."

This was news to me, but I trotted out a warm smile.

"It's all right, Mrs. M," I told her. "They know not what they do."

Very deliberately, Father closed the latest issue of *The London Philatelist* which he had been reading, picked it up, and left the room. A few moments later, I heard his study door closing quietly.

"Now you've done it," Feely said.

Father's money problems had become more pressing with each passing month. There had been a time when his worries made him merely glum, but recently I had detected something which I feared was far, far worse: surrender.

Surrender in a man who had survived a prisoner-of-war camp was almost unthinkable, and I realized with a sudden twinge in my heart that the bone-dry little men of His Majesty's Board of Inland Revenue had done to Father what the Empire of Japan had failed to do. They had caused him to give up hope.

Our mother, Harriet, to whom Buckshaw had been left by her great-uncle Tarquin de Luce, had died in a mountaineering accident in the Himalayas when I was a year old. Because she had left no will, His Majesty's Vultures had descended upon Father at once, and had been busily pecking out his liver ever since.

It had been a long struggle. From time to time, it had looked as if circumstances might take a turn for the better, but recently, I had noticed that Father was tiring. On several occasions, he had warned us that he might have to give up Buckshaw, but somehow we had always muddled through. Now, it seemed as if he no longer cared.

How I loved the dear old place! The very thought of its wilting wallpaper and crumbling carpets was enough to give me gooseflesh.

Uncle Tar's first-rate chemistry lab upstairs in the unheated east wing was the only part of the house that would pass inspection, but it had long been abandoned to the dust and the cold of neglect until I had discovered the forgotten room and commandeered it for my own.

Although Uncle Tar had been dead for more than twenty years, the laboratory which his indulgent father had built for him had been so far in advance of its time that it would even now, in 1951, be considered a marvel of science. From the gleaming brass of the Leitz binocular microscope to the rank upon rank of bottled chemicals, from the forest of flasks and flagons to the gas chromatograph which he had caused to be built, based upon the work of the enviably named Mikhail Semenovich Tswett, Uncle Tar's laboratory was now mine: a world of glass and wonder.

It was rumored that, at the time of his death, Uncle Tar had been at work upon the first-order decomposition of nitrogen pentoxide. If those whispers were true, he was one of the pioneers of what we have recently come to call "The Bomb."

From Uncle Tar's library and his detailed notebooks, I had managed to turn myself into a cracking good chemist, although my interests were not so much given over to the splitting of atoms as to the concocting of poisons.

To me, a jolly good dose of potassium cyanide beats stupid old spinning electrons any day of the week.

The thought of my waiting laboratory was impossible to resist.

"Don't bother getting up," I said to Daffy and Feely, who stared at me as if I had sprouted a second head.

I walked from the room in utter silence.

·TWO·

VIEWED THROUGH A MICROSCOPE at low power, human blood looks at first like an aerial view of the College of Cardinals, dressed in their scarlet birettas and capes, milling about in Vatican Square, waiting for the Pope to appear on the balcony. Not that they have to, of course.

But as the magnification is increased, the color fades, until at last, when we are looking at the individual red corpuscles in close-up, we see that, in reality, each one has no more than a pale pink tint.

Blood's red coloration comes from the iron contained in the hemoglobin. The iron bonds easily with oxygen, which it carries to the most far-flung nooks and crannies of our bodies. Lobsters, snails, crabs, clams, squids, slugs, and members of the European royal families, by contrast, have blue blood, due to the fact that it's based on copper rather than iron.

I suppose it was finding the dead frog that had given me the idea in the first place. The poor thing had probably been trying to make its way from the river that ran behind St. Tancred's to the small marsh across the road, when it experienced a major misadventure with a motorcar.

Whatever the case, the thing had been squashed flat even before I stuffed it into my pocket and brought it home for scientific purposes.

In order to make the corpuscles more transparent under the microscope, I had mixed a sample of its blood with a one-in-four solution of acetic acid; then, as I adjusted the fine focus, I could see clearly that the frog's corpuscles were flat disks—rather like pink pennies—while my own, which I had extracted with a quick jab of a safety pin, were twice the size, and concave, like dozens of red doughnuts.

The idea of comparing my *own* blood to that of my father and sisters had come later, and indirectly from Daffy.

"You're no more a de Luce than the man in the moon," she had snapped when she caught me snooping in her diary. "Your mother was a Transylvanian. You have bat's blood in your veins."

As she snatched the leather-bound book from my hand, she gave herself a rather bad paper cut with the edge of one of its pages.

"Now look what you've made me do!" she'd shrieked, holding out for my inspection her bleeding, quivering finger as it dripped spectacularly onto the drawing-room carpet. In order to increase the dramatic effect even further, she had milked a few extra drops from the wound. And then, without another word, she'd dashed, half sobbing, from the room.

It had been a simple matter to sponge up a good bit of the gore with my handkerchief. Father was always going on about the importance of carrying a clean honking-rag, and there had been several occasions upon which I'd offered up silent praise for such excellent advice. This was another of them.

I had dashed at once to my laboratory, prepared a microscope slide from the blood sample, and made several quite good sketches of my observations, coloring them neatly with a boxed set of professional artist's pencils that Aunt Millicent had given to Feely several Christmases ago.

Then, through an incredible stroke of good luck, Feely, who was uncommonly vain about her hands, ripped a hangnail at the breakfast table a few days later, and it was Flavia on the spot—which is rather a good witticism, when you come to think of it.

"Watch out! You've stained the table linen," I said, whisking the napkin out of her fingers and handing her a wad of woolly lint from my pocket. "I'll rinse this out in cold water before it sets."

In my laboratory, I had added another set of colored sketches to my notebook.

The circular flattened disks of the red corpuscles, I had written, *have a tendency to stick together. They display their characteristic red color only where they are seen to overlap. Otherwise, they are the pale yellow of the western sky after an evening rain.*

Obtaining a sample of Father's blood had been more tricky. It wasn't until the following Monday, when he appeared at the breakfast table with a ragged little patch of toilet tissue stuck to his throat where he had cut himself shaving, that I saw a way.

It was the morning after Dogger had suffered one of his awful midnight episodes, crying out every few minutes in a shockingly hoarse voice, followed by long, horrid periods of whimpering which were even more unnerving than his screams.

Dogger was Father's general factotum. His duties varied according to his capabilities. He was sometimes valet and sometimes gardener, depending upon how the winds were presently blowing in his brain. Dogger and Father had served together in the army, and together they had been imprisoned at Changi. It was something that they never spoke of, and what few details I knew of those ghastly years had been pried, bit by painful bit, from Mrs. Mullet and her husband, Alf.

In the morning, I realized that Father had not slept—that he had stayed at Dogger's side until the terrors subsided. Father would never normally dream of allowing himself to be seen with lavatory paper clinging to his person, and the fact that he had done so said more about his distress than he could ever put into mere words.

It had been a simple matter to retrieve the stained scrap from the refuse container in his dressing room, but I must admit that in doing so, I'd never felt more guilty in my life.

Our red and white corpuscles, Father's, Feely's, Daffy's, and mine, I had written in my notes, although I hardly wanted to believe it, *are identical in size, shape, density, and coloration.*

From a battered and interestingly stained book on microscopy in Uncle Tar's library, I knew that the corpuscles of a bat's blood were approximately 25 percent smaller in size than those of humans.

Even magnified a thousand times, my corpuscles were identical with those of my father and my sisters.

At least in appearance.

I had read, in one of the popular magazines which littered our drawing room, that human blood is identical in chemical composition to the seawater from which our remote ancestors are said to have crawled: that seawater, in fact, had sometimes been used for temporary transfusions in emergency medical situations in which the real thing was not available.

A French researcher and artillery officer, René Quinton, had once replaced a dog's blood with diluted seawater and found that not only did the dog live—to a ripe old age, evidently—but that within a day or two of the experiment, the dog's body had replaced the seawater with blood!

Both blood and seawater are composed primarily of sodium and chlorine, although not in the same proportions. Still, it was amusing to think that the stuff which flowed in our veins was little more than a solution of table salt, although, to be fair, both also contain dribs and drabs of calcium, magnesium, potassium, zinc, iron, and copper.

For a short time, this so-called fact had made me immensely excited, suggesting, as it did, the possibility of any number of daring experiments, some of them involving humans.

But then Science had set in.

An extensive and carefully calibrated set of chemical tests using my own blood (I was faint for weeks) showed clearly the differences.

I had demonstrated quite conclusively that what flowed in the veins of the de Luces was not seawater, but a different blend of the elements of creation.

And as for Daffy's accusation of my having a Transylvanian mother—well, that was simply ludicrous!

My sisters had attempted, on numerous occasions, to convince me that Harriet was not my mother: that I had been adopted, or left by the Little People as a changeling, or abandoned at birth by an unknown mother who couldn't bear the thought of weeping every day at the sight of my ugly face.

Somehow, it would have been much more comforting to know that my sisters and I were not of the same tribe.

Bat's blood, indeed! That witch Daffy!

However, all that now remained, in order to conclude my experiment in the correct scientific manner, was to add a few firsthand notes based upon my observations of the juices of an actual bat.

And I knew precisely where to find one.

I would get an early start in the morning.

·THREE·

It was one of those glorious days in March when the air was so fresh that you worshipped every whiff of it; that each breath of the intoxicating stuff created such new universes in your lungs and brain you were certain you were about to explode with sheer joy; one of those blustery days of scudding clouds and piddling showers and gum boots and wind-blown brollies that made you know you were truly alive.

Somewhere, off to the east in the woods, a bird was singing: *Cuckoo, jug-jug, pu-we-to-witta-woo*.

It was the first day of spring, and Mother Nature seemed to know it.

Gladys squeaked with delight as we rattled through the rain. Even though she was considerably older than me, she loved a good run on a damp day as much as I did. She had been manufactured at the bicycle branch of the British Small Arms factory in Birmingham before I was born, and had originally belonged to my mother, Harriet, who had named her *l'Hirondelle*, "the swallow."

I had rechristened her Gladys because of her happy nature.

Gladys did not usually like to get her skirts wet, but on a day such as this, with her tires singing on the wet tarmac and the wind shoving at our backs, it was no time for prissiness.

Spreading my arms wide so that the flaps of my yellow mackintosh became sails, I let myself be swept along on a river of wind.

"Yaroo!" I shouted to a couple of dampish cows, who looked up at me vacantly as I sped past them in the rain.

In the misty green light of early morning, St. Tancred's looked like a Georgian watercolor, its tower floating eerily above the bulging churchyard as if it were a hot-air balloon casting off its moorings and bound for heaven.

The only jarring note in the quiet scene was the scarlet van pulled up onto the cobbled walk which led to the front door. I recognized it at once as Mr. Haskins's, the church sexton's. Beside it, on the grass under the yews, was a gleaming black Hillman, its high polish telling me that it didn't belong to anyone in Bishop's Lacey.

To the west of the church, almost hidden in the mist, a blue lorry was parked over against the chapel. A couple of battered ladders and a load of filthy weathered boards protruded from its open tailboard. *George Battle*, I thought. The village stonemason.

I skidded to a stop and leaned Gladys against the worn chest tomb of one Cassandra Cottlestone, 1685–1750 (an exact contemporary of Johann Sebastian Bach, I noted).

Sculpted in stone and sadly weathered, Cassandra lay atop her mossy tomb, her eyes closed as if she had a headache, her fingertips pressed together under her chin, and a faint smug smile at the corners of her mouth. She did not look as if she minded too much being dead.

On the base was carved:

I didd dye
And now doe lye
Att churche's door
For euermore
Pray for mye bodie to sleepe
And my soule to wayke.

I noted the two different spellings of "my," and remembered that Daffy had once told me some far-fetched story about the Cottlestone tomb. What was it?

My thoughts were interrupted by the sound of raised voices from the church's porch. I walked quickly across the grass and stepped inside.

"But a faculty was granted," the vicar was saying. "There can be no going back now. The work is already under way."

"Then you must stop it," said a large man in a dark suit. With his lumpy potato face and mane of white hair, he had the appearance of a dust mop dressed in its Sunday best. "You must put a stop to it at once."

"Marmaduke," the vicar said, "the bishop has assured me on several occasions that there would be no—oh, good morning, Flavia. You're out and about early, as it were."

The large man swiveled his head slowly and let his

light-colored eyes come to rest on my face. He did not smile.

"Good morning, Vicar!" I burbled. Being overly cheery at the crack of dawn is extremely upsetting to a certain kind of person, and I knew instantly that the white-haired man was one of them. "Lovely old morning, eh wot?—in spite of the rain?"

I knew I was laying it on with a trowel but there are times when I just can't help myself.

"Wot?" I added for emphasis.

"Flavia, dear," the vicar said. "How nice to see you. I expect you're looking for Mr. Haskins. It's about the floral baskets, isn't it? Yes, I thought as much. I believe he's up the ringing chamber tidying the bell ropes and so forth. Mustn't have chaos for Good Friday, must we?"

Floral baskets? The vicar was including me in some little drama of his own creation. I was honored! I had barged in at an indelicate moment and he obviously wanted me to buzz off.

The least I could do was play along. "Righty-ho, then. I thought as much. Father will be ever so glad to know the lilies are all sorted out."

And with that I leapt like a young gazelle onto the first step of the tower's steep spiral staircase.

Once out of sight, I trudged upward, recalling that ancient stairs in castles and churches wind in a clockwise direction as you ascend, so that an attacker, climbing the stairs, is forced to hold his sword in his left hand, while the defender, fighting downward, is able to use his right, and usually superior, hand.

I turned back for a moment and made a few feints and thrusts at an imaginary Viking—or perhaps he was a

Norman—or maybe a Goth. When it comes to the sackers and raiders I am quite hopeless.

"Hollah!" I cried, striking a fencer's pose, my sword arm extended. "*En garde*, and so forth!"

"Blimey, Miss Flavia," Mr. Haskins said, dropping something and putting a hand to where his heart was presumably pounding. "You gave me a fair old start."

I'm afraid I gave a small smirk of pride. It's no easy matter to startle a grave-digger, especially one who, in spite of his age, was as sturdily constructed as a sailor. I suppose it was his corded arms, his knotted hands, and his bandy legs which made me think of the sea.

"Sorry, Mr. Haskins," I said, as I removed my mackintosh and hung it on a handy coat hook. "I should have whistled on my way up. What's in the trunk?"

An ancient and much-battered wooden chest stood open against the far wall, a length of rope snaking over its lip where the sexton had let it drop—rather guiltily, I thought.

"This lot? Not much. Bunch of rubbish, really. Left over from the war."

I craned my neck to see round him.

In the chest were several more lengths of rope, a folded blanket, half a pail of sand, a stirrup pump with a rotted rubber hose, a second length of India rubber hose, a rather dirt-clodded shovel, a black steel helmet with a white "W" on it, and a rubber mask.

"Gas mask," Mr. Haskins said, lifting the thing and holding it in the palm of his hand like Hamlet. "The ARP lads and the fire-watchers had a post up here during the war. Spent a good many nights here myself. Lonesome, like. Strange things, I used to see."

He had my undivided attention. "Such as?"

"Oh, you know . . . mysterious lights floatin' in the churchyard, and that."

Was he trying to frighten me? "You're pulling my leg, Mr. Haskins."

"P'raps I am, miss . . . an' p'raps I amn't."

I grabbed the grotesque, goggle-eyed mask and pulled it on over my head. It stank of rubber and ancient perspiration.

"Look, I'm an octopus!" I said, waggling my tentacles. Muffled by the mask, my words came out sounding like "Mook, mime um mocknofoof!"

Mr. Haskins peeled the thing from my face and tossed it back into the chest.

"Kids have died playing with them things," he said. "Smothered 'emselves to death. They're not meant for toys."

He lowered the lid of the chest, and, slamming shut the brass padlock, he pocketed the key.

"You forgot the rope," I said.

Giving me what I believe is called a narrow look, he dug in his pocket for the key, snapped open the hasp, and retrieved the rope from the chest.

"Now what?" I asked, trying to look eager.

"You'd best run along, miss," he said. "We've work to do, and we don't need the likes of you underfoot."

Well!

Ordinarily, anyone who made such a remark to my face would go to the top of my short list for strychnine. A few grains in the victim's lunch pail—probably mixed with the mustard in his Spam sandwich, which would neatly hide both the taste and the texture . . .

But wait! Hadn't he said "we"? Who was "we"?

I knew, from hanging round the church, that Mr. Haskins usually worked alone. He called in a helper only when there was heavy lifting to be done, such as shifting fallen tombstones—at least the heavier ones, or burying someone who—

"Saint Tancred!" I said, and made a dash for the door.

"Hang on—" Mr. Haskins protested. "Don't go down there!"

But his voice was already fading behind me as I clattered down the winding stairs.

Saint Tancred! They were opening Saint Tancred's tomb in the crypt, and they didn't want me butting in. That's why the vicar had shunted me off so abruptly. Since he had directed me straight to Mr. Haskins in the tower, it didn't make any sense, but then he hadn't really had time to think.

Floral baskets, indeed! Somewhere below, they were already breaking open the tomb of Saint Tancred!

The vestibule, when I reached it, was empty. The vicar and the white-haired stranger had vanished.

To my left was the entry to the crypt, a heavy, wooden door in the Gothic style, its curved frame an arched, disapproving eyebrow of stone. I pushed it open and made my way quietly down the stairs.

At the bottom, a string of small, bare electric bulbs, which had been strung temporarily from the low roof, led off in the distance toward the front of the church, their feeble yellowish gleam only making the surrounding shadows darker.

I had been down here just once before, upon the occasion of a winter's evening game of hide-and-seek with the

St. Tancred's Girl Guides. That, of course, had been before my dishonorable discharge from the troop. Still, even after all this time, I couldn't help thinking of Delorna Higginson, and how long it had taken them to make her stop screaming and foaming at the mouth.

Ahead of me now, lurking in the darkness, crouched the hulking heap of scrap metal that was the church's furnace.

I edged uneasily round it, not willing to turn my back to the thing.

Manufactured by Deacon and Bromwell in 1851 and shown at the Great Exhibition, this famously unpredictable monstrosity squatted in the bowels of St. Tancred's like the giant squid that attacked Captain Nemo's submarine, *Nautilus*, in *20,000 Leagues Under the Sea*, the tin tentacles of its ducts snaking off in all directions, its two round windows of isinglass in the cast-iron door glowing like a pair of savage red eyes.

Dick Plews, the village plumber, had for years been having what the vicar called "an affair of the heart" with the brute, but even *I* knew that to be sadly optimistic. Dick was afraid of the thing, and everybody in Bishop's Lacey knew it.

Sometimes, during services, especially in the long silences as we settled for the sermon, a stream of four-letter words would come drifting up through the hot-air ducts—words that we all knew, but pretended not to.

I shuddered and moved on.

On both sides of me now were bricked-up arches. Behind them—stacked like cordwood, according to Mr. Haskins—were the crumbling coffins of those villagers who had gone before us into death, including a good many defunct de Luces.

I must admit that there were times when I wished I could hoist those dry, papery ancestors of mine out of their niches for a good old face-to-face—not just to see how they compared with their darkened oil portraits which still hung at Buckshaw, but also to satisfy my private pleasure in confronting the occasional corpse.

Only Dogger was aware of this unusual enthusiasm of mine, and he had assured me that it was because in tackling the dead, the pleasure of learning outweighs the pain.

Aristotle, he assured me, had shared my keenness for cadavers.

Dear old Dogger! How he sets my mind at ease.

Now I could hear voices. I was directly underneath the apse.

"Easy!" someone was saying in the gloom ahead of me. "Easy now, Tommy lad."

A dark shadow leapt across the wall as if someone had switched on a torch.

"Steady on! Steady on! Where's Haskins with that bloody rope? Pardon my French, Vicar."

The vicar was silhouetted in an open archway, his back to me. I craned my neck to peer round him.

On the far wall of the small chamber, a large, rectangular stone had been pried from the wall and pivoted outward. One end of it was now being supported on a wooden sawhorse, while the other still rested on the lip of the stone below. Behind the stone were visible a couple of inches of cold darkness.

Four workmen—all of them strangers, except for George Battle—stood at the ready.

As I moved in for a closer look, I bumped against the vicar's elbow.

"Good heavens, Flavia!" the vicar exclaimed with a start, his eyes huge in the strange light. "I almost leaped out of my skin, dear girl. I didn't know you were there. You oughtn't to be down here. Far too dangerous. If your father hears of it, he'll have my head on a platter."

Saint John the Baptist flashed into my mind.

"Sorry, Vicar," I said. "I didn't mean to startle you. It's just that, since Saint Tancred is my namesake, I wanted to be the first to see his blessed old bones."

The vicar stared at me blankly.

"Flavia Tancreda de Luce," I reminded him, injecting a dollop of fake reverence into my voice, folding my hands modestly across my chest, and casting my eyes downward, a trick I had picked up by watching Feely at her devotions.

The vicar was silent for a long moment—and then he chuckled. "You're having a game with me," he said. "I remember distinctly officiating at your baptism. Flavia Sabina de Luce was the name we bestowed upon you, in the name of the Father, and of the Son, and of the Holy Ghost, amen, and Flavia Sabina de Luce you shall remain—until such time, of course, as you choose to change it by entering into a state of Holy Matrimony, like your sister Ophelia."

My jaw fell open like a bread box.

"Feely?"

"Oh, dear," the vicar said. "I'm afraid I've let the cat out of the bag."

Feely? My sister, Feely? Entering into a state of Holy Matrimony?

I could scarcely believe it!

Who was it to be? Ned Cropper, the potboy from the Thirteen Drakes, whose idea of courtship was to leave offerings of moldy sweets at our kitchen doorstep? Carl Pendracka, the American serviceman who wanted to show Feely the sights of St. Louis, Missouri? ("Carl's going to take me to watch Stan Musial knock one out of the park.") Or was it to be Dieter Schrantz, the former German prisoner of war who had elected to stay behind in England as a farm laborer until such time as he could qualify to teach *Pride and Prejudice* to English schoolboys? And then, of course, there was Detective Sergeant Graves, the young policeman who always became tongue-tied and furiously red in the presence of my dopey sister.

But before I could question the vicar further, Mr. Haskins, rope in hand, his torch producing weird, swaying shadows, came pushing into the already crowded space.

"Make way! Make way!" he muttered, and the workmen fell back, pressing themselves tightly against the walls.

Rather than moving out of the chamber, I used the opportunity to squirm my way farther into it, so that by the time Mr. Haskins had fixed the rope round the outer end of the stone, I had wedged myself into the farthest corner. From here, I would have a front-row seat for whatever was going to happen.

I glanced across at the vicar, who seemed to have forgotten my presence. His face was strained in the light of the small, swaying bulbs.

What was it that Marmaduke, the man in the dark suit, had said? *"You must stop it. You must put a stop to it at once."*

It was obvious that, in spite of Marmaduke, whoever he may be, the work was going ahead.

The vicar was now gnawing distractedly at his lower lip.

"Where's your friend, then?" Mr. Haskins asked suddenly, turning from his work, his words echoing oddly from the crypt's curved arches. "I thought he wanted to be here for the main event?"

"Mr. Sowerby?" the vicar said. "I don't know. It's most unlike him to be tardy. Perhaps we should wait a while."

"This here stone's waitin' on nobody," Mr. Haskins said. "This here stone's got a mind of her own, and she's comin' out whether we likes it or not."

He gave the heavy block a familiar pat, and it made a most awful groan, as if it were in pain.

"She's hangin' by her toenails, and no more. Besides, Norman and Tommy need to get back to Malden Fenwick, don't you, lads? They're here to work, and work they shall."

He waved grandly toward his workers, one exceedingly tall, the other quite unremarkable.

Down here, in the depths of the crypt, Mr. Haskins was the ruler of his own dark kingdom, and nobody dared raise a voice against him.

"Besides," he added. "This here's only the wall. We won't get to the sarcophagus till we're through it. Fetch the rope, Tommy."

As Tommy worked the rope up and round an overhanging shelf of masonry, Mr. Haskins turned his attention full upon me. For an awful moment, I thought he was going to tell me to leave. But he had his audience.

"Sarcophagus," he said. "Sar-coph-a-gus. Now there's a rare old word for you. Bet you don't know what it means, do you, miss?"

"It comes from two Greek words meaning 'eater of flesh,'" I said. "The ancient Greeks used to make them of a special stone brought from Assos, in Turkey, because it was said to consume the entire body, except the teeth, in forty days."

Although I didn't do it often, I offered up a little prayer of thanks to my sister Daffy, who had read this fascinating snippet aloud to me from one of the volumes of a coffin-black encyclopedia in Buckshaw's library.

"Aha!" said Mr. Haskins, as if he had known it all along. "Well, there we have it then, straight from the horse's mouth," he said, meaning me.

Before I could protest what I took to be an insult, he had given the rope a fierce tug.

Nothing happened.

"Lend a hand, Norman. Tommy, give the other end a nudge—see if we can swing 'er out."

But in spite of their hauling and pushing, the stone wouldn't budge.

"Seems to be stuck fast," the vicar said.

"Stuck ain't the word for it," Mr. Haskins said. "Well and truly bloody—"

"Little pitchers, Mr. Haskins, little pitchers," the vicar said, putting a forefinger to his lips and giving an almost imperceptible nod in my direction.

"Something jammin' it up, like. Let's have a dekko."

Mr. Haskins dropped the end of the rope and snatched the torch away from Tommy.

Holding the lamp just behind its lens, he shoved his face against the crack.

"No good," he announced at last. "Wants more of an opening."

"Here—let me," I said, taking the torch from his hands. "My head's smaller than yours. I'll tell you what I can see."

They were all so astonished, I think, that nobody tried to stop me.

My head went easily in through the gaping crack, and, like a contortionist, I maneuvered the light until it was beaming into the tomb from over my head.

A cold, dank draft brushed at my face, and I wrinkled my nose at the sharp, brackish stink of ancient decay.

I was looking into a small stone chamber of perhaps seven feet long and three wide. The first thing I saw was a human hand, its dried fingers tightly clutching a bit of broken glass tubing. And then the face—a ghastly, inhuman mask with enormous, staring acetate eyes and a piggish rubber snout.

Beneath it was a white ruffle, not quite covering the ink-black vessels of the neck and throat. Above the eyes was a shock of curly golden choirboy hair.

This was most definitely not the body of Saint Tancred.

I turned off the torch, withdrew my head, and turned slowly to the vicar.

"I believe we've found Mr. Collicutt," I said.

·FOUR·

IT WAS THE HAIR, of course, that gave it away. How many Sundays had I watched Feely galloping down the aisle for first dibs on the pew from which she would have the best view of Mr. Collicutt's golden locks?

Perched on the organ bench in his white surplice, his head illuminated by the light of a morning sunbeam streaming in through stained glass, he had often seemed like a Botticelli cherub brought to life.

And he knew it.

I remembered the way he would toss his head and quickly run all ten fingers through his glowing curls before making them pounce on the keys for the anthem's opening chord. Feely once told me that Mr. Collicutt reminded her of Franz Liszt. It was not so long ago, she said, that there used to be found, in the keepsake boxes of ancient ladies who were freshly dead, the remnants of reeking cigar butts that had been smoked in another century by Liszt. I had meant to have a poke through Feely's belongings to see if she were hoarding the cork tips of Mr. Collicutt's Craven A's, but it had slipped my mind.

All of this went whizzing through my brain as I waited for the men to enlarge the opening and confirm my discovery.

Not that I wasn't shocked, of course.

Had Mr. Collicutt died because I'd counted corpses on my fingers? Had he been made a victim by some dark and unsuspected magic?

Stop it at once, Flavia! I scolded myself. *The man was obviously dead for ages before you tempted Fate to hand you another cadaver.*

Still, the man was dead. There was no getting round that.

While part of me wanted to break down and cry at the death of Feely's golden-haired Prince Charming, another part—a part I couldn't quite explain—was awakening eagerly from a deep sleep.

I was torn between revulsion and pleasure—like tasting vinegar and sugar at the same time.

But pleasure, in such cases, always wins. Hands down.

A hidden part of me was coming back to life.

Meanwhile, the workmen had brought a number of sturdy planks to lever the heavy stone forward, as well as to serve as a makeshift ramp, down which it could be manhandled to the floor.

"Easy, now—easy," Mr. Haskins was telling them. "Don't want to squash 'im, do we?"

Mr. Haskins was completely at home with corpses.

At last, after much grating and a couple of curses, the stone was removed, and the chamber's contents became clearly visible.

The gas mask strapped to the corpse's face glinted horridly, as only wet rubber can, in the shuddering light.

"Oh dear," the vicar said. "Oh dear. I'd best ring up Constable Linnet."

"No great rush, I'd say," said Mr. Haskins, "judgin' by the smell of him."

Harsh words, but true. I knew in great detail from my own chemical researches the process by which the human body, after death, digests itself, and Mr. Collicutt was well along the way.

Tommy and Norman had already produced handkerchiefs and clapped them to their noses.

"But before I do so," the vicar said, "I would ask each of you to join with me in a short prayer for this most—this most—ah, *unfortunate* individual."

We bowed our heads.

"O Lord, receive the soul of this, thy faithful servant, who has come to great misfortune alone and in a strange place."

A strange place indeed! Although I didn't say so . . .

"And perhaps, also, in fear," the vicar added, after taking a few moments as if fishing for the proper words. "Grant him, we beseech thee, eternal peace and the life everlasting. Amen."

"Amen," I said quietly.

I almost crossed myself, but I fought down the urge. Although our family patronized St. Tancred's because the vicar was one of Father's dearest friends, we de Luces, as Daffy liked to say, had been Catholics for so long that we sometimes referred to Saint Peter as "Uncle Pete" and to the Blessed Virgin Mary as "Cousin May."

"Flavia, dear," the vicar said, "I'd be indebted to you if

you'd come up and help me deal with the authorities. You're so much better at this sort of thing than I."

It was true. There had been several occasions in the past upon which I had pointed the police in the proper direction when they were hopelessly stumped.

"I'd be happy to, Mr. Richardson," I said.

For now, I'd seen all I wanted to.

Outdoors, it had rained, and the vicar and I stood waiting side by side in the porch, strangely tongue-tied by what we had just witnessed.

The police, when they arrived in their familiar blue Vauxhall saloon, were wearing their best poker faces. Inspector Hewitt gave me a curt nod and a fraction of a smile as he stepped from the car. Detective Sergeants Woolmer and Graves were their usual selves: Woolmer like a large and surly dancing bear (the Vauxhall groaned audibly with relief when he hoisted himself ponderously out of it!) while Graves, young, blond, and dimpled, was grinning at me ear to ear. As I have said, Sergeant Graves had a first-rate crush on Feely, and in a number of ways, I hoped he would be the one to march the divine Ophelia (Ha ha! Pardon me if I laugh!) to the altar. *One more detective in the family would give us something to talk about during the long winter evenings,* I thought. *Guts, gore, and Tetley's tea.*

Sergeant Woolmer gave me barely a glance as he hauled his photo kit from the car's boot. I looked away, and nodded pleasantly at Sergeant Graves, who was carrying a familiar case.

"Got the dabs organized, have you?" I asked pleasantly, showing him I remembered that his specialty was fingerprints.

The sergeant colored nicely, even though I was merely Feely's sister.

Like Santa Claus in the American poem, they spoke not a word but went straight to their work. They filed into the porch, bound for the crypt, leaving the vicar and me standing alone together at the door.

"How long has he been missing? Mr. Collicutt, I mean."

"Missing?"

In spite of having telephoned for the police, the vicar still seemed somewhat in a daze.

"We hadn't really thought of him as missing. Departed, I should say. Oh dear! No—that's hardly the correct word, either."

I said nothing: a useful tool that I had added to my kit by closely observing Inspector Hewitt at his work.

"Mrs. Battle said he came down that last morning for breakfast just as he always did. A single slice of toast only. He was always careful of his figure. Needed to keep his waist in shape for the pedal work. Oh dear, I'm gossiping."

"When was that, exactly?" I asked, as if I'd known it all along, but forgotten.

"The Tuesday after Quinquagesima, as I have reason to remember," the vicar said.

"About six weeks ago," I said, counting rapidly backward in my head.

"Yes. Shrove Tuesday."

"Pancake Day," I said with a dry gulp as I remembered for an instant the plate of rubbery flat tires Mrs. Mullet had set before us on that unfortunate morning.

"Indeed. The day before Ash Wednesday. Mr. Collicutt was to have picked up Miss Tanty and driven her to Hinley for her ophthalmological examination."

Miss Tanty, who sang in the choir, was a retired music mistress whose sheer physical bulk and full-strength spectacles gave her the appearance of an ancient omnibus with enormous acetylene headlamps bearing down upon you in a narrow country lane.

Hers was the voice that could always be heard rising above the rest of the choir during the *Magnificat:*

"*My soul doth mognify the Lord . . .*"

Everything about Miss Tanty was mognified.

Both her glorious soprano voice and her bottle-glass gaze were capable of making wet chills ooze down your spine.

"When he hadn't arrived by nine-fifteen," the vicar went on, "she rang up Mrs. Battle, and was told by Florence, the niece, that he had gone out the front door at eight-thirty on the dot."

"Did no one report him missing?"

"No. That's the thing. Crispin—Mr. Collicutt, I mean—was so much involved in various music festivals that he was seldom at home during the week. 'You shall make great savings on the kippers and cabbage,' he told Mrs. Battle, when she first took him in as a boarder. And then, of course, there was that rather odd comment he made about—but I must say no more. Cynthia is forever telling me that I have a propensity to prattle, and I do believe she's right."

Cynthia Richardson, the vicar's wife, was Bishop's Lacey's equivalent of smallpox, but I didn't let that thought distract me.

"Who was the man with the white hair?" I asked, changing the subject abruptly. "The one you were talking to in the porch?"

A shadow crossed the vicar's face. "Marmaduke Parr," he said. "From the Diocesan Office. He's the bishop's—"

"Hit man!" I blurted. I had learned about hit men from listening to the detective Philip Odell on the wireless: "The Case of the Copper Cupcake."

"—secretary," the vicar said, trying not to smile at my little joke. "Although I must admit Marmaduke *is* rather a—how shall I put it?—*determined* individual."

"He doesn't want Saint Tancred's tomb to be opened, does he? He's ordered you to stop."

But before the vicar could answer, Constable Linnet, Bishop's Lacey's arm of the law, came pedaling up the path and swung off his bicycle directly in front of us as neatly as a cinema sheriff dismounting his horse. He leaned the bike against a yew tree, flipped open his notebook, and licked the tip of his pencil.

Here we go again, I thought.

The constable began by asking both of us for our full names and complete addresses. Although he knew them perfectly well, it was important, because of his superiors, to have an unblotted notebook—even if it *was* written in pencil.

"Stay here, mind," he said, unbuttoning the breast pocket of his uniform and tucking the notebook away. He waved an official forefinger at us, and disappeared into the porch.

"Poor Crispin," the vicar said after a very long time, as if thinking aloud. "Poor Crispin. And poor Alberta Moon. She's going to be devastated—simply devastated."

"Alberta Moon?" I asked. "The music mistress at St. Agatha's?"

I had once heard Miss Moon play a Schubert sonata at

a village concert, and I have to say that she wasn't a patch on Feely.

The vicar was in the middle of nodding glumly when Constable Linnet reappeared at the door.

"Downstairs," he ordered, jabbing his thumb toward the ground like a Roman emperor breaking the bad news to a defeated gladiator. "Inspector Hewitt would like a word. In the crypt."

The Inspector stood with his chin cupped in his hand, a forefinger extending along his cheekbone. In the crypt's dim light he looked rather like John Mills, I thought, although I'd never tell him so to his face.

The ghastly remains of Mr. Collicutt were illuminated every few seconds by the blinding flashes of Sergeant Woolmer's camera.

"Who discovered the body?" the Inspector asked, which seemed to me a reasonable place to begin.

"Er . . . Flavia here," the vicar told him, placing a protective hand on my shoulder. "That is, Miss de Luce."

"I might have known," the Inspector said.

Then the miracle happened. As the vicar glanced uneasily at the remains of Mr. Collicutt, the Inspector slowly closed and reopened his right eye so that only I could see it.

He had winked at me! Inspector Hewitt had winked at me!

Somewhere, church bells rang. Somewhere cannons boomed. Somewhere fireworks exploded crazily in a darkened sky.

But I did not hear them: My ears were too stopped up with the roaring of my own blood.

Inspector Hewitt had actually winked at me!

But wait—

Now he was rubbing at his eye, pulling down his lower eyelid, examining something—a bit of grit, perhaps—on his fingertip.

Curses!

It was nothing more than a bit of crypt dust, or perhaps a particle of some ancient citizen of Bishop's Lacey—even one of my own ancestors.

I gave him a look of professional concern and handed him my handkerchief.

"Thank you," he said. "I have my own."

"Now then," he went on, as if nothing had happened, "describe to me, from the beginning, what took place—from the time that you arrived at the church this morning."

And so I did: I told him about the van in the churchyard, the vicar and Marmaduke Parr in the porch, Mr. Haskins in the tower, George Battle and Norman and Tommy and the other workman in the crypt. I told him about the levering out of the stone, and of my peering behind it. The only detail I withheld was the wooden chest over which I had found Mr. Haskins hovering.

After all, I had to leave *something* for the poor man to discover for himself.

"Thank you," the Inspector said when I had finished. "If there's anything else, I shall send someone to Buckshaw."

Even just a few months ago, I should have spat and stalked off at such an abrupt dismissal. But things had changed. I'd come to know, even if only a little, the Inspector's wife, Antigone, and their personal little tragedies.

"Right, then," I said. "Cheerio!"

I thought that I had pitched it just right.

Gladys was waiting in the weeds, and she gave a small squeak of delight as I grabbed her handlebars and pointed her toward the road.

It was still barely breakfast time as we splashed our way home, me whistling "Land of Hope and Glory," and Gladys happily clanking out the beat with her rattling chain.

·FIVE·

IT WASN'T UNTIL I was nearly home—not, in fact, until I was sweeping past the great stone griffins that guarded the Mulford Gates—that I realized I had overlooked two very important things. The first was that business of the bat, and how it had managed to get into the church. The second was this: If the tomb in the crypt was occupied by the remains of Mr. Collicutt, where on earth, then, were the bones of Saint Tancred?

As Buckshaw loomed up at the end of the long avenue of chestnut trees, I realized with a shock that I was thoroughly soaked. The morning mist had slowly and almost imperceptibly, as the English mist loves to do, transformed itself into a downright drizzle. I'd left my mackintosh in the church tower and now my cardigan, my blouse, my skirt, and my socks were stuck to my body like saturated bath sponges.

Gladys, too, was caked with mud and other bits of road debris.

"We need a bath, old girl," I told her, as we crunched across the sweep of gravel at the front door.

Father, Daffy, and Feely, I knew, would still be at breakfast. Wheeling Gladys through the foyer was out of the question because of the mud, and the kitchen entrance, at least at this time of day, was under the very nose of Mrs. Mullet.

I put a finger to my lips and, rolling Gladys silently round the corner and along the east side of the house, propped her directly below one of my bedroom windows.

"Wait here. I'll scout out the territory," I whispered.

I whipped back round to the front and crept silently into the foyer.

I needn't have worried. The usual breakfast-time hush hung over the dining room. Father would be poring over the latest philatelic journal, and Daffy would by now have her nose in *The Monk,* which Carl Pendracka had given her for Christmas. I couldn't help thinking he must have some ulterior motive.

Was he trying to gain her support for the begging of Feely's hand? Or could it be that Daffy was his second choice? At thirteen, Daffy was far too young for courtship, but Americans have far more patience than we British, who, after six years of war, want the earth and want it now, at least according to Clarence Mundy, who operated the only taxicab in Bishop's Lacey. Clarence had confided this bit of information as he drove Mrs. Mullet and me over to Hinley to replace a copper cooker which I had ruined with a chemical experiment involving the preservation of frog skins.

"War brides!" he'd said. "That's all the Americans think about nowadays is making off with a war bride. If they keep on the way they're going, why, there won't be nothing left for the home-born working lad."

"It's the bomb," Mrs. Mullet had replied. "That's what my Alf says. Everybody's afraid of 'em since they've got the bomb."

"Arrr," Clarence had grumbled before falling into silence.

I tiptoed up the staircase to the east wing, where my laboratory and bedroom were located. All of the bedrooms at Buckshaw were vast, windblown wastelands which were more suited to the mooring of airships than to the dreaming of sweet dreams, and mine was more remote and desolate than most.

This part of the house had been largely abandoned: Its unheated immensity, its sprung floors, its blank, blind windows, its billowing wallpaper, its smell of mildew, and its eternal drafts made it the perfect place to be left alone. I dwelt there by choice in privacy and peace.

I stripped the sheets from my bed, and with the addition of a couple of old afghans, quickly fashioned a makeshift rope with a large loop in one end.

Throwing open the sash, I lowered the loop until I was able to lasso Gladys's handlebars.

"Easy, now . . . easy!" I whispered as I hauled her slowly up the outside wall and dragged her in at the window.

In less time than you could say "cyanide," Gladys was leaning against the end of my bed, filthy of fender and still a little giddy from her ascent, but happy to be home and indoors.

I wound up the gramophone, dug out from the pile under my bed a recording of "Whistle While You Work," and dropped the needle into the scratchy grooves.

With a bucket of water fetched from the laboratory, I partially filled the tin hip bath and swabbed Gladys down with a loofah. I used my toothbrush to get into the tight places.

Although she was quite ticklish, Gladys tried to pretend that she wasn't. It is not a weakness that one likes to advertise. I still shuddered at the memory of being tickled by Feely and Daffy until I was foaming at the mouth.

"Steady on," I said. "It's only hog bristles."

I polished her briskly with my flannel nightgown until she fairly gleamed.

"*La la* lah *la la la la*," I sang along, even managing to whistle a bit of harmony.

I was the eighth dwarf.

Sneaky.

With the dirty work done, I breathed on Gladys's plated parts, gave them an extra polish, and stepped back to admire my handiwork.

"You'll do," I said.

I rinsed the sheets in a bucket of clean water, wrung them out, and strung them up to dry in a series of long loops from the picture frame of Joseph Priestley to the chandelier.

After a quick sponge bath in the sink, I put on clean clothing, brushed my hair and my teeth, and went down for breakfast.

"Morning, all," I said in a sleepy voice, rubbing my eyes.

I needn't have bothered. Feely was gazing into her teacup, admiring her own reflection. She insisted on drinking it plain, "no cream, thank you," the better to see herself in the shimmering liquid surface. At the moment, she was blowing on it gently to see what she'd look like with wavy hair.

Daffy peered at the pages of her book, which was propped open on a toast rack, wiping her jammy fingers on her skirt before turning the next page.

I lifted the lid on a serving dish and examined its rather grisly contents: a few scraps of burned bacon, a couple of kippers, a small scrap heap of curdled omelet, and what appeared to be a bundle of boiled bindweed.

I reached for the last piece of cold toast.

"Put some parsnip marmalade on it," Mrs. Mullet said as she hurried into the room. "Alf's sister grows 'em in 'er allotment garden. There's nothin' as'll put 'air on your chest like parsnips, Alf says."

"I don't want hair on my chest," I said. "Besides, Daffy has more than enough for all of us."

Daffy made a rude sign with her fingers.

"So when's the wedding?" I asked in a cheerful voice.

Feely's head came up like a sow's at the sound of the swill bucket.

Her wail began somewhere low down in her throat and rose, then fell, like an air-raid siren in distress.

"Faaa-aaa-aaa-ther!"

It faded finally and ended in tears. It fascinated me the way in which my sister was able to transform herself from Health Queen to hag in less than the twinkling of an eye.

Father closed his journal, removed his spectacles, put them back on again, and fixed me with that crippling de Luce stare of coldest blue.

"Where did you happen upon that bit of information, Flavia?" he asked in an Antarctic voice.

51

"She's been listening at keyholes!" Feely said. "She's always listening at keyholes."

"Or at hot-air registers," Daffy added, *The Monk* forgotten for a moment.

"Well?" Father asked, his voice an icicle.

"I just assumed," I said, thinking more quickly than I've ever thought before, "now that she's eighteen—"

Father had always said that no daughter of his would ever marry until she was at least eighteen, and even then . . .

Feely's eighteenth birthday had been not long before, in January.

How could I forget it?

To celebrate the happy occasion, I had planned a small display of indoor fireworks: just a few bangers, really, and a couple of gaily colored carpet rockets. I had mailed written invitations to everyone in the household and watched, hugging myself in secret delight, as each person took their hand-printed summons from the mail salver in the foyer, opened them, and then set them aside without a word.

I had followed up with a series of handmade posters placed strategically throughout the house.

On the day itself, I set up a row of five wooden chairs: one for Father, one for Feely, one for Daffy, and a pair together at one end for Mrs. Mullet and Dogger.

I had prepared my chemicals. The appointed time had come and gone.

"They're not coming, Dogger," I'd said after twenty minutes.

"Shall I fetch them, Miss Flavia?" Dogger had asked. He was sitting calmly in one of the chairs with a charged seltzer bottle in his hands in case of small fires.

"No!" I said, far too loudly.

"Perhaps they've forgotten," Dogger suggested.

"No, they haven't. They don't care."

"You may put on the show for me," Dogger had said after a while. "I've always fancied a nice display of drawing-room pyrotechnics."

"No!" I'd shouted. "It's canceled."

How bitterly, in time, I was to regret my words.

"Well?" Father asked again, bringing me back to the present.

"Well, now that she's eighteen," I went on, "it's only natural that . . . that her thoughts should turn to thoughts of—

"—of Holy Matrimony!" I finished triumphantly.

From behind her book, Daffy let off a wet snicker.

"No one was to know," Feely groaned, tearing at her hair dramatically. "Especially *you*! Damn and blast! Now it will be all over the village."

"Ophelia . . ." Father said, not really putting much into it.

"Well, it's true! We wanted to announce it ourselves at Easter. Other than clapping your ears to keyholes, the only way you could have heard was from the vicar. That was it! The vicar told you! I saw you sneaking in through the foyer an hour ago, and don't tell me you didn't. You were at the church and you weaseled it out of the vicar, didn't you? I should have known. I should have known!"

"Ophelia . . ."

Once my sister got wound up, you might as well take a chair. I certainly didn't want the blame to fall on Reverend Richardson. His life was hard enough, what with Cynthia and so forth.

"You little beast!" Feely said. "You filthy little beast!"

Father got up from the table and left the room. Daffy, who loved a good argument but hated squabbling, followed.

I was alone with Feely.

I sat for a moment enjoying her red face and her bugging blue eyes. She didn't often allow herself to go to pieces like that.

Although I wanted to get back at her, I didn't want to be the one to break the news to her about the unfortunate Mr. Collicutt.

Well, actually, I *did*—but I didn't want to be blamed for shattering her world.

"You're quite right," I heard myself saying. "I *was* at church this morning. I went early to say a few private prayers, and just happened to be there when Mr. Collicutt's body was discovered."

Teach you *to accuse me of listening at keyholes*, I thought.

The blood drained out of Feely's face. I knew instantly that my sister was not the murderer. You cannot fake pallor.

"Mr. Collicutt? Body?"

She leaped to her feet and sent the teapot crashing to the floor.

"'Fraid so," I said. "In the crypt. Wearing a gas mask. Most peculiar."

With a truly terrifying wail, Feely fled the room.

I followed her upstairs.

"I'm sorry, Feely," I called softly, tapping at her door. "It just slipped out."

Her sobs were muffled by the wooden panels. How long would she be able to resist begging for the gory details? I'd have to wait it out.

"I know you're upset, but just think how Alberta Moon is going to take it."

A long, shuddering sob ended abruptly in a hiccup.

I heard the sound of shoes on the carpet and the turning of a key. The door swung open and there stood Feely, damp and devastated.

"Alberta Moon?" she asked, her hand trembling in front of her mouth.

I nodded sadly. "Better let me come in," I said. "It's a long story."

Feely threw herself facedown on the bed. "Tell me everything. Start at the beginning."

Oddly enough, she used nearly the same words as Inspector Hewitt had, and I told her, as I had told him, my gripping tale, leaving out only those essentials which I wished to keep to myself.

"A gas mask," she sobbed as I finished. "Why in heaven's name would he be wearing a gas mask?"

I shrugged. "I don't know," I said.

Actually, I *did* know—or at least I had a fairly good idea.

In the past eight or nine months I'd spent a good many hours poring over the pages of Taylor's *Principles and Practice of Medical Jurisprudence*, whose photographically illustrated volumes I had been fortunate enough to find hidden away on a high shelf in the stacks of the Bishop's Lacey Free Library. By a remarkable stroke of fortune, these were similar enough in size to Enid Blyton's *The Island of Adventure*, *The Castle of Adventure*, and *The Sea of*

Adventure that, through a clever bit of jiggering with the dust jackets, I was able to study them closely for as long as I pleased in a remote corner of the reading room.

"My goodness, Flavia!" Miss Pickery, the head librarian had said. "You *are* a bookworm, aren't you?"

If only she knew.

"Perhaps there was a gas leak," Feely said, her voice muffled by the comforter. "Perhaps he was trying to escape the fumes."

"Perhaps," I said, noncommittally.

Although a carbon monoxide leak from the iron monster in the church basement was a distinct possibility, the problem was this: Since the gas is odorless, colorless, and tasteless, how could Mr. Collicutt have been aware of its presence?

And it seemed unlikely that, after six weeks, there would be measurable traces of the stuff in whatever was left of his blood. In cases of carbon monoxide poisoning, as I had good reason to know, the gas (CO) bonded to the blood's hemoglobin, displacing the oxygen it was meant to carry to the body's cells, and the victim died of simple suffocation. As long as he remained alive (once dragged from the gaseous atmosphere, of course) the carbon monoxide would pass off fairly quickly from the blood, its oxygen being replenished by normal breathing.

Dead bodies were a different kettle of fish. With respiration at a standstill, carbon monoxide could remain in the body for a considerable length of time. Indeed, it was a fairly well-known fact that the monoxide could still be detected in the gases given off by a cadaver that had been dead for months.

With no easy access to the late Mr. Collicutt's blood,

or his inner organs, it would be nearly impossible to be sure. Even if there *had* been a pool of blood hidden beneath his body, it would long ago have been reoxygenated by exposure to the air of the crypt, however foul that may be.

I thought of the moment I first stuck my face into that abyss—of the wave of cold, acrid decay that was swept into my nostrils.

"Eureka!" I shouted. I couldn't help myself.

"What is it?" Feely asked. She couldn't help herself, either.

"The bat in the organ!" I said excitedly. "It got into the church somehow. I'll bet there's a broken window! What do you think, Feely?"

As an excuse, it was as stale as yesterday's toast, but it was the best I could come up with on such short notice.

It's just as well she couldn't read my mind. What I was thinking was this: The cold draft coming out of what ought to have been a closed crypt reminded me of what Daffy had told me about the verse on Cassandra Cottlestone's tomb.

I didd dye
And now doe lye
Att churche's door
For euermore
Pray for mye bodie to sleepe
And my soule to wayke.

"She lies at the church's door," Daffy had said, "because she was a suicide. That's why she's not buried with the rest of the Cottlestones in the crypt. By rights, she shouldn't have been buried in the churchyard at all, but her father was a magistrate, and was able to move heaven and earth, as it were."

I thought for a moment of poor Mr. Twining, Father's old schoolmaster, who lay in a plot of common ground on the far side of the riverbank behind St. Tancred's. *His* father, evidently, had not been a magistrate.

"Mrs. Cottlestone, though, had arranged for a tunnel to be dug between Cassandra's tomb and the family crypt, so that her daughter—or at least the soul of her daughter—could visit her parents whenever she wished."

"You're making this up, Daffy!"

"No, I'm not. It's in the third volume of *The History and Antiquities of Bishop's Lacey.* You can look it up yourself."

"A tunnel? Really?"

"So they say. And I've heard rumors—"

"Yes? Tell me, Daffy!"

"Perhaps I shouldn't. You know how cross Father can be when he thinks we're filling your mind with specters."

"I won't tell him. Please, Daffy! I swear!"

"Well . . ."

"Pleee-ase! Cross my heart with a silver dart!"

"All right, then. But don't say I didn't warn you. Mr. Haskins told me that once, when he was digging a new grave next to Cassandra Cottlestone's tomb, the edge gave way, and his shovel fell in the hole. When he found he couldn't fish it out with his arm, he had to crawl in headfirst and—you're quite sure you want to hear this?"

I pretended to be biting off my fingers at the knuckles.

"At the bottom of the grave, beside the shovel, was a mummified human foot."

"That's impossible! It couldn't have lasted for two hundred years!"

"Mr. Haskins said it could—under certain conditions. Something to do with the soil."

Of course! Adipocere! Grave wax! How could I have forgotten that?

When buried in a damp location, a human body can be wonderfully transmogrified. The ammonia generated by decay, in which the fatty tissues break down into palmitic, oleic, and stearic acids, working hand in hand with sodium and potassium from the grave soil, could turn a corpse into a lump of hard laundry soap. It was a simple matter of chemistry.

Daffy lowered her voice and went on. "He said that not long before this, he had sprinkled red brick dust on the crypt floor to see if rats from the riverbank were finding a way into the church."

I shuddered. It was less than a year since I'd been locked in the pit shed on the river's edge, and I knew that the rats were no figment of my sister's imagination.

Daffy's eyes widened, her voice now no more than a whisper. "And do you know what?"

"What?"

I couldn't help it: I was whispering, too.

"The sole of the foot was tinted red, as if it had stepped in—"

"Cassandra Cottlestone!" I almost shouted, the hair at the nape of my neck standing on end as if suddenly blown by a cold, invisible breeze. "She was walking—"

"Exactly," Daffy said.

"I don't believe it!"

Daffy shrugged. "Why should I care what you believe?

I give you a fact and you give me a headache. Now buzz off."

I had buzzed off.

While I was lost in recollection, Feely's sobs had subsided, and she was now staring sullenly out the window.

"Who's the victim?" I asked, trying to cheer her up.

"Victim?"

"You know, the poor sap you're going to carry down the aisle."

"Oh," she said, tossing her hair and coughing up the answer with surprisingly little urging on my part. "Ned Cropper. I thought you'd have already heard that at the keyhole."

"Ned? You despise him."

"Wherever did you get that idea? Ned's going to own the Thirteen Drakes one day. He's going to take it over from Tully Stoker and rebuild the whole place: dance bands, darts on the terrace, lawn bowling . . . blow a breath of fresh air into that coal hole . . . bring it into the twentieth century. He's going to be a millionaire. Just you wait and see."

"You're warped," I said.

"Oh, all right, then. If you must know, it's Carl. He's begged Father to let me be Mrs. Pendracka and Father has agreed—mostly because he believes Carl to be of the bloodline of King Arthur. Having an heir with those credentials would be a real feather in Father's cap."

"Sucks to you," I said. "You're pulling my leg."

"We're going to live in America," Feely went on. "In St. Louis, Missouri. Carl's going to take me to watch Stan Musial knock 'em out of the park for the Cardinals. That's a baseball team."

"Actually, I was hoping it was Sergeant Graves," I said. "I don't even know his first name."

"Giles," Feely said, looking dreamily at her fingernails. "But why ever would I marry a policeman? I couldn't bear the thought of living with someone who came home every night with murder on his boots."

Feely seemed to be getting over poor Mr. Collicutt's death quite nicely. Perhaps there was a drop of de Luce blood in her after all.

"It's Dieter," I said. "He's the one who gave you the friendship ring at Christmas."

"Dieter? He has nothing to offer but love."

As she touched the ring, I noticed for the first time that she was wearing it on the third finger of her left hand. At the very mention of his name, she couldn't keep from smiling.

"It is!" I'm afraid I shrieked. "It *is* Dieter!"

"We shall make a fresh start," Feely said, her face more soft than I had ever seen it before. "Dieter is going to train as a schoolmaster. I shall teach piano and the two of us shall be as happy as dormice in cotton."

I couldn't help hugging myself. *Yaroo!* I was thinking.

"Where is Dieter, by the way?" I asked. "I haven't seen him for a while."

"He's gone up to London to sit a special examination. Father arranged it. If you breathe a word I'll kill you."

Something in her voice told me that she meant it.

"Your secret's safe with me," I told her, and for once I meant it.

"We shall be engaged for a year, until I'm nineteen," Feely went on, "simply to please Father. After that it's all cottages and columbines and a place to turn handsprings whenever one feels the urge."

Feely had never turned a handspring in her life, but I knew what she meant.

"I shall miss you, Feely," I said slowly, realizing that my heart was in every word.

"How too, too touching," she said. "You'll get over it."

· S I X ·

WHENEVER I'M A LITTLE blue I think about cyanide, whose color so perfectly reflects my mood. It is pleasant to think that the manioc plant, which grows in Brazil, contains enormous quantities of the stuff in its thirty-pound roots, all of which, unfortunately, is washed away before the residue is used to make our daily tapioca.

Although it took me an hour to admit it to myself, Feely's words had stung me to the quick. Rather than brooding about it, though, I took down from the shelf a bottle of potassium cyanide.

Outdoors, the rain had stopped, and a shaft of warm light now shone in through the window, causing the white crystals to sparkle brightly in the sudden sun.

The next ingredient was strychnine, which, coincidentally, came from another South American plant, and from which curare—arrow poison—was derived.

I've mentioned before my passion for poisons and my special fondness for cyanide. But, to be perfectly fair, I must admit that I also have something of a soft spot for strychnine, not just for what it *is*, but for what it's capable of becoming. Brought into the presence of nascent oxygen, for instance, these rather ordinary white crystals become at first rich blue in color, then pass in succession through purple, violet, crimson, orange, and yellow.

A perfect rainbow of ruin!

I placed the strychnine carefully beside the cyanide.

Next came the arsenic: In its powdered form, it looked rather drab beside its sisters—more like baking powder than anything else.

In its arsenious oxide form, the arsenic was soluble in water, but not in alcohol or ether. The cyanide was soluble in alkaline water and dilute hydrochloric acid, but not in alcohol. The strychnine was soluble in water, ethyl alcohol, or chloroform, but not in ether. It was like the old puzzle about the fox, the goose, and the bag of corn. To extract their various essences, each poison needed to be babied along in its own bath.

With the windows thrown wide open for ventilation, I sat down to wait out the hour it would take for all three solutions to be complete. Solutions in more than one sense of the word!

"Cyanide . . . strychnine . . . arsenic." I spoke their names aloud. These were what I called my "calming chemicals."

Of course I wasn't the first to think of compounding several poisons into a single devastating drink. Giulia Tofana, in seventeenth-century Italy, had made a business of selling her Aqua Tofana, a solution containing, among other ingredients, arsenic, lead, belladonna, and hog drippings, to more than six hundred women who wished to have their marriages chemically dissolved. The stuff was said to be as limpid as rock water, and the abbé Gagliani had claimed that there was hardly a lady in Naples who did not have some of it lying in a secret phial among her perfumes.

It was also said that two popes had been among its victims.

How I adore history!

At last my flasks were ready, and I hummed happily as I mixed the solutions and decanted them into a waiting bottle.

I waved my hand over the still steaming mixture.

"I name thee Aqua Flavia," I said.

With one of Uncle Tar's steel-nibbed pens, I wrote the newly coined name on a label, then pasted it to the jar.

"A-qua Fla-via," I said aloud, savoring each syllable. It had a nice ring to it.

I had created a poison which, in sufficient quantities, was enough to stop a rogue elephant dead in its tracks. What it would do to an impertinent sister was almost too gruesome to contemplate.

One aspect of poisons that is often overlooked is the pleasure one takes in gloating over them.

Then, too, as some wise person once said, revenge is a dish best eaten cold. The reason for this, of course, is that while you're gleefully anticipating the event, the victim has plenty of time to worry about when, where, and how you're going to strike.

One thinks, for instance, of the look on the victim's face as she realizes that what she is sipping from the pretty glass is more than just orange squash.

I decided to wait a while.

. . .

Gladys was standing patiently where I had left her, her fresh-washed livery gleaming handsomely in the morning sunlight from my bedroom windows.

"Avaunt!" I shouted. It was an ancient word meaning "Begone!" which I had learned when Daffy read *The Bride of Lammermoor* aloud to us at one of our compulsory Cultural Evenings.

"Both of us!" I explained, although it wasn't really necessary.

I leaped into her saddle, pushed off, pedaled out the bedroom door, wobbled along the hall, made a sharp left turn, and moments later was at the top of the east staircase.

From astride a bicycle, stairs appear to be much steeper than they actually are. Far below, in the foyer, the black and white tiles were like winter fields viewed from a mountaintop. I got a firm grip on the front braking handles and started down at an alarming angle.

"Bucketa-bucketa-bucketa-bucketa," I exclaimed, one for each stair, all the way down, my bones rattling pleasantly.

Dogger was standing at the bottom. He was wearing a canvas apron and holding a pair of Father's boots. "Good morning, Miss Flavia," he said.

"Good morning, Dogger," I replied. "I'm happy to see you. I have a question. How does one go about disinterring a dead body?"

Dogger raised one eyebrow a fraction. "Were you thinking of disinterring a dead body, miss?" he asked.

"No, not personally," I told him. "What I mean is, what permissions must be obtained, and so forth?"

"If I remember correctly, consent must first be given by the church. It is known as a faculty, I believe, and must be obtained from the Diocesan Council."

"The bishop's office?"

"More or less."

So that's what the vicar had been talking about. A faculty had already been granted, he told Marmaduke Parr, the man from the bishop's office. The bishop's secretary, in fact.

"There can be no going back now," the vicar had said.

It seemed obvious that a faculty had been granted for the exhumation of Saint Tancred, and then for some reason withdrawn.

Who, I wondered, would stand in the way? What harm could there be in digging up the bones of a saint who had been dead these past five hundred years?

"You're a corker, Dogger," I said.

"Thank you, miss."

Out of respect, I dismounted, and wheeled Gladys discreetly across the foyer, and out the front door.

On the lawn, at the edge of the gravel, was a folding camp stool, and beside it, several rags and a tin of boot polish. The day was warmer now, and Dogger had obviously been working outside in the fresh air, enjoying the sunshine.

I was about to push off for the church when I saw a car turn in at the Mulford Gates. It was the odd shape of the thing which had caught my attention: rather boxy, like a hearse.

If I left now, I might miss something. Better, I thought, to stifle my impatience and wait.

I sat down on the camp stool and studied the machine

as it came flouncing along the avenue of chestnuts. Viewed head-on, it was certain from the tall Corinthian radiator of gleaming silver that it was a Rolls-Royce landau—in some ways, very like Harriet's old Phantom II which Father kept stored away as a sort of shrine in the dimness of the coach house: the same broad skirts and the same gigantic headlamps. And yet there was something different.

As the car turned side-on, I saw that its paint was apple green, and that the roof had been peeled away from just behind the driving seat, like a tin of opened sardines. Where the backseats had once been were rows of gray, unpainted wooden boxes, each crammed cheek by jowl with flowerpots, all of them open to the weather, rather like a gallery of cheap seats atop a charabanc from which the seedlings and the growing plants could view the passing world.

Since Father had lectured us so often about the evils of staring, I instinctively pulled my notebook and pencil from the pocket of my cardigan and pretended to be writing.

I heard the tires crunch to a heavy stop. The door opened, and closed.

I snuck a quick peek from the corner of my eye and registered a tall man in a tan mackintosh.

"Hullo," he said. "What have we here?"

As if I were a waxwork figure in Madame Tussauds.

I went on scribbling nothings in my notebook, resisting the urge to stick my tongue out the corner of my mouth.

"What are you doing?" he asked, coming dangerously close, as if to look at the page. If there's one thing I despise, it's a person who snoops over your shoulder.

"Writing down number plates," I said, snapping my notebook shut.

"Hmmm," he said, gazing slowly round at the empty landscape. "I shouldn't imagine you add many to your collection in such an out-of-the-way place."

In what I hoped was a properly chilling manner I said, "Well, I've got yours, haven't I?"

It was true. GBX1066.

He saw me staring at the Rolls.

"What do you think of the old bus?" he asked. "Phantom II, 1928. The former owner, requiring something to transport a racehorse in comfort, took a hacksaw to her."

"He must have been mad," I said. I couldn't help myself.

"*She*, actually," he said. "Yes, she was. *Quite* mad. Lady Densley."

"Of Densley's Biscuits?"

"The very one."

As I was thinking about how to respond, he produced a silver case from his pocket, flipped it open, and handed me a card.

"My name's Sowerby," he said. "Adam Sowerby."

I glanced at the bit of pasteboard. At least it was tastefully printed in small black type.

Adam Tradescant Sowerby, MA., FRHortS, etc.
Flora-archaeologist
Seeds of Antiquity—Cuttings—Inquiries
Tower Bridge, London E.1 TN Royal 1066

Hmmm, I thought. *The same four digits as his number plates. This man has connections.*

"You must be Flavia de Luce," he said, extending a hand. I was about to give back his card when I realized that he intended us to shake.

"The vicar told me I'd likely find you here," he went on. "I hope you don't mind my barging in like this, unannounced."

Of course! This was the vicar's friend, Mr. Sowerby. Mr. Haskins had asked about him in the crypt.

"Are you related to Sowerby & Sons, our village undertakers?"

"The present incumbent is, I believe, a third cousin. Some of us Sowerbys have chosen Life, and others Death."

I took his hand and gave it an intelligent shake, looking directly into his cornflower-blue eyes.

"Yes, I'm Flavia de Luce," I said. "I don't mind you barging in at all. How may I help you?"

"Denwyn is an old friend," he said, not letting go of my hand. "He told me that you could very likely answer my questions."

Denwyn was the vicar's name, and I mentally blessed him for being so frank.

"I shall do my best," I replied.

"When you first looked into that chamber behind the stone, what did you see?"

"A hand," I said. "Rather dried. Clutching a broken bit of glass tubing."

"Rings?"

"No."

"Fingernails?"

"Clean. Well manicured. Although his hands and clothing were filthy."

"Very good. And then you saw?"

"The face. At least, a gas mask *covering* the face. Golden-blond hair. Dark lines on the throat."

"Anything else?"

"No. The torch was throwing quite a narrow beam."

"Excellent! I see that your reputation—which precedes you—is well deserved."

My reputation? The vicar must have told him about those several earlier cases in which I had been able to point the police in the right direction.

I preened a little, inwardly.

"No dried petals . . . vegetation . . . anything of that sort?"

"Not that I noticed."

Mr. Sowerby gathered himself, as if he were about to ask a tender question. In a hushed voice, he said, "It must have been quite a shock to you. The poor man's body, I mean."

"Yes," I said, and left it at that.

"The police have made quite a hash of the scene— removing the remains and so forth. Anything that may have been of interest to me is now no more than—"

"Dust on the sergeant's boots," I suggested brightly.

"Precisely. Now I shall have to go over the ground with a magnifying glass, like Sherlock Holmes."

"What are you hoping to find?"

"Seeds," he said. "Remnants of Saint Tancred's interment. The mourners often tossed fresh flowers into the tomb, you know."

"But there was nothing in the tomb," I said. "It was empty. Except for Mr. Collicutt, of course."

Adam Sowerby gave me a quizzical look. "Empty? Oh, I see what you mean. No, it's hardly likely to be empty.

The crevice where you found Mr. Collicutt is actually a chamber above the tomb proper. Its lid, if you like. Saint Tancred will still be nicely nestled somewhere down below."

So that was why there had been no bones! My question was answered.

"Then it's quite likely that you'll still find seeds and so forth?"

"I should be surprised if we didn't. It's just that, in any investigation, one likes to start at the outside and nibble one's way in."

I couldn't have put it better myself.

"And these seeds," I said. "What shall you do with them?"

"I shall coddle them. I shall put them in a warm place and provide them with the nourishment they need."

I could tell by the passion in his voice that seeds were to him as poisons were to me.

"And then?" I asked.

"They might well germinate," he said. "If we're extraordinarily lucky, one of them will be brought to blossom."

"Even after five hundred years?"

"A seed is a remarkable vessel," he told me. "Our one true time machine. Each of them is capable of bringing the past, alive, into the present. Think of that!"

"And then?" I asked. "After they've blossomed?"

"I sell them. You'd be surprised what some people will pay to be the sole possessor of an extinct flower.

"Oh, and then there are the academic trumpets, of course. Who can live nowadays without the academic trumpets?"

I had no idea what he was talking about, but the part about the flowers was intriguing enough.

"Would you mind giving me a lift into the village?" I asked suddenly. It was still early in the day and an idea was taking shape.

"Does your father allow you to beg rides from complete strangers?" he asked, but there was a twinkle in his eyes.

"He won't mind, if you're a friend of the vicar's," I said. "May I put Gladys in the back, Mr. Sowerby?"

"Adam," he said. "Since we're both under the vicar's spell, I expect that it's all right to call me Adam."

I climbed up into the front passenger's seat. There was a prolonged and grinding judder as Adam trod on the clutch and coddled the shifting lever down into first gear, and then we were off.

"Her name is Nancy," he said, indicating the instrument panel, then, glancing at me, he added, ". . . after Burns's poem."

"I'm afraid I don't know it," I said. "My sister Daphne is the bookish one."

" *'Though poor in gear, we're rich in love,'* " he quoted. "From 'The Soldier's Return.'"

"Ah!" I said.

The churchyard was, if anything, more vividly green than it had been in the early morning light. The Inspector's blue Vauxhall was still parked in the same spot, as was Mr. Haskins's van.

"I'll drop you off here," Adam said at the lych-gate. "I have odds and ends to discuss with the vicar."

It was a way of saying "I want to speak with him privately," but he handled it so politely that I could hardly object.

Although I could see that Gladys was excited about her first ride in a Rolls-Royce, I sensed that she was glad to be on solid ground again. I waved as I wheeled her away.

I had no sooner set foot in the church when a large, dark figure loomed up, barring the way.

"Hold on," growled a voice.

"Oh, good morning, Sergeant Woolmer," I said. "Lovely day, isn't it? In spite of the rain earlier, it's actually turned out quite well."

"It's no good, miss," he said. "You're not getting in. The place is closed. Off-limits. It's the scene of a crime."

"I just want to say a few prayers," I said, going all stoop-shouldered and mousy like Cynthia Richardson, the vicar's wife, and injecting a bit of a whine into my voice. "I won't stay long."

"You can pray in the churchyard," the sergeant said. "The Lord has large ears."

I sucked in my breath as if I had been shocked at his blasphemy.

Actually, he had given me an idea.

"Very well, Sergeant," I said. "I shall remember to mention your name."

That would give the brute something to think about!

Cassandra Cottlestone's tomb had the appearance of a massive Elizabethan dresser which had been made off with by culprits who, being caught in the act, had abandoned the thing in the churchyard where, over the centuries, it had turned to stone.

Longish grass sprouted all round the limestone base, a clear sign that this part of the churchyard was seldom visited.

The sun went behind a cloud, and I realized with a shiver that just under my feet was the secret tunnel through which the wraith of the dead Cassandra was said to walk.

Pray for mye bodie to sleepe
And my soule to wayke.

As I went round toward the north side of the monument, my heart gave a little leap.

An adjacent grave had sunk, and the turf no longer wholly covered the base of the Cottlestone tomb.

It was just as Daffy had said!

At the northwest corner, a large stone slab had been leaned at an angle against the monument, parts of it draped with a weathered tarpaulin which had filled with pools of rainwater. The sheeting was held down at the corners with broken chunks of stone and, by the amount of sediment that had already settled, I deduced that it had been left lying like this for some time.

Either Mr. Haskins had been diverted from repairing the cave-in, or he was simply lazy.

From where I now stood at its north end, the bulky tomb blocked the view of the church, and vice versa. As I have said, nobody ever came to this part of the churchyard anyway. It might as well have been on another planet.

I got down onto my hands and knees and peered under the tarpaulin. What lay beneath was a gaping hole.

Around it, in the disturbed soil, were a number of foot-prints, some of them blurred by the recent rain, others protected by the tarpaulin and remarkably clear. They had not all been made by the same person.

I removed the stones and pulled back the covering, taking care to let the puddled water run off to one side in the grass.

Now the hole was fully revealed.

Once more on hands and knees, I was able to see into the opening.

Had I been expecting bones? I wasn't quite sure, but what lay beneath the tomb was a stone chamber, most of which was filled with darkness.

Oh, for a torch! I thought.

Why didn't nature provide us with a headlamp in the middle of our foreheads, something like the glowworm, but with our lights on the opposite end? And more pow-erful, of course—it would have been a matter of simple phosphorescent chemistry.

I was craning my neck for a better look when the soil gave way beneath my pressing hands.

I grabbed wildly at the long grass to save myself, but the blades either broke off or slipped wetly through my fingers.

For an instant I tottered, arms windmilling, fighting madly to gain my feet. But it was no use. My shoes slith-ered and slipped one last time on the muddy turf and I plummeted into the grave.

·SEVEN·

I MUST HAVE HAD the wind knocked out of me. For what seemed like ages, but was in fact probably no more than a few seconds, I'm sure I lay there in a daze.

And then the smell. Oh, the *smell*!

It was like being hit in the nose with a brick.

My nostrils felt suddenly raw, as if they were being forcibly bored out with a brace and bit.

I clapped a hand to my nose and scrambled to my knees, but that only made things worse. I realized instantly that the smelly sludge which I had just smeared onto my face was all that remained of Cassandra Cottlestone and her neighbors.

I knew that the instant life ends, the human body begins to consume itself in a most efficient manner. Our own bacteria transform us with remarkable swiftness into gas bags containing methane, carbon dioxide, hydrogen sulfide, and mercaptan, to name just a few. Although I had for some time been making notes toward a future work to be called *De Luce on Decomposition*, I had not had until that moment any real, so to speak, firsthand experience.

Now, I was learning quickly that the stuff acts as smelling salts.

I leapt to my feet, gagging, and fell back against a hard stone wall.

As my eyes became accustomed to the darkness, I saw that the opening through which I had fallen was actually no larger than the entrance to a fox's den. In the weak light, I could see that the walls of the tomb were all of crumbling stone.

Except for a few bits of rubble on the floor, the rectangular cavern was empty. On the side opposite the hole, set into the wall, was a small but surprisingly ordinary-looking wooden door.

I took hold of the knob and gave it a turn. The door was locked.

In other circumstances, I would have taken a handy bit of wire and picked the lock—an art which Dogger had taught me in exchange for helping him clean flowerpots in the greenhouse during one long winter.

"It's all in the fingers," he used to say. "You must learn to listen to your fingertips."

Unfortunately, a person who has just tumbled headfirst into a grave is ill equipped with tools of the lock-picking trade. I had once improvised by removing my braces and forming the wire into a passable pick, but today I was not wearing them.

I could, in a pinch, crawl out of the grave and beg Gladys's permisson to borrow one of her spokes. But with the place crawling with police, it was more than likely I would be spotted and the game would be up.

So far, it seemed as if Inspector Hewitt's men had been kept so busy in the crypt that they had not yet discovered this end of the hidden tunnel.

I pressed an ear against the door and listened intently. The acute sense of hearing which I had inherited from Harriet was seldom more useful than painful, but this was one such occasion.

On the other side of the door there was nothing but silence: no burly policemen trampling their way along the tunnel in search of its origin.

I gave the door one last powerful tug, but it barely moved. *Someone meant to keep someone out,* I thought.

Or to keep someone in.

I would need to come back at night: back to the churchyard with a hooded torch and dressed all in black.

It would need to be done quickly. Tonight. If I was lucky, I would be one step ahead of the police.

For now, all that remained was to climb out of this stinking pit and get home to Buckshaw for a bath. My clothing would probably have to be burned.

I went to the hole, reached up, grasped its edge, and gave a great upward leap, my toes pedaling like mad against the wall for traction.

For an instant, my fingers touched the ledge at the bottom of the monument, but I couldn't quite catch hold of it.

I fell back into the muck. If I had been just an inch or two taller . . .

I could see only one solution—other than screaming for help, of course, and I certainly didn't want to do that.

With filthy fingers I untied my laces and removed my

shoes and socks. Shoving one of the socks into one of the shoes to give it additional thickness, I used the other to tie the shoes together, soles outermost, into a makeshift rubber brick. This I positioned tightly against the stone wall and stepped on top of it.

I took a deep breath, prayed to Saint Tancred to give wings to my heels—and made a mighty leap.

This time, my fingers caught the marble ledge easily, and with feet furiously paddling behind me, I rose up out of the grave.

Standing there in the grass, staring at me in shock, her face as white as a shroud, her open mouth a black "O," was Cynthia Richardson, the vicar's wife.

I suppose I should have said something polite: uttered some comforting reassurance. But I didn't.

I don't know what must have been running through her mind at the sight of this filthy, black-faced, foul-smelling apparition that suddenly came clawing its way up out of the grave under her very nose, but at that particular instant, I didn't care. I did what any sensible girl would do under the circumstances. I took to my heels.

Any thoughts I *might* have had of washing off the worst of the crud in the river behind the church were set aside.

Oh, Flavia! I thought. *Oh, Flavia!*

And then in one of those blinding flashes of inspiration that come from fear of punishment, I remembered that I had left my mackintosh on a hook in the tower room. With any luck I could retrieve it without being spotted. Yes, that was it! I would wear it home to conceal the filthy rags that my clothing had become.

At the corner of the tower, I shot back a glance at

Cynthia, who was still standing frozen as I had left her, as white as all the rest of the boneyard angels.

I edged slowly along the tower wall, my back pressed tightly against the stones. A quick peep round the corner revealed Sergeant Woolmer sitting with his behind on the back seat of the Vauxhall, his feet outside in the grass. He was writing in his notebook.

Trying to make myself paper-thin, I slipped round the corner and darted in at the door. If anyone was in the porch, I was sunk.

But Fate was on my side. The porch was empty and the church beyond lay in dim silence. The police were obviously still going about their work in the crypt.

I tiptoed up the winding stone staircase and stepped into the chamber at the top. My mackintosh was hanging exactly as I had left it.

I folded it into as flat and compact a bundle as possible and shoved it under what was left of my sweater. No point in catching anyone's eye with a fluorescent yellow coat which simply screamed for attention.

If I ran into anyone on my way out, I would simply wrap my arms tightly round my tummy and concoct some sort of story. Stomach pain, for instance. I would blame it on Mrs. Mullet's Hasty Pudding.

Down the winding stairs I crept . . . stopping at every step to listen.

Sergeant Woolmer was still absorbed in his notebook, and I flitted out the door and round the corner of the tower in a wink. Even though it is considered unlucky to do so, I worked my way counterclockwise ("widdershins," as Daffy calls it) round the church, pausing before I attempted the north side. But the coast was clear. Cynthia Richardson was gone.

Gladys was basking happily in the sun, and I wheeled her slowly through the churchyard, dodging from tombstone to tombstone, westward and south, along the winding riverbank. My normally drab cardigan and skirt, further camouflaged with splotches and smears of grave mud, should make me nearly invisible among the weathered monuments. When we reached the stone wall that marked the boundary, I lifted Gladys over and set her down gently on the other side, and moments later, we were spinning happily home along the road to Buckshaw.

I had not noticed until now, as I cycled along the avenue of chestnut trees, how seedy and run-down our home had begun to look. Its grass uncut, its hedges untrimmed, its gravel unraked, and its windows unwashed, the place had a look of neglect that snagged at my heart.

Not that it was Father's fault. His lack of ready funds had caused him to narrow his personal world until there was little left to him but his own small study: a little haven—or was it a prison?—in which he could insulate himself from a demanding world behind a barricade of ancient and changeless postage stamps.

Nor could Dogger be blamed: He did as much as he was physically and mentally able. Sometimes, when he was up to being gardener, the house and its grounds looked as spruce as they did in those long-gone days when they had been photographed for *Country Life*. At other times, functioning simply as Father's man was more than enough of a strain on his shattered nerves, and I, for one, gave thanks that Dogger was able even to manage Father's boots.

His camp stool was nowhere in sight. Dogger had vanished to wherever it is that he vanishes.

As before, it was a matter of getting across the foyer and upstairs without being seen. If Daffy or Feely saw the state of my clothing, it would be a matter of seconds before Father had been tattled to, and if Father himself were the first to catch a glimpse of my filthy condition . . . well, I shuddered at the very thought of the tongue-lashing.

Thankfully, my mackintosh, having been washed by yesterday's rain, was spotless. I turned up the collar and buttoned it from top to bottom. Who knows? I might even be praised for dressing warmly and keeping dry.

My feet were the only problem. Not only were they bare, shoeless, and sockless, they were also caked with the reeking remains of Cassandra Cottlestone.

I bent at the knees until the hem of my coat was touching the floor tiles, then waddled awkwardly across the foyer like a penguin, or perhaps like Mr. Pastry making his exit at the end of his pantomime, "The Passing Out Ceremony." I must have looked as if I'd been sawn off at the knees, or driven into the ground like a tent peg.

I was halfway up the stairs when I heard footsteps in the upstairs hall.

Curses! I thought.

Legs appeared between the upper banisters: legs wearing black trousers.

A moment later, the rest of Dogger appeared.

"I shall be up directly with the hot water," he said quietly from the corner of his mouth as he passed me on the stairs.

The man was uncanny.

I was soaking in my tin hip bath, trying not to think too hard about the various bits that were floating to the surface of the steaming stew. The hot water, in addition to my fatigue, must have caused me to nod off. One instant I was wrinkling like a dumpling and the next I was again at St. Tancred's, sitting on the organ bench.

I watched with fascination as long white fingers stroked the keys, illuminated only by a pair of candles, one at each end of the music rack.

The rest of the church was in darkness.

Black notes flying across a white page. Black shadows of the hands flying like spiders across white ivory.

I recognized the music as Chopin's funeral march: Feely had played it just two weeks ago as old Mrs. Fuller was led down the aisle for the last time.

Dum-dum-da-DUM, dum-da-DUM-da-DUM-da-DUM.

It had such an air of finality about it. Once you're sent to the grave there's no going back. Unless you're dug up again, of course.

"Feely," I said with a shudder, "do you think—"

I turned to look at my sister—but it was not Feely beside me on the organ bench.

The black, piggish snout turned slowly toward me in the darkness, its glassy eyes brimming with blood. Even before it spoke, I could smell its filthy rubber skin, the graveyard reek of its hot, rotting breath.

"Harriet," the thing croaked. "Ha-r-r-i-et."

I awoke screaming, my hands flailing the water and my feet thrashing. I leapt out of the tub, sending a tidal wave splashing onto the floor.

My teeth were chattering. My skin, in spite of the now tepid water, was icy cold. I lurched across the room, struggled into my bathrobe, and collapsed into a huddle on the bed.

It was all I could manage. My breath was still coming in ragged gasps, my heart pounding like a madman beating away on a drum.

There was a light knock at the door, but I could not find within myself whatever it took to answer. After a few moments, it opened slowly and Dogger's face appeared.

"Are you all right?" he asked, sizing me up as he came across the room toward me.

I overcame the iron muscles in my neck just enough to nod stiffly.

Dogger touched my forehead with the inside of his wrist, then placed a thumb under the angle of my jaw.

"You've had a fright," he said.

"It was a dream."

"Ah," he said, wrapping a quilt round my shoulders. "Dreams will sometimes do that. Lie down, please."

As I stretched out on the bed, Dogger placed a pillow beneath my feet.

"Dreams," he said. "Very beneficial things, dreams. Most useful."

I must have looked at him with begging in my eyes.

"Fright can be remarkably healing," he said. "It has been known even to cure gout and to alleviate fever."

"Gout?" I murmured.

"A painful disease of elderly gentlemen who love their wine more than their livers."

I think I smiled, but my eyelids were suddenly made of lead.

Iron neck, leaden eyes, I thought. *I'm growing stronger.*

And then I slept.

·EIGHT·

When I opened my eyes, there was daylight at my windows, although the sun had not yet risen. The hands of my brass alarm clock pointed sleepily to five-thirty.

Rats! I had slept straight through my intended midnight visit to the crypt. Now I should have to wait another twenty-four hours, by which time, the police would probably—

"Good morning, Miss Flavia," said a voice at my elbow, and I nearly jumped out of my skin.

"Oh! Dogger! I didn't know you were here. You startled me."

"I'm sorry. I didn't intend to. I trust you slept well?"

By the slow, stiff way in which he was unfolding himself from the chair at my bedside, I knew that he had been sitting there all through the night.

"Very well, thank you, Dogger. I think I rather overdid things yesterday."

"Indeed," he agreed. "But I believe you are much improved this morning."

"Thank you, yes."

"In ten minutes I shall be breakfasting on tea and toast in the kitchen if you care to join me," Dogger said.

"Bags I the crust!" I said, fully aware of what a tremendous honor it was to be asked.

When Dogger had gone, I washed my face and neatly rebraided my pigtails, going so far even to tie each one with a bit of fresh white (for Easter) ribbon. After Dogger's sleepless night, the least I could do, I thought, was to look decent at the breakfast table.

We were seated in the kitchen, Dogger and I. The rest of the household was not yet awake, and Mrs. Mullet wouldn't arrive from the village for another hour.

There had fallen between us what Dogger once referred to as "a companionable silence," a little parcel of time during which neither of us felt any particular need to talk.

The only sound in the kitchen was the scratching of our knives on toast, and the slight ticking of the silver toaster as the little red snakes of its innards turned white bread to brown. It was quite wonderful, when you came to think of it: the way in which the red-hot electric element's dry heat caused the bread's sugars to interact with its amino acids, producing a whole new set of flavors. The Maillard reaction, it was called, after Louis-Camille Maillard, the French chemist who had made a study of toasting and suntanning.

As my teeth crunched into the tasty crust, I realized suddenly that toast eaten hot and fresh from the toaster is vastly superior in taste to toast brought to a distant table. Although there seemed to be a lesson here, I couldn't for the moment think what it might be.

I was the first to break the silence.

"Have you ever heard of a person named Adam Sowerby?" I asked.

"An acquaintance of your father's, I believe," Dogger said. "Rather a well-known botanist nowadays. They were at school together."

A friend of Father's? Why hadn't Adam told me so? Why had Father never mentioned his name?

"His work often takes him to old churches," Dogger continued, not looking at me.

"I know," I said. "He's hoping to find old seeds in Saint Tancred's tomb. He gave me a lift into the village yesterday."

"Yes," Dogger said, helping himself to another piece of toast and spreading the honey with surgical precision. "I watched you from an upstairs window."

No one looked up as I entered the dining room. Father, Feely, and Daffy were sitting as they always sat, each in their own invisible compartment.

The only difference this morning was Feely's appearance: Her face was chalky white, with purplish rims round her red eyelids. She had, without a doubt, spent the night grieving for the late Mr. Collicutt. I could almost smell the candles.

Evidently, she had not yet shared the news of his demise with Father. For some complicated reason she was keeping it to herself. Almost as if she were treasuring it.

A shiver of cold air told me I had just brushed shoulders with a ghost.

I slipped into my chair and lifted the lid of the patent food warmer. This morning's main dish consisted of Mrs. Mullet's Omelets Royale: those flat rubber pancakes of pale egg embedded with particles of red and green peppers and chunks of chutney, which, when Father was not present, we called "toad-on-the-road."

I speared one of these squidlike monstrosities with my fork and passed it on a plate to Feely.

She covered her mouth with the palm of her hand, made a slight but still detectable retching noise, pushed back her chair, and hurried from the room.

I raised a quizzical eyebrow at Father as he looked up from *The London Philatelist*, but he was not to be distracted from his hobby. For a moment he listened to Feely's retreating footsteps, as if hearing the baying of a distant hound, then went back to reading his journal.

"I met a friend of yours yesterday, Father," I said. "His name is Adam Sowerby."

Father came slowly up again out of the depths.

"Sowerby?" he said at last. "Wherever did you meet him?"

"Here," I said. "At Buckshaw. In the forecourt. He has the most remarkable old Roller—full of plants."

"Mmm," Father said, and returned to reading about engravings of Queen Victoria's head.

"He gave me a lift into the village," I went on. "He's here to look for ancient seeds when they open Saint Tancred's tomb."

Again Father surfaced. It was like carrying on a conversation with a deep-sea diver who resubmerged after every sentence.

"Sowerby, you say?"

"Yes, Adam Sowerby. Dogger says he's an old friend of yours."

Father closed his journal, removed his reading spectacles and tucked them into his waistcoat pocket. "An old friend? Yes, I daresay he is."

"Speaking of Saint Tancred's tomb, by the way," I said casually, now that I had Father's undivided attention, "Mr. Collicutt was found dead in it yesterday."

Daffy's head snapped up from her book. She had been listening all along.

"Colly?" she said. "Colly dead? Does Feely know?"

I nodded. I did not say that she had known since yesterday at breakfast. "He appeared to have been murdered."

"Appeared?" Father asked instantly. I had to give him full marks for lightning-quick perception. "Appeared? Do you mean you were there? That you saw him—dead?"

"I discovered the body," I said modestly.

Daffy's jaw fell open like a hangman's trap.

"Really, Flavia," Father said. "This is simply too much."

He fished out his spectacles, put them on, removed them, and put them on again. In the past, he had seemed rather proud of the corpses I had happened upon, but even corpses, I suppose, have their limit.

"Collicutt, you say? The organist chap? What's he doing dead?"

It was a silly question, but also an excellent one.

Mrs. Mullet, who had come in from the kitchen as Father spoke, sniffed: "They say as 'ow 'e 'ad it comin', that one. All them carryin's-on in the churchyard. Turned into a sow by devils, 'e was, like them gaberdine swine in the Bible."

Carryings-on in the churchyard? Whatever could she mean by that? When I talked to him in the tower, Mr. Haskins had mentioned mysterious lights seen floating in the churchyard by the ARP and the fire-watchers, but that had been years ago, during the war. Could these strange ceremonies, or whatever they were, still be taking place?

One thing of which I was almost certain which connected that remote past with the present was this: Since there was now only one mask left in the trunk, the gas mask strapped to poor dead Mr. Collicutt's face must have come from that same wooden chest in the tower. There would surely have been more than one, originally.

In fact, I would be willing to bet my Bunsen burner that the two were identical.

Not that I was an expert on gas masks.

There was Daffy's, of course, a gaily colored Mickey Mouse mask of red India rubber with a blue tin nozzle that had been issued to her when she was no more than three years old, and which she still kept hanging close at hand from its straps at the side of her looking glass.

"You never know," she once told me, with rather an odd look on her face.

Then, too, there was that mask of early vintage which was kept in my laboratory in case of certain chemical accidents. It had been given personally to Uncle Tar not long before his death in 1928, by Winston Churchill, who was, at the time, chancellor of the exchequer. I had gleaned the details of their meeting from one of Uncle Tar's extensive diaries, a volume of which I always kept at hand on my night table for gripping bedtime reading.

Churchill had paid an autumnal visit to Uncle Tar at Buckshaw, and as they strolled together beside the Ornamental Lake, Churchill had offered a cigar (which, since his particular weakness was Pimm's No. 2 Cup, Uncle Tar had politely refused) and said: "There is war in the wind, Tarquin. I can smell it. England can ill afford to lose a de Luce."

I could almost hear the voice of that bulldog man uttering the words, which certainly had a Churchillian ring to them.

"Thank you, Mrs. Mullet," Father was saying as my thoughts came back to the present. He was thanking her not for her tales of dire doings in the churchyard, but for the toad-on-the-road whose remains she was now removing from the table.

Daffy, marking her place in *The Monk* with one of the crepe paper serviettes we had been forced to adopt since "Hard Times" (her words) had fallen upon us, slipped silently from the room.

Father was not far behind her.

"Tell me about the sows in the churchyard, Mrs. Mullet," I said, now that we were alone. "I've become quite keen on Bible studies recently. In fact I've been thinking of starting a scrapbook of New Testament animals and their—"

"That isn't safe for ears the likes of yours," she replied, rather snappishly, I thought. "Alf says Mr. Ridley-Smith, the magistrate, tipped 'im off that 'tisn't safe to be 'angin' about that church till a elephant of justice 'as been served, which makes good sense to me."

"Oh, piffle," I said, changing tactics. "It's no more than village gossip. Father's always warning us about village gossip, and I think he's quite right."

I could hardly believe my mouth was saying this.

"Oh, village gossip, is it?" Mrs. Mullet snorted, putting down the stack of dishes she had been carrying and planting her hands on her hips. "Then tell me, if you please, miss, why they 'ad to call Dr. Darby to give Missus Richardson a shot after what she seen in the churchyard?"

I let my mouth loll open. If I could have drooled at will, I would have.

"Tell me," I begged. "Please—what was it?"

Mrs. Mullet bit her lip, fighting like mad the urge to be discreet.

"A ghost a-comin' up out of 'er grave! That's what!" she said in a low, harsh voice, her eyes, wide as saucers, nervously scanning the four corners of the room.

"In daylight!" she added. *"In broad daylight!*

"Mind you, I've said nothin'."

Although I was still a little shaky from my nightmare, I was soon pedaling back toward the church, as if drawn by a magnet. The fresh air would do me good, I thought: a bit more oxygen to spike the old seawater.

Even as I approached the churchyard, I could see that my way was barred. Although the blue Vauxhall was parked in a different spot from where it had been yesterday, it was still uncomfortably close to the front door. It was not Sergeant Woolmer who sat in it this time, but Sergeant Graves, my sister's failed suitor.

I skidded to a stop, dismounted from Gladys, and ducked down behind the stone wall. How could I get past the man?

It is remarkable how the human mind works.

I was thinking of the church—which reminded me of hymns—when what popped into my head, as if by magic, were these words: *"God moves in a mysterious way, his wonders to perform."*

Hymn 373.

Of course!

Right there, growing wild along the wall, were the first flowers of spring: crocuses, snowdrops, primroses—even a huddle of daffodils which had likely been turfed out after some funeral or another and had taken wild refuge in the shelter of the stones.

I picked a sampling of these and gathered them into a quite decent bouquet, whose blues, yellows, and whites were dazzling in the morning sun. As a final touch, I removed one of my white hair ribbons and gave it several turns round the stems, tying it into an elaborate, and actually quite pretty, bow.

Then I walked up the path to the church door as bold as you please.

"Flowers for the altar," I said, waving the bouquet under the sergeant's nose as I swept past him.

What man would dare stand in my way?

I had almost reached the door when Sergeant Graves spoke.

"Hold on," he said.

I stopped, turned, and raised an eyebrow. "Yes, Sergeant?"

He suddenly went all casual, shrugging and examining his fingernails as if what he were about to say didn't matter, as if it were nothing—no more than an afterthought.

"Is it true what they say about your sister? I've heard she's getting married."

"Why, whoever told you that?"

I was fishing.

"The police hear things," he said sadly, and as he spoke the words, I noticed that for the first time since I had met him, Sergeant Graves was not wearing his perpetual boyish smile.

"It might be only a rumor," I said, unwilling to be the one to break the sergeant's heart.

For a moment we stood staring into each other's eyes: just a couple of human beings.

And then I turned away and stepped into the church.

To keep from hugging him.

The interior was a cool, dim, tinted twilight, and was filled with that vague and unnerving vibration that churches have when they are empty, as if the souls of those in the crypts below are singing—or perhaps cursing—at a pitch too high or too low for the rest of us to hear.

But what I was detecting now was no choir of souls. A choir of hornets was more like it: a rising and falling—what was that word that Daffy loved to use? Ululation? Yes, that was it, ululation: a faint howling, like the wail of distant air-raid sirens snatched away now and then by the wind.

I stood motionless beside a stone pillar.

The sound continued, echoing back from the vaulted roof.

I could see no one. I took a cautious step or two—and then a few more.

Was it coming from the organ casing in the chancel? Had a pipe become stuck? Or could it be the wind howling through a hole?

I remembered suddenly that I had come back to the church yesterday—before being distracted by the corpse of Mr. Collicutt—to look for a broken window through which a bat might have entered.

I tiptoed up the carpeted steps and into the chancel. The humming was louder here.

How odd! It almost seemed as if—yes, it *was* a tune. I recognized the melody: "Savior, When in Dust to Thee."

Feely had been singing it as she practiced on the piano just a few days ago:

"Savior, when in dust to thee, low we bow the adoring knee."

I had lingered in the hall to listen to the rather gruesome words:

"By the anguished sigh that told, treachery lurked within thy fold . . ."

Feely sang it with such feeling.

I remember thinking, *They just don't write hymns like that anymore.*

The haunting words were running through my head now as I crept stealthily along the nave, all of my senses on alert for the source of the weird whining.

A floorboard creaked.

I turned my head slowly, the hair at the back of my neck standing on end.

There was nobody there. The humming stopped abruptly.

"Girl!"

It came from behind me. I spun round on my heel.

She was sitting in an oak clergy chair at the end of the choir stalls, whose elaborately carved wings had kept her hidden until I had come directly alongside. Hugely magnified eyes stared out at me through thick lenses which were also reflecting, in a most unsettling way, the dripping stained-glass colors of John the Baptist's severed head.

It was Miss Tanty.

"Girl!"

Except for a starched white doily for a collar, she was dressed all in black bombazine, as if her clothing had been stitched together from the cloth under which the photographer hides his head before squeezing the rubber bulb.

"Girl! What are you up to?"

"Oh, good morning, Miss Tanty. I'm sorry, I didn't see you there."

My words were greeted with rather a rude grunting noise.

"You were skulking, and don't pretend you weren't."

In ordinary circumstances, someone who spoke to me like this never saw another sunrise. In my mind, at least, I dealt out poisons with a happy hand.

But in this case, because I needed information, I decided to make an exception.

"I wasn't skulking, Miss Tanty. I brought some flowers to put on the altar."

I shoved them almost into her face and the huge goggles moved from side to side, examining the blooms and stems as if they were colored serpents.

"Hmph," she said. "Wildflowers. Wildflowers have no place on the altar. A girl of your breeding ought to know that."

So she knew who I was.

"But—" I said.

"But me no buts," she said, holding up a hand. "I am Chairman of the Altar Guild, and as such, it is my business to know what's what. Give them here and I shall throw them on the rubbish heap on my way out."

"I heard you humming," I said, putting the flowers behind my back. "It sounded lovely, what with all the echoes and so forth."

Actually, it hadn't sounded lovely. "Eerie" was more the word. But Rule 9B was this: Change the Subject.

"Savior, When in Dust to Thee," I said. "One of my favorite hymns. I recognized it even without the words. You have such a wonderful voice, Miss Tanty. They must always be simply pleading with you to make phonograph recordings."

You could feel the thaw. In an instant, the temperature in the church went up by at least 10 degrees Celsius (or 283 degrees Kelvin).

She patted her hair.

And then without a word of warning, she drew in a deep breath and, with her hands clasped at her waist, began to sing:

"*Savior, when in dust to thee, low we bow the adoring knee.*"

There was no doubt she had a remarkable voice: a voice that, because of the way in which (at least at close range) it rattled your bones, might even have been called "thrilling." It seemed to originate from somewhere deep in her body; from down among her kidneys, I guessed.

"*By thy deep expiring groan, by the sad sepulchral stone,*
"*By the vault whose dark abode . . .*"

Her voice swept over me in waves, enveloping me in a kind of warm dankness. She sang all five verses.

And what feeling Miss Tanty put into the words! It was almost as if she were taking you on a guided tour of her own life.

When she had finished, she sat transfixed, as if dazed by her own powers.

"That was super, Miss Tanty!" I said—and it was.

I don't think she heard me. She was staring up into the colored light, at Herodias and Salome, those two triumphant women etched in acid into glass.

"Miss Tanty?"

"Oh!" she said with a start. "I was somewhere else."

"That was magnificent," I said, having had time to choose a more refined word.

Her great bulging eyes swiveled round and focused on me like a pair of spotlights. "Now then," she said. "The truth. I want the truth. What are you up to?"

"Nothing, Miss Tanty. I just brought these flowers . . ."

I produced them from behind my back. ". . . to place on the altar . . ."

"Yes?"

"In memory of poor Mr. Collicutt."

A hiss came out of her.

"Give them here," she rasped, and before I could protest, she stood and snatched the posies from my hand.

"Don't waste your crocuses," she said.

·NINE·

Boom!

A cannon-shot from the back of the church.

Miss Tanty and I blinked at each other in surprise, then swiveled our heads toward the source of the noise.

The great church door, a massive thing of oak and studded iron straps, had slammed shut. There was a scurrying in the shadows.

"Who's there?" Miss Tanty called out in a commanding voice.

There was no answer. A kind of feverish mumbling came from somewhere back among the shadowy pews.

"Who's there? Make yourself known at once."

"The vials of wrath. The blood of a dead man!"

The words came to our ears in a weird whisper made louder by the towering glass and the surrounding stone.

"Come into the light!" Miss Tanty commanded, as a bundle of animated rags worked its way jerkily along the kneeling-benches.

"*For they have shed the blood of saints and prophets, and thou hast given us blood to drink!*"

"It's Meg," I said. "From Gibbet Wood."

Mad Meg (I hesitated to use her nickname in front of Miss Tanty) lived in a hovel in the wood on Gibbet Hill, not far from the rotting remains of the eighteenth-century gibbet that had given both hill and wood their names.

"*Mad* Meg, you mean," Miss Tanty said loudly. "Meg, come out here at once, into the light, where we can have a look at you."

"*The blood of saints, given for Meg to drink,*" Meg said with a horrible wet snicker.

"Rubbish!" Miss Tanty said. "You're talking nonsense."

Meg had now reached a spot of light that fell at the end of a row of pews. Dressed in a rusty black garment which might have been one of Miss Tanty's castoffs, she began moving toward us, her head nodding, the red glass cherry on her flowerpot hat bobbing with saucy detachment. She pointed with a filthy crooked finger to the timbers of the hammer-beam roof that arched above our heads.

"*The blood of saints and prophets,*" she repeated, again nodding her head at us as if to confirm her words, looking eagerly from Miss Tanty's face to mine for some sign of understanding.

"The Book of Revelation," Miss Tanty said. "Chapter sixteen."

Meg looked at her blankly.

"*Saints and prophets,*" she said in reply, her voice now a hoarse but confidential whisper. "*Blood!*"

Her pale staring eyes were almost as bulbous as Miss Tanty's.

At the back of the church a long finger of dazzling daylight fell suddenly into the porch as the door swung open and two dark figures appeared. One of them I recognized at once as the vicar. The other . . . of course! It was Adam Sowerby. I had almost forgotten about the man.

They came strolling casually up the center aisle together, as if they were out for a pleasant walk in a country lane.

"Of course," the vicar was saying, "as dear old Sydney Smith pointed out, bishops are fond of talking of '*my* see, *my* clergy, *my* diocese,' as if these things belonged to them, as their pigs and dogs belong to them. They forget that the clergy, the diocese, *and* the bishops themselves all exist only for the public good."

"The tormenting bishop and the tormented curate, and so forth," Adam said.

"Exactly. 'A curate trod on feels a pang as great as when a bishop is refuted.' It is quite clear that something must be done."

"Perhaps it already has," Adam said.

The vicar stopped in his tracks.

"Oh dear!" he said. "Oh dear! I hadn't thought of that."

"Nor had I—until now," Adam said.

"Hullo!" he added, as he glanced up and spotted the three of us, Meg, Miss Tanty, and me, standing like abandoned brides at the altar. "What have we here? The Three Graces, if I'm not mistaken."

The Three Graces? Which one was I? I wondered: Charm, Beauty, or Creativity?

And which was Miss Tanty? And Mad Meg?

"Hello, Meg," Adam said. "It's been a long old while, hasn't it?"

Meg sank down in a deep and stately curtsy, her grubby fingers pulling her skirt out into an elaborate black tent and revealing striped stockings and a pair of shockingly battered workman's boots of the Victorian lace-up variety.

"You've met?" I'm afraid I blurted. I couldn't help myself. I could hardly believe that someone like Adam Tradescant Sowerby, MA., FRHortS, etc., Flora-archaeologist and all the rest of it, could possibly know the madwoman who lived in Gibbet Wood.

"Meg and I are old acquaintances, aren't we, Meg?" Adam said, with a genuine smile, touching his hand to her tattered shawl. "More than acquaintances, really—colleagues, I should say. Pals, actually, when it comes right down to it."

Meg's mouth stretched wide in a smile which is best not described.

"Her consultations have kept me, on at least one occasion, from making a pharmacological fool of myself."

"*Blood,*" Meg remarked pleasantly. "*The blood of saints and prophets. Blood to drink.*"

Her hand waved vaguely toward the shadows.

"And Miss Tanty, if I'm not mistaken," Adam went on. "I've heard nothing but paeans of praise for the way in which you've breathed new life into the Altar Guild."

Miss Tanty pulled a tight smile which, if anything, was more ghastly than Meg's.

"One does one's best," she said, drawing herself up with rather a fierce glance at the vicar. I was afraid for a moment that the ferocity of her gaze, focused by the bottle-bottom thickness of her spectacles, would shrivel him up like a bug under a burning-glass.

"One can only hope," she added, "to do one's best in spite of all—"

"Dear me!" the vicar said loudly, consulting his wristwatch. "It *is* getting on, isn't it? Wherever does the time go? Cynthia will be waiting for my contribution to the church leaflet. She's become quite the Cassandra ever since the bishop donated his hand-me-down spirit duplicator to replace our dear old superannuated hectograph."

Cassandra? Was he making an unwitting reference to the ghost of Cassandra Cottlestone, whose sudden uprising from the grave may or may not have been the cause of Cynthia's alleged collapse? The only other Cassandra I could think of was the one used by William somebody as a pen name for his sometimes scandalous column in the *Daily Mirror*.

"Like the *Times*," the vicar was saying, "Cynthia's sheets are put to bed at midnight."

I could hardly believe my ears! What was the poor dear man thinking about?

"'The Vicar's Vegetables,' I'm calling my piece," he continued. "Something for the congregation to *chew on* during the week, do you see? I thought that perhaps a bit of levity would go a long way to—but now—oh dear! Whatever will Cynthia think?"

What will Cynthia think? indeed! I thought.

The last I'd heard of Cynthia Richardson, she'd been given a sedative by Dr. Darby after being scared out of her bloomers in the churchyard by the ghost of Cassandra Cottlestone.

Either the injection was just another bit of village gossip, or the vicar was covering up. Cynthia could hardly be stupefied by chloral hydrate and yet still, at the same time, be churning out church bulletins on her Banda machine. It made no chemical sense.

"I should have thought you'd be printing something about Mr. Collicutt," Miss Tanty said, with a sly glance at the vicar.

Hold on, I thought. *What's going on here?*

Just minutes ago the woman had been telling me not to waste my crocuses and now here she was practically begging on bended knee for Mr. Collicutt to be given screaming headlines in the church bulletin.

Adults can sometimes behave in the most peculiar ways.

I'll have to admit that I'd almost forgotten about Mr. Collicutt myself. As discoverer of his corpse, I felt a certain responsibility toward him, but circumstances in the meantime had kept me from giving him more than a moment's thought.

Later, when I was back at Buckshaw, I would turn to a fresh page in my notebook and jot down the pluses and the minuses of the deceased Mr. C. But first, I would need to pump Miss Tanty for details. She, after all, was the one who had made an appointment with the dead man.

I was quite certain that, given time, I could extract enough gossip from her to shock even the most hardened tabloid editor in London. If only I could pry her away from Adam and the vicar.

"Yes, well . . ." the vicar was saying to Miss Tanty, "you really must excuse me," and with that, he turned and trudged slowly down the aisle toward the door.

The image which trickled into my mind was of the plowman homeward plodding his weary way.

"*Sowerby! Blood!*" Meg was calling excitedly from the east aisle. As the others were still chatting, she had made her way back into the shadows among the pews and was beckoning with an unwashed finger.

Adam walked toward her and I followed. After a moment, so did Miss Tanty.

The vicar stopped in his tracks and turned.

I shall never forget that moment. It is etched into my memory like the image on a treasured Christmas card: the three of us, me, Adam, and Miss Tanty, hovering round the crouching Meg like some weird nativity scene carved in wood; the vicar motionless, keeping watch over his flock by night in the far, shadowy fields of the darkened center aisle.

"*Blood,*" Meg said again, looking up at us, as if for approval, jabbing at the floor with her filthy finger.

On the stones at her feet was a red ooze.

"The blood of saints and prophets," she said in a matter-of-fact voice.

In my memory, we are frozen in our places, although there must have been some bending and jostling for a better view of the red puddle at our feet.

Meg, complacent now that her work of convincing us is done, squats happily beside the mess, looking up at our faces in turn.

"For drinking," she explains.

A shaft of sunlight struggles through the colored glass, illuminating the liquid.

A fresh drop falls from above, lands with an audible plop, sending out a tiny, but perfectly circular wave of ripples on the surface of the red puddle.

Meg's bony finger points upward, to where the dark

timbers of the hammer-beam roof stretch like the underside of the floorboards of heaven.

Up there, far above our heads, the carved wooden face of Saint Tancred stares down at us as yet another red drop falls from it into our midst.

And another.

"Old man's crying," Meg says, simply.

·TEN·

ODDLY ENOUGH, THE FIRST to react was Miss Tanty, who, with astonishing flexibility for someone her age, climbed down onto her knees and dipped a finger into the shimmering liquid.

With this she crossed herself, first on her forehead and then again on her breast. *That smeared red stain on her white starched collar is going to be a bugger to get out,* I thought.

"Forgive me, O Lord," she said, clasping her hands under her chin and staring up rapturously for some reason at the kaleidoscope of colors that was the head of John the Baptist.

Adam produced a white linen handkerchief from his jacket pocket and dipped a corner of it into the ruby-colored ooze. After examining it closely, he touched it to his tongue.

Well, why not? I thought. *Since everyone else is sampling the stuff . . .*

Reaching round for my pigtail and untying the remaining white ribbon, I dipped it into the edge of the spreading pool just as another drop fell from the face of the saint in the rafters.

Adam caught my eye and gave me a look which said nothing and yet said everything—an invisible wink.

I don't think the vicar actually saw any of this. He was still making his way toward us, shuffling awkwardly sideways through the long row of pews which separated us from the center aisle. It seemed to take him forever but when he reached us at last and was finally standing between Adam and me, he stared without a word at the bloody mess on the floor.

Now here's a fine pickle! he must have been thinking. *When the wooden head of a saint begins suddenly weeping blood in a remote village church, who do you call? The police? The Archbishop of Canterbury? Or the* News of the World?

"Flavia, dear," he said, laying a quivering hand on my shoulder, "run outside and fetch Sergeant Graves, there's a good girl."

Instantly I felt my face becoming hot, the pressure building up inside my head like Mount Vesuvius.

Why were people always doing this to me? Ordering me about as if I were some kind of specialized chambermaid kept on hand for emergencies?

I counted to eleven. No, twelve.

"Certainly, Vicar," I said, biting my spiritual tongue. Not until I was almost at the door did I add, under my breath, "Would you like a nice cup of tea and a biscuit while I'm at it?"

Sergeant Graves was nowhere in sight. The blue Vauxhall was gone, which meant, I supposed, that the police had done what they had come to do, and then had vanished.

Which explained why the sergeant had allowed me into the church. My cleverly conceived "flowers-for-the-altar" scheme had been a waste of time. Then, too, Meg had come in and slammed the door explosively without so much as a village constable raising an eyebrow.

I should have known it. The police had already been leaving, and now they were gone.

Which was a shame, in a way. If I were completely honest, I would admit that I had been looking forward to renewing old acquaintances with Inspector Hewitt. The Inspector and I had what might presently be described as a lukewarm relationship—mental note: Look up origin of "lukewarm." Possibly biblical? One of the finest passages in the Bible, at least to my way of thinking, was from Revelation: *Because thou art lukewarm, and neither cold nor hot, I will spue thee out of my mouth*—a relationship which seemed, somehow, to blow hot and cold depending upon the Inspector's glorious wife, Antigone. I had not yet sorted out the cogs and levers of our somewhat shaky triangular relationship, but it was certainly not for want of trying.

I had more than once thrown myself upon this warm cool goddess, hoping that she would—

Would what? Pledge herself to be my true sworn friend and secret sharer, forever and ever, world without end, Amen?

Something like that, I suppose. But it had not quite worked out that way.

I had blundered badly by asking her if, on an Inspector's salary, they could not afford to have children. Gracious as she had been in her response, I knew that I had hurt her.

Although I was not accustomed to apologizing, I had done my best, but her lost babies had haunted my sleep for weeks.

What had they looked like? I wondered. Had their hair been dark like hers, or fair and wavy, like his? Were they boys or girls? Did they smile when she cooed at them, and kick up their little feet? What pet names had she whispered to them, and, when it came to that, what final names were given to them before they were placed into the earth?

Motherhood could be a grim old business, I decided, and one that could never, really, be shared. In spite of her gentle exterior, there was a part of the Inspector's wife that was forever beyond knowing.

Perhaps it was like that with all mothers.

I was thinking that when a black Hillman turned in from the main road and came rushing toward me up the church walk, which was not meant to be used by motorcars. I recognized the driver at once: It was Marmaduke Parr, the bishop's secretary.

His car was so well washed that, as he climbed out of it, I could see the back of his white mane reflected in its polished paint.

"Good morning, Mr. Parr," I said, instinctively anxious to keep him from going into the church. The vicar had troubles enough without having a petty bureaucrat from the Diocesan Office barging in on what might yet prove to be a miracle.

An oaken saint whose eyes wept blood would put an end forever to St. Tancred's chronic financial problems. The Roof Fund, after half a century, would be liquidated, and with any luck, those never-ending concerts, fêtes in the churchyard, and games of Tombola in the parish hall would be laid to rest.

"*Reverend* Parr," he corrected, in response to my greeting. "Or *Father* Parr, if you prefer."

The man was biting off more than he could chew. Although he meant it as a snub, he was obviously not aware that for we de Luces, who had been Roman Catholics since the Resurrection, there could never be too many bells, books, and candles.

Because the vicar was one of Father's few friends, we attended St. Tancred's by choice, rather than force. Father looked favorably upon the many innovations that Denwyn Richardson had brought to the parish and had, in fact, once told the vicar to his face, perhaps joking, that he'd always thought of the Oxford Movement as the fold returning to the sheep. All of this, though, was far too complicated to be discussed while standing about in the churchyard.

Marmaduke Parr was staring at me petulantly, impatient to be on about his bullying.

"Then good morning to you," he said, and strode off toward the door.

"I wouldn't go in there if I were you," I called out cheerily. "There's been a murder. The place is closed. Off-limits. It's the scene of a crime."

I used Sergeant Woolmer's exact words, although I didn't bother mentioning that the ban had already been lifted.

He stopped in mid-stride and came slowly back toward me. His face and his eyes seemed paler than ever.

"What do you mean?" he demanded.

"A murder," I explained patiently, one word at a time. "Someone's been killed in the crypt."

"Who?"

"Mr. Collicutt," I whispered importantly. "The organist."

"Collicutt? The organist? That's impossible. Why, he was just—"

"Yes?" I said, waiting.

"Collicutt?" he asked again. "Are you sure?"

"Quite sure," I told him. "Everybody in Bishop's Lacey is talking about it."

This was not quite true, but I had come to believe that there's no harm in spreading a little fear where fear is due.

"Good lord," he said. "I hope not. I surely hope not."

Now we were getting somewhere.

"Is there anything I can do to help?" I asked. "I was hoping to volunteer to assist with digging out Saint Tancred—sorting the bones, and so forth, but it looks as if that's off."

"I should say it's off!" he said. His face went in an instant from the color of curds to a blazing shade of beetroot. "It's desecration! Those who are asleep in the Lord are not to be rousted from their graves for the idle entertainment of a pack of vacant villagers."

Vacant villagers, were we? Well! We shall see about that!

"I understand you've put a stop to it," I said.

"The bishop has put a stop to it," he said, drawing himself up to his full height—which was fairly substantial—as if he were wearing the bishop's miter on his head and gripping the bishop's crosier in his closed fist.

"And not only the bishop," he added, as if a clincher were needed. "The chancellor, too, is dead set against it. He has withdrawn the faculty and forbidden the disinterment. The archaeologists have been sent packing."

"Forbidden?" I asked. I was interested in the word, and not just because it had an amusing sound.

"*Strictly* forbidden." He said this with a note of dooms-day finality.

"And who is the chancellor?" I asked.

"Mr. Ridley-Smith, the magistrate."

Mr. Ridley-Smith, the magistrate? I thought.

Cassandra Cottlestone's father had been a magistrate, Daffy had told me, and as such, was able to move heaven and earth—to the extent even of having his suicide daughter buried in consecrated ground.

"That would be the Ridley-Smiths of Bogmore Hall," I said.

Everyone knew about the Ridley-Smiths of Bogmore Hall, at Nether-Wolsey. They were the subject of stories that had once been whispered behind elaborate paper fans, but were now likely chattered about over cigarettes in the ABC Tea Shop.

I had heard, for instance, from Feely's friend Sheila Foster, about Lionel Ridley-Smith, who thought he was made of glass, and his sister, Anthea, whose pet crocodile had eaten a chambermaid.

"That, of course, was before the First War," Sheila had said, "when chambermaids were thicker on the ground than they are nowadays."

And didn't Miss Pickery, the librarian, have a married sister, Hetty, who lived in Nether-Wolsey?

Hetty had suffered what Miss Mountjoy, the former li-brarian, had once referred to as "a tragic accident" with a sewing machine. And what was it Miss Cool, at the con-fectionery, had contributed to my storehouse of knowl-edge about the mysterious but absent Hetty?

". . . the Singer, the needle, the finger, the twins, the wayward husband, the bottle, the bills . . ." she had told me.

That, of course, had been almost a year ago, but with any luck, Hetty would be more than ever on the lookout for someone who was willing to babysit twins.

"Yes, that's right," Marmaduke Parr said with a sniff. "The Ridley-Smiths of Bogmore Hall."

And before you could say "antitransubstantiational-ist," Gladys and I were speeding along the narrow tarmac on our way to Nether-Wolsey.

By hook or by crook, by fair means or foul, I would make Chancellor Ridley-Smith eat his words. Strictly forbidden, indeed!

To the south and west of Buckshaw was a crossroads, its left arm being, by way of Nether Lacey, more or less a backroad to Doddingsley. To the right was St. Elfrieda's, and beyond it, a little farther to the south, lay Nether-Wolsey.

I saw at once, as I approached, that it was not the prettiest village in England. Not by a long chalk. Even the trees looked tired.

The most notable landmark was an ancient butcher's shop huddled among terraced houses, its gray, unpainted boards sagging like a wooden drape, giving the place the pallor of the undead. In the flyblown window hung an odd arrangement of sausages, tied into strings and loops, and it took me more than a few moments to realize that they spelled out rather distastefully the word MEATS.

A bell tinkled as I opened the door, and then, except

for the buzzing of a solitary fly in the window, the shop fell back into silence.

"Hello?" I called.

The fly buzzed on.

A glass case stretched halfway across the back of the narrow room, and in it were stretched out various slabs of raw meat in a grisly display of red, white, and blue that made my stomach wince.

Behind the counter, mounted in an ornate wrought-iron stand, was a roll of pinkish butcher paper. A length of heavy string dangled handily down from a small wire cage fastened to the ceiling.

At the rear of the shop, in a corner, stood a bloodied butcher block, and behind it was an open door which obviously led to the area behind the shop.

"Hello?" I called again.

There was no answer.

I edged round the glass case and stuck my head out the door.

The garden was littered with empty wooden crates. A reddened tree stump was obviously being used as a chopping block whose victims came from the chicken coops beyond.

As I stood there not quite knowing what to do next, a tiny woman in a skirt, blouse, and bandanna emerged from the largest chicken coop, gripping a large brown hen by its feet.

The bird hung struggling upside down, its stubby wings flapping helplessly.

As she placed its neck on the block and reached for the hatchet, she spotted me in the shop's open doorway.

"Go back inside," she said. "I shall be there directly."

Her bare spindly arm raised the polished blade.

"No! Wait!" I heard myself saying. "Please . . ."

The woman looked up, the ax poised.

"Please," I said. "I want to buy that bird . . . but I want it alive."

What on earth had come over me? Although I didn't mind dead humans—in fact, in some ways I delighted in them—I knew in that instant I could not bear the thought of harm coming to any other creature.

It hadn't been all that long since I had been attacked in Bishop's Lacey by a maddened rooster, and yet, in spite of that bloody free-for-all, my protective wings seemed at this very moment to be sheltering every chicken in the universe. It was a most peculiar feeling.

"Alive . . ." I managed, my head spinning like a toy top.

The woman put down the hatchet and flung the bird away from her. It flew—actually flew!—across the yard, made a half-decent landing, and began pecking at the hardened earth as if nothing had happened.

I knew that if Daffy were here, she would have said *"Curfew shall not ring tonight."* This particular hen, at least for now, would live to cluck another day.

I had saved my first life.

Is there life after death for chickens? I wondered. Given the prospect of the ax, the plucking, the seething pot, the heat of the oven, and the gnawings of our hungry teeth at the Sunday table, it seemed somehow unlikely.

And yet . . . and yet, in spite of all that, perhaps there really was the reward of a heavenly roost somewhere above the bright blue sky.

"I came away without my money," I said. "I'll bring it to you as soon as I can."

"Not from around here, are you?" the woman asked, walking toward me.

"No, but not far," I said, waving a vague hand toward the north.

"Haven't I seen you before?" she asked, close enough now to peer into my face.

It was at that moment that I was struck with a brilliant thought: *Tell the truth.* Yes, that was it—tell the truth. What did I have to lose?

"Perhaps you have," I told her. "My name is Flavia de Luce."

"Of course," she said. "I should have known. The blue eyes, the—"

She stopped as if she had run into a stone wall.

"Yes?"

"We used to take poultry to Buckshaw," she said slowly, "to Mrs. Mullet. I suppose she's long gone?"

"No," I said. "She's still with us.

"Fortunately," I was quick enough to add.

"But that was years ago," the woman said. "Years ago. Before— But tell me, what brings you to Nether-Wolsey?"

"I'm looking for a woman named Hetty. I don't know her last name, but she's—"

"Patsy Pickery's sister."

Patsy? Was "Patsy" Miss Pickery's name?

I put my hand in front of my mouth to suppress a smile.

"Yes," I said. "That's the one. Patsy Pickery's sister."

I enjoyed pronouncing the name, the way it rolled off my tongue in a limping rhyme: "Pat-sy Pick-ery's sister."

"Gone," she said. "She's took the kids and gone. Lived right across the road next the petrol station till Rory

belted her once too often and she took the kids and—
What do you want with her, anyway?"

"I wanted to ask her a question."

"Maybe I can answer it."

"It's about Bogmore Hall," I said, and I could see the
woman's face closing even before the words were out of
my mouth.

"Keep clear of Bogmore Hall," she warned. "It's not the
kind of place for someone like you."

Someone like me? Whatever could she mean by that?

"There's something I need to discuss with Mr. Ridley-
Smith, the magistrate."

"Got yourself into some kind of trouble, have you?"
she asked, closing one eye like Popeye.

"No, not really."

"Well, all the same—don't go hanging round. Things
aren't right up there, if you take my meaning." Her finger
came, almost automatically, it seemed, to her head.

"The Ridley-Smiths, you mean? The crocodile? The
man who was made of glass?"

The woman snorted. "Made of glass my fanny!" she
said. "You listen to me. There are things that are worse
than glass and crocodiles. You keep away from that place."

She waved her hand toward what I guessed was the
southwest.

"All right," I said. "Thank you. I will."

As I turned and went back into the shop, she was not
far behind me.

"I'll be back for the chicken as soon as I can," I told her
over my shoulder.

I was already in the street with a foot on one of Gladys's pedals when the woman came scurrying out of the

shop, a wooden crate in her hands. Through its slats, the brown hen was craning her neck in all directions, her yellow eyes glaring fiercely out at this vast new and unsuspected world.

"Her name's Esmeralda," she said, hurriedly strapping the crate to Gladys's rear carrier.

"The money—" I began.

But before I could finish, the woman had scurried back into the shop and slammed the door.

To the south of Nether-Wolsey, the road ran gently downhill. To the west, another rose steeply to a prominent ridge which brooded like a single dark eyebrow over the village. It might well have been an old hill fort.

This was the direction the woman had indicated as she warned me about Bogmore Hall. It couldn't be far away.

I turned to the west.

After a while the rising road became steeper and steeper, and was now little more than a stony path. Even in first gear Gladys was wobbling dangerously. I climbed off and shoved her slowly ahead of me up the steep slope.

As I came up out of a deep cutting onto a flat plateau, there was no doubt that the dark Gothic pile ahead of me was Bogmore Hall. A crazy conglomeration of spiky gables gave it the look of a bundle of ancient lances shoved carelessly, points uppermost, into an oversized umbrella stand.

Cut off from the rest of the world, the house stood in the middle of a sea of wild grass from which protruded mossy chunks of broken stone which might once have been the cherubs and nymphs of urns and fountains.

A chubby white arm stuck up out of the earth like a dead baby trying to escape its grave.

Windows without curtains stared at me blankly, and the idea crept into my head that I was being watched by more than glass. A worn block of stone served as a doorstep, as if renovations had been begun in another century and then abandoned.

It seemed rather a rum place for a magistrate to live.

I leaned Gladys against a ruined railing and tugged at the rusty bellpull. Although I could not hear it, I knew that somewhere in the depths of the house a bell would be jangling.

Nobody, of course, answered.

I rang again: once . . . twice . . . three times.

Even by putting my ear to the door I could hear nothing inside. And yet there remained that uneasy sense of being watched.

Turning my back to the house, I strolled casually out onto what once might have been the front lawn, but which was now a tangle of clods embedded with last year's weeds. I put a flattened hand above my eyes and pretended to be gazing out at the view, which, from this elevation, really was quite spectacular.

Then suddenly I whipped round.

A white face shrank back from an upstairs window.

I hauled at the bellpull again, this time ringing ever more insistently. But as before, the house remained in silence.

I tried the door but it was locked.

So that I could not be seen from inside, I flattened myself against the wall and made my way slowly, one step at a time, all the way round the house to the kitchen door, where, as Mrs. Mullet had once assured me, "There's always a key under the mat."

She was wrong. The key was not under the mat, but it *was* hidden under a broken flowerpot not two feet away from the doorsill.

I was never more happy that Dogger had taught me so much about the art of locks.

This was no ordinary household skeleton key, but one of the patent Yale variety. Whoever had this lock installed had meant to keep people out.

Odd, though, that they should leave the key so handily under a broken flowerpot.

I slid the key's jagged teeth quietly into the lock, turned it, and slipped into the house.

The kitchen was a dim box, lighted coldly by a single window high on the wall. The gray slate floor made the room seem like a prison cell. The unlit stove offered no warmth or comfort.

I shivered at the general clamminess of the place and pulled my cardigan tight round my shoulders.

A broad door, designed, I supposed, for the wheeling-in of ancient feasts—boars' heads and so forth—led into a short corridor and then, on the left, to a breakfast room in which two places were partially set with knives, forks, spoons, and eggcups. Someone was ready for tomorrow, I thought.

I moved silently through into the dim foyer: cracked tiles, dark portraits of sour old men in judge's wigs, and the faint smell of kippers. A tall clock ticked unnervingly, as if counting the seconds to an execution. Perhaps my own.

What would I do if I were caught? Pretend that I had seen smoke at an upper window? But if that were the case, why hadn't I called out to alert the house's occupants? Or, for that matter, shouted to them from outside?

How had I managed to find the key?

Perhaps I needed to use the telephone. Perhaps, while cycling, my blood pressure had fallen suddenly, leaving me dizzy and confused. Perhaps I was in urgent need of a doctor.

A bell went off!—and then another, echoing horribly in the empty foyer. Now my heart really *was* pounding. Had I set off a hidden alarm? A family of judges was likely to be well up on the subject of burglars.

But no, it was only the stupid clock, bonging away in the corner to keep itself company in the oddly empty house.

I looked into one or two of the rooms and found them much the same: high ceilings, bare floors, a stick or two of furniture, and the tall uncurtained windows I had noticed from outside.

It was evident from the very feel of the downstairs rooms that no one was about, and within a few minutes I was walking round as freely as if I owned the place.

Billiards room, ballroom, drawing room, library—all of them as cold as ashes. A small dark study was stacked to the ceiling with legal papers and folders, the lower, heavier ones of vellum and the lighter upper layers of yellowed paper.

Strata of people's lives, I thought, *heaped up in piles awaiting judgment. Or already judged. How many of these million documents*, I wondered, *have the name de Luce inked upon their dusty pages?*

I sneezed and a floorboard creaked.

Was someone here?

No—not, at least, in this room. It was just a pile of papers settling in the corner.

I made my way back to the foyer. The house was, I thought with a shudder, as silent as a tomb.

"Hello?" I shouted, my voice echoing as if I were in a cave.

I knew, somehow, that nobody would answer, and they didn't.

And yet someone was here—I was sure of it. That white face shrinking away from the upstairs window had hardly been in my imagination.

A chambermaid, perhaps, too frightened at being caught alone in the place to show herself. Or could it have been the ghost of that earlier chambermaid who had been devoured by Anthea Ridley-Smith's crocodile? Or the transparent spirit of Lionel Ridley-Smith, who had been made of glass?

Whoever or whatever it was awaited me upstairs.

Did I think of bolting?

Well, yes, I did.

But then I thought of how Marmaduke Parr had bullied the vicar, and of how disappointed the entire village of Bishop's Lacey would be—most of all myself—not to have the bones of our very own saint visibly present among us at the feast of his quincentennial.

When they finally saw the light, I might even become something of a village heroine, with banquets, etc. held in my honor, with after-dinner speeches by Father, the vicar, the bishop, and, yes, perhaps even by Magistrate Ridley-Smith himself, thanking me for my dogged persistence, and so forth.

I believe Daffy referred to such an extravagant

outpouring of praise as an *encomium*, and I realized that I had not been given an encomium for a very long while.

If ever.

I started up the stairs—one slow step at a time, listening for the slightest sound of life.

Whether it's a whole house or just a single drawer, there's a deep and primitive pleasure that comes from snooping through someone else's belongings. Although part of me was scared silly, the greater part was having the time of my life. I wanted to whistle, but I didn't dare.

At the top of the stairs, like the passageway of an ocean liner, a long hall led off to the right into some remote distance, its floor covered with pockmarked linoleum. Bedrooms, I guessed, each with a dismal four-poster, a table with ewer and basin, and an enamel chamber pot.

A quick peek into several of these on each side of the hall proved that I was correct.

Back at the head of the staircase, a solid wooden door with a small porthole seemed to promise another long hall running in the opposite direction. The servants' quarters, perhaps. I cupped my hands and peered through the glass but could see only darkness.

I wiggled the knob and to my surprise, the door swung open.

Behind it hung a heavy pair of green velvet drapes which, by their musty smell, had last been cleaned when Henry VIII was a bachelor.

I pulled them reluctantly aside, dusting my hands, and found myself face-to-face with another door. This one, too, had a circular porthole which, unlike the other, was made of frosted glass.

I wiggled the knob but this second door was locked.

Locked doors seemed to be everywhere, I thought. First, the wooden door in the churchyard tunnel, and now these.

Was it a coincidence?

Ordinarily, I should have skipped down the stairs to the kitchen, pocketed a cheap fork and a bottle brush, and made quick work of the thing.

But again the lock was a Yale.

There was no way of getting into this wing of the house other than by scaling an outside wall. Unless there was another entrance from the back stairs.

In momentary frustration, I stretched my hand wide and flattened my fingers against the cold glass.

There was a flicker—a mere shifting of light—and then the black shadow of a hand materialized, spread itself against the other side of the pane, matching my hand, finger for finger—except that these fingers were webbed!

Save for the quarter-inch thickness of the glass, this whatever-it-was and I were almost touching.

I gasped.

But before I could move, the bolt clicked. The knob turned with maddening slowness and the door swung open, inch by inch.

He was small, and dressed in a Norfolk jacket with baggy plus fours, a yellow checkered vest, and a high white celluloid collar—someone's cast-off clothing which must have been found in a trunk.

The corners of his eyes and—as I had already noted—his fingers were webbed. He had a round face which rose above a tiny chin and a large tongue which his mouth couldn't quite contain. His ears, small and round, were set low on his head, and his skin looked as if it had been rubbed all over with candle wax.

Was he a man or was he a boy? It was difficult to tell. His face was young and unlined, but his neatly combed hair was completely white. Like Dogger's, I realized with a shock.

I hadn't moved. I stood frozen, my arm outstretched, fingers spread as if I were stopping a runaway horse, my hand still in the same position it had been against the glass.

For an uncomfortably long time we stood staring at each other.

And then he spoke.

"Hello, Harriet," he said.

·ELEVEN·

A COLD SHIVER SHOOK me. A goose had waddled over my grave.

Not knowing that she was dead, this poor man was obviously under the impression that I was Harriet. Would I be able to act out the lie, or should I simply tell him the truth?

He stepped back and beckoned me in through the open door.

It's at moments like this that you find out what you're made of: moments when everything you've ever been taught is fighting against your heart. On the one hand, I wanted to run—down the stairs, out of this house, home to Buckshaw, up to my room, lock the door, and dive under the blankets. On the other I wanted to throw my arms about this round little person, let him put his head on my shoulder, and hug him until the sun burned out.

I stepped inside and he shut the door abruptly behind me, as if he had captured a rare butterfly.

"Come," he said. "Sit."

I followed him into the room.

"You have been gone a long time," he said as I perched on an offered armchair.

"Yes," I said, deciding in that instant to follow my instincts. "I've been away."

"I beg your pardon?" He cocked his head toward me.

"I've been away," I repeated, louder this time.

"Are you well?" he asked.

His voice was quite deep: too deep for a boy, I decided.

"Yes," I said. "Quite well. And you?"

"I suffer," he said. "But otherwise I am quite well also.

"Tea!" he added suddenly.

He went to a sideboard where an enamel teapot stood on a small hot plate. He switched it on and stood wiping his fingers nervously on his trouser legs as it heated.

I took the opportunity to look round the room: bed, dresser with black Bible, clothespress. On the wall above the bed were a couple of photographs. The first, in a black frame, was of a man in robes, standing with the knuckles of one hand pressed white against a tabletop, an open book in the other, staring with contempt at the camera. Magistrate Ridley-Smith—I was sure of it.

The second photograph, smaller than the other, was in an oval frame of what looked like bamboo. In it, a pale-faced woman in a frilly white dress looked up with haunted eyes from her needlework, as if someone had just broken some tragic piece of news. She was seated on a verandah from which glimpses of exotic trees were visible, but out of focus in the background.

There was something familiar about her.

I maneuvered myself as casually as I could for a closer look.

The little man turned off the switch, lifted the kettle, and poured some of the tar-black liquid for each of us.

"Your favorite cup," he said, handing me a china tea-cup and saucer decorated with large blue pansies. The cup was badly chipped along the rim, black cracks running out from each nick like a map of the Amazon and all its tributaries.

"Thank you," I said, turning away from the photograph. I would need to be better acquainted before summoning up enough boldness to ask about her. "It's been ages since I had a good cup of tea."

Which, except for my breakfast with Dogger, was true.

I forced myself to raise it to my mouth and smile pleasantly as the acrid sludge ate away at my taste buds. This brew had been steeping for months.

After a very long pause he asked, "How is Buckshaw?"

"Much the same as ever," I said.

Which was also true.

He was staring at me eagerly over the rim of his cup.

"It's lovely in the spring," I said. "It's always lovely in the spring."

He nodded sadly, as if he didn't quite know what spring was.

"Is the magistrate at home today?" I asked. I did not want to risk guessing whether this curious man with whom I was sipping tea was the son or the brother of Mr. Ridley-Smith. I had never seen him at St. Tancred's, whose parishioners I knew on sight from the oldest gaffer to Mrs. Lang's latest baby.

"Father?" he said. "Mr. Ridley-Smith? Mr. Ridley-Smith is never at home."

"I was hoping to see him about a church matter," I said.

He nodded wisely. "About the saint?"

I almost dribbled my tea. "Yes," I said. "Actually it is. How did you know?"

"Mr. Ridley-Smith talks to Benson in the air."

"I beg your pardon?"

"In the air," he repeated, waving a hand. "Mr. Ridley-Smith talks to Benson."

"I see," I said, although I didn't see at all.

"The saint must not be wakened!" he said in a suddenly loud, gruff voice, and I realized he was mimicking his father.

"Why not?" I asked.

He did not reply, but stared up at the ceiling.

"Shhh!" he said.

My ears had already picked up a change in the sound of the room, as if it had suddenly become larger. There was a humming—a hiss . . .

"Ottorino Respighi," a flat, hollow voice announced, seeming to come from nowhere. *"The Pines and Fountains of Rome."*

The words were spoken without expression, as if the person who spoke them were tired of breathing. He also mispronounced "Respighi."

There was a *click!* and then the crackling of a needle in the grooves of a spinning phonograph record.

The tinny music began. I located its source at last as a grilled opening high on the wall.

"Why—" I began, but he stopped me instantly with a raised hand.

"Listen!" he said, putting a webbed finger to his lips.

Perhaps there was another announcement to come, I thought. It was obvious that someone else was in the house. The dull voice had not been that of a BBC commentator, and it certainly hadn't the sound of a magistrate or a chancellor.

What if he caught me here?

The Pines and Fountains of Rome spun on, providing a dramatic sound track to my teeming thoughts.

Who was it that kept this unfortunate man locked away in an upper room? And why? Why did they force music upon him from a hidden loudspeaker? Who was Benson? Why must the saint not be wakened?

"Was that Benson speaking?" I asked, but again my words were met with the finger to the lips and an urgent "*Shh!*"

Why not help this man escape? I thought. I would simply lead him out through the two doors, down the stairs, through the foyer, and outside. I would balance him on Gladys's seat, let him hang onto my waist, coast downhill to Nether-Wolsey, then pump us, standing up, all the way to Bishop's Lacey. I would take him to the vicarage and—

"Wait a minute," a voice said inside my head. "The door to this room was locked. He let you *in*!"

Which of us then, was the captive?

If the second door was able to be opened with an inside bolt, what was its purpose? To keep someone out?

Was the outer door also able to be opened from the inside? Had there been a bolt? I hadn't noticed. It certainly hadn't been locked. Perhaps Benson, or whoever the disembodied voice belonged to, had accidentally left it open.

Two doors, two locks: one open and one not.

It was like a puzzle in *The Girl's Own Annual*.

I was thinking this when the music came to an end.

"Music teaches. Music soothes the savage beast," my host (or was he my captor?) said, and again I thought I detected the mimicking of a harsher voice.

Before I could ask him another question, the disembodied voice spoke again, riding above the hum and buzz of the loudspeaker:

"Peter Ilyich Tchaikovsky," it said. "*Swan Lake* overture."

There was a muted crash, as if someone had dropped a piece of china in another room.

"As you were," the voice ordered, and there was an uneasy silence.

"Franz Schubert," it said at last in a swamp-flat tone. "*Death and the Maiden.*"

Again the needle was dropped into the record's grooves and the sounds of a string quartet came straining out through the sievelike covering of the speaker.

Death and the Maiden? I thought. Could it be a warning? What kind of madhouse had I stumbled into?

My host was now sitting perfectly still, absorbed totally in the music, his eyes closed, his hands folded in his lap, his lips pronouncing silent words.

His hardness of hearing made it unlikely that he would detect faint noises which, thanks to Franz Schubert, would also be masked by the music. As long as I didn't cast a shadow across his face, I should be quite safe. I got slowly to my feet and moved with glacial slowness across the room, going round to his right and behind him to avoid passing in front of the window.

When I reached the dresser, I opened the cover of the heavy black Bible.

Hallelujah!

As I had hoped, the branches of the Ridley-Smith family tree coiled like jungle vines across the page. At the very bottom, under "Births," was this entry:

Vivian Joyous Ridley-Smith—1 January, 1904.

Vivian. So that was his name. He was forty-seven years old.

I was closing the Bible when my fingers scraped against a sharp corner. Something was projecting slightly beyond the edges of the next two pages.

An envelope. I slipped it out.

On its front was written in a flowing—and obviously feminine—hand: *Dearest Jocelyn.*

It must have been from an earlier time: something removed from the family papers. But who was Jocelyn, the recipient?

There was no postage stamp, so obviously no date on the envelope. It must have been delivered by hand.

I held it to my nose and gave a sniff and my heart almost froze as my nostrils were filled with the odor of small blue flowers, of mountain meadows, and of ice.

Miratrix!

Harriet's scent!

I had smelled it often enough in her boudoir. It was as familiar to me as the back of my own hand.

With clumsy fingers I opened the envelope and extracted the single sheet of paper.

Dearest Jocelyn, it began.

Jocelyn?

And then I saw! Of course! "Jocelyn"—"Joss"—was a variation of "Joyous."

A nickname. A name that only his family and his closest friends—or perhaps only Harriet—would have called him.

> Dearest Jocelyn,
> I shall be going away for a time, and unable to visit you. I shall miss the two of us reading together, and hope that you will keep on with it. Remember what I told you: Books make the soul float.
> Your friend,
> H.

> p.s. Burn after reading.

Oddly enough, it was only then that my brain admitted that this was Harriet's handwriting.

My hands were suddenly shaking like a leaf in winter. My mother had written this note as she was about to set out on her final journey.

I shoved the paper back into its envelope and replaced it in the Bible.

The music slowly floated back into my consciousness: the sawing away of the strings at that mournful melody.

Death and the Maiden.

Jocelyn was still listening intently, his eyes closed.

How often had Harriet visited him here? I wondered. How had she managed to get in through all those doors—at least two of them locked?

Perhaps, eleven or twelve years ago, things had been different. Perhaps, like Buckshaw, Bogmore Hall had once been a happy home.

But somehow I doubted it. The place was what I imagined an abandoned courtroom would be like: cold and empty and smelling of judgment, the last prisoner dragged away for punishment.

Except Jocelyn, of course. It seemed as if he had been sentenced to life.

I began to think what a horrid existence he must lead when my mind began sending me an urgent message—something about the double doors. What was it?

The locks! If Benson, or whoever Jocelyn's jailer was, *had* in fact forgotten to lock the outer door, and should happen to return for any reason, I would be locked in, too.

I had to get out of this place at once! Any thoughts I might have had of questioning Jocelyn about his father, or Harriet, or the saint who must not be wakened would have to be put off until another day.

As long as he stayed inside his instructional musical bubble, I could leave quietly without his noticing.

I plotted my course and began moving slowly toward the door. I was halfway across the room when the music ended.

Jocelyn swiveled his head a little to the right—and then to the left. He got up out of his chair and turned completely round just as my hand touched the doorknob.

His eyes met mine, his face expressionless. It was impossible to tell what he was thinking.

I don't know what made me do it, but it must have been some primitive memory that caused me, without even thinking, to raise three fingers to my lips and blow him a kiss.

And then I went out the door.

Now I was back in the small chamber, the dusty curtains dragging across my face like the cobweb of some obscene, mammoth spider. I fought free of them and shot back the bolt of the outside door. There *had been* a bolt, after all.

Hold on, though!

Would Benson be lying in wait on the other side? Catching an intruder red-handed would be a real feather in his cap.

Keeping my eye well back from the glass porthole, I moved my head slowly from side to side, viewing the outer room piece by piece, yard by yard.

It was empty.

I eased the door open and was stepping through it when I heard the sound of footsteps. A moment later, seen through the banisters, a head appeared. An oddly familiar head.

Someone was coming up the stairs! A man.

There was nowhere to hide. It was too late.

Good job I hadn't yet closed the door behind me. I dodged back into the cubicle and quietly eased the bolt shut.

Had he seen me?

I couldn't get back into Jocelyn's room—the inner door had locked behind me. I was stuck in the dark, airless space between the two doors: trapped among the moldering velvet curtains.

A key scratched at the lock.

The dust was eating at my nostrils like black pepper—I could feel it. I was going to sneeze.

I pinched my nose between thumb and forefinger and tried to breathe through my mouth as I huddled into the corner behind the door, shrinking back, trying to make myself as small as possible.

The door opened, jamming me against the wall, crushing the air out of my lungs.

There was a pause—and then the sound of a key in the second lock.

I couldn't breathe. I was going to suffocate.

Then suddenly the pressure eased as the outer door was closed.

I was now locked into the cubicle with the man. He was so close I could smell his breath. Tobacco and kippers.

There was a shuffling, and the curtains billowed.

"Open the door, will you?" he called out loudly, almost in my ear. "I've got a tray."

There was a banging, as if he were kicking at the inner door with his toe.

After an eternity, a bolt clicked back.

"Benson?" Jocelyn's voice called through the door.

"Who else did you think it was," the man growled. "The king of Siam?"

And then he was gone and I was alone in the stuffy cubicle.

I counted to three and slid open the bolt of the outer door, which I left ajar behind me as I made for the top of the stairs.

Fourteen, fifteen, sixteen: Down the stone steps I flew as if the hounds of Hades were barking at my backside. I counted the treads as they flew by beneath my feet. Now I was at the landing. *Twenty-two, twenty-three, twenty-four—* two at a time—*twenty-six.* Across the foyer and out the front door, and only then, I think, did I begin to breathe.

Gladys was where I had left her, leaning against the crumbling stone railing. Esmeralda was pecking at the bottom of the crate, absorbed in her own thoughts.

As I pedaled away, I risked a glance back over my shoulder at the upper windows. They were empty.

No face at the window. No Jocelyn, and thankfully, no Benson.

I knew that I had seen him somewhere before as soon as I saw him coming up the stairs.

The problem was this—I could not for the life of me remember where.

·TWELVE·

THE SUN WAS ALREADY far down in the west as I pedaled home to Buckshaw.

Father, I knew, would be furious. He demanded that all of us, with no exceptions, no excuses, be seated, properly dressed, and on time for the evening meal. Now, because of my tardiness ("tardiness" is one of those ten-shillings-sixpence words that Daffy loves to fling at me), Mrs. Mullet would have been kept late, and Father, who had been trying desperately to slash expenses by reducing her working hours, would be on the hook for additional overtime.

Even before I reached the Mulford Gates I knew that something was wrong. A knot of people had gathered in the road at the turn-in.

Had there been an accident?

I put on such a burst of speed that I was forced to jam on both hand brakes and come skidding to an undignified sideways stop to avoid hitting them.

Still astride Gladys, but with both feet on the ground, I came waddling over toward the group. I could scarcely believe my eyes.

Father, Feely, Daffy, Dogger, and Mrs. Mullet stood in a ragged semicircle. Not one of them even looked at me.

The center of their attention was a man in an undersized vest with a tight celluloid collar and watery, protruding eyes who was pounding a sign into the ground with a sledgehammer.

FOR SALE, it said, in awful black letters.

DOOM! DOOM! DOOM! the hammer went, and every blow was a stake through my heart.

Buckshaw for sale! I couldn't believe it!

There had been threats, of course, and Father in the past had warned us that he was losing his long battle with the government department he once referred to in a lighter moment as "His Majesty's Leeches." But somehow we had always muddled through; something had always turned up.

Just a few months ago, for instance, a First Quarto of Shakespeare's *Romeo and Juliet* had come to light in our library, but because his own initials and Harriet's had been entwined in ink in the front of the book—a memorial to their courtship—Father had refused to part with it.

The actor Desmond Duncan had besieged him with one outrageous offer after another, but Father had brushed them aside. The British Museum had then been enlisted to make a combined proposal that would probably have bought the whole town of Stratford-upon-Avon right down to the last swan.

But Father wouldn't budge.

And now it had come to this.

There were times when I wanted to shake Father: wanted to pick him up by his lapels and shake him until the feathers flew out.

"You stubborn fool!" I wanted to shout into his face.

And then, as reason seeped back into my overheated brain, I would realize how much alike we were: that my father angered me the most when he was most like me.

It didn't make the slightest bit of sense, but there it was.

And now here we were, all of us standing round in the road like yokels at the fair, watching a stranger pound a signboard into our ancestral earth.

It was only then, as I realized that my family, every last one of them, had been drawn out of doors and had walked the considerable distance along the avenue of chestnuts from the house to the Mulford Gates to watch a bailiff seize our property, that the gravity of the situation hit home.

It was the first time I could remember us ever being truly together.

And there we stood: we de Luces all grim as death, Dogger looking on, his jaw muscles tense, and Mrs. Mullet in tears.

"'Tisn't right," she muttered, shaking her head. "'Tisn't right at all."

She was the only one to speak.

After a time, Father moved slowly off toward the house, followed by Feely and Daffy, then Dogger.

The bailiff, his work finished, dusted his hands and threw his sledgehammer into the boot of a muddy Anglia that was parked at the roadside. Moments later, he was gone.

Mrs. Mullet and I stood there silently together in the darkening world.

"Your supper's in the warming oven, dear," she said, then turned and walked away, ever so slowly, in the direction of Bishop's Lacey.

Later, in my bedroom, I was sitting hunched up among the pillows picking at my plate, tossing the occasional tinned pea to Esmeralda on the floor, when there came a light tapping at the door.

It was Dogger.

"I've brought some bread and water for your friend," he said, putting down one of the two bowls he was carrying onto the floor.

"Her name is Esmeralda," I said. "They were going to kill her."

With Dogger, there was no need for long, detailed explanations. He understood things as quickly and as easily as if he absorbed them through his skin.

"A very fine example of a Buff Orpington," he said, tossing her a bread crumb. "Are you not, Esmeralda?"

Esmeralda pounced upon the crumb and it vanished. Dogger threw her another.

"She wouldn't eat," I said. "I tried her with some of my corn."

"She may be broody," Dogger said. "Certain varieties are more inclined than others to go broody in the spring."

"What's broody?" I asked. I'd never heard the word.

"It means being short-tempered and with a strong inclination to sit on one's nest," Dogger said.

"Like Father," I blurted. I couldn't help myself.

Dogger threw another fat crumb to Esmeralda. "A very strong breed, the Buff Orpington," he said. "Very British. The Queen is said to be very fond of them. She keeps a flock at Windsor Castle, I believe."

"Perhaps we could go in for chickens at Buckshaw!" I said with sudden inspiration. "We could knock together some cages in the coach house and sell eggs at the market in Malden Fenwick. It would be jolly good fun."

"I'm afraid it will take more than chickens," Dogger said, with a long sigh, and then, after what seemed like an eternal pause he added, "No, I'm afraid that chickens are not enough."

"But what's to be done?" I asked.

"We must pray, Miss Flavia. That's all that's left."

"Good idea," I said. "I'll pray before I go to sleep tonight that nobody sees the 'For Sale' sign. Then, first thing in the morning, I shall go out and chop it into kindling wood."

"That would do no good," Dogger said. "The notice will appear in all the papers."

"Perhaps if we prayed to Saint Tancred . . ." I said, my mind bubbling with ideas. "After all, he *is* our patron saint. Do you think it will hurt that we're not Anglicans?"

"No," Dogger said. "In Tancred's day there was no Church of England. He was as Roman Catholic as ever you could wish for."

"Are you sure?" I asked.

"*Quite* sure."

"Then it's settled. I shall be there when they open his tomb and pray for Buckshaw before anyone else has a chance to stick in a request."

Which brought me, with something of a jar, back to the church's crypt and the dead Mr. Collicutt.

Last night, I had slept through my opportunity to re-visit the churchyard and to explore the tunnel which connected the church with the tomb of Cassandra Cottlestone.

Was it now too late? Had the police already discovered the secret passage? Or had they overlooked it in their rush to find the murderer?

There was only one way to find out.

"Good night, Dogger," I said, making a counterfeit yawn. "A good sleep will help me get an early start."

I didn't say *how* early.

At a quarter past two in the morning, the road was a ribbon of moonlight, just as it was in Mr. Noyes's poem "The Highwayman." In my long, dark, winter churchgoing coat, I might have been the highwayman himself, except for the fact that I was riding a bicycle and wasn't planning to end up dead like a dog on the highway.

"Bundle up warm," Mrs. Mullet was forever telling me, and this time, I was taking her advice. In heavy brown stockings and a woolen sweater underneath my Sunday coat, I was as warm as toast, perfectly kitted out for a descent into the underworld.

The cold air of the early morning rushed past my face and a hunting owl swooped low across the road in front of me. I wanted to shout "Yaroo!" but I didn't dare risk it. You never know who's listening in the darkness.

I pulled the torch from my pocket and carried out a quick test. Rather than beaming it onto the road and making my presence known for miles around, I shoved the lens end into my mouth and clicked the switch. I was rewarded with a rich red glow from my puffed-out cheeks. It was working.

To anyone abroad at this forsaken hour, such as poachers, I would look like the skull of a ghastly jack-o'-lantern floating along the road to Bishop's Lacey, with hollow black eyes and a head lit from within by an unearthly fire.

I swiveled my head from side to side and glared horribly into the ditches.

Legends would spring up: "The Huntsman from Hell," they would tell their children in hushed voices, and claim that they had even heard the hoofbeats of a ghostly horse.

They would warn them against stealing sweets and telling lies.

Although it was pleasant to tell myself such tales, part of me knew that I was only doing it to fight off fear.

Who knew what horrors I would find in that dank, earthy passage beneath the church? It wasn't so much the thought of undead spirits that troubled me as much as the knowledge that a killer was still on the loose in Bishop's Lacey.

At this early hour, there would be no police at the scene of the crime: nobody to rescue me if I got myself into a jam.

The churchyard, when I got to it, was like the nerve-jangling illustrations in one of Daffy's Gothic novels: all sunken shadows, tombstones leaning like broken teeth, and everywhere that eerie graveyard moss which has an almost invisible luminescent glow of stale greenish-blue in the cold light of a nearly full March moon.

I parked Gladys on the north side of Cassandra Cottle-stone's tomb and gave her leather seat a pat. The silver glint of her handlebars reminded me of a frightened horse showing the whites of its eyes.

"Keep a sharp lookout," I whispered. "I'll be right back."

The mound of earth and the tarpaulin looked much as I had left them. As nearly as I could tell by moonlight, there were no new footprints, no fresh impressions of official boots.

So far, so good, I thought.

I worked my way under the tarpaulin, let my feet dangle in empty air for a few seconds—then dropped into the grave.

As before, my nostrils were pinched instantly by the stink, but this time I had decided to switch it off in my brain.

Little danger now of having the light of my torch spotted, so I clicked it on and turned my attention to the heavy wooden door.

I had brought with me one of my favorite lock-picking tools: a set of my wire dental braces which I had ruined forever last summer by putting them to good use for a similar purpose at Greyminster School. Those and a bent pickle fork—which nobody, I hoped, would ever miss—were all that a person would ever need to open nearly every lock in Christendom.

The problem was that this lock was rusty. It couldn't be too badly oxidized, I thought, since, if my theory was correct, it had been used at least as recently as six weeks ago. Still, the stupid thing was stuck.

Where was I going to find a decent lubricating oil in the bottom of a reeking tomb at two-thirty in the morning?

The answer came to me almost as quickly as the question.

There is an unsaturated hydrocarbon with the molecular formula of $C_{30}H_{50}$ and the unlovely name of "squalene," which is found in yeast, olive oil, fish eggs, the liver of certain sharks, and the skin of the human nose.

Because of its extremely high viscosity, it has been used by clockmakers to oil cogs, by butlers to polish ebony, by burglars to lubricate revolvers, and by smokers to baby the bowls of their favorite pipes.

Good old, jolly old everyday nose oil to unstick a good old, jolly old everyday mortise lock.

The door itself had been banged together from heavy planks and I could still see the marks of the chisel with which the lock had been roughly installed. It was of the warded type, which opens with a skeleton key.

A piece of cake.

I raked a thumbnail across the side of my nose and wiped the oily deposit onto one end of my mangled braces. Holding the torch between a hunched shoulder and my chin, I inserted the hooked end of the wire into the keyhole and jiggered it about until I judged the wards and levers had been sufficiently lubricated.

Then, after pushing and pulling the hooked end of my improvised lock-pick in and out until it was lined up with the levers, I gave it a sudden twist.

At first . . . nothing. Resistance. And then . . . a satisfying *click!*

I turned the knob and the door swung open with a hollow groan.

I stepped over the rough wooden sill and into the tunnel.

Dank and *acrid* are the two words that best describe the smell of the place. I was now about five or six feet beneath the surface, and from this point onward, the tunnel sloped downward toward the church. Whoever had dug it, I supposed, had wanted to get well below the graveyard's grisly contents.

I was well aware, as I moved slowly along, that the earth above my head and on both sides contained all that remained of Bishop's Lacey's dead, most of whose bones had long ago leached and whose fluids had seeped over the centuries into the spongy soil.

One of the vicar's sermons popped unexpectedly into my mind: the one about how we are the clay and the Lord our potter—a lesson that only now was coming vividly to life here in this country churchyard. Everywhere I looked, bone fragments of the dead, like broken bits of kitchen crockery, reflected whitely in the beam of my torch.

It was as astonishing a display as any of the three-dimensional geological exhibits in the Science Museum.

Hold on, Flavia, I thought: *This is not the time to be thinking about the wonders of putrefaction.*

I made my way slowly along the tunnel, going deeper into the earth with every step. Underground, the distance seemed much farther than it did in the churchyard above. Surely by now I must be close to the foundation of the church.

Perhaps the tunnel didn't lead to the church—perhaps it was taking me off in a different direction altogether.

But no—I had been moving in a straight line, at least, as far as I could tell.

Now the tunnel's floor began rising quite steeply. Ahead was what looked like a stone archway.

And another locked door.

This lock was older and much more difficult to pick. The mechanism was more massive—heavier—more stiff— and almost impossible to move with the thin wire of my braces.

I congratulated myself on bringing the pickle fork as a backup.

A bit more squalene from my nose, a bit of twiddling the lock's wards with my mouthware, a couple of deft twists with the cutlery and—Bob's your uncle!—the levers lifted and the door swung inward.

I was no longer in the tunnel.

Now, I found myself in a low stone chamber which was obviously part of the crypt.

Iron sconces on the walls had once held torches: massive blotches of black soot on the ceiling, probably hundreds of years old, showed that flaming brands had once been used.

The walls were scratched with names and initials: D.C., R.O.; Playfayre; Madrigall, Wenlock: some of them ancestors of families who still lived in Bishop's Lacey.

Not a de Luce among the lot.

At the back of the chamber was what I took at first to be a hole: a rectangle of darkness about five feet above the floor. I shone the torch into it, but could not see far. I wasn't tall enough.

Luckily, someone had made a makeshift stepping-stone of broken granite—old tombstones, perhaps—directly beneath the opening.

Even without the footprints which were everywhere in the dust, it was clear that this opening had been used quite recently.

I climbed up and peered into the chamber. It was surprisingly roomy.

I boosted myself into the darkness, clicked on the torch, and began scraping along on hands and knees. I thought for a moment of Howard Carter crawling through those puzzling passages in the pyramids.

Hadn't he died by ignoring a curse?

In the cramped stone passageway I could hear the beating of my own heart.

Tanc-red, Tanc-red, Tanc-red, Tanc-red . . .

Had the saint, like Shakespeare, put a curse on his own grave? *Curs't be he that moves these bones,* and so forth?

Is that what had happened to poor Mr. Collicutt?

It seemed unlikely. Even if the spirits of the dead *were* capable of killing, I doubted that they were able to strap gas masks onto the faces of their victims.

A shiver shook my shoulders at the thought of Mr. Collicutt, who, if my theory was correct, had been dragged, dead or alive, through this very passageway.

I tied a mental string onto my forefinger. I would remember to pray for him properly on Easter Sunday.

And now, quite abruptly, the narrow crawl space branched, and I found myself peering down from above into a large chamber. As with the outer room, someone had piled broken stones handily below the opening, and I was easily able to scramble down onto the rubble-covered floor.

This part of the passage went no farther: This was the end.

I let the torch's beam sweep slowly round the room, but aside from more names and initials scratched into the stone of the walls, there was little to see.

The place was empty.

Empty, that is, except for a pair of iron brackets that projected from the wall.

Two handgrips had been drilled into opposite ends of a single stone; they could have no purpose other than to shift it.

A quick examination showed that I was right: A razor-thin gap ran across the top of the stone and down both sides. Unlike the other stones in the wall, this one, although it was snug-fitting, had no mortar.

It was meant to come out.

As I traced out the gap, I could feel the draft on my fingertips: the same draft—I was sure of it!—I had felt in the crypt.

Unless I was sadly mistaken, I was now directly behind the wall of the chamber in which Mr. Collicutt's body had been hidden.

This was how his killer—or killers, more likely—had maneuvered him into an unopened tomb.

The sound came at first as no more than a stirring of the air about my ears. The acute sense of hearing I had inherited from Harriet was like that: imperceptible at first, a kind of audible silence.

Only when I acknowledged its presence did it fully take form, as it now did.

Someone was talking.

The voice was that of a fly in a bottle—a hollow tinny buzzing that rose and fell . . . rose and fell.

I could not make out the words, only the drone of the insect voice.

My immediate reaction was to switch off the torch.

Which left me in darkness.

I could see instantly that there were beads of light coming through the cracks.

Had they seen the light from my torch? It seemed unlikely: They were in a crypt illuminated by a string of bulbs. Little enough of my torchlight would have been visible.

But who would be in the crypt in the middle of the night? I decided that there must be at least two of them, since one would hardly be talking to himself.

I pressed an ear against the crack and tried to make out the words.

But it was no use. The narrow slit between the stones had a strange filtering effect: It was as if I were hearing only a thin slice of the speaker's voice—not quite enough to make out the words.

After half a minute or so, I gave it up and, using only my fingertips, began a closer examination of the stone itself.

It was about eighteen inches wide and about a foot high. The depth, I knew, must be the thickness of the wall, which I guessed to be another eighteen inches.

One and a half times one and a half times one equaled two and a quarter cubic feet. How much would it weigh?

That, of course, depended upon its specific gravity. From the tables in Uncle Tar's handbooks, I knew that gold had a specific gravity of more than twelve hundred, and lead about seven hundred.

St. Tancred's was famous for the beauty of its sandstone, which, if I remembered correctly, had a specific gravity of somewhere between two and three, and weighed about a hundred and fifty pounds per cubic foot.

The whole stone, then, would weigh somewhere between three and four hundred pounds.

Would I be able to shift it? Obviously, with someone on the other side, now was not the time.

But still, I needed to know, without a doubt, that this tunnel and this stone connected directly with the cavity in which I had found Mr. Collicutt's corpse.

I didn't dare pull on the iron handles for fear of being heard.

Perhaps I would have to sit here in darkness and wait until the light went out on the other side of the stone.

How long would it take? I wondered. What on earth could they be doing in there?

I might as well make myself comfortable. I would press my back against the wall behind me and slide down it until I was seated on the floor.

Then, in darkness, I would wait.

I was halfway through this simple maneuver when my feet slipped on a pebble.

I dropped down heavily upon my behind.

Worse, I dropped the torch.

·THIRTEEN·

CLANG! IT WENT, THE sound chillingly loud in the darkness.

I held my breath.

The insect buzzing of voices stopped instantly.

I strained my ears, but the only sound I could hear was the beating of my own heart.

And then a grinding noise—a grating of stone, echoing from wall to wall. I crawled forward and touched my fingers to the block.

It was moving!

They were shoving the stone inward—toward me!

I scrabbled for the torch but my fingers could not locate it in the darkness. I was clutching uselessly at bits of rubble, my nails tearing at the hard stone floor.

The block was still moving. I could not see it, but I could hear it grating. In less than a minute they would be climbing through the opening.

If only there were some way to stop the stone: a stout

length of timber, for instance, to wedge against the opposite wall.

But there was nothing in this echoing chamber.

Nothing but Flavia de Luce.

The thought came out of nowhere—or so it seemed at the time.

Later, I would realize that my mind had vomited up a sudden memory of snooping through Feely's unmentionables drawer in search of her diary. Having given up, I was annoyed to find that the drawer would not close completely. No matter how hard I pushed it would not budge.

When I slid it forward and off the tracks, I found the diary taped to the back with strips of sticking plaster. A lesson learned.

I threw myself down onto my back, my feet against the moving stone, and jammed my shoulders against the opposite side of the chamber.

I stiffened every muscle of my body and made myself into a human wedge.

The stone stopped moving.

There was a moment of silence, and then renewed effort from the other side.

Again the stone began inching inward.

Had they brought a lever? I wondered.

Perhaps they were now both shoving.

My knees were beginning to bend. I tried to keep them straight but they were quivering like bowstrings.

Daffy had once read me a story in which the victim was tortured with a device called the Scavenger's Daughter which, rather than stretching the body like the rack, compressed it into a ball until its fluids caused it to burst like an enormous pimple.

I stretched out both arms full length, trying desperately to grip onto the floor. Anything to increase the resistance.

A sliver of light appeared. The stone was almost clear of the wall.

Now I could hear their voices.

"Bloody thing's stuck," one of them said. "Give me the crowbar."

There was a metallic clanking and I felt the stone move even more powerfully against my feet. I couldn't hold out much longer.

And then the light went out—and, a few seconds later, came back on again.

"Someone's coming!" a voice hissed, and the stone grated to a stop.

"Someone's at the top of the stairs," another voice said. "They've turned the switch off and on."

"Let's get out of here!" the first voice whispered, frantically.

"Go round back of the furnace. Use the coalhole."

There was a scuffling, and then absolute silence.

I knew that they were gone.

I counted slowly to a hundred.

No point in crawling like a Commando all the way back through the Cottlestone tomb, I thought, when I was so close to freedom.

I seized the iron handles of the stone and gave it a hard tug. It might have moved a quarter of an inch.

I sat down on the floor so that the stone was between my knees, planted my feet against the wall, and pulled again. Perhaps half an inch, this time, or a little more.

If I concentrated on pulling at one end, it would swing

in like a door, just far enough, if I were lucky, to allow me to squeeze past.

At last I had made a gap of about four inches: not wide enough to pass through, but enough to have a look outside. I dropped to my hands and knees and peered out into the crypt. The crowbar was lying where they had dropped it, about two feet from the opening.

I got down onto my stomach and shoved an arm through the opening as far as it would go. My face was crushed so tightly against the stone that I must have looked like something from the ocean depths.

My fingers found the beveled end of the crowbar, but just barely. I didn't want to shove the thing completely away.

A fraction of an inch at a time, I hooked my fingernails onto the crowbar's edge and pulled it ever so slowly toward me.

Feely had been nagging me about biting my nails since I was in a pram, and quite recently I had decided she was right. A chemist who is going to be photographed by *The Illustrated London News* holding up a test tube and peering into it intently needed half-decent hands.

My nails were not yet as long as I liked, but they were enough to do the job.

The crowbar crept toward me. When it was safely within reach, I hauled it in through the opening and gave thanks to the good Saint Tancred who lay somewhere just a few feet below me.

From there on, levering the stone all the way into the chamber was a piece of cake.

A *piece of* rock *cake*, I thought, with what was probably a silly grin.

There was now light enough to spot the torch, which had rolled away into a far corner. I flicked the switch to see if it was still working—which it was—then crawled through the wall and into the crypt.

As I stood up straight I realized for the first time how stiff and sore my body had become. My hands and knees were scratched and scraped.

I was quite proud of myself. I understood how the veterans felt who had suffered war wounds.

Before moving on into the main part of the crypt, I stopped to listen.

Not a sound.

Whoever had been in the crypt was gone. There could be no doubt about it. The place was filled with that special stillness that is found where all the occupants are dead.

Still, I'll admit that, as I crept past the furnace, the hair on the back of my neck bristled—but only a little.

Now I was at the bottom of the steps that led up to the church. Was there anything else to worry about? Would the crypt's midnight visitors be lying in wait for me outside the church?

They needed only to hide behind the tombstone where Gladys was parked and pounce on me as soon as I appeared—abducting a girl in a churchyard in the middle of the night would not be difficult.

Perhaps I'd better stay in the church: Curl up in a pew, catch forty winks, and race home just as the sun was coming up. No one would even know I'd been away.

Yes, that's what I'd do.

Up the stone staircase I trudged—one slow step at a time.

In the porch, the outer door was closed, but unlocked, as it probably had been since the time of Henry VIII when the churches of England were looted and vandalized.

To my left, illuminated only by the light which shone down through the stained-glass windows, the carpet of the center aisle was a ribbon of red in the moonlight.

I thought again of the poem, and of the Highwayman, who had, at the end, been shot down like a dog on the highway.

And I thought—for some peculiar reason—of the dead Mr. Collicutt.

Mr. Collicutt, of course, had not lain in his blood on the highway with a bunch of lace at his throat—but he might as well have.

It came back to me in a flash like a news reporter's camera.

He *had* been wearing a bunch of lace at his throat.

Or something very much like it.

The Highwayman had died for love, hadn't he? To warn him that the inn was swarming with King George's men, the landlord's black-eyed daughter, Bess, had shot herself in the breast.

They had both died.

Would there be another victim in Bishop's Lacey? Were Mr. Collicutt's killers already plotting to silence someone else—someone who had loved the unfortunate organist?

I moved slowly up the center aisle, touching the ends of every row of pews with my fingertips, absorbing the security of the ancient oak.

There was just enough light to make my way up the chancel steps to the organ without using the torch.

Back to business, I decided.

Although the wall panel was nearly invisible, Feely had opened it easily. Would I be able to find the latch?

I ran my fingers over the polished wood and the carved moldings, but they were as solid as they looked. I pressed here and there—it was no use.

The face of a carved wooden imp grinned at me saucily in the shadows. I touched his puffed-out polished cheeks and gave them a twist.

There was a *click* and the panel slid open.

I stepped carefully inside.

Closing the panel behind me, I switched on the torch.

Praise be to Saint Tancred, the patron saint of Evidence!

There on the floor, in the beam of light, were Feely's footprints and my own in the dust. Nobody had walked over them. The police had seen no reason to examine the organ case. Why should they, after all? It was nowhere near the spot where Mr. Collicutt's body had been hidden.

Even Mr. Haskins hadn't been in here to extract the bat from the organ pipe—I could spot the prints of his grave-digger boots a mile away—which meant, most likely, that the bat's carcass was still at the bottom of the sixteen-foot diapason.

Rest in peace, little creature, I thought.

The thing had got in through the coalhole, I supposed, during the nighttime comings and goings of whoever had stuffed Mr. Collicutt into the wall of the crypt.

I gave the pipe a tap with my knuckles, but nothing stirred. The bat was almost certainly dead.

My torch illuminated a couple of fresh gouges in the wood of the organ frame. I dropped to my knees for a closer look.

Yes, there could be no doubt about it—

"Crikey!"

I nearly leaped out of my skin as, in the far corner, the wind chest gave out a dry wheeze. The tombstone of Hezekiah Whytefleet had settled, forcing wind into the organ's works.

There was also a hissing behind me.

I swung round the torch's beam and at once spotted the source of the noise. Set into the wooden ductwork was a round, drilled hole, slightly smaller in diameter than a lead pencil, and it was through this that the air was hissing.

On the floor directly beneath it was a dried red stain.

As I took a step forward, something crunched under the sole of my shoe.

I knew even without looking that it was glass.

My own laboratory work had made me quite familiar with the principle of the manometer: that liquid-filled, U-shaped glass tubing which was used to measure air pressure.

It made good sense that the organ would have been fitted with such a device to measure the pressure from the wind chest. The tube, marked in inches, would, until recently, have been partially filled with colored alcohol, its level giving the required reading, very much like an outdoor thermometer.

All that now remained of the manometer, besides the gritty glass crumbs on the floor, was the jagged ring of hollow glass where it had been snapped off level with its wooden socket.

The rest of the glass tubing, if I were any judge at all, I had seen clutched in the hand of the late Mr. Collicutt.

It was here on this spot, in the very heart of the great

organ that he had loved and played, that the organist met his death.

I was sure of it.

I didn't have a pocketknife to scratch away a sample of the red-colored stain, but that wasn't much of a problem. To avoid contaminating it with my fingers, I would unscrew the back of the torch and use the tin casing as a makeshift scraper.

It was only as I pointed the beam at my knees that I realized what I had done to my clothing. My best black coat looked as if I had been rolled in ashes. It was streaked with slime from the grave, caked with mud from the tunnel, and covered over with a layer of dust. Another item to be consigned to the flames.

My face, I supposed, was no better. I ran the back of my hand across my forehead and it came away darkened with disgusting juices.

Better have a good washup, I thought. I hoped there was a source of water somewhere in the church. If so, and given the number of hours until daylight, I might even manage to make myself respectable in time for breakfast.

Of course! I thought. *The font!*

I stepped carefully out of the organ chamber and into the apse, taking care not to wipe myself against the ecclesiastical furniture.

If need be, I might even make a raid on the Communion wine to use as a spotting solution.

I let out a dry snort at the thought of the vicar's likely reaction. The look on his face—

A piercing scream shattered my thoughts.

I spun round and found myself face-to-face with an apparition dressed all in black.

My blood ran cold. It took my startled brain several seconds to recognize this seeming phantom.

It was Cynthia Richardson.

She had seen me come floating out of a blank wall, my clothing, if anything, more grave-stained than before.

Her mouth was still hanging open from the scream, her eyes bugging out.

"Hannah!" she gasped.

Her eyes rolled up into her head and she crumpled to the floor as if she had been shot in the heart.

My spine was suddenly a trickle of ice water.

"Hannah" had been the name the vicar had cried out in his sleep, the night he and Cynthia had been trapped by a storm at Buckshaw.

"Hannah, please! No!"

I could still hear his tortured whisper in my mind.

I had wondered then who Hannah might be, and I wondered now as I stared down at the unconscious Cynthia Richardson.

Unconscious? Or was she dead?

Had she died of fright? People had been known to do that.

I knelt down beside her and put a finger to the angle of her jaw, just as I had seen Dogger do on more than one occasion. The strong, steady pulsing was impossible to miss.

I breathed a sigh of relief. I hadn't killed her after all.

Next thing was to make sure that she was comfortable and breathing properly. From my Girl Guide training in first aid I remembered that shock victims must, at all costs, be kept warm.

I peeled off my heavy coat and covered her, thinking how pitifully small the woman was: scarcely bigger than me.

As I listened at her mouth to the breath rushing in and

out—in and out—I thought about the time Cynthia had caught me climbing the altar to scrape a sample of blue zafre from a medieval stained-glass window for chemical analysis. Cynthia had put me over her knee and spanked me on the spot, making improper use of a copy of *Hymns Ancient and Modern*.

It was almost comical, in retrospect, but not quite. I had still never completely forgiven her for the first real punishment—other than from my sisters, of course—that I had ever received in my life.

Now, as I knelt beside her, I wanted to feel revenge.

But I couldn't. I just couldn't.

Should I stay beside her? Keep watch over her until the sun came up?

Perhaps I should run to Dr. Darby's house for help. Or rouse the vicar from the vicarage.

These thoughts were racing through my mind when there was a soft footstep behind me. I leapt to my feet and spun round.

There stood the vicar, his face white as ashes.

"Oh dear," he was saying. "Oh dear. I feared it would come to this."

Not *What are you doing creeping round the church in the middle of the night?* Not *Why are you crouching over my beloved wife?* Not *What have you done to her?*

Just "Oh dear. I feared it would come to this."

Come to what? I wondered.

And when it came to that, what was *Cynthia* doing creeping round the church in the middle of the night? Could it have been she who—

I couldn't allow myself to complete that impossible thought.

"I think she fainted," I said rather stupidly, and I caught myself, incredibly, wringing my hands.

"This is not the first time," the vicar said, almost as if to himself, shaking his head. "No, I fear it is not the first."

Not knowing what to do, I stood there like a lug.

"Flavia, dear," he said at last, kneeling beside Cynthia's crumpled body. "You must help me get her home."

The words seemed odd and strained. Why not let her regain consciousness before hauling her back to the vicarage?

It wasn't as if she were drunk in a public place and needed to be whisked out of sight before the parishioners found her out.

Or was it?

No, it couldn't be. I hadn't detected the slightest smell of alcohol, and I prided myself on my ability to sniff out the ketones.

"Of course," I said.

The vicar lifted his wife as easily as if she were a doll and moved quickly with her down the center aisle toward the door.

I followed him through the churchyard's cold wet grass to the vicarage, glancing round to see if there were faces peering out from behind the ancient tombstones, but there were not. The intruders had made their getaway.

I dashed ahead up the vicarage steps and held open the door.

"In the study," the vicar said as I flicked on the dim bulb in the little foyer.

The study, as usual, was a landslide of books. I shifted several stacks of tinder-dry volumes from the horsehair sofa to the floor: the same sofa, I noted, upon which Mad

Meg had been stretched out at the time of the Rupert Porson affair.

The vicar arranged my coat as carefully round his wife's body as if he were tucking a child into bed.

She stirred slightly and gave out a little moan. He touched her face tenderly.

Cynthia's pale eyes opened and moved uneasily from side to side.

"It's all right, darling," the vicar said. "Everything is all right."

Her eyes found his, and it was then that the miracle happened.

She smiled!

Cynthia Richardson smiled!

I had always thought of the woman as rat-faced, although perhaps I was a little prejudiced. The fixed grin of her protruding teeth, canceled out by a perpetual frown, gave her the look of a terrible-tempered rodent.

Yet Cynthia had smiled!

And to be perfectly fair, I would have to admit that her smile was of the sort that is generally described as radiant.

No Madonna had ever gazed down upon her child with such a tender look; no bride had ever smiled up at her groom with such love as Cynthia Richardson gave to her husband.

It almost brought tears to my eyes.

"Shall I run for Dr. Darby?" I asked. "I can be there and back in a jiff."

The truth was that I wanted to leave them alone in this moment. I was an intruder.

"No," the vicar replied. "Rest is what she needs. Look, she's already asleep."

And it was true. With part of that wonderful smile lingering at the corners of her mouth, Cynthia had nodded off.

A small snore confirmed it.

"What happened?" the vicar asked, rather tentatively. "She must have—had a shock."

"It's a long story," I said.

"Tell me," he said gently. "We have all night."

One of the things I love about our vicar, Denwyn Richardson, is the fact that he accepts me as I am. He does not ask idiotic questions.

He does not want to know, for instance, what I was doing at two or three o'clock in the morning, emerging, covered in grave dirt, from the paneling of his church.

He does not want to know why I am not at home, tucked up into my own little bed, dreaming childish dreams.

In short, he treats me as a grown-up.

It is a gift.

To both of us.

Which is why I broke my long-standing rule and not only took responsibility, but also volunteered information.

"I'm afraid it's my fault," I said. "I gave her a start. She thought I was someone else."

The vicar raised a sad eyebrow. He didn't need to do more.

"She said 'Hannah,'" I told him. "And then she collapsed."

There was one of those long silences during which,

through embarrassment, you're aching to say something but, for fear of even greater embarrassment, you don't.

"Hannah," he said slowly. "Hannah was . . . our daughter."

I felt something horribly heavy descend upon me: as heavy as all the universe, and yet invisible.

I said nothing.

"She died when she was four," the vicar said. "I killed her."

·FOURTEEN·

I COULD HARDLY FIND the breath to speak.

"Surely not," I managed.

Another eternity passed before the vicar spoke again.

"Seven years ago, Christmas week. I had taken her with me to the railway station in Doddingsley to pick up the holly for the church, as I always do. Hannah loved Christmas . . . always wanted to be a part of everything.

"Someone stopped me on the platform—a former parishioner—hadn't seen her for years—wanted to wish me compliments of the season, you see, and I let go of Hannah's hand—only for a moment, you understand—but—

"The train . . . the train—"

Suddenly tears were rolling down his cheeks.

I watched my hand reaching for his.

"I shouted at her—tried to call her back—"

"I'm sorry," I said, aware even as I spoke, what useless things, really, words of sympathy are, even though they're sometimes all we have.

"I'm sorry," I repeated.

"Had she lived," the vicar said, his eyes swimming, "she would have been your age. Cynthia and I often think how much you—" He stopped abruptly. "Cynthia and your mother were great friends, you know, Flavia. They were to become mothers at the same time."

Another part of the puzzle that was Harriet fell into place.

"I'm sorry," I said again. "I didn't know."

"How could you?" the vicar asked. "The good people of Bishop's Lacey have conspired to silence. Hannah's death is not to be spoken of. They think we don't know, you see—but we do."

"But you mustn't blame yourself," I blurted, filled with a rising anger. "It wasn't your fault. It was an accident."

The vicar gave me a sad smile which signaled that my words changed nothing.

"Where is she buried?" I asked with sudden boldness. I would take flowers and place them with great ceremony on the little girl's grave. I would put an end to this pathetic silence.

"Here," the vicar said simply. "In the churchyard. Close by the Cottlestone tomb. We couldn't, at first, afford a stone, you see. A country vicar's purse does not— and later . . . well, later was too late. Still, Cynthia goes there often to visit, but I'm afraid I—"

I shivered as the full horror of his words crept upon me.

Their child was buried at the very spot from which Cynthia had seen me burst forth from the earth. And later, in the church—

How could I ever make amends?

"She thought I was Hannah," I said, taking the first step.

"I was looking round inside the organ casing for clues. I must have seemed to her to have come through the wall."

As I spoke, Cynthia gave a soft moan and rolled her head from side to side.

"I'm glad you were in the church," I said. "I wasn't quite sure what to do."

"I followed her there," the vicar said softly. "I often do. To ensure that she comes to no harm, you see."

Cynthia stirred.

Gently, he lifted my disgusting coat from her shoulders and handed it to me, replacing it with the afghan that was folded at the end of the sofa.

"I'd best be going," I said, taking the hint.

As I shrugged into my coat, small clods of clay fell to the carpet.

I was already at the door when the vicar spoke: "Flavia—" he said.

I turned back. "Yes?"

His eyes, still wet, met mine. "Be careful," he said.

That's another one of the things I love about Denwyn Richardson.

Buckshaw by moonlight was a scene from a dream. As I rode toward it along the avenue of chestnut trees, the house was half illuminated by a pale silvery light, the other half in darkness, its long black shadow crawling away across the Trafalgar Lawn toward the east, as if trying to reach the safety of the distant trees.

I parked Gladys against the brick wall of the kitchen garden and glanced at the upstairs windows. There were no lights and no white faces staring down at me.

Perfect, I thought. I needed time to concoct a chemical cleaning solvent. I would mix something in a coal scuttle—something involving ammonia and one of the chlorine-based oxydizing agents. Or perhaps petrol: I could easily siphon a gallon from Harriet's Phantom II. I would ball up my filthy coat, immerse it for half an hour, then hang it out the window of my laboratory to dry in the wind. It would be as spotless and fresh-smelling as if it had been dry-cleaned by Armfields, in Belgravia.

As I opened the door and stepped into the kitchen, I realized how hungry I was. I hadn't eaten for ages and my stomach was hanging against my spine like an empty saddlebag. I would cut some bread from the pantry and take it upstairs to toast over the open flame of a Bunsen burner.

I was halfway across the kitchen when a solemn voice, like the tolling of a passing-bell, said: "Flavia."

It was Father.

At first I hardly recognized him. He was seated at the table in dressing gown and slippers. I had never before seen him dressed in anything other than his usual outfit of shirt, tie, vest, jacket, trousers, and mirror-polished boots.

"I was at the church," I began, hoping to gain some advantage, even though I couldn't imagine what it was. "Talking to the vicar," I added lamely.

"I'm quite aware of that," he said.

Aware? Had the vicar turned rat on me?

"The chancellor telephoned."

I could hardly believe it! Father forbade use of "The Instrument" as he called it, except in the most dire emergency. He felt about the telephone the way a condemned man feels about the scaffold.

"He advised me to stop your messing round the church during these excavations. Thinks you're liable to do yourself an injury."

And how did he know I was messing round the church? I wanted to ask.

The answer was obvious: His toady, Marmaduke Parr, had told him.

"It's not only that," Father went on. "As you very well know, a murder has been committed in the crypt."

I offered up a small prayer of thanks. At least it hadn't been Inspector Hewitt who had rung up, ordering me to keep away.

"Did he mention poor Mr. Collicutt? The chancellor, I mean?"

"As it happens," Father answered, "he did not. But nevertheless, I want you to stay—"

"Mrs. Richardson fainted at the altar," I put in before he could say another word. "She mistook me for her daughter, Hannah."

Father looked up at me, his face harshly lined in the cold moonlight. He had not shaved, and the stubble of his whiskers glittered cruelly. Never had he looked so old.

"The vicar told me about her," I said. "I didn't ask."

The kitchen clock ticked. Father let out a long sigh.

"I can't see you," he said, after a while. "My eyes are not what they once were. Bring a candle from the pantry. Don't put on the electric light."

I fetched a pewter candlestick and a box of wooden matches, and a minute later, by the flickering light of a wax candle, we were facing each other across the kitchen table.

"Denwyn and Cynthia have not had the easiest of lives," Father said.

"No," I replied. I was learning that the best conversations consisted of keeping quiet and listening, and speaking, when one spoke at all, in words of a single syllable.

"He blames himself," we both said at the same time.

It was incredible! Father and I had spoken the same three words at the same instant—as if we were reciting in unison.

I did not dare smile.

"Yes," we both said.

It was downright eerie.

Father had only talked to me—really talked, I mean—on one other occasion, which was the time he was incarcerated in a jail cell in Hinley, charged with the murder of Horace Bonepenny. On that day, he had talked and I had listened.

Now both of us were speaking at the same time.

"It was an accident pure and simple, or at least as pure and simple as any accident can be. Tragic. Still, in the circumstances, there was nothing for it but to get on with things. There was a war on. Everybody, in one way or another, was suffering loss. It was a bad time to be deprived of a little girl."

"Were you here when it happened?" I asked, shocking myself. Where did this sudden boldness come from?

A shadow crossed Father's face. The kitchen clock ticked on.

"No," he said after a moment. "I wasn't."

He had, as I well knew, been with Dogger in a prisoner-of-war camp. It was not a topic of discussion at Buckshaw.

How odd, I thought: Here were these four great griev-
ers, Father, Dogger, the vicar, and Cynthia Richardson,
each locked in his or her own past, unwilling to share a
morsel of their anguish, not even with one another.

Was sorrow, in the end, a private thing? A closed container? Something that, like a bucket of water, could be
borne only on a single pair of shoulders?

To make matters worse, there was the fact that the entire village was sheltering each of them in a cocoon of
silence.

Those dear damned people! Both the blessers and the
blessed!

I felt the color rising in my face as I remembered that I
had vowed to place flowers, publicly, on Hannah Richardson's grave.

But I would not trouble Father by telling him that. He
had enough to worry about.

"What are we going to do with you?" he asked suddenly.

"I don't know, sir," I replied.

The "sir" came out of nowhere. I had never addressed
my father in that way before, but it seemed perfectly the
right thing to do.

"It's just that sometimes . . . sometimes—I think that I
am very like my mother."

There! I had said it!

I could only wait now to see what damage I had done.

"You are not like your mother, Flavia."

I gulped at the blow.

"You *are* your mother."

My mind was a swarm—a beehive, a tornado, a tropical storm. Were my ears actually hearing this? For the

past several years my sisters had increasingly tried to convince me that I was adopted; a changeling; a lump of coal left by a cruel Father Christmas in their stockings.

"I've been meaning to talk to you about this for some time," Father said, fidgeting as if he were looking for something lost in the pockets of his dressing gown. "I may as well come straight to the point."

My chin was trembling. What was going to happen? What was he going to say?

Was he about to tear a strip off me for ruining my best coat?

"I am aware that your life has not always been—" he began unexpectedly. "That is to say, I know that you sometimes . . ."

He looked at me in misery, his face flickering in the candlelight. "Damn it all," he said.

He began again. "As was your mother, you have been given the fatal gift of genius. Because of it, your life will not be an easy one—nor must you expect it to be. You must remember always that great gifts come at great cost. Are there any questions?"

Dear Father! Even the most tender of his moments was a parade-square lecture. How I loved him.

"No, sir," I said, as if I were a sapper being charged with blowing up the enemy lines. "No questions."

"Very good. Very good," Father said, standing up and rubbing his hands together. "Well, then, you'd better get some sleep."

And with that he was gone, leaving me alone at the table.

I thought over all that he had said.

His remarks about Harriet were not the sorts of things

one ponders at a kitchen table. I needed to review them later, in the privacy of my room. In the comfort of my bed.

One thing, though, was clear. Father had not expressly forbidden me to go near the church.

·FIFTEEN·

"THEY SAY 'E'S BLEEDIN' cause 'is bones 'as been bothered!"

Mrs. Mullet ladled another dollop of her lavalike porridge into my bowl. Thoughts of being an Oliver Twist in reverse crossed my mind: *"Please, ma'am, I don't want any more."*

"Eat it up, dear, while it's 'ot. There's a good girl. Remember:

"*Margaret Mullet tells no fibs*
"*'Ot por-ridge sticks to the ribs.*
"'Ere! I'm a poet and I don't know it."

She giggled at her own wit.

The very thought of this gray guck sticking to my ribs—or anything else—was enough to make my stomach go into hibernation.

"Thank you, Mrs. M," I said groggily, adding a generous slosh of milk to the oatmeal. Perhaps I could sip away at the liquid and leave the quivering horror hidden beneath the surface like the Loch Ness Monster.

I'd barely slept and wasn't at my best. The cleaning of my coat had been more chemically complicated than I had supposed and had, in the end, required me to duplicate Michael Faraday's famous 1821 experiment in which he had synthesized tetrachloroethylene by extracting it, by thermal decomposition, from hexachloroethane.

Consequently, I had been up all night.

"Actually, his bones haven't been disturbed," I told her. "They haven't dug that deep yet."

"Well, 'e bloomin' well knows they're on the way," Mrs. Mullet said. "Mark my words. Saints aren't like your ordinary people. They knows things. They can see and 'ear things at a distance just like the television. They 'ear when Mrs. Frampton is prayin' to 'ave 'er Elsie's Bert win the pools so's she can send 'er mother to Blackpool on 'oliday come June and get 'er out of 'er 'air for a fortnight so's she can scrub the floors and beat the rugs. Mind you, I've said nothin'."

I was eating breakfast in the kitchen because, by the time I dragged myself out of bed, Mrs. Mullet had already cleared the table in the dining room.

"I 'eard all about it from my friend, Mrs. Waller. She says there was blood all over the place like a abbotory."

"There wasn't all that much," I said. "I saw it myself."

Mrs. Mullet's eyes widened.

"No more than a couple of teaspoonsful if you collected it all together. Blood always seems greater in volume than it actually is."

If it *was* blood, in fact. I could hardly wait to get upstairs to my laboratory and analyze the residue of the stuff into which I had dipped my white ribbon.

"Still an' all," she said. "Miss Tanty 'ad to be put to bed

and the doctor called. A real fright, she 'ad, babblin' on about Mr. Collicutt and the four 'orsemen of the pocket lips. Made no sense at all. Shock, if you ask me."

"I think you're quite right, Mrs. M," I said, my plans changing even as I spoke. "I'll take her some flowers. I'll tell her they're from all of us here at Buckshaw."

"That would be nice, dear," Mrs. Mullet said. "You're always such a thoughtful child."

Of course I was a thoughtful child. If Miss Tanty's lips had been loosened by laudanum, I wanted to be among the first to hear what came spilling out.

Miss Tanty lived in a small house on the west side of Cater Street, which ran north from the high street, just west of the Thirteen Drakes.

I pulled up and parked Gladys at the gate just as Miss Gawl, the Treasurer of the Altar Guild, was coming out the front door.

"I'm afraid she can't see anyone, child. Doctor's orders. Here, give me those flowers. I'll put them in a vase and bring them round later."

I knew she wouldn't. She would toss them out her back door and onto the rubbish heap. Not that it mattered. I had picked the wild bouquet in the same spot in front of the church as I had the first lot.

"That's very kind of you, Miss Gawl," I said, handing over the flowers and pulling a look of worried concern down over my face like a balaclava. "How *is* she?"

"She's resting comfortably now," she replied. "But she mustn't be disturbed. We've given her an injection to help her sleep."

We've given her an injection?

And then I remembered. Of course—Miss Gawl was the retired District Nurse. Which was why she had used the word "injection." Anyone else would have said "We've given her *something* to help her sleep." Or "given her a *sedative* to help her sleep." And they wouldn't have said *we*—they would have said "The *doctor's* given her something to help her sleep."

What wonderful things can be deduced from a simple four-letter word!

I gave the woman my best village idiot grin.

"I'd best be getting along then," I said, resisting the urge to add, "to the Easter Cow Show."

There is a limit even to sauciness.

I wheeled Gladys along toward the place where the street ended at the river. With elaborate stupidity, I picked up a handful of pebbles and, with tongue hanging out of the corner of my mouth, skipped them across the water's surface.

One . . . two . . . three . . .

When I looked back, Miss Gawl was gone.

I walked quickly back to Miss Tanty's house, looked both ways to be sure that no one was in sight—then opened the door and slipped inside.

The place was overheated—sweltering like a tropical jungle.

On the right was a dining room with an oversized table and more chairs than we had in all of Buckshaw.

To the left, a drawing room-cum-music room with all the usual fittings: small grand piano, music stands, plaster busts of Beethoven and Mozart and another I didn't recognize—aha!—Wagner; his name was engraved on the base—all three of them as cold-looking as if they had been molded from moon rubble. Beyond the study was a small conservatory, overflowing with exotic-looking plants. A parrot sat hunched in an elaborate wire cage.

"Pretty Polly," I said, trying to make friends.

The parrot gave me a surly look.

"Who's a pretty bird, then?" I asked, feeling like a fool, but there are only so many topics of conversation one can have with a bird.

The thing ignored me. Perhaps it was hungry. Perhaps Miss Tanty had been so disturbed that she had forgotten to feed it.

I took hold of a chunk of suet which was jammed between the wires of the cage.

The bird made a sudden lunge and I jerked back my hand before I lost a finger.

I'm afraid I called Polly a nasty name.

"Starve, then," I told it, and turned back to the front entrance.

The kitchen, at the back of the house, was the source of the high temperature. A great black stove was throwing off as much heat as the *Queen Elizabeth*'s boilers and the smell of cooking filled the air. I opened the largest oven and peered inside. An enormous roast of beef was basking in a bed of potatoes, carrots, onions, swedes, and apples.

The meat was well browned. It had been baking for at least an hour.

Miss Gawl had said Miss Tanty was resting, which probably meant upstairs.

I returned to the front hall.

"Hello, Quentin," the parrot said conversationally from the conservatory. The stupid thing had probably realized I'd intended to feed it, and was now trying to suck up to me. But it was too late.

Forgiveness is not one of my better qualities.

To my left, the stairs had been painted to resemble the keys of a piano, the treads black and every riser white.

I climbed slowly up the sloping keyboard, glancing as I went at each of the many black-framed photographs which crowded the walls on both sides: a younger Miss Tanty singing onstage in a long evening gown, her hands clasped at her ample waist; Miss Tanty being given a trophy by a sour gentleman whose expression indicated that he thought someone else should have been the winner; Miss Tanty standing in front of a medieval half-timbered house that looked as if it might be somewhere in Germany; Miss Tanty conducting a choir of girls, all of them—including Miss Tanty herself—dressed in school uniform of jumper, blouse, and black stockings; Miss Tanty front and center in the choir stalls of St. Tancred's, to one side, the back of Mr. Collicutt's blond, curly hair just visible as he sits at the organ console. High in the background, just out of focus, is the carved wooden face of Saint Tancred.

He is not bleeding.

At the top of the stairs I turned to my right and made for the room at the front of the house. Miss Tanty would never settle for a back bedroom.

Most of the doors were standing open; only one, the bedroom at the very front of the house, was closed.

I twisted the knob and stuck my nose round the door.

Hands crossed on her breast, the mountainous Miss Tanty was lying motionless on the bed. Although her thick spectacles were perched on her nose, her eyes were closed.

I tiptoed across the room.

It worried me somewhat that she was not snoring. Miss Tanty struck me as the kind of person who did nothing by halves, and I guessed that she was not likely a quiet sleeper. But then, perhaps, trained singers were taught to control their uvulas—those little fingers of flesh that dangle like pink icicles at the back of one's throat—even when they were asleep.

Was Miss Tanty asleep? Or had someone done her in? Had Mr. Collicutt's killer returned for a repeat performance? Was someone killing choirs, one musician at a time? Would Feely be next?

All of these thoughts were milling round in my mind at the same time.

I had already spotted the dark bottle that stood on top of an overflowing bookcase which was wedged between the bed and the wall. I was leaning across the bed for a closer look when one of Miss Tanty's eyes came slowly open.

I almost swallowed my tongue.

Magnified by the thick lenses, her watery eye was as large as the sudden rising of a bloodshot harvest moon.

She blinked and the other eye came open, which was even more alarming than the first. Her pupils swiveled, floating in their soupy liquid, and settled on me.

She seemed not at all surprised to see me. It was almost as if she had been waiting.

"I—I let myself in. To see if you were all right," I said. "I was worried about you."

Miss Tanty's substantial body began shaking with silent tremors, beginning with her shoulders and her ample breasts, and working their way down to vanish at her ankles. It reminded me, if only for an instant, of one of Mrs. Mullet's failed gelatin aspics.

"*Did* you," she said, and it was not a question.

It took me a moment to realize that she was laughing. As her cheeks convulsed, she bit her bottom lip and her great wet eyes thrashed about in their sockets.

It was a gruesome spectacle.

"Ho!" she said. "Did you indeed."

She rolled over toward the night table and picked up the bottle. She worked the cork out with her thumbs and poured an inch of reddish-brown liquid into a handy glass.

"For my vocal cords," she said, and tossed it back with a single gulp.

She made a token gargling noise as if to convince me.

I recognized at once the smell of sherry. Mrs. Mullet used it in Christmas pudding as well as in what she called her "Sinful Stew."

"The vocal folds must be rewarded now and then," Miss Tanty said, shoving the cork back into the bottle. "They must be treated like trained lions: the frequent whip tempered with the occasional reward."

Could this be the Miss Tanty who had to be put to bed and the doctor called? The Miss Tanty who had been given an injection to help her sleep?

If that were true, she was the second woman in Bishop's Lacey within a remarkably short time to require the needle. The first had been Cynthia Richardson, who'd had a fright in the churchyard. And now Miss Tanty, who'd had a fright in the church itself.

The same Miss Tanty who was now treating her vocal folds to a second slug of sherry.

"I'm sorry to walk in without an invitation," I said,

without mentioning Miss Gawl. "I knew what a great shock you'd had with the blood in the church, and so forth. I wanted to—"

"Codswallop!" she said, fixing me with her swivel eyes. "I was no more shocked than you were."

"But—"

The woman was laughing again, her flesh forming whitecaps.

"Of *course*, I went to great pains to put it about that I *was*. A few words babbled from the Book of Revelation can be remarkably convincing. Well . . . not so much *great* pains when you come right down to it. In any village, a single telephone call is as good as a leader in the *Times*."

"But—"

"It was a *performance*, dear girl. A *performance*! And a magnificent one, if I do say so myself. I was especially pleased that even *you* were taken in by it.

" '*Forgive me, O Lord.*' You *were* quite taken in, weren't you? Admit it. And I must say that crossing myself with the drippings, as it were, was a touch of sheer genius— although I must tell you that I thought for a few moments you had seen through me."

My mind was racing in circles. I felt like the last to cross the line in a sack race. This horrid old woman had beaten me at my own game.

"Taken in by it?" I managed. "Of course I wasn't taken in by it. That's why I'm here."

It was a feeble recovery, but the best I could do under the circumstances.

Miss Tanty's heaving billows had by now worked themselves up into a full-fledged tropical storm.

"Dear me!" she said, removing her spectacles and

mopping at her streaming eyes with the corner of a mauve sheet. "Dear me!

"Why," she asked, waving a hand at the bookcase, "should we leave all the glory of detection to Miss What's-her-name?" and I noticed for the first time that her library consisted of nothing but green-covered paperback mysteries, like the ones Daffy kept hidden away from prying eyes at the back of her knickers drawer.

"I've always fancied myself a more than intelligent woman," Miss Tanty went on. "Not brilliant, but not half bad. I'm always the first to work out who put the poisoned plums into the Christmas pudding; who left the backward footprints in the paddock—that sort of thing.

"Much like you," she added with a withering and focused glare.

My heart sank.

I had a rival.

"There we were, the three of us, detecting away like billy-ho and no one the wiser."

The three of us? What was the woman talking about?

"I was first out of the gate, I believe," Miss Tanty said. "I was on my knees and had a sample of 'the red stuff,' as I believe Jack the Ripper called it, on my finger, on my collar and—you'll have to admit it was a masterstroke, Flavia—in the sign of the cross on my forehead."

Blast the woman!

"The man Sowerby almost beat me to it with his handkerchief. His tasting the stuff was a nice touch, although a trifle showy. And then, of course, there was you, dipping your white ribbon, hoping desperately that no one would notice."

Blast the woman again!

"Like three great sleuths, we were, thrown together unexpectedly over a pool of blood at the scene of a crime. What a tableau it was! What an immortal moment. What a snapshot for a book's dust jacket. I wished I'd brought my Kodak!"

Now here was a fine kettle of fish. I suppose I should have been happy to find a kindred soul in Bishop's Lacey, but I was not.

Far from it.

How could I hope to get to the bottom of Mr. Collicutt's unfortunate demise with someone like Miss Tanty muddying the waters?

To say nothing of the police.

"We could form a type of club," she went on with increasing enthusiasm. "Call ourselves 'The Big Three.' Or a corporation: 'TSD,' we shall name it: Tanty, Sowerby & de Luce. With an ampersand, of course."

That did it!

I was not going to spend the rest of my hard-earned life playing third fiddle to a couple of amateurs.

Or were they?

Miss Tanty *had* raised an interesting point.

I had completely overlooked Adam Sowerby.

I closed my eyes and tried to visualize his business card. What had it said?

Adam Tradescant Sowerby, MA., FRHortS, etc.
Flora-archaeologist
Seeds of Antiquity—Cuttings—Inquiries
Tower Bridge, London E.1 TN Royal 1066

Inquiries!

I had missed that. Drat and double drat!

The man was a *private detective*.

Which put a whole new light on things. How much, for instance, did he already know about the death of Mr. Collicutt? And how was I going to worm it out of him?

Miss Tanty, too, if she had been snooping round the village in search of clues, might well be an even richer source of information than I had imagined.

I would need to remain on best of terms with her.

At least for now.

"I've already heard, of course," I said, "of how you solved the case of the missing knitting needles."

Mrs. Mullet had told us the story as she served the fish. "Mind the bones," she had said. And then she had told us about the village mystery solved.

"It's true," Miss Tanty was saying, preening a little. "Poor Mrs. Lucas. She was so *distrait*. Couldn't for the life of her. Where had she left her knitting needles? They had completely vanished, you see. In a flash.

"'Have you looked in your hair?' I asked her. She's always worn her hair bunched up in a great knot like those dreadful dancers in Toulouse-Lautrec. *La Goulue*, and so forth . . . *The Queen of Montmartre*.

"Mrs. Lucas gave me ever so odd a look and reached up and, lo and behold! She had shoved them without thinking into her *coiffure* when the postman came to the gate. 'You're a regular Sherlock Holmes, you are,' she told me."

I gave Miss Tanty a professional courteous smile.

"About Mr. Collicutt—" I began.

But there was no need to prime *this* pump. One touch of the handle and the whole story came gushing out.

"It was on a Tuesday," she said. "The Tuesday before Ash Wednesday, to be precise. It's always so lovely to be precise, isn't it, dear? One finds it so helpful when one is involved in the art of pervigilation."

Get on with it! I wanted to shout. But I had to be on my best behavior. I gave Miss Tanty a weak smile.

"The Tuesday before Ash Wednesday, as I have reason to recall, since we were going to be singing the Chaillot setting of the *Benedicte* the next morning at Matins. We had been working it up for some time, but as your sister Ophelia will tell you, it's a fiendishly difficult piece. It sounds easy, I know, as all great music does, but it is, in fact, a trap and a snare for the unwary.

"Because I had not had sufficient time to master the score—odd, isn't it, how printed music is called a score, as if it were a game of cricket, which I suppose, in a way, it is: runs, and so forth—I knew that I should have to rely upon my sight-reading ability, which is generally considered, by those who have witnessed it, to be quite remarkable.

"The only difficulty—the fly in the ointment, if you will—was the fact that my eyes had been playing up. There were times—especially times of great emotion—when the notes on the page were little more than a wretched blur. I knew that either my lenses or my medication needed to be adjusted posthaste, and hence, my appointment with the good Mr. Gideon, in Hinley.

"Usually, whenever I found it necessary to make 'the Pilgrimage,' as I like to call it, Mildred Battle was kind enough to run me over in her Austin. A regular saint, she is: a most appropriate conductor to one on a Pilgrimage, don't you think?"

I smiled dutifully.

"But on the morning itself, her niece, Florence, rang me up before breakfast. 'Auntie Mildred's sick,' she said. 'It must have been something she ate.' 'Oh, dear,' I told her, 'I'm sorry to hear that. I shall have to telephone for Clarence Mundy's taxicab, although I shudder to think of the cost of keeping him waiting all day in Hinley.'

"I suppose I ought to have been more sensitive to Mildred's predicament, but there it is. I suppose I was thinking of the keen disappointment of the parishioners, and yes, the vicar, too, should I be unable to lend my voice to the *Benedicte*. You do see my dilemma, don't you?"

I said that I did.

"'But don't worry,' Florence said, almost before the words were out of my mouth. 'Mr. Collicutt's offered to drive you, and Auntie Mildred's kindly agreed to let him take her car. He'll pick you up at twenty-five minutes to nine.'"

I had forgotten that Mr. Collicutt lodged with Mr. and Mrs. Battle. Thank goodness Miss Tanty had reminded me. That made two more people—three, counting Florence, the niece—to be questioned.

"Which couldn't have been more perfect," Miss Tanty went on. "My appointment with Mr. Gideon was set for nine-thirty, and although it's only a ten- or fifteen-minute drive to Hinley, I always like to be well ahead of the clock. Sometimes, if one is early, and there should happen to be a cancellation, they'll take one before one's time and one will be home all that much earlier and save three shillings in the bargain.

"'I shall be waiting at the gate,' I told Florence. And so I was.

"When Mr. Collicutt hadn't arrived by nine o'clock, I

tried to ring Florence back, but the line was engaged. Miss Goulard at the telephone exchange said that, as there were no voices on the line, someone had likely left the receiver off its cradle. I was beside myself, I can tell you. But when I tried again at quarter past, the call went through with no trouble at all. Florence picked up at once and told me that Mr. Collicutt had left the house at eight-thirty sharp.

"I was furious, I can tell you. I could have killed the man—"

I must have looked shocked. Miss Tanty flustered.

"A figure of speech, of course. I'd no more kill dear Mr. Collicutt—or anyone else, of course—than sprout wings and fly. Surely you know that."

"Of course," I said, suddenly wary of the woman.

Dear Mr. Collicutt? Could this be the same Miss Tanty who had told me not to waste my crocuses?

There was something strange at work here, and it wasn't love.

"He was a very competent musician," she went on, "but like all competent musicians, he tended to overwork himself. If he wasn't teaching his private pupils, or working with the choir, or off adjudicating one music festival or another, he was in the throes of composition. Mildred says she and George used to hear him pacing back and forth in his room overhead no matter the time of night. They'd have had words with him if it weren't for the fact that they needed the money. Lodgers are not as easy to find as they were during the war, but one that creeps out to go walking in the dark of the moon is surely a sore trial to a stonemason who works long, hard hours and has to be up before the crack of dawn."

"The dark of the moon?" I asked. "Why would he do that?"

"Restlessness, I suppose. Working out harmonies and counterpoint in his head. I know that he sometimes went to the church. At times, when the wind was in the west, I would catch snatches of organ music at odd hours. I more than once thought of taking the dear man a thermos flask of hot tea but I hated to intrude. Music can be such a harsh mistress, you know."

She fixed me with a gigantic eye.

Was she trying to extract information?

Mistresses were a topic Daffy had sometimes spoken of, but they did not hold the same interest for me as they did her. Unless there was murder involved, or poison, such as in the case of Madame de Brinvilliers and the Chevalier de Sainte-Croix, I didn't give a fig what people got up to in their spare time.

"I sometimes walk in the darkness myself," Miss Tanty was saying. "Even though the night air is said by some to be deleterious to the voice. One simply walks with one's mouth closed, breathing calmly through one's nose."

I shuddered at the very thought of Miss Tanty drifting about the village in the darkness with her mouth closed, breathing calmly through her nose.

No wonder people claimed to have seen ghosts!

Those mysterious lights the ARP members and the fire-watchers had seen floating in the churchyard during the war were probably, in reality, no more than the glinting of the moon off Miss Tanty's gigantic lenses.

Or were they something far more sinister?

"I'd better be getting along," I said. "I'll see myself out. I'm relieved to hear that you're all right, Miss Tanty."

This shameless toadying was like playing the game even after the last seats in the pavilion had emptied. But my seeming generosity of spirit would leave the door open for later questioning, should it be necesssary.

"Think about what I said," Miss Tanty called out when I was already at the door. "The three of us with our heads together would be a force to be reckoned with."

I gave her a noncommittal smile and started down the stairs, past the musical portrait gallery. I paused for a moment to have a second squint at the vinegarish gentleman presenting Miss Tanty with the music trophy. I had seen his face somewhere before, but I couldn't for the life of me remember where.

Just for fun I jumped down the last three steps and landed on my feet with a bang in the foyer.

"Geronimo!" I shouted. It was a battle cry made famous by the American paratroopers, or so Carl Pendracka had told me.

To my right, in the drawing room, a man standing at Miss Tanty's desk straightened with a jerk and spun round in surprise. He had been rifling through her papers.

It was Adam Sowerby.

He stared for no more than a split second before a broad grin began spreading across his face.

"By Jove!" he said. "Caught in the act. You gave me a jolly good start."

"You're a private detective," I said.

"Well," he replied, "I shall have to admit that there are certain aspects of my career which do not involve gillyflowers."

"You're a private detective," I repeated. I was not going

to be circumlocuted, or whatever the word was. I would have to ask Daffy.

"Yes. Since you put it that way, yes."

"I thought as much," I said. "It's printed on your card: inquiries."

"Very astute of you."

"Please don't condescend to me, Mr. Sowerby, I'm not a child. Well, actually—strictly speaking, and in the eyes of the law—I suppose I *am* a child, but still, I resent being treated like one."

"I shall throw myself prostrate before you and weep hot tears into the carpet," he said with a grin, waving his arms like a madman.

I marched toward the door.

"Flavia—wait."

I stopped.

"Sorry. It's hard to quit being an ass in an instant. Rather like running a motorcar off the road and into a hayfield: It takes a few yards to come to a halt."

"Perhaps we should step outside," I said, "before Miss Tanty comes downstairs and finds you burglarizing her belongings."

"Good lord!" he said. "You mean to say she's at home?"

"Upstairs," I said, pointing with my chin.

"Then it's *exeunt omnes* for us," he whispered, putting a long forefinger to his lips and taking high, exaggerated steps toward the door like a black-masked housebreaker in the pantomime.

"You really are silly," I told him. "I wish you'd stop."

·SIXTEEN·

WE WERE STANDING ON the riverbank at the end of Cater Street, well away from Miss Tanty's ears. We had walked there in total silence.

Now, the only sound was that of the running river, and the muted muttering of a few ducks that paddled round in circles on the current.

"I'm sorry," he repeated. "Old habits die hard."

"Is that part of your cover?" I asked. "Being an ass?"

I had heard the term "cover" used in one of the Philip Odell mysteries on the BBC wireless. "The Case of the Curious Queen," if I remembered correctly. It meant pretending to be someone else. Someone that one wasn't.

I had only occasionally had the opportunity to try the technique myself, since nearly everybody in Bishop's Lacey was as well acquainted with Flavia de Luce as they were their own mothers. It was only when I was a safe distance from home that I was able to take on another character.

"I suppose it is," Adam said, giving his nose a twist with his fingers. "There. I have switched it off. I am quite myself again."

His grin was gone and I took him at his word.

"Miss Tanty thinks we should join forces," I told him. "Form some sort of detection club."

"Share information?" Adam asked.

"Well, yes, I suppose that's what she was getting at."

"I wasn't aware of her detective aspirations," he said. "Perhaps I should have been. Which means, of course, that that ghastly performance in the church yesterday was all a sham. As was her well-advertised breakdown this morning. Very clever of you to have spotted it."

"I didn't spot it," I said. "She confessed before I was halfway in the door."

"But why? It makes no sense. Why go to all that trouble and then blow the gaff with no provocation whatsoever?"

Now he was talking to me as if I were a grown-up and I have to say I loved it.

"There can be only one reason," I told him, returning the favor. "She needs to make an ally of me."

Adam's eyes went hooded for a moment, and then he said, "I think you may be right. Are you prepared to play along?"

Up until that moment, my usual response would have been to nod, but I did not.

"Yes," I told him.

"Good," he said. "And so shall I."

He stuck out a hand and I shook it to avoid making a scene.

"Now that we're partners, so to speak, there's something you ought to know, but before letting you in on it,

I must have your most solemn pledge that you won't breathe a word."

"I so pledge," I said. I had heard the expression somewhere and thought that it suited the occasion admirably. We were *not* partners, but I wasn't about to tell *him* that.

"I also want you to promise me that you will not go prowling about the church—at least not alone. If you feel that you need to go there for any reason, let me know and I shall come with you."

"But why?"

I was hardly going to saddle myself with someone old enough to be my father.

"Have you ever heard of the Heart of Lucifer?"

"Of course I have," I said. "We were taught it in Sunday School. It's a legend."

"How much of it do you remember?"

"Following the Crucifixion of Our Lord," I began, parroting almost word for word Miss Lavinia Puddock's account to our childish ears, "it is said that Joseph of Arimathea brought to Britain the Holy Grail, the vessel which had contained the Blood of Christ. When Joseph laid down his staff at Glastonbury Abbey, it took root and there sprang forth a bush whose like had never before been seen. This was the famous Glastonbury Thorn, and from its branches was carved the crosier, or shepherd's staff, of our own dear Saint Tancred, into which was set a precious stone called 'the Heart of Lucifer,' which was said to have fallen from the sky and thought by some to be the Holy Grail itself.

"It all seems rather a muddle," I added.

"Well done," Adam said. "You can see the crook of his crosier beside his face in the carving."

"The one that's leaking blood," I said enthusiastically.

"Have you confirmed that in your laboratory?" Adam asked.

"I was about to, but I was interrupted. I saw you taste the stuff in the church. What did you think?"

"I shall wait upon your chemical analysis. Then we shall see if your test tubes agree with my taste buds."

"What were you going to tell me?" I asked. "The thing that you said I ought to know?"

Adam's face was suddenly serious. "In the latter years of the war, a person named Jeremy Pole, whom I had known slightly at university, was doing research at the Public Record Office when he made rather a startling discovery. While sifting through bales of quite boring charters from the Middle Ages he came upon a small book which had once been in the library, or scriptorium, of Glastonbury Abbey, which had been sacked—there's no other way of putting it—by Henry the Eighth in 1539, in spite of the fact that the Benedictine monks were said to be at ease among royalty. I suppose that proves, if nothing else, that royalty was not at ease among the Benedictines. Westminster Abbey, as you will remember, began life as a Benedictine monastery.

"Their libraries were known to have been a treasure trove of rare and unique documents; that of Glastonbury, specifically, contained a number of early and original histories of England."

As a matter of fact, I didn't remember. It was a bit of history that I had never known, but I loved it that Adam pretended I did. He was definitely improving.

"Here was the odd thing about Pole's discovery: Although this ancient little leather-bound book was sandwiched between many packets of moldy cowhide court rolls, there were no corresponding marks either above it or below."

"It had been put there recently," I said.

"Excellent. That, also, was Pole's conclusion."

"Someone had hidden it there."

"Full marks, Flavia," Adam said. "Well done."

I resisted brushing off my shoulders.

"When he leafed through it, he found that it was a household book, written in Latin and kept by the Cellarer at Glastonbury, a certain Ralph: expenses, and so on, and so on. Nothing very exciting. A few notes here and there on what was happening at the abbey: great storms, deaths, and droughts. Not a chronicle, as such, but more a notebook kept by a busy man who was more concerned with the stillroom, the bees, and the state of the herb garden—which is why Pole brought it to my attention.

"As with many monastic documents, it was filled with scribbling round the edges—marginalia, we call it nowadays—little notes jotted in the margins about this and that: such things as 'don't forget the eggs,' 'metheglin for Father Abbot's stomach'—metheglin was a kind of spiced mead, a fermented honey offshoot of beekeeping— all the craze in the monasteries—the Guinness stout of its day.

"At any rate, Pole was leafing idly through these notes—they weren't really his field, you know—when the word *adamas* caught his eye: Latin for 'diamond.' A most uncommon word to find among monkish writings.

"The text noted, in surprisingly few matter-of-fact words, the death of the bishop: Tancred de Luci."

For a few moments, my mind did not register what my ears had heard.

"De Luci?" I said at last, slowly. "Could it be—?"

"It's altogether quite possible," Adam said. "The de Luce name is, as you know, an ancient one, of Norman French origin. It has appeared in many different forms. There was, of course, famously, Sir Thomas Lucy, of Charlecote Park, in Warwickshire, who was said—probably wrongly—to have had a young man named William Shakespeare brought up before him on a charge of poaching the Charlecote deer."

"Damn!" I said.

"Quite," Adam agreed.

He picked up a pebble and shied it to one side of the dabbling ducks. There was a sudden excited quacking, a flutter of wings, and then they settled once more into their eternal dipping and diving.

"But there's more," he added. "Would you like to hear it?"

I gave him *such* a look.

"A few pages later, Ralph the Cellarer records that the bishop has been laid to rest—you'll be interested in this— 'att Lacey.'"

"Not *Bishop's* Lacey?"

"No. It wasn't given that name until after his death.

"He was laid to rest, according to Ralph, who must have attended the funeral, 'with greatte and soleymne pomp in hys mitre, cope and crosier.'"

"The crosier having the Heart of Lucifer set into it?"

"The very same," Adam said in a low voice, as if there were some danger of us being overheard. "In the margin, Ralph made the note: '*oculi mei conspexi*' and the single word 'adamas'—which means, more or less, 'I have seen this diamond with my own eyes.' It's interesting that he chose to write the marginalia in Latin."

"Why?" I demanded.

"Because it would have been as easily understood by everyone at the abbey as the English in which his note-book was kept."

"Perhaps someone else made the note."

"No, it was in the same handwriting. What it means is that we have an eyewitness report—or as near as damn it—to the fact that Saint Tancred was interred with his miter, cope, and crosier, the Heart of Lucifer, and all."

"But why has nobody ever found this out?"

"History is like the kitchen sink," Adam answered. "Everything goes round and round until eventually, sooner or later, most of it goes down the waste pipe. Things are forgotten. Things are mislaid. Things are cov-ered up. Sometimes, it's simply a matter of neglect.

"During the last century and a half, there have been amateur sportsmen who made a hobby of digging through the rubble of our island's history, mostly for their own enlightenment and amusement, but with two recent wars, that's come almost to a halt. Nowadays the past is a luxury which nobody can afford. No one has the time for it."

"Do you?" I asked.

"I try to," he said. "Although I am not always success-ful."

"Is that all, then?" I asked.

"All?"

"All that you wanted to tell me? All that I've given you my pledge not to repeat?"

A shadow came over his face. "I'm afraid," he said, "that it is only the beginning."

He picked up another pebble, as if he were going to toss it carefree among the ducks, but thought better of it and let the stone drop from his fingers.

"The thing of it is," he said, "that someone else within the past—say, ten years—has happened upon the scribblings of Ralph the Cellarer, and found them important enough to hide in a pile of old vellum. As is so often the case, I fear that there's a diamond at the bottom of it all."

"Saint Tancred's crosier!" I let out a whistle.

"Precisely."

"It's in his tomb!" I said, hopping from one foot to the other.

"I believe it is," Adam said. "Do you know anything about diamonds in history?"

"Not much," I told him. "Other than that they were once thought to be both poison and antidote to poison."

"Quite true. Diamonds were also thought to confer invisibility, to defend against the evil eye and, at least according to Pliny the Elder, to give men the power to see the faces of the gods: '*Anancitide in hydromantia dicunt evocari imagines deorum.*' They were believed at the beginning of the sixteenth century, by a Venetian named Camillus Leonardus, to be '*a help to lunaticks and such as are posessed with the Devil.*' He also believed they could tame wild beasts and prevent nightmares. The diamond in the breastplate of the Jewish High Priest was once believed to become clear in the presence of an innocent man and turn cloudy in the presence of a guilty one. And Rabbi Yehuda, in the Talmud, was said during a voyage to have placed a diamond on some salted birds which came back to life and flew away with the stone!"

"Do you believe those things?"

"No," Adam said. "But I like to keep in mind that when a thing is believed to have a certain effect, that it often does. It is also wise to remember that when it comes to diamonds, there *is* one power which they possess without a doubt, and that is the power to make people kill."

"Are you talking about Mr. Collicutt?" I asked.

"To be blunt, yes. Which is why I want you to keep well away from the church. Let me deal with it. That's why I'm in Bishop's Lacey. It's my job."

"Is it?" I asked. "I should have thought it Inspector Hewitt's."

"There are more things in heaven and earth than Inspector Hewitt," Adam said.

"May I ask you one question?" I said, screwing up my courage.

"You may try."

"Who are you working for?"

The air between us went suddenly cool, as if a phantom breeze had blown upon us from the past.

"I'm afraid I can't tell you that," he said.

·SEVENTEEN·

Back home at Buckshaw, I hunched over my note-book in the laboratory. I had found by experience that putting things down on paper helped to clear the mind in precisely the same way, as Mrs. Mullet had taught me, that an eggshell clarifies the consommé or the coffee, which, of course, is a simple matter of chemistry. The albumin contained in the eggshell has the property of collecting and binding the rubbish that floats in the dark liquid, which can then be removed and discarded in a single reeking clot: a perfect description of the writing process.

I glanced up at Esmeralda, who was perched on a cast-iron laboratory stand, cocking her head to keep an eye on the two eggs she had laid in my bed: two eggs which I was now steaming in a covered glass flask. If she was saddened by the sight of her offspring being boiled alive, Esmeralda did not show it.

"Stiff upper lip—or beak," I told her, but she was more

interested in the bubbling water than in my false sympathy. Chickens are much less emotional than humans.

Steamed Eggs Deluxe de Luce, I called my invention.

Mrs. Mullet's ghastly hard-boiled eggs, with their green circle around the yolk, looking for all the world like the planet Saturn with its rings poisoned—the very thought of the things gives me the hoolibobs—had forced me to find a chemical solution to the problem.

An eggshell, I reasoned, is composed chiefly of calcium carbonate, $CaCO_3$, which, although it does not itself boil until it reaches a very high temperature, begins to decompose nevertheless at 100 degrees Celsius, the boiling point of water.

Steamed, covered, for ten minutes, the crystalline structure of the calcium carbonate is weakened. After another ten minutes or so in cold water, the egg can then be given a light tap on a hard surface and rolled lightly under the hand along its equator until the shell shatters into crystals and can be peeled away almost in a single piece as easily as skinning a tangerine. The white is firm without being rubbery, and the yolk a perfect daffodil yellow.

Farewell hard-boiled eggs. Hail *Steamed Eggs Deluxe de Luce!*

It was a perfect solution for anyone who hates struggling with the shells of boiled eggs, or who bites their fingernails. I would write a cookbook and become famous. *Flavia Cooks!* I would call it, and I would become known as The Egg Lady.

"*Better Living Through Chemistry*," as the people at DuPont are forever telling us in their adverts in the *Picture Post*.

I picked up my pencil.

The Heart of Lucifer, I wrote, then crossed it out. On second thought, I tore out the page and held it to the flame of a Bunsen burner, then washed the black ashes down the sink. Much as I was aching to set down in writing the story of that priceless stone, I realized that I didn't dare. It was not safe nor was it wise to commit certain things to paper. Diaries and notebooks could always be read by prying eyes. It had been known to happen.

For now I would confine myself to people.

ADAM TRADESCANT SOWERBY, I wrote on a new page, and underlined it. This was going to be difficult. I had such tangled feelings toward the man.

—admits he's a private investigator, but who is employing him? And how much does he know?

It was odd, wasn't it, that he had asked me no questions about my own findings. He seemed not in the least curious about anything I might have discovered.

I drew a line, leaving more space for Adam Sowerby. I would come back to him later.

—Miss Tanty fancies herself an amateur detective. Fortunately, she believes that Adam and I are, also.

As Chairman of Altar Guild, has unquestioned access to the church at all hours. Admitted to being furious with Mr. Collicutt about not picking her up for her appointment, but hardly reason enough to kill him. Other motives? Musical ones, perhaps? She had cried out at the sight of dripping blood in the church, "Forgive me, O Lord"—then tried to convince me that it was staged. What did she need to be forgiven for? (NB: Pry it out of Feely.)

Which reminded me—I had still not analyzed the red residue on my hair ribbon. I reached into my pocket.

It was empty.

I leapt up from the bench and dug desperately in both pockets. The ribbon was gone.

Surely it had been there this morning while I was talking to Mrs. Mullet. Or had it? I had certainly thought about beginning my chemical analysis, but had I actually touched the ribbon with my hand? Probably not.

Had I lost it on the riverbank while talking to Adam? Or somewhere in Miss Tanty's house?

"Bugger!" I said.

I might have dropped it anywhere: in the crypt, in the churchyard, in the tunnel, on the road to Nether-Wolsey, or in the butcher's shop of that peculiar village. Or could it have fallen out of my pocket at Bogmore Hall? Was it still lying somewhere in those dusty corridors—or even in the prison cell of Jocelyn Ridley-Smith's room—waiting to betray the fact that I had been there? Perhaps it had already been found by his father, the magistrate—or by the servant. What was the man's name? Benson?

No matter. I needed to get on with my notes before I forgot the details.

Mad Meg—quite harmless. At least I believe she is. Although she was the first to spot the falling blood, she didn't seem at all surprised. In fact, she immediately began quoting the Book of Revelation—as if she had come there especially to announce the miracle.

Marmaduke Parr—Without even knowing the man, I can tell that he is one of those persons Father would call "an ecclesiastical chameleon." Altogether a nasty piece of furniture. Why is he so determined to stop the exhumation of Saint Tancred? Or is it really the bishop who wishes to do so? Or the chancellor?

Which brings us to:

Magistrate Ridley-Smith—I've never clapped eyes on the man but I already dislike him intensely, if only for the fact that he keeps his poor son, Jocelyn, captive like a princess in a tower.

My hand stopped writing.

Wasn't it "passing strange," as Daffy would say, that although Harriet had visited Jocelyn Ridley-Smith at Bogmore Hall—frequently, it would appear—that she had never demanded he be set free? Why not? That, perhaps, was the greatest question of all.

My pencil broke with a snap!

I realized suddenly that, between words, I had been gnawing on it and chewed the thing almost in half. I would have to continue later.

Esmeralda gave a cluck and I saw that the eggs had

boiled nearly dry. I had probably ruined them. I turned off the Bunsen burner and extracted the steaming eggs from the flask with a pair of nickel-plated laboratory tongs.

Using a glass funnel stuck into a flask as an eggcup, I gave the first egg a sharp crack with a graduated measuring spoon I had pinched from the kitchen, and lifted off the top.

The smell of hydrogen sulfide filled the air.

Rotten egg gas.

"A overcooked egg smells like a you-know-what," Mrs. Mullet had told me, and she was right, even though she didn't know the chemical details.

Besides fats, an egg contains magnesium, potassium, calcium, iron, phosphorus, and zinc, along with a witches' brew of the amino acids, vitamins (which were not believed in by the Royal Navy until quite recently), and a long list of proteins and enzymes including lysozyme, which is found in milk as well as in human secretions such as tears, spit, and snot.

It made no difference: I was hungry.

I was spooning out the first mouthful when the door flew open and Daffy stormed into the room. I must have forgotten to lock it.

"Look at you!" she shouted, her pointing finger trembling.

"What?" I said. As far as I knew I hadn't committed any recent wickedness.

"Look at you!" she said again. "Just look at you!"

"Would you like an egg?" I asked, gesturing to an empty stool. "They're a little overdone."

"No!

"Thank you," she added. Good manners were as persistent in Daffy as a speck of dust stuck in the eye.

"Well, sit down anyway," I said. "You're making me nervous."

"What I have to say to you needs to be said standing up."

I shrugged.

"Shoot *yourself*," I said, but she gave me not so much as the ghost of a smile.

"Have you no sense?" she shouted. "Have you no sense at all?"

I waited for the explanation, which I suspected would not be long in coming.

"Can you not see what you're doing to Father? He's crushed, he's ill, he doesn't sleep, and you're off stirring up trouble. How can you live with yourself?"

I shrugged. I could have told her, I suppose, that just last evening, I'd had a perfectly civilized chat with him.

And then I remembered that I had found Father sitting alone in the kitchen in the dark.

Better to wait out Daffy's anger. Even a flying bomb runs out of fuel eventually. But for the moment, Daffy was so infuriated that, even though she had glanced at her several times, she had not really registered Esmeralda.

I listened for what must have been ten minutes as Daffy raged, pacing up and down the room, waving her arms, citing chapter and verse of my offenses since the day that I was born, dredging up incidents that even I had forgotten.

It was an impressive spectacle.

And then suddenly she was in tears, sobbing like a

little girl lost, and I found myself at her side, my arm around her, and my own vision inexplicably blurred.

Neither of us spoke a word and we didn't need to. We stood there clinging to each other like squids, damp, quivering, and unhappy.

What was going to become of us?

It was a question I had been hiding from myself for longer than I cared to remember.

Where would we go when Buckshaw was sold? What were we going to do?

These were questions which had no answers. There were no happy outcomes.

If we were lucky, the sale of Buckshaw would bring in enough to pay off Father's debts, but we would be left homeless and penniless.

Father, I knew, would never accept charity. It was not in his blood.

There was that word again: *blood*. It was everywhere, wasn't it?—dripping from the severed head of John the Baptist, falling from the face of a wooden Saint Tancred, staining my hair ribbon, oozing in all its red wonder on glass plates under my microscope . . .

Everywhere. Blood.

It was what tied us together, Daffy and Feely and Father and me.

I knew for certain in that instant that we were one. In spite of the stupid tales with which my sisters had tormented me, my blood was now screaming out to me that all of us were one, and that nothing could ever tear us apart.

It was the happiest and yet the saddest moment of my life.

We stood there for the longest time, Daffy and I, hugging each other, not wanting to break away and have to look at each other. Faces, at times like these, were best left buried in shoulders.

And then, incredibly, I heard myself saying, "There, there," and patting Daffy's shoulder.

We might have laughed at that but we didn't. Daffy at last, snuffling, pulled away and made for the door. Our eyes did not meet.

Things were back to normal.

I felt rather odd as I walked slowly down the east staircase. What was happening to me?

On the one hand, something had made me follow Daffy from the room: some need to continue the contact that we had just made. On the other, I wanted to kill her.

Of my two sisters, Daffy was the one of whom I was most afraid. It was, I think, because of her silences. She was most often to be found curled up with a book which in itself was a pretty enough picture, but curled up, nevertheless—coiled, like a snake.

One never knew when she was going to attack, and when she did, her words were poisonous.

I stopped on the landing to reflect.

I was being torn apart from the inside: pressed with a sort of dopey gratitude which was trying to expand me, and at the same time crushed in from the outside by the enormous weight of our situation.

Would I explode or would I be squashed?

I continued, half in a daze, to the bottom of the stairs and made my way, without realizing it, to the kitchen.

Mrs. Mullet was up to her elbows in a sink full of pots.

"What's the matter with you, dear?" she asked, drying

her hands and turning toward me. "You look as if you'd seen a ghost."

Perhaps I had.

Perhaps I had seen the ghost of what our family life might have been if all of us were not who we were.

It was all so damnably complicated.

Mrs. Mullet did something she had not done since I was a little girl. She knelt down and put her hands on my shoulders and looked up into my face.

"Tell me about it," she said softly, pushing my hair back out of my eyes. "Tell Mrs. M all about it."

I suppose I could have, but I didn't.

"I think it's just the thought of Feely getting married and moving away," I said, my lower lip trembling. "I'm going to miss her."

Why is it, I wondered, even as I spoke, that we lie most easily when feelings are involved?

It was a thought that I had never had before, and it frightened me. What do you do when your own brain vomits up questions to which you don't know the answers? Questions that you don't even understand?

"We're all goin' to miss 'er, dear," Mrs. Mullet said. "We shall miss 'er lovely music in the house."

That did it. I burst into tears.

Why?

It's hard to explain. It was partly the thought that Mrs. Mullet was going to miss Ludwig van Beethoven and Johann Sebastian Bach, that she was going to miss Franz Schubert and Domenico Scarlatti and Pietro Domenico Paradisi and a hundred others that had been hanging round the halls of Buckshaw for as long as I could remember.

How empty the place was going to be. How bloody, awfully empty.

Mrs. Mullet wiped my eyes with her apron.

"There, there, dear," she said, just as I had said to Daffy. "I've got some 'ot scones comin' out the oven directly. There's nothin' like scones to dry up tears."

I smiled at the thought, but not very much.

"Sit up the table and I shall put the kettle on," she said. "A nice cup of tea is good for the gizzard, as the bishop said to the chorus girl. Oh! Sorry, dear! I oughtn't to 'ave let that slip. It's one of them sayin's Alf picked up at 'is regimental dinner that makes you smile. I can't think what come over me."

What was she going on about? There was nothing remotely amusing about what she had said. In fact, it made no sense at all.

And yet it reminded me of something: the bishop.

And the bishop reminded me of the chancellor.

"Do you know anything about Magistrate Ridley-Smith?" I found myself asking.

"Just that 'e's a Tartar," she said. "Them Ridley-Smiths are an odd lot. Not right, like."

"I've heard about the one who was made of glass," I offered, "and the one whose pet alligator ate the chambermaid."

Mrs. Mullet sniffed. "They were nothin' compared with 'im," she said. "'E's a bad lot, magistrate or no. You keep clear of 'im."

"But Harriet used to visit Bogmore Hall," I said.

Mrs. Mullet stopped halfway to the Aga, the teakettle frozen in her hand.

"Wherever did you 'ear that, miss?"

The room had gone suddenly cold, as it does when you've gone too far.

"Oh, I don't know," I said lightly. "Daffy or Feely must have mentioned it."

"Miss Daphne and Miss Ophelia know nothing about it. It was a secret between Miss 'Arriet and me. Not even the Colonel knew. I used to make up the food 'ampers and she delivered 'em."

"To Jocelyn Ridley-Smith?" I asked.

"Now, you listen to me, Miss Smartpants. Don't you mention that name again in this 'ere 'ouse. They'll think it's all my fault and I'll be given the sack for blabberin'. Now, off you go—and get them Ridley-Smiths off your brain."

"Do you think it's a sin that Harriet made friends with Jocelyn?"

"It isn't a question of what I think. 'Tisn't my place to think. I drags myself in 'ere every day and cooks for you lot and then I goes 'ome, and there's an end of it."

"But—"

"There's an end of it," Mrs. Mullet said loudly. "If I comes 'ome and tells Alf I've lost my place, I 'ate to think what 'e'd say. Now off you go."

And off I went.

Mrs. Mullet had given me an idea.

Mrs. Mullet and Alf lived in a picturesque cottage near the end of Cobbler's Lane, a narrow track which ran off the high street and went nowhere in particular.

"It's what they call a 'colder-sock,' Alf says," she had once told me. "Ends all of a sudden, like a sock."

A ginger cat sat in a window, watching me with one open eye.

I knocked at the door and tried to look respectful.

I didn't know much about the home life of the Mullets except those titbits that Mrs. M inevitably let leak. I knew, for instance, that Alf loved custard pie; that their daughter, Agnes, had left home in the last year of the war to study Pitman shorthand, and that her bedroom had been kept ever since as a shrine to the powers of the type-writer, but I knew little else.

The door opened and there stood Alf. He was a man of middle age, middle height, middle hair, and medium build. His only unusual feature was in the way he stood: ramrod straight. Alf, I remembered, had been in the army and, like Father and Dogger, knew a lot of things which must never be spoken of.

"Well, miss," he said. "To what do we owe this prodigious great pleasure?"

The precise same words with which he had greeted me the last time I visited, six months ago.

"I'm doing some research," I said. "And I'd appreciate having your advice."

"Research, eh? Best come in and tell me about it."

Before you could whistle the first two bars of "Rule, Britannia," we were sitting in a tiny kitchen that was as neat as a pin.

"Pardon me for not layin' on the ballroom," Alf said, "but the missus don't like havin' 'er cushions made a mess of."

"It's all right, Mr. Mullet," I said. "I don't, either."

"Sound girl," he said. "Wizard good sense."

I plunged right in. "I was chatting with Mrs. Mullet today about the Ridley-Smiths," I said, matter-of-factly.

Which was true, as far as it went, but only just barely.

"Ah," Alf said, noncommittally, not looking at me. "Anything else?"

"No—just the Ridley-Smiths. Magistrate Ridley-Smith, in particular."

"Ah," Alf said again.

"His wife was very beautiful," I said. "I think I've seen a photograph of her."

"Funny old thing, isn't it," Alf asked, "'ow every village has its secrets? Some things just not talked about. Ever noticed that? I 'ave."

"And this is one of them, isn't it?" I asked.

Alf busied himself with the teakettle, in exactly the same way Mrs. Mullet had in the kitchen at Buckshaw. I suppose when people have been married for centuries, they become like joined paper cutouts of each other.

"Lovely day," Alf said, sitting himself down at the kitchen table. "Bit windy. Not bad for March, though."

"I've been to Bogmore Hall," I said. "I've seen Jocelyn Ridley-Smith. I've talked to him."

There was only the slightest hesitation. If I hadn't been looking out for it, I'd have missed it.

"'Ave you, by George."

"Yes," I said.

It was a bit of a stalemate.

Alf flicked a crumb off the tabletop, then bent down and picked it up from the floor, examining it as intently as if it were a bit of fallen moondust.

"I need your help, Mr. Mullet," I said. "I'm doing ge-nealogical research for an article I'm thinking of writing:

The Norman Roots of Certain Families Residing in the Parish of—"

I could see by his grin, even before I finished speaking, that it wasn't going to work.

"The truth is, I know that you were in the army," I said, changing tactics. "I know that because of the Official Secrets Act there are things you are still forbidden to speak of. I am not going to ask you about them. I am not going to ask you about my father, for instance, and I am not going to ask you about Dogger. It would be putting you on the spot."

Alf nodded.

"But I *am* going to ask you about Mrs. Ridley-Smith because . . . well, because I need to know. It's important to Jocelyn, too. I hope you'll understand. It could be a matter of life and death.

"Secrets or no secrets," I added.

I could tell by the way he avoided my eyes that he was wavering.

"I know that you're a great expert on the British military. Everybody in Bishop's Lacey says so. 'A walking encyclopedia,' they call you."

"Is that a fact?" Alf said.

"Yes," I told him, crossing my heart with my first two fingers crossed, and extending my other hand so that he could see I wasn't canceling out the cross with a negative sign behind my back. "It's a fact. Mrs. Mullet says so, too."

I could see him softening.

"You've 'eard of the Battle of Plassey," he said. It was a statement, not a question.

I shook my head no. Once I'd got him started, I didn't dare interrupt.

"How about Clive of India?"

I shook my head again.

"Shocking," he said. "We shall correct that PDQ."

What could this possibly have to do with the Ridley-Smiths?

I couldn't begin to guess.

·EIGHTEEN·

"INDIA, IN THEM DAYS, was like 'eaven and 'ell tossed into a stone kettle and boiled. Still an' all, everyone was dyin' to get into it—the French, the Dutch, the Portuguese, and yes, the English, too, all clawin' away at one another to be top dog. To say nothin' of the Mohammedans and the Moghuls what were tryin to 'ang onto what was rightly theirs.

"More wars than you could count on all your toes and fingers put together, fought over a country full of snakes, elephants, lions, leopards, tigers, rivers, mountains, monsoons, and malaria."

"But why?" I asked.

"Business," Alf said. "Agriculture. Tea and timber. Rice. Coffee and cotton. Opium."

"Ah," I said, as if I understood. "Who won?"

"We did, of course."

"At the Battle of Plassey?" I asked, trying to be one jump ahead of him.

"Among others," Alf said. "That was just one of 'em. One of the best, though. Bengal, Trichinopoly, Pondicherry, Coromandel . . . they don't make names like that nowadays."

He got up from the table and, opening a kitchen drawer, pulled out two handfuls of cutlery—a dozen knives, forks, and spoons, which he dumped with a clatter on the tabletop.

"The Black 'Ole of Calcutta," he said, sitting himself down again. "You must have 'eard of that?"

"No," I said.

"'Undred and forty-six Englishmen packed into a cell no bigger than your butler's pantry at Buckshaw. June. 'Ottest month of the year. Next mornin', no more'n twenty-three of 'em left alive."

I tried for a moment to imagine myself opening the door of Dogger's pantry and having a hundred and twenty-three dead bodies come tumbling out onto the kitchen floor, leaving another two dozen or so poor human beings cringing terrified in the shadowy corners. But I couldn't. It was unthinkable.

"'Eat somethin' awful," Alf went on. "No air. It's murder, plain and simple. What do you do?"

"Revenge?" I asked. It seemed to me the logical answer.

"Revenge is right!" Alf said, slamming his fist down onto the tabletop, causing the cutlery to jump.

"'Ere's the Bhagirathi River," he said, quickly placing a knife. "And 'ere . . ." positioning a salt shaker, "is Suraj-ud-Dowlah, the last Nawab of Bengal. The enemy. He's nineteen years old and 'as the temper of a cobra with a festered fang. 'As an army of fifty thousand foot, eighteen thousand horses, fifty-three pieces of cannon, and forty Frenchmen to work 'em."

Alf had suddenly come to life. It was easy to see that he was as passionate about British military history as I was about poisons.

"Over 'ere, to the west, is Clive, with the Thirty-ninth Regiment. Robert Clive. Not even a military man by profession, when you come right down to it. 'E's a bookkeeper. A *book*keeper! But 'e's a *British* bookkeeper.

"But for all that, 'e once marched his men to battle through a storm—thunderin' and lightnin' to beat blue blazes. Natives thought 'e was some kind of a war god."

Alf sighed. "Those were the days, those were.

"Now then, at Plassey, he's got thirty-two 'undred men and nine guns. It's the monsoon season. Rainin' cats and dogs again. Outnumbered more than fifteen to one. What do you suppose 'e did?"

"He attacked," I said, guessing.

"Too bleedin' well true 'e attacked," Alf said, swiveling a sugar spoon and hopping it across the table. "Suraj-ud-Dowlah took to 'is 'eels on a camel."

He swept the spoons and forks of the Nawab's army off the table and onto the floor.

"I'll wash up later," he said. "Five 'undred dead. British losses? Twenty-two dead and fifteen wounded."

I let out a low whistle. "How could that be?" I asked.

"Nawab didn't keep 'is powder dry," Alf said. "Can't fight with wet powder."

I nodded wisely. "Very interesting," I said. "Whatever became of him?"

"The Nawab? 'E was executed about a week later by 'is successor."

"And Clive?"

"Slit 'is own throat years later in London."

"Ugghhh!" I said, even though I was interested.

"I suppose you're wonderin' why I'm tellin' you all this," Alf said.

"Just a little," I admitted.

"Because," Alf said, watching carefully to see my reaction, "one of them officers of 'Is Majesty's (that'd be George the Second, mind) Thirty-ninth Regiment of Foot was an ancestor of Mrs. Ridley-Smith."

I sucked in my breath. "Mrs. Ridley-Smith? The magistrate's wife? Jocelyn's mother?"

"One and the same," Alf said. "Funny old world, i'n't it?"

"But how do you know that?" I asked.

"Old Beatty told me. 'E was gardener at Bogmore Hall, man and boy, for sixty years or more. I worked 'longside him as a lad. Just a nipper, I was, but old Beatty enjoyed 'avin' someone to rattle off his stories to. A great storyteller, was old Beatty. Put a lot of trust in 'im, the Ridley-Smiths. The magistrate brought 'im out to India to see to 'is garden. Up-country from Calcutta, it was. Marvelous flowers, old Beatty used to say. Bleedin' marvelous."

"Just a minute," I said. "I'm confused. Was Magistrate Ridley-Smith in India?"

"When 'e was a young man. Some kind of district magistrate. Met 'is wife out there. Ada, 'er name was. 'Er family 'ad been in India for donkey's years. British, of course, but they'd been there for generations. Jocelyn was born while they were out there."

"And his mother?"

"She died."

"She died when he was born?"

"So old Beatty told me."

Aha! So that was it! Mrs. Ridley-Smith *was* the sad-eyed woman in the photograph on Jocelyn's wall.

"Was she ill?" I asked. "Before Jocelyn was born, I mean."

"She was nervy," Alf said. "Kept to 'erself, like. Spent all 'er time with 'er soldiers."

He was watching me to see my reaction.

"Soldiers?"

"Tin soldiers. Thousands of 'em."

I couldn't believe what I was hearing. Tin soldiers? A grown woman playing with tin soldiers?

"She bought them for Jocelyn?" I asked.

"No, she died when 'e was born, remember."

"Perhaps she was keeping them for when he was older."

Alf smiled. "No. She had 'em since she was a girl. 'Anded down from 'er military ancestors. Each one 'ad added to the collection. It was 'er 'obby, like."

"Soldiers," I said. I could scarcely believe it.

"Soldiers," Alf said, bending and picking up, piece by piece, the scattered pieces of cutlery from the floor. These he replaced in neat rows on the table, naming each as he set it gently into position.

"First Division 'ere," he said. "First Madras European Regiment. Second Division here—First Madras and Bombay European Regiments.

"Third Division, 'Is Majesty's Thirty-ninth Regiment of Foot, one of 'em—and God only knows which one— bein' 'er great-great-great, or whatever 'e was, grandfather.

"Fourth Division, the Bombay European Regiment, and 'ere, two thousand sepoys, the native foot soldiers, the First Bengal Regiment, Royal Artillery.

"That's us, then," he finished. "All present and accounted for."

"But what about the Nawab?" I asked. "What about his fifty thousand fighters?"

"Oh, they were there, right enough," Alf said quietly. "Old Beatty said she 'ad a little toy figure for every one of 'em. Every last blinkin' one."

He let this sink in.

"You mean—?" I asked.

"That's right, miss," he said. "'Ad a room built special. Kept it locked up tight as the Treasury, she did. Nobody allowed in but 'erself. Old Beatty only knew about it 'cause 'e was called in one time to carry 'er out when she'd fainted. That didn't stop 'im 'avin' a good look round, though."

I edged forward on my chair, begging with my eyes for more.

"The whole battlefield at Plassey, she 'ad, laid out like a model. Exact scale replica of the real thing. 'Uge, it was. Rocks, 'ills, pipe-cleaner trees. The Bhagirathi River was a mirror, tinted blue. Wonderful clever with their 'ands, the Indians. Filled the whole room, wall to wall to wall to wall. Marvelous to see, Old Beatty said."

"And Mrs. Ridley-Smith—?"

"Locked 'erself away in there from mornin' to night, movin' the figures around, fightin' the Battle of Plassey over and over and over again."

"But her husband," I said. "The magistrate, the chancellor—did he think she was—"

"Right in the 'ead? Nobody knows. 'E never mentions 'er name."

A chill went through me. I would not think why until later.

"'Depressed,' they calls it nowadays. Back then it was more likely 'the vapors' or some suchlike."

"What about her family? Were they like that, too?"

"Solid as rocks, the lot of 'em. Soldiers, lawyers, nabobs in the East India Company back to the year dot. They left 'er pretty well alone with 'er toys, at least accordin' to old Beatty."

"Thank you, Mr. Mullet," I said, scraping back my chair and giving his hand a shake. "I'd better be getting along. I don't want anyone to be worrying about me."

The truth was, I needed to talk to Dogger immediately.

It was a matter of life and death.

As I pedaled past St. Tancred's, my eye was caught by a crowd milling outside the front door of the church.

I skidded to a stop.

The vicar was standing in the porch, his hands raised.

"Gentlemen . . . gentlemen," he was saying.

I parked Gladys against the wall and crept slowly forward through the crowd, trying not to be noticed. Most of the people were from Bishop's Lacey, but a few of them were not.

One of the strangers was a tall, thin man in a gray trench coat and red bow tie with a notebook in his hand. At his side was another, shorter man, similarly dressed, holding a press camera up to his eyes.

"But they're saying it's a miracle, Vicar. Surely you can spare us a few words?"

The vicar tried without success to smooth down his disarranged hair, which was blowing in the wind. As he did so, a flashbulb went off.

"What did you think when you saw the blood?" another man called out. "We were told someone threw away their crutches. Is it true?"

A murmur went through the crowd.

"Gentlemen, please. All in good time."

"What about the corpse in the crypt, Vicar?"

I could already see the sensational headlines in tomorrow's *Hinley Chronicle* and *The Morning Post-Horn* and so, I knew, could the vicar.

THE CORPSE IN THE CRYPT! SAINT WEEPS BLOOD!

With that kind of publicity, the bishop would soon have him paddling to a new post somewhere up the Amazon. The press was ruthless, but then so was the Church.

"Gentlemen, please . . . we must remember that today is Good Friday. Nothing must be allowed to profane—"

"Let me through," I shouted. "It's an emergency. Please let me through."

I pushed my way into the crowd and stepped up beside the vicar. Taking his elbow in my hand, I said in a stage whisper just loud enough to be overheard by the newspaper reporters, "I'm afraid she's taken a turn for the worse, Vicar. The doctor says she may not last. They need you to come at once."

I hopped from foot to foot, squinting horribly, trying to force a tear to my eye.

The vicar looked at me as if he had just awakened suddenly on another planet.

"Please," I whimpered, then added in a loud and rising wail, "before it's TOO LATE!"

I pulled at his arm, swung him round, dragged him into the porch, slammed the heavy door shut, and shot the iron bolt.

"Phew!" I said. "What a siege. Just like in *Ivanhoe*. We can sneak out through the vestry."

The vicar looked at me for a moment with empty eyes. He was even more shaken than I had thought. This whole business was taking its toll, to say nothing of his troubles with Cynthia.

I walked him to one of the back pews and sat down beside him.

"Everything's going to be all right," I told him. "I've almost got it figured out."

His face, shaded with mauve from the colored windows above, turned reluctantly toward me.

"Oh, Flavia," he said. "If only that were true."

·NINETEEN·

IT WAS NOT UNTIL I was halfway home that the indignation struck me.

"If only that were true," indeed! It was obvious from his words that in spite of his calling, the vicar was a man of little faith.

I had taken him by the hand and led him out through the vestry, tiptoed with him through the churchyard, and delivered him safely to the vicarage door. I had lurked behind a large tombstone and watched as the grumbling crowd slowly broke up and drifted away.

Not one of them had even thought of looking round behind the church. Not one had thought to follow us on our sad procession to the imaginary deathbed. They had all been so touched by my pretended mission of mercy, that nobody—not even the most hardened of the newspapermen—had tried the church door.

And yet the vicar had no faith in me.

I hate to admit how much that stung.

. . .

The best thing for soothing a disappointed mind is oxygen. A couple of deep inhalations of the old "O" rejuvenates every cell in the body. I suppose I could have gone upstairs to my laboratory for a bit of the bottled stuff, but to me, that would have been cheating. There is nothing like oxygen in its natural form—oxygen which has been naturally produced in a forest or a greenhouse, where many plants, by the process of photosynthesis, are absorbing the poisonous carbon dioxide which we breathe out, and giving us oxygen in exchange.

I had once remarked to Feely that, because of the oxygen, breathing fresh air was like breathing God, but she had slapped my face and told me I was being blasphemous.

The greenhouse at Buckshaw, I had found, always cheered me up instantly, although how much of that was due to Dogger's presence and how much to oxygen I couldn't say. Probably half and half. This much was certain: A greenhouse is a placid place. You never hear about ax murders taking place in a greenhouse.

My theory is that it is because of the "O."

I found Dogger among the flowerpots, lashing gardening tools into bundles with heavy twine.

"Dogger," I said casually, stifling a yawn as I bent over to inspect a potted polyanthus, "what would you say if I asked you the cause of wasted thumb muscles and drooping hands?"

"I should say you'd been at Bogmore Hall, Miss Flavia."

I suppose I should have been dumbfounded, but somehow I wasn't.

"You've seen the photograph of Mrs. Ridley-Smith?"

"No," Dogger replied, "but I *have* overheard the idle chatter of servants."

"And?"

"Most unfortunate. By what I have been able to piece together, a classic case of lead poisoning. The flexor muscles and, to a lesser degree, the extensors are affected. But you will have spotted that already, won't you, miss?"

"Yes," I said. "But I needed you to verify it."

There was a silence as each of us considered how to handle what was inevitably coming next.

"You've known about it all along." I ventured not to make my words sound like an accusation.

"Yes," he said, and there was a sadness in his words, "I've known about it all along."

There was another silence and I realized suddenly that it was because both of us were avoiding any mention of Harriet.

"She used to visit him, didn't she?" I asked. "Jocelyn, I mean."

"Yes," Dogger said, simply.

"And you went with her!"

"No, miss. You must remember, I wasn't yet at Buckshaw in those days."

Of course! How stupid of me. What was I thinking of? Dogger hadn't come to Buckshaw until after the war. He must have heard about the Ridley-Smiths, as I did, from someone else.

"But he's a prisoner! How could they keep him locked up like that?"

"Is he locked up—" Dogger began.

"Of course he is," I said, perhaps too loudly. "Behind a set of double doors!"

"—or is he being protected?"

Now I found myself speaking too quietly. "I hadn't thought of that," I admitted.

"No," Dogger said. "People often don't. One reads these stories in the daily press and jumps to conclusions. Facts are often in direct opposition to assumptions."

"To the headlines," I said, thinking for an instant of the vicar.

"Yes," Dogger said. "As you know from your own studies, lead poisoning is not a pretty thing."

It was true. I had read about what happened to women who had used it in hair dyes, or had slathered quack cosmetics containing carbonate of lead onto their faces: stuff with names like *Cosmetique Infallible*, and *Ali Ahmed's Treasures of the Desert*.

I let my mind fly back to those fat books in Uncle Tar's library in which I had first come across the details: Christison's *A Treatise on Poisons*, Taylor's *Principles and Practice of Medical Jurisprudence*, and Blyth's *Poisons: Their Effects and Detection*, which, since I had discovered them, had become my Old and New Testaments and my Apocrypha.

I thought of the gruesome but fascinating horrors that lay within their pages: the wrist drop, or lead palsy; the paleness, the bloodlessness, the headaches, the foul taste in the mouth, the cramping legs, the difficulty in breathing, the vomiting, the diarrhea, the convulsions, the unconsciousness. I knew that if by some magic we had been able to peel back the lips of Ada Ridley-Smith in that old black-and-white photograph, we should have spotted at least a trace of the blue line where her gums met her teeth, the classic sign of plumbism, better known as lead poisoning.

No wonder the woman was depressed!

"Lead toy soldiers painted with lead paint," Dogger said. "Intended to be looked at, not played with—not, at least, in such great numbers."

"But Jocelyn—" I said.

"Unfortunately, the damage is already done." Dogger shook his head. "He was born poisoned."

It seemed too shocking a thought to be put into mere words.

"The brain of an unborn baby is a most susceptible target," Dogger said. "Women suffering from lead poisoning, more often than not, lose the child.

"But not always," he added. "Not always."

"Tell me about the 'not always,'" I said quietly.

"Children born of a lead-poisoned mother seldom survive more than two or three years. The odds are less than three in a hundred."

"But what's to be done?" I asked. "Surely we can't allow him to be cooped up like that. It isn't right."

Dogger put aside the rakes and hoes. "Sometimes," he said, "a jackstraw family life is the best that can be hoped for."

He paused, and then went on as quietly as if he were dusting furniture. "It may not be ideal, but still, it might be the best possible under the circumstances. The slightest interference might bring the whole thing tumbling down entirely like a house of cards."

Suddenly I didn't want to talk about this anymore. It was odd. Perhaps I was overtired. Father had more than once lectured us about overexertion, but perhaps he was right. I *had* had rather a hectic day.

"I have taken the liberty of preparing a nest for

Esmeralda," Dogger said, neatly changing the subject, "and laying on a supply of the approved feed."

He pointed to a wooden box in the corner, where Esmeralda was nestling in a luxurious bed of straw. I hadn't even noticed her.

"Dogger," I said, "you're a darling!"

I don't know what came over me. It just slipped out. I was mortified. It was the sort of thing Feely's friend Sheila Foster might have said.

"I'm sorry," I told him, "I didn't mean—"

And then I fled, leaving Dogger placidly at work amidst his atmosphere of oxygen.

What was happening to my world? Everything was topsy-turvy. Buckshaw was to be sold. Father had told me I was Harriet and so more or less had Jocelyn Ridley-Smith. Daffy had hugged me. The vicar had doubted me. I had learned that I was likely a collateral descendant of a saint. I had already begun to love the hated Cynthia. I had allowed myself to burst into tears in front of Mrs. Mullet. And now I had spoken down to Dogger as if I were a cinema star and he a mere hireling. The universe was changing in ways that I did not necessarily approve of.

If only we could go back to the good old days of a week ago when, as unpleasant as they might have seemed, we were revolving securely in our dusty old orbits.

Feely, it seemed, was, as Sherlock Holmes once called Dr. Watson, "the one fixed point in a changing world." Throughout the events of the past few days, Feely had somehow managed to remain her same unpleasant self.

Could it be that goodness waxes and wanes like the moon, and that only evil is constant?

If I could find the answer to that question, perhaps everything else would come clear.

It was, in a way, the same problem that was now facing Inspector Hewitt and me, and to a lesser degree, I suppose, Adam Sowerby and Miss Tanty.

Could it be that some person with an otherwise spotless record had suddenly become unhinged and committed murder? Or had Mr. Collicutt met his end at the hands of someone who had killed before?

A professional, say?

His death did not seem to fit what one thinks of as a village murder: the jealousy, the angry words, the blow, the strangulation, the poisoning, the booby-trapped bed warmer.

Instead, he had been brutally murdered within the closed casing of a historical pipe organ, his body hauled out of doors and through the churchyard, dropped down into an open grave, dragged through a tunnel, and tossed at last into a hidden chamber atop the tomb of a long-dead saint.

It didn't make any sense.

Or did it?

The truth, I suspected, was in a bit of cloth.

The white ruffle I had seen protruding from the gas mask at Mr. Collicutt's throat.

I flung myself down on my bed to rest my eyes.

When I opened them again, it had grown dark outside.

I came slowly down the east staircase rubbing my eyes after a restless night. My dreams had been of Buckshaw— dark dreams in which holes were appearing everywhere, as if some monstrous mole were blindly digging away at the house and its grounds, relentless and unstoppable.

I had awakened to find it well past nine in the morning. I would need to find Father and apologize, not just for missing yesterday's supper, to say nothing of lunch, but also for this morning's breakfast.

Father, as I have said, was a stickler for attendance. Excuses not allowed.

I dawdled along the corridor, dragging out the inevitable confrontation as long as I possibly could.

I stopped outside the drawing-room door and listened. If Father were not here, he would be in his study, and I certainly didn't want to disturb him there.

In a way, I would be off the hook.

I put my ear to the door and listened to the low murmer of voices. Although I could not hear what was being said, I knew by the way the paneling vibrated that one of the speakers was Feely.

I knelt down and applied my eye to the keyhole, but it was no good: The key was in the lock and my view was blocked.

I listened at the door again—pressing my ear tightly against the wooden panel—but it was no use. Even my supersensitive hearing was not enough.

The solution came—as brilliant solutions often do—in a flash.

On tiptoe, I loped back to the foyer and upstairs to my laboratory, chuckling as I went.

From a cupboard under one of the sinks I extracted a screwdriver, a length of rubber hose, and two funnels, used ordinarily for filling bottles but now destined for a much more exciting role.

Back along the upstairs corridor I went, along the unused north wing and through the baize door that led to family quarters. Directly across from Harriet's boudoir, which Father kept untouched as yet another shrine to her memory, was Feely's room. Besides Harriet's it was the largest bedroom at Buckshaw, and the most luxurious.

I tapped at the door with a fingernail, to check that the coast was clear.

If Feely were inside—if it happened to be someone else's voice I had heard in the drawing room—she would instantly answer the slightest sound with a loud and surly "What?"

Feely was the most territorial of all we de Luces, and as fearsomely protective of her domain as God is of Heaven.

I tapped again.

Nothing.

I tried the door and, miracle of miracles, it swung open. Feely must have gone downstairs in an almighty rush to overlook such a basic point of privacy.

I closed the door quietly behind me and tiptoed across the room. I was now directly above the drawing room, and didn't want the sound of my footsteps to give me away. Not that they would, of course. Buckshaw was as solid as any ancient cathedral—high ceilings, thick floors—but still, one didn't want to trip on the carpet and give away the game.

One of the marvels of Buckshaw, at least in its Victorian days, had been the conversion of its chimneys from their original smokestack design to a patent draft-regulating scheme. Through the ingenious knocking together of flues on the ground and second floors, by means of a crude valve—actually, no more than a cast-iron plate—the inhabitants could be protected against the danger of carbon monoxide poisoning from coal fires in the grate, should one of the chimneys become blocked by a jackdaw's nest.

I had discovered these plates almost by accident while investigating in my laboratory a more efficient way than opening a window of venting poisonous gases, such as hydrogen cyanide, and so forth, to the outside air without killing my own flesh and blood.

These iron plates at the back of each fireplace, coated with generations of soot, could with a little persistence be easily unscrewed and removed.

I should have brought something to catch the soot— an old quilt or blanket, perhaps—but it was too late now. I needed to listen in on Feely's conversation with someone I was quite sure had to be the only visitor Buckshaw had received in months. The topic was almost certainly her wedding, whose details were, for some inexplicable reason, being kept from me. I didn't want to miss a word more than was necessary.

I had heard somewhere that chimney sweeps had used sheets to drape the furniture which, from my viewpoint, couldn't have been more convenient. Because it was closest to hand, I stripped back her comforter and whipped off the top sheet from Feely's bed. I would replace it with a fresh one later.

I spread the sheet on the cold hearth, ducked down as if I were passing through a low door, and stood up with my head inside the fireplace.

Ah! Here it was—just above my head. By climbing up onto the grate I could easily get at the screws that held the plate in position. I felt out the slots with my thumbnails.

It is important to remember, when removing cast-iron fittings in chimneys, to be quiet about it, since brick transmits the slightest sound with wonderful efficiency.

The plate came away without a struggle, and I put it down carefully on the sheet.

Next I took the two funnels—a large one of tin and a small one of glass—and shoved the spout of each into opposite ends of the rubber hose.

I slipped the larger funnel into the new opening and then, playing out the rubber hose as if it were a rope, slowly . . . carefully . . . inch by inch . . . foot by foot—lowered away.

After what seemed like forever, the full length of the hose was dangling down the chimney. If my calculations were correct, the large funnel was now about level with the drawing-room fireplace.

I put the small funnel to my ear, just in time to hear Feely say, "I thought perhaps something from Elgar. 'The Angel's Farewell.' It's very British."

"Yes, but rather too Catholic, don't you think?" the stranger's voice replied. "Based on a poem by the turncoat Newman. It would be tantamount to doing 'Ave Maria.' Don't want to put wrong ideas into the girls' heads. They'll all be there, you know. They all adored him."

I knew instantly that I was eavesdropping on a conversation between Feely and Alberta Moon, the music mistress at St. Agatha's—Alberta Moon, who the vicar had said would be devastated to hear of Mr. Collicutt's death. They were not discussing Feely's wedding, but rather Mr. Collicutt's funeral.

"Perhaps the *Nunc Dimittis*," Feely said. "'Lord now lettest thou thy servant depart in peace.' He played it so often at Evensong. I thought we might ask Miss Tanty to sing it as a solo."

There was a cold silence, made colder and longer by the length of rubber tube through which I was listening.

"No, I think not, Ophelia. Miss Tanty, to be quite plain about it, hated his intestines."

This was followed by a brittle laugh.

Feely said something which I couldn't quite make out, but it sounded as if she were upset. I removed the glass funnel from the hose and jammed the end of the rubber tubing directly into my ear.

". . . had many a jolly old girl-to-girl with her at the school before she hung up her hatchet," Miss Moon was saying. ". . . in the days when we were still managing to be civil to each other."

I'd forgotten that Miss Tanty had been Miss Moon's predecessor at St. Agatha's.

"And as difficult as it may be for you to believe, it is perhaps my bounden duty to inform you that she had what my girls would call 'a mad pash' for Crispin."

Crispin? Aha! She was talking about Mr. Collicutt.

"Oh, don't look shocked, Ophelia. Of *course* she was old enough to be his mother but still, as you ought to know by now, one must never underestimate the juices of a soprano."

To my ears—or rather to my *ear*, since I was eavesdropping with a rubber tube shoved into just one of them—Miss Moon sounded more angry than devastated.

"I will not have that woman singing a solo at Crispin's funeral! The would-be lover scorned being allowed to warble over the loved one's remains? It is simply not on, Ophelia. You may put it out of your head. No, I shall do the honors myself. Purcell, I think. 'When I Am Laid in Earth,' from *Dido and Aeneas*. The very thing. I shall accompany myself and sing from the organ bench, so there shall be no need for you to learn the piece.

"No, no. No need to thank me. I'm sure you have quite enough on your plate these days without— Such a pity about Buckshaw, isn't it? I saw the sign at the gates. Too shocking. But then we must look on the bright side. A little birdie tells me that you yourself will soon have cause to celebrate. We're all so happy for you, Ophelia, really we are.

"What's his name, from up at Culverhouse Farm? Victor? I know that you and Victor will—"

It was too much!

I picked up the small glass funnel from the grate and rammed its end back into the hose. I put it to my mouth and shouted into it, "Dieter! It's *Dieter*, you stupid old sea cow!"

What had I done? Had I let a moment of anger destroy the de Luces' last scrap of dignity? Was Saint Tancred, in the church, shaking his wooden head in bloody disbelief that one of his descendants could behave like such a drip?

I put the funnel to my ear again and listened. There was nothing but silence.

And then a door slammed.

A moment later came the sound of heels on the hearth and then the unmistakable grating of fingers on the distant end of my rubber hose.

Strangled by the narrow tube, Feely's thin voice, like that of an angered elf, came leaking from between my fingers and out the tiny trumpet of the funnel.

"I hate you!" it said.

·TWENTY·

How could a single village, nestled miles from anywhere in the English countryside, contain both a Miss Tanty and a Miss Alberta Moon? Mathematically speaking, of course, Providence should have placed them at opposite ends of the country—one at Land's End and the other at John o' Groat's.

I was thinking this as I came down the west staircase, Feely's bagged sheet full of soot in my hand. I would scatter the stuff somewhere on the Visto, where it would sooner or later be washed away by the rain. I had already found a clean sheet in a cupboard and installed it quite neatly on Feely's bed. I would wash this one in the laboratory, hang it up to dry in my bedroom, and return it to storage at my leisure. No one would be any the wiser.

Feely was standing at the bottom of the stairs, tapping her foot.

I almost turned and ran, but I did not. Something in me froze my legs. Oh, well, sooner or later, she would find me anyway. There was no real escape. I might as well take my medicine now and get it over with.

As I stepped awkwardly off the last step, Feely came flying at me.

I dropped the sheet, soot and all, and covered my eyes.

She seized me by the shoulders. She was going to crush the breath out of me—break my ribs, like the hulking American wrestlers we had seen in the newsreel at the cinema.

"You were magnificent!" she said, giving me a squeeze. "Thank you!"

I broke free, not trusting her.

"A few minutes ago, you hated me," I pointed out.

"That was then—this is now," Feely said. "I've had time to consider it. Perhaps I was a bit hasty."

I knew that this was as close to an apology as I was likely to receive from Feely in this or any other lifetime.

"'Stupid old sea cow'!" Feely said, shaking her head. "You ought to have seen her face. I thought for a moment she was going to have an accident on our carpet."

My sister could be remarkably crude when she forgot herself.

"You're welcome," I said, still basking a bit in Feely's unexpected thanks and wanting the feeling to last for as long as possible.

With this abrupt ending of hostilities, my brain was suddenly bubbling over with goodwill, simply dying to share with her the news that she might have the blood of a saint flowing in her veins—to tell her about poor little Hannah Richardson, the tomb of Cassandra Cottlestone, and my discovery of Jocelyn Ridley-Smith.

I wanted to hug her, as I had hugged Daffy. I wanted to embrace her bones.

But I could not. It was as if both of us had been born north poles of the same magnet—as if, because of it, we should have been identical but were, in fact, repellent to each other—forever pushed apart by some mysterious but invisible power.

"When's the funeral?" I asked lamely.

"Next Tuesday," Feely said. "After Easter is out of the way."

Although I was a little surprised to hear my pious sister refer to one of the greatest festivals of the Church as something to be got out of the way, I said nothing. I was learning, at least where Feely was concerned, to hold my tongue.

"Will they be having an open coffin?" I asked.

I was certainly hoping they would. *It would be better,* I thought, *to remember Mr. Collicutt without the gas mask.*

"Heavens, no," Feely said. "The vicar does not approve of open caskets. In fact, he strongly discourages the practice. The Order for the Burial of the Dead emphasizes the resurrection, not the death. *'I am the resurrection and the* life, *saith the Lord.'* "

"I expect it puts a bit of a damper on things to have a corpse lying there bang in the middle with a poker face," I said.

"Flavia!"

"Speaking of poker faces," I said, "I ran into Miss Tanty in the church."

I did not mention that there had been blood dripping from the rafters.

"So I am given to understand," Feely said.

Blast! Was there no privacy in this village?

But who could have told her? Certainly not the vicar, and even more certainly not Adam Sowerby. She didn't even know the man. Mad Meg, of course, was out of the question.

Feely must have seen the look of puzzlement on my face.

"'The successful organist,'" she quoted, "'must have fingers long enough to reach the stops, legs long enough to reach the pedal board, and ears long enough to reach into the lives of every choir member.' *Whanley on the Organ and Its Amenities*, chapter thirteen, 'Management of the Choristers.'"

"Actually, I heard it from the lips of Jezebel herself," she admitted.

"Jezebel?"

I had made a note to pry Miss Tanty's details out of Feely, but had hardly expected them to come gushing out before I had even, so to speak, fingered the lock.

"Oh, surely you must have noticed," Feely said. "Those two old harpies, Miss Moon and Miss Tanty, primping and preening, hurling themselves onto the ashes at the feet of poor Mr. Collicutt. It was like watching a Roman chariot race."

"And the perfumes!" I said, eager to join in the game. "*Backfire* and *Evening in Malden Fenwick*."

"*Jealousy*," Feely added, and I wondered for a moment why I didn't talk to my sister more often.

But our laughter faded quickly, as it often does when it is artificial, and we were left in an embarrassed silence.

"Why would Miss Tanty cry out, 'Forgive me, O Lord,' when she saw the blood?"

I was assuming Miss Tanty had told Feely about the blood.

"Because she needs to be the center of attention—even when a saint bleeds."

"She told me it was a performance," I said, not volunteering that I had heard this later at Miss Tanty's house. "She fancies herself a detective and wants to become involved in the case—wants someone to think she may even be the killer."

"The killer?" Feely snorted. "Horse eggs! She couldn't see to kill an elephant if it were standing on her toes. And as for being a detective, why, the woman couldn't find her own bottom if it weren't buttoned on."

"God bless her all the same," I said. It was a formula we used whenever we had gone too far.

"God bless her all the same," Feely echoed, rather sourly.

"Which leaves Miss Moon," I suggested subtly.

"Why would Miss Moon kill Mr. Collicutt?" Feely asked. "She doted on him. She brought him bags full of her dreadful homemade saltwater toffee. She even took it upon herself to wash his surplices and handkerchiefs."

"Really?" I asked, my mind flashing instantly to the white ruffle protruding from the gas mask.

"Of course," Feely said. "Mrs. Battle has always drawn the line at doing her boarders' laundry."

Which gave me an idea.

"Your ears are already long enough to reach into the lives of every choir member," I said with a grin. "You're going to make a whizzo organist, Feely!"

"Yes, I expect I am," she agreed. Then, pointing to the sooty bundle on the floor, she added, "Now clean up this god-awful mess before I tell Father."

Mrs. Battle's boardinghouse, an ancient structure of warped, weathered clapboards and peeling paint, stood in a rutted yard on the south side of the road, halfway between St. Tancred's and the Thirteen Drakes. In earlier times it had been a public house, the Adam and Eve, its name and the words "Ales & Stouts" still faintly visible in faded letters above the door. The whole place sagged in the middle like a serpent and had a general air of dampness.

I knocked and waited.

Nothing happened and I knocked again.

Still nothing.

Perhaps, I thought, as with the butcher's shop in Nether-Wolsey, the owner was in the garden.

I strolled casually round the back as if I were a rather dopey tourist who had lost her way.

The area behind the house was like an archaeological dig: heaps of sand like giant hedgehogs, their backs bristling with shovels. Everywhere were untidy piles of boards and bags of cement. Everywhere broken rocks were strewn about as if in a temper tantrum by a baby giant.

The home of George Battle's stonemasonry business.

I peeped into a dim shed which stood to one side. More cement, a wooden box of trowels, an old-fashioned sloping desk with accounting books and inkwells, a row of pegs upon which hung various pieces of black rubber rainwear, an electric ring and enamel teakettle, and a blanket flung into the corner which might once have been lain upon by a long-dead dog.

No point in snooping too much, I thought. *Someone might be watching from a back window of the house.*

I shoved my hands into the pockets of my cardigan, looked up at the sky as if carelessly checking the weather, and sauntered, whistling, back round to the front door.

I knocked again . . . and again. A regular volley of knocks.

After what seemed like an hour, heavy footsteps came lumbering toward the door and a lace curtain fluttered in one of the side windows.

An eye peered out and then withdrew.

After another painfully long moment, the cracked china doorknob turned slowly through a few degrees and the door swung inward to reveal a long tunnel of darkness that led away almost to infinity, ending in a small scrap of distant daylight somewhere at the back of the house.

"Well?"

The voice came from somewhere in the gloom.

"Mrs. Battle?" I said. "I'm Flavia de Luce, from Buckshaw. May I come in?"

Ask and ye shall receive, I had been told to believe, but it didn't work. It's difficult for the average person to refuse such a direct request, but Mrs. Battle was obviously not an average person.

"Why?" she demanded.

"It's about Mr. Collicutt," I said. "Actually, it's rather private. I'd prefer to discuss it indoors where we can't be overheard."

Step two: Insinuate that your message is both secret and juicy.

"Well . . ." she said, wavering.

"I don't want anyone to see me here," I said, lowering my voice and looking back over both shoulders as if checking for eavesdroppers.

"Come," she commanded, and a fleshy hand from the shadows behind the door beckoned me into the gloom.

After the bright light of the outdoors it took several

seconds for my eyes to adjust to the darkness, but when they did, I found myself face-to-face with the lady of the house. Or at least half face-to-face. The other half was still hidden in shadows behind the door.

Although I had seen Mrs. Battle now and then about the village, it had always been at something of a distance, and I had never actually spoken to the woman. Up close, she was larger than I remembered, and more red-faced.

"Well?"

"Actually . . ." I said, using the word a second time.

The word "actually," like its cousin "frankly," should, by itself, be a tip-off to most people that what is to follow is a blatant lie—but it isn't.

"Actually . . ." I said again, "it's about my sister Feely. Ophelia, I mean."

"Yes?"

The eye widened a little in the gloom. So far, so good. I had rehearsed the entire conversation in my mind as I pedaled to the village from Buckshaw.

I shifted from foot to foot, glancing uneasily about the dark-paneled hallway as if in fear of being overheard.

"She's . . . she's getting married, you see, and there are certain letters . . ."

Daffy had once read us a French novel in which this was the plot.

I held my breath and strained to make my face red, although my effort was probably wasted in the darkness.

"Mr. Collicutt—" I began to explain.

"Letters, is it?" Mrs. Battle said. "I see. And you want them back."

Just like that!

I bit my lip and nodded my head.

"For your sister."

I nodded again, trying to remember how to look desolate.

"Very sweet," she said. "Very touching. You must love her."

I brushed away an imaginary tear and wiped my finger elaborately on my skirt.

That did it.

"Not that it will do much good," she went on, waving a hand at the dark staircase. "The police have already had a good root through everything."

"Oh, no!" I said. "Feely will simply *die*."

I had an odd feeling even as I spoke the words.

Nobody ever simply dies.

Mr. Collicutt, for instance, had met his death at the hands of a couple of killers—I was now sure of it—and had been dragged, gas-masked (or had the mask been put on later?) through the churchyard, through the much-trampled grave of Cassandra Cottlestone, through a dank and earthy tunnel, to be dumped in the tomb of a long-dead saint.

Nothing simple about that.

"Turned everything upside down, Inspector Whatsis and his lot. Haven't had the heart to straighten up. Whole thing has been such a—"

"Frightful shock," I put in.

"Taken the words right out of my mouth," she said. "Frightful shock."

I let a few moments pass in silence so that we could bond to each other as sisters in sorrow.

"I hope you're feeling better," I told her. "Miss Tanty

told me you've been a regular saint in driving her to her appointments. You have a very large heart, Mrs. Battle."

"Yes. Since you put it that way, I suppose I do."

Not even Saint Francis de Sales, whose dying word was "Humility," could have refused a compliment like that.

"I had a touch of the megrims that day," she went on without being prompted. "I hated to let her down but Florrie—that's my niece—offered to run her over since she didn't start work till noon that day.

"'No, Florrie,' Crispin—Mr. Collicutt, I mean—told her. 'I need to have a word with the woman anyway. You deserve your half-day, and I shall be back well before noon.'"

"The woman?" I asked. "Did he always refer to Miss Tanty as 'the woman'?"

Mrs. Battle's eyes slowly came round and lighted on mine.

"No," she said. "He didn't. Not always."

Was this, I wondered, "the rather odd comment" the vicar had mentioned?

"Gosh, it must have been a worry for both you and Florence—having your car go missing like that, I mean. As well as Mr. Collicutt, of course."

"Car never went missing," she said. "He never took it. Not far, anyway. Florrie found it parked in front of the church."

"Huh," I said in a bored voice.

Then I let out a sigh.

"The letters . . ." I said, almost apologetically.

She waved a hand toward the stairs.

"First door left," she said. "At the top."

I found myself creeping slowly up the dark staircase as if points were being given for silence, even though the fourth and seventh steps groaned horribly. The first door on the left was so small and so close to the top of the stairs that I almost missed it.

I turned the china doorknob and stepped into Mr. Collicutt's bedroom.

I suppose I had been expecting something spacious. Having been accustomed to the stadium-sized bedrooms at Buckshaw, this tiny space beneath the eaves came as something of a shock. It was as if a few feet of attic had been banged into an extra bedroom for an emergency, and no one afterward had ever quite got round to putting things back the way they were. An altogether peculiar room.

But what a room!

It was full to bursting with organ pipes. Like the rats in "The Pied Piper of Hamelin," they were everywhere: great pipes, small pipes, lean pipes, brawny pipes, brown pipes, black pipes, gray pipes, tawny pipes, grave old plodders, gay young friskers, fathers, mothers, uncles—a thicket of wood, tin, zinc, lead, and brass—a maze of leaning tubes and cylinders. Racks of stops, like ribs of beef in the butcher's window, each with its name engraved on an ivory disk: Trumpet, Gemshorn, Violin, Nason Flute, Rohrflöte, Bourdon, and a handful of others. Wedged into a corner beneath a sloping ceiling was a pitifully small bed, neatly made.

For a sudden spinning moment I thought I was back inside the organ chamber at St. Tancred's—the chamber where Mr. Collicutt had been murdered.

A wooden tea chest, standing on end, served as a desk,

and on it was an untidy pile of papers. I climbed over something which might have been a diapason and picked up the top sheet, which was covered with tiny, antlike handwriting—what Daffy would have called "miniscule."

The Coming-to-light of the 1687 Renatus Harris Organ at Braxhampstead With an Account of its Restoration, it said. This was underlined twice in red ink, and beneath it was written, *by Crispin Savoy Collicutt, Mus. B., F.R.C.O.*

After that, in black, and in another hand, someone had added the word *Deceased*.

·TWENTY·ONE·

WHO COULD HAVE DONE such a thing?

The black word must have been added within the past few days—since the discovery of Mr. Collicutt's body.

Unless, of course, someone had written it earlier as a warning.

Had Inspector Hewitt seen it? Surely he must have done. But if he had, why had he not taken it away with him as evidence?

I riffled quickly through the pile of pages. I guessed that there were five hundred of them. Yes, here it was—they were numbered. Five hundred and thirteen sheets, each one covered closely with Mr. Collicutt's microscopic handwriting. He must have been working on this thing since he was a schoolboy in short trousers.

In spite of the density of his handwriting, thousands of additions and corrections crammed the margins of almost every page, each with a spidery line joining it to the place in the text where the change was to be made, "disarrangement" changed to "derangement," "device" to "contrivance," and so forth.

Very straightforward.

Were these scribbles what Adam's friend Pole had called marginalia? Probably not. Marginalia were notes on everyday life, while these scribbles were Mr. Collicutt's revisions to his own manuscript.

At least that's what I was thinking until I noticed the word *adamas*.

At first I thought it said Adam. Was Mr. Collicutt making a note in his book about Adam Sowerby? Was *adamas* meant to stand for "Adam A. Sowerby"?

But no—it couldn't be. Adam's middle name was Tradescant. I had seen it on his calling card.

And then the penny dropped! Dropped so hard that I felt it hit the bottom of my brainpan!

Adamas was the Latin word for diamond. Adam had said so!

The word was circled and linked with an arrowed line to a listing of the various stops which had once been part of the ancient organ at Braxhampstead. He had meant to insert the word between "Gemshorn" and "Violin."

"Have you found them yet?"

Mrs. Battle's voice, and her heavy tread on the creaking stairs.

I sprang to the door and stuck my head out into the hall.

"I'm just coming, Mrs. Battle," I called, and I heard her footsteps stop. Stairs were probably difficult for her, and she wouldn't want to climb any more than were necessary.

"Would it be all right to use the WC while I'm up here?" I shouted, with sudden urgency. "I'm afraid I—"

I did not elaborate, nor did I need to. The human imagination is capable of anything when left on its own to fill in the blanks.

I prayed desperately that there was a loo up here. There had to be—it was a boardinghouse.

"End of the hall," she muttered, and her footsteps retreated downward.

I turned back to my examination of Mr. Collicutt's belongings. For a cluttered room, there were surprisingly few of them, aside from the scrapyard of organ parts.

Piles of music books, a metronome, a pitch pipe, a bust of Johann Sebastian Bach—who had been born and died in the same years as Cassandra Cottlestone, I remembered with a delicious shiver.

On a side table an upright toothbrush was stuck into a water glass, and nearby, a tin of tooth powder. A nail file and a pair of nail scissors were perfectly aligned side by side, as you would expect. More than anything, organists needed to look after their hands.

I thought of Mr. Collicutt's shriveled fingers as I had seen them in the tomb at St. Tancred's, and of the clean nails on the hand that clutched the broken bit of glass tubing.

He had been dead when he was dragged through the tunnel. He had not clutched at the soil of the graveyard.

I got to my knees and looked under the bed. It was too dark to see anything. I flattened myself with my cheek to the floorboards, edged forward, and reached as far as I could under the wooden frame. My fingers touched something—felt it—seized it—and pulled it slowly toward me.

It was a flat tin cigarette box. Players Navy Cut. One hundred cigarettes.

Surely the police had seen it. But if they had, why would they have shoved it back under the bed?

Perhaps they had only looked, rather than felt—relied on eyes rather than fingers. A large police sergeant would not be as accustomed as I was to slithering about under beds on his belly. A thin tin would be easy enough to miss in a dark corner.

I got to my knees and sat back on my heels. Judging by its weight, the box was not completely empty.

I fiddled with the hinge and the lid popped open.

Something fluttered into my lap.

Paper banknotes! Half a dozen of them—one hundred pounds each.

Six hundred pounds, in all. More money than I had ever seen in my entire life. I must confess that a number of ideas popped into my mind as quickly as the banknotes had spilled into my lap, but since every one of them involved theft I stifled the urge almost at once.

The notes had been folded double in an envelope which had sprung out like a jack-in-the-box when I opened the lid.

Six hundred pounds!

So much for Mr. Collicutt being as poor as a church mouse—this was no village organist who had to scrape by on fifty quid a year.

I picked up the notes one by one and was about to replace them in the tin when I noticed something odd about the envelope. The flap had been ripped off, leaving a raw edge.

"Are you finished up there?"

Mrs. Battle again. Impatient now.

"Yes, just coming," I called out. "I'll be right down."

I folded the banknotes and pressed them back into the cigarette tin. Getting down onto my stomach again, I shoved the box back into the far corner behind one of the legs of the bed.

I pocketed the envelope and made for the door.

I tiptoed silently to the far end of the hall, stepped into the loo, pulled the chain and flushed . . . waited . . . pulled it again . . . and again, then slammed the door and sauntered casually down the stairs trying to look grateful.

"Well?" Mrs. Battle demanded, hands on hips.

I shook my head grimly.

"Nothing," I said. "Feely is going to be devastated. Please promise you'll keep this confidential."

Mrs. Battle glared at me for a long moment, and then suddenly she softened. What might have been a smile flickered across her face.

"Believe it or not, I was young once," she said. "I'll not breathe a word."

"Oh, thank you!" I told her.

"By the way," I added, "is your niece at home? I'd like to thank her personally for her great kindness toward Miss Tanty. I know my sister greatly appreciates it, what with the choir, and so forth. Miss Tanty is such a treasure, don't you think?"

"Florence is at work," Mrs. Battle said, holding the door open for me. "I'll give her the message."

"Oh, yes," I said, scrambling madly to gather every slightest scrap of information. "She's housekeeper at Foster's, isn't she?"

It was a shot in the dark.

"Housekeeper?" She sniffed. "I should say not. Florence is private secretary to Magistrate Ridley-Smith."

. . .

Home again, home again, jiggedy-jig. If it hadn't been for Gladys, my feet would long ago have been worn down to the nubs.

In my laboratory, I took a torch from a drawer and went into the photographic darkroom which Uncle Tar had built in one corner.

Light-tight. Dark as pitch.

I flicked on the torch and pulled the envelope from my pocket.

In Mr. Collicutt's bedroom, my fingertips had detected the faintest irregularity of the paper's surface. Why, I had wondered, would someone remove a flap from an envelope used to carry money? The answer seemed obvious: to dispose of something that was written on it.

I placed the envelope faceup and laid the torch down flat on the worktable beside it. A bit of card narrowed the beam.

I now had a slit of light shining at a very low angle of illumination—a right angle, actually—across the paper. Any slight indentations should spring into view.

I took up a magnifying lens and bent closer.

Voilà! as Daffy would say.

The paper was old and of high quality, the sort used before the war for personal correspondence. Not at all the kind of cheap, thin, glazed stuff in which Father's creditors now sent him their frequent bills.

The missing flap had been embossed with a crest or a monogram, and long storage in a press, or box, had transferred a slight impression to the envelope's blank front.

Slight, yes, and very faint, but the monogram was just decipherable in the oblique beam of the torch:

QRs

Something Ridley-Smith.

Ridley-Smith, I wrote in my notebook. *Ridley-Smith the father, not the son. What is the man's first name?*

Magistrate Ridley-Smith—*Chancellor* Ridley-Smith— had given, or sent, six hundred pounds in banknotes to Mr. Collicutt, who was said in the village to be too poor to have his handkerchiefs and surplices cleaned and pressed at the steam laundry.

Too much of a coincidence that Mrs. Battle's niece, Florence, works for Ridley-Smith, I wrote. Perhaps she was unwittingly mixed up in this, too.

Perhaps all of them were.

Why on earth, I wondered, would one of His Majesty's magistrates, a chancellor of the Church of England, give a village organist such an enormous sum, only to have it hidden under the bed? Whatever the money was meant for, why had Mr. Collicutt not deposited it safely in the bank?

The answer seemed obvious.

Someone was being secretly paid to do something.

But what?

I was just about to write down my suspicion when there was a light knock at the door. It was Dogger.

"Mr. Adam Sowerby wishes to see you, Miss Flavia. Shall I show him up?"

"Thank you, Dogger. Of course," I replied, trying to keep my excitement in check until the door had closed.

Adam Tradescant Sowerby, MA., FRHortS, etc., making a professional call upon Miss Flavia de Luce! Just fancy!

I closed my notebook and shoved it into a drawer, then flew to the darkroom to put away the torch and the envelope.

I had barely time to return to the window and hold a test tube of colored liquid up to the light—tea, as it happened—when the door opened and Dogger intoned, "Mr. Sowerby, Miss Flavia."

I counted slowly to seven, then turned round.

"Come in," I said. "How nice to see you again."

Adam gave out a low whistle as he looked round at my laboratory.

"Good lord," he said. "I had, of course, heard about your famous Closet of Chemistry, but I had no idea—"

"Very few do," I said. "I try to keep it as private as possible."

"Then I am very much privileged."

"Yes, you are," I told him.

No point in wasting time with false vanity when you possess the real thing.

He drifted over to my microscope.

"Ernst Leitz, by Jove," he said. "And binocular, too. Very nice. Very nice indeed."

I nodded graciously and kept my mouth shut. *Let's wait and see*, I thought, *what the cat's brought home*.

"I saw you at the church," he said. "Quite ingenious, the way you rescued the vicar from those baying reporters."

"You were there?" I asked, surprised.

"Lurking among the funerary entablature," Adam said. Then when he saw the look on my face, he added quickly, "Hiding behind a tombstone, I mean. You were magnificent."

I flushed slightly. This was twice I had been told I was magnificent—first by Feely, and now by Adam Sowerby.

I was not accustomed to dealing with such unexpected praise. I didn't know what to say.

"I expect you're wondering why I've come," Adam said, rescuing the moment.

"Yes," I said, although I hadn't been.

"Reason the first . . ."

He reached into his pocket and pulled out a test tube, in which something was twisted.

"Abracadabra," he said, handing it to me.

I recognized it at once. "My hair ribbon!" I said.

"Stain and all." Adam grinned.

"Where did you find it?"

"Where you dropped it. In the church porch."

I am not a person given to blaspheming, but I came perilously close.

"Thank you," I managed, setting it aside. "I shall analyze it later."

"Why not do it now, so that I can watch?"

I was tempted to refuse, but the thought of glory did me in. Chemistry is such a lonely occupation that there is never an audience for its greatest moments.

"All right," I said, with no further persuasion.

I put a bit of distilled water into a clean test tube, then carefully unscrewed the hair ribbon inch by inch from the glass container Adam had brought it in.

"Stolen from one of my germinating samples," he said. When he saw my look of alarm he added, "I sterilized it first."

With scissors, I snipped off the rather brownish-stained end of the ribbon and, with tweezers, immersed it in the water.

I lit a Bunsen burner and handed Adam the test tube and a pair of nickel-plated tongs.

"Hold it in the flame," I instructed. "Keep it moving. I'll be there in a jiff."

I went to a row of bottled chemicals and took down the nitric acid.

"Take it off the flame," I told him. "Keep steady."

I added a few drops of acid to the water in the test tube.

"Thank you," I said, taking over.

I heated the liquid slowly, swirling the test tube and watching as the water and the nitric acid quickly took up the stain.

I did this until the liquid had nearly evaporated, leaving not much more than a residue of sludge at the bottom of the tube. To this, I added a bit of alcohol, then filtered and set the mixture aside to cool.

"What kind of blood would you expect to get from a wooden saint?" I asked as we waited. "Blood from the arteries has more oxygen and less nitrogen, while blood from the veins is the opposite. Since a carved saint doesn't breathe, what's most likely to be the chemical composition of his blood?"

Adam said nothing, but he caught my eye and did not look away.

He had known at once that there was more to my question than chemistry.

When it was ready, I placed a drop of the residue on a clean glass slide and slipped it under the microscope. I was smiling even as the image came into focus.

Adam was breathing pleasantly over my shoulder.

"Look," I said. "Four-sided prisms. Made up of acicular crystals. Like little needles," I explained, in case he didn't know the meaning of the word. "CH_4N_2O."

"Clever," Adam said. "Damned clever of you to think of it."

I agreed with him totally.

"You said the hair ribbon was only 'reason the first' for coming. What was reason the second?"

"Reason the second? Oh, yes, I thought you'd like to know. They're hoisting Saint Tancred from his tomb even as we speak."

"What?" I said it with several exclamation marks.

"I thought you'd like to watch," he said. "May I give you a lift?"

"Ra-ther!"

·TWENTY-TWO·

WE WERE BUCKETING ALONG the road to Bishop's Lacey in Adam's open Rolls-Royce, Nancy, the wind whistling round our ears.

"They decided to do it straightaway before anyone's the wiser. The vicar tipped me off," Adam said, shouting above the noise of the car's cutaway body. "I knew you'd never forgive me if I didn't let you in on it."

"But why?" I asked, perhaps for the third time. "You didn't have to."

"Let's just say I'm a kindly old gaffer."

"No," I told him firmly. "I want the truth."

"Well," Adam said, "I've always believed that when the bones of the great are exhumed, it should always be done in the presence of the youngest person practicable— the one who is going to live the longest; the one who will carry down the years the memory of coming face-to-face, as it were, with history."

"And I'm the youngest person practicable? Is that the only reason?"

"Yes," Adam said.

Blast the man!

"Then, too," he went on, "I thought you might like to be first in the queue to have a squint at the Heart of Lucifer."

Now I was grinning like a fool.

The Heart of Lucifer!

I was struck with a sudden and remarkable idea.

"If what you say is true," I told Adam, "and it turns out that Saint Tancred *was* a de Luce, doesn't that mean that the Heart of Lucifer would belong rightfully to Father?"

"The Church might think otherwise," he said, after thinking about it.

"Oh, bother the Church. If they're stupid enough to dump a priceless diamond in the grave, they can't have wanted it very badly. It's probably under one of those peculiar laws like flotsam and jetsam. I'll ask Daffy. She'll know."

Daffy had read aloud to us one of Victor Hugo's novels in which the laws of flotsam and jetsam were explained to the point that you became seasick.

"One way or another, it's bound to be interesting," Adam said, "although if I were you, I shouldn't get my hopes up much."

He must have seen at once the dampening effect his words had on me.

"Tell you what," he said. "I've been thinking."

I kept quiet.

"Thinking that perhaps we should make a swap. Scandal for scandal. Tit for tat."

"I'm afraid I don't know what you mean," I said, not willing to give up my advantage a second too soon.

"You tell me what you found in Collicutt's bedroom, and I'll tell you the results of his autopsy."

He grinned at me, daring me to say no.

"Done!" I said. "It was money—and quite a lot of it. Six hundred pounds, hidden under his bed in a Players cigarette tin."

"Phew!" Adam whistled, and then he laughed. "And the police missed it?"

"Evidently," I said, and he laughed even more.

"Now, then," I told him, "it's your turn. The autopsy. How did you find out about it? Did you pump Dr. Darby?"

"Dear me, no! The good Dr. Darby is much more discreet than that. I merely had a word with my cousin Wilfred."

I must have looked blank.

"Wilfred Sowerby, of Sowerby & Sons, your local undertakers. *Furnishers of Funerals and Furniture*. Bit of a tongue twister, that."

Of course! I had forgotten about their connection.

"The ones who chose Death while your side of the family chose Life," I said. "Yes, I remember now."

How like the de Luces, I wanted to say, but it was not a thought I wanted to share.

"Yes," Adam said. "The *Dismal* Sowerbys."

"And?"

"And what?"

He was playing the fool again.

"Ah, yes. The autopsy," he said when I did not rise to

his stupid bait. "Cousin Wilfred was most enlightening. Rupture of the internal organs. Everything from the esophagus to points south of the equator. Wilfred said he'd never seen a blowout anything like it. Quite spectacular, he said."

"Caused by?"

I could hardly contain myself, but I kept still.

"They haven't a clue. At least, not so far."

I needed to change the subject. Quickly.

"Huh," I said, as if I weren't interested. "Fancy that."

We went along without speaking for a minute or so, each of us wrapped in our own thoughts, and then I said, "Hold on—how can they be going ahead with opening Saint Tancred's tomb? I thought the bishop had forbidden it."

"The bishop, it seems, has had a change of heart. As has Chancellor Ridley-Smith."

"What?"

"It's true," Adam said. "Although bishops are not generally known for their flexibility, this one, it seems, has gone into reverse on the matter. He has withdrawn the withdrawn faculty."

"But why? Why would he do such a thing?"

" 'There are more things in heaven and earth, Horatio, than are dreamt of in your philosophy,' " Adam said with a cinema-star grin.

Why were people always quoting this tired old line to me? The last time I'd heard it was from Dr. Darby, and before that, my sister Daffy.

Why do people always quote Hamlet when they want to seem clever?

Altogether too much Shakespeare, methinks!

"Meaning?" I'm afraid I snapped, without really intending to.

"Perhaps he was made to do so," Adam said.

"Ha!" I told him. "Nobody orders a bishop about."

I was no expert in theology, but even *I* knew that.

"Do they not?" Adam asked, a little smugly, I thought.

"You know something you're not telling me," I said.

"Perhaps," he said, looking more like the Cheshire cat with every passing second.

What a maddening man he was!

"You know who's bossing the bishop and you won't tell me?" I asked him.

"*Can't* tell you," he said. "There's a difference."

We were now approaching the marshy land which surrounded the church. Adam applied the brakes and stopped for a mallard that was waddling across the road.

I jumped out and slammed the door.

With eyes fixed straight ahead, I marched off toward the church, leaving Adam Tradescant Sowerby, MA., FRHortS, etc., to stew in his own clever juices.

"Ah, Flavia," the vicar said as I picked my way over the rubble into the crypt. "We've been expecting you."

"It's awfully good of you to let me know," I said, craning my neck to see over his shoulder. George Battle and his workers had drilled eyebolts into the bottom stone of the chamber—the slab upon which Mr. Collicutt's corpse had been lying.

"It's actually the lid of the sarcophagus," the vicar explained in a hushed voice, as if he were a BBC

commentator covering some particularly solemn ceremony on the Home Service.

A compact winch had been set up to lift the stone, and
the ropes were already straining under its weight.

"You're just in the nick of time. Dear me, to think
that in just a few moments we shall be looking into the
face of—of course, given your proclivities, I knew you
wouldn't want to miss a moment of what promises to be—"

"Heave!" said George Battle.

With a hollow groan, the stone rose half an inch.

"It is said that when certain Royal tombs were opened,
the workers found the occupant unchanged by time,
clothed in armor, crowned with gold, their faces as fresh
as if they had just fallen asleep. And then suddenly,
within a minute or so of being exposed to the air, they
crumbled away to dust. The Royal personages, that
is—not the workers."

"Heave!"

The stone came up another grating inch.

"You may be interested to hear, George," the vicar
said, "that the stonemason who opened the tombs of the
regicides Cromwell and Ireton was paid seventeen shillings for his trouble."

George Battle said nothing, but hauled grimly again
on his rope.

"*Heave!*"

Now a dark crack was showing round the edges of the
slab.

"Good heavens," the vicar said. "I'm as excited as a
schoolboy. Here, let me give a hand."

"Watch your fingers, Vicar!" George Battle shouted.
"You'll lose 'em if this bugger drops."

The vicar sprang back.

The stone was now free of its channel, swinging slowly and heavily from side to side, like a two-ton marble pendulum.

I felt the draft at once and smelled the tomb's cold stink.

"Swing now, Norman. Grab that bar, Tommy. Easy! Easy!"

The stone swung out of its setting, revealing a black and gaping pit. I leaned forward but could see only a few of the bricks that lined its side. The vicar put his hand on my shoulder and smiled at me. Was he imagining that I was his daughter, Hannah, returned from the grave to be at his side for this wonderful but terrifying moment?

He squeezed, and I put my hand on his. We neither of us spoke a word.

"And down . . . down . . . down—that's it . . . down . . . down."

With an unnerving grinding noise, the stone settled onto the floor.

"Well done," Norman said, to nobody in particular.

"Let's have that torch," Tommy said, and George Battle handed it over.

Tommy scrambled up onto the ledge, straddling the pit, and shone the beam down into the abyss.

"Blimey," he murmured.

The vicar was next. He stepped slowly forward, leaned in, and, dodging Tommy's legs, stared for a long moment downward.

Without a word, he crooked his forefinger and beckoned me to come.

Although only a couple of days had passed, it seemed

as if I had been looking forward to this moment forever. Now that the moment had arrived, I found myself wavering.

What was I about to see? A fresh-faced Saint Tancred? A diamond as big as a turkey's egg—the Heart of Lucifer?

I eased my face slowly over the edge of the pit and looked down.

At the bottom, in the torch's beam, perhaps ten feet deep in the earth, covered with dust and reeking slightly, was a heap of moldy fabric and old green bones.

They lay in a lead sarcophagus whose lid had been ripped off and stood on end in a corner.

A shriveled stick of carved black wood, shaped vaguely like a shepherd's crook, had been tossed carelessly atop the pile, like a withered and badly weathered tree branch thrown onto the remains of a dead fire.

Saint Tancred's crosier, carved from the Glastonbury Thorn, fashioned, it was said, from the Holy Grail itself.

At its thicker end, a gaping oval hole with twisted metal clasps showed clearly where something had been wrenched away. The Heart of Lucifer was gone.

Someone had been here before us.

· T W E N T Y - T H R E E ·

"My word," the vicar said. "Someone has been here before us."

The two of us were shoulder to shoulder at the very edge of the pit, staring down into the shaft as if we were looking down a well. A cold, acrid draft blew up into our faces from a ragged opening halfway down the side. At the bottom of the pit, pitiful tatters of Saint Tancred's robe shivered in the moving air.

"They've knocked a hole in the wall," I said.

"A cave-in," George Battle said, edging me aside and taking my place. "You get cave-ins in old churches."

Suddenly and quietly, Adam was behind us. He was wearing a soft peaked cap, rubber boots, and a sort of explorer's vest covered in pockets bursting with scientific supplies. A bulky camera bag completed his kit.

"If I may," he said quite abruptly to the vicar, "I need to make my descent before anything else is disturbed."

"By all means. Albert, if you wouldn't mind fetching Mr. Sowerby a ladder . . ."

He was speaking to Mr. Haskins, who had come into the crypt behind Adam.

"Ladder?" Mr. Haskins asked, as if he didn't know the meaning of the word, or as if he didn't want to be bothered.

"There's a ladder on the back of Mr. Battle's lorry," I said helpfully. "Several of them, actually."

"Norman," Mr. Battle said, with a glance at his helpers. Norman, tall in the crypt, ducked his head and stepped out through the archway.

Nobody said anything for the longest time, each of us shifting from foot to foot, looking everywhere but at one another.

I wondered why.

I glanced casually round at the remaining workers. Tommy from Malden Fenwick took advantage of the lull to light a cigarette. The other man, whose name I did not know, shook his head as Tommy held out the pack and offered him a smoke.

There was no idle chatter. Just a couple of workmen waiting restlessly to get on with the job.

Then Norman was back with the ladder, clattering through the crypt, breaking the spell of silence. With much banging and a few muttered instructions, the ladder's end was maneuvered down into the saint's grave.

Adam sprang up onto the ledge and placed a foot on one of the upper rungs.

"Wish me luck," he said, and taking the torch from Tommy, he began his descent.

"Adam—" the vicar said.

Adam stopped, already almost out of sight. He seemed surprised.

"Let us pray," the vicar said, in a remarkably strong voice, and we all of us bowed our heads.

"Lord, Thou hast been our refuge, from one generation to another. Before the mountains were brought forth, or ever the earth and the world were made, Thou art God from everlasting, and the world without end. Thou turnest man back to the dust, and Thou sayest, 'Return, ye children of men.' For a thousand years in Thy sight are but as yesterday when it is past, and as a watch in the night. Amen."

"Amen," we echoed.

Adam's face looked up at us quizzically, strangely pale in the light of the torch.

"Just in case," the vicar said.

"Thank you," Adam said quietly, and was gone.

I recognized the vicar's words as being from the Order of the Burial of the Dead. Psalm 90. But why had he chosen them? Was he thinking of Saint Tancred? Of Adam? Of his lost Hannah?—or of himself?

The ladder trembled as Adam descended. I peered over the edge to watch as he pulled an elaborate flash unit from the bag. The shaft and even the chamber where we stood were soon illuminated by a series of white lightning flashes from the pit.

There wasn't much to see from directly above. I was content to linger and listen. At first there was silence and an occasional muffled exclamation. And then Adam began to whistle.

I knew the tune at once. It was a song we had sung in Girl Guides, and its words went through my mind.

*Pack up your troubles in your old kit bag, and smile,
   smile, smile.
While you've a lucifer to light your fag, smile boys, that's
   the style . . .*

A lucifer, of course, was a type of match used during the First World War, tipped with sulfur and a dried paste made up of phosphorus and potassium chlorate. It was also a nickname of Satan. And of Saint Tancred's stolen diamond.

No one in the chamber above was smiling as the song urged us to do. The workmen looked uneasily at one another as if some great taboo had been broken by Adam's whistle, which was still echoing eerily up from the pit.

"Adam . . ." the vicar called down.

"Sorry." The word floated up from the grave and hung echoing in the air.

Was he whistling without thinking, or was there a message in his choice of song? If so, who was it meant for?

It was then that I became aware that several others had joined us in the crypt. One was a large man wearing a black suit, a clerical collar, and a look of stressed holiness.

The bishop. There could be no doubt about it.

"Your Grace," the vicar said. "And Chancellor Ridley-Smith."

He shook hands with each of them, neither with any real joy.

So this was Chancellor—or Magistrate—Ridley-Smith. Jocelyn's father.

The first thing I noticed about him was that I had seen

him before. He was the man in the photo presenting the trophy to Miss Tanty.

I studied him carefully.

A rigid man, I thought, with hard but watery brown eyes, which shifted sideways professionally, going constantly from one of us to another, like the carriage on a typewriter. The sockets in which they were mounted were round and staring, and I pitied at once all the accused who had ever been made to stand before him in the dock.

His brow was permanently wrinkled, like that of a person who had just got a whiff of something nasty, an impression that was heightened by the fact that he hadn't a trace of eyebrows or eyelashes. His blotchy nose was flattened, as if he had boxed in his youth, but not very well.

A *boozer,* I decided.

Although he was not physically large, Magistrate Ridley-Smith's very presence seemed to use up all the remaining air in the crypt, which was suddenly stifling.

He stood teetering on curiously tiny feet, glaring impatiently at his surroundings.

"Let's get on with it, then," he said in a remarkably hoarse, thick voice, pulling a half-hunter watch from his waistcoat pocket and consulting it with protruding lower lip. "Where are the remains?"

As he fumbled to put the watch away, I couldn't help noticing that his wrist, like that of Mrs. Ridley-Smith in the photograph at Bogmore Hall, was peculiarly weak and floppy.

What was it Dogger had said? A *classic case of lead poisoning.*

Had the magistrate, in those long-ago days in India, been exposed to his wife's toy soldiers?

"We haven't brought them up yet," the vicar said. "I thought it best if we waited until you—"

"Yes, well, then, you are keeping the Church, the Judiciary, and the Constabulary waiting. I suggest we proceed."

By the Church, he meant the bishop; by the Judiciary, himself. Who on earth was representing the Constabulary?

And then I saw Inspector Hewitt. He was standing in the shadows behind the bishop. I smiled at him but he did not appear to have noticed me. His eyes were moving as coolly round the crypt as Magistrate Ridley-Smith's. Perhaps even more coolly.

"Proceed," the bishop ordered, licking his lips.

At that very instant Adam's head appeared at the top of the ladder, his chin just level with the stone edge of the saint's grave. I was reminded for an instant of the head of John the Baptist.

"Right, then," he said, destroying the illusion. "All clear below."

"Who is this . . . man?" Magistrate Ridley-Smith demanded. "He oughtn't to be mucking about down there. Who gave him permission?"

"We did," the bishop said. "You may recall—"

But Magistrate Ridley-Smith was not listening. His face was a thundercloud.

"Come along, Martin," he growled, and stepped clumsily out through the archway.

Martin, the fourth workman—Martin the silent one, Martin who had not spoken a word since I had first seen him—said in a flat, frayed voice, "Now we're in for it."

Five words. But that was all it took to set my mind

spinning like a Catherine wheel, sending off showers of sparks in all directions.

That voice! I had heard it before. But where?

My sense of hearing had never let me down in the past and I did not expect it to do so now.

I replayed the man's words in my mind. "Now we're in for it."

In a back room of my brain something went click, and I heard that same voice saying, "*Peter Ilyich Tchaikovsky . . . Franz Schubert . . . Swan Lake . . . Death and the Maiden.*" It was the voice I had heard issuing from the concealed loudspeakers in Jocelyn's room at Bogmore Hall.

Benson!

This otherwise silent workman was Jocelyn's keeper! He had been sent here right from the very beginning to spy on the opening of Saint Tancred's tomb!

I knew when I saw the side of his face on the staircase that I'd seen him before, but couldn't think where. It had, of course, been right here in the crypt, where his silent presence in the shadows drew little attention.

Now he was leaving the stony chamber, shuffling away in his master's footsteps.

As if to confirm what I already knew, Tommy said, "Ta-ta for now, Benson."

"Yes, well, then," the bishop said. "I propose we get on with it. It's late. Easter is tomorrow. We have only a few hours left and much to do. Please inform us when the relics have been collected, Mr. Haskins, and we shall prepare the ossuary."

Then he, too, was gone.

Adam climbed up onto the ledge, and sat with his legs dangling into the pit.

From somewhere down below came a wooden banging, and the ladder rattled against the stone edges.

"Hullo!" Adam said, looking down into the pit. "Something stirreth in the grave."

Again the ladder shook, and a red face appeared, streaked with mud and surprised to see us.

It was Sergeant Graves.

"Right you are, chief," he said to Inspector Hewitt, pointing the beam of his torch back down the way he had come. "It goes right the way through from here to the churchyard."

Brilliant, I wanted to say, but I kept my mouth shut. It was obvious that the other branch of the tunnel—the one I had not taken—led down into the actual tomb of Saint Tancred.

The sergeant scrambled up off the ladder and sat himself beside Adam on the edge, brushing the filth from his clothing.

The Inspector nodded, his face a mask. He did not say what must surely have been on his mind: that the sergeant's passage like a pipe cleaner through the tomb had almost certainly destroyed traces of those who had looted it.

But then, too, so had my own explorations, so I decided to say nothing. Perhaps the Inspector didn't even know about the Heart of Lucifer. Nor, perhaps, did the bishop or the chancellor.

I had once heard a saying that went like this: "Least said, soonest mended."

I would keep my tongue tamed and my lip zipped. Never let it be said that Flavia de Luce was a blabbermouth.

But what was this? Inspector Hewitt had caught my eye and was motioning with a sideways jerk of his head and an upward rolling of his eyes, a message I could read as clearly as if it were a newspaper headline.

UPSTAIRS, it said. NOW.

We were strolling pleasantly in the long grass at the back of the churchyard, the Inspector and I.

"Your footprints are everywhere in that tunnel," he said, pointing back toward Cassandra Cottlestone's busy tomb.

I pretended surprise and bafflement. I could easily point out that there were plenty of people who wore plimsolls.

"Don't bother," he said. "We have your footprints on file.

"As well as your fingerprints," he added.

"Well," I said, "it's a long story. There was a bat in an organ pipe and I was trying to find out how it got into the church. I was afraid it might be rabid. I didn't want anything to happen to Feely. She's engaged to be married, you know, and I was afraid—"

I flipped on the switch marked "Shuddering Sobs," but nothing came.

Damnation! I used to be a dab hand at water on demand. What on earth was happening to me? Was I becoming hardened? Was this what being twelve was going to be like?

"Very commendable, I'm sure," the Inspector remarked. "And what did you discover while you were down the rabbit hole?"

When tears fail, I decided on the spot, dazzle them with details.

I rattled off a quite decent reply. "The tunnel leads from the Cottlestone tomb to the space where I found Mr. Collicutt's body. There was another branch, but I didn't follow it. There's a stone that can be moved with iron handles. That's how they dumped him there. He was murdered in the organ chamber and brought down either through the crypt or outdoors through the churchyard. By the footprints that were there before mine, I suspect there was more than one killer."

"Anything else?" the Inspector asked.

"No," I said, lying through my teeth.

How could I possibly even begin to tell him about Miss Tanty or Mad Meg, or Jocelyn Ridley-Smith, or Mrs. Battle, or even, for that matter, about Adam and the Heart of Lucifer?

As I had noted before, I needed to leave him something to discover for himself. It was only fair.

"Flavia—"

I loved it when he said my name.

"You must remember that there are dangerous killers on the loose."

My heart accelerated.

"Dangerous killers on the loose!" The words which every amateur sleuth lives in eternal hope of hearing. Ever since I first heard them spoken on the wireless by Philip Odell in "The Case of the Missing Marbles," I had longed for someone to say them to me. And now they had. *"Dangerous killers on the loose!"* I wanted to shake the Inspector's hand.

"Yes," I said. "I know. I'll be careful."

"It's not just a matter of being careful. It's a matter of life and death."

"*A matter of life and death!*" That other great phrase! Perhaps even greater than *"dangerous killers on the loose."*

My cup of crime runneth over, I thought.

"Flavia, you're not paying attention to me."

"Yes I am, Inspector," I assured him. "I was just thinking how grateful I am that you warned me."

"You're to stay strictly away from the church. Do you understand?"

"But tomorrow is Easter!"

"You may attend with your family. That is all."

That is all? Was I being dismissed? Chopped like a chambermaid who'd been surprised with her snout in the sherry?

He was already striding away through the long grass when I thought to call after him, "Inspector, how is *Mrs. Hewitt?*"

He did not stop and turn around. In fact he didn't even slow his steps.

It was obvious he hadn't heard me.

·TWENTY-FOUR·

I KNEW, DON'T ASK me how, even as I steered Gladys between the stone griffins of the Mulford Gates, that something else had gone wrong at Buckshaw.

It's hard to explain, but it was as if the house were vanishing between heartbeats—as if it were being partially erased, and then restored, by the unseen artist who was drawing it.

I had never in my life experienced anything like this.

The avenue of chestnuts seemed never-ending. The harder I pedaled, the slower seemed my approach.

But at last I reached the front door and opened it.

"Hullo?" I called out, as if I were a traveler coming unexpectedly upon a witch's cottage in the woods— as if I hadn't lived here all my life. "Hullo? Anyone here?"

There was, of course, no answer.

They would be in the drawing room. They were always in the drawing room.

I raced into the west wing, my feet thudding along the carpets.

But the drawing room was empty.

I was standing puzzled in the doorway when something bumped behind me.

The sound must have come from Father's study, one of the two rooms at Buckshaw that were off-limits. The other was Harriet's boudoir which, as I have said, Father had preserved as a memorial in which every scent bottle, every last nail file and powder puff was kept in precisely the same position as she had left it on that last day.

The boudoir was not to be entered under any circumstances, and Father's study was to be entered only upon command.

I knocked and opened the door.

Dogger looked up, surprised. Hadn't he heard me running in the hall?

"Miss Flavia," he said, putting down a stamp album he had been about to place in a packing box.

The truth was, I had still not got over the shyness I had created by calling Dogger a pet name to his face, and at that moment, I thought that I might never, ever get over it.

"What's wrong?" I asked. "Where is everybody?"

"I believe Miss Ophelia has gone to her room with a headache. Miss Daphne is sorting books in the library."

I didn't need to ask why. My heart sank.

"And Father?"

"The Colonel has gone, likewise, to his room."

"Dogger," I blurted. "What's wrong? I knew something was not right as soon as I came through the Mulford Gates. What is it?"

Dogger nodded. "You sense it, too, miss."

Neither of us could find words and then Dogger said, "Colonel de Luce has received a telephone call."

"Yes? From who?"

I was too edgy to say "From whom?"

"I'm afraid I can't answer that," Dogger said. "The calling party would not identify himself. He insisted on speaking directly, and only, to Colonel de Luce."

"It's the house, isn't it?" I demanded. "Buckshaw has been sold."

My bones were boiling. My soul was freezing. I was going to vomit.

"I don't know," Dogger said. "The Colonel did not confide in me. I will admit that I thought as much myself."

If I were anyone other than Flavia de Luce, I would have marched up to Father's room and demanded an explanation. After all, it was my life, too, wasn't it?

But I could feel myself growing older by the minute.

Admit it, Flavia, I thought. *You simply don't have what it takes to beard the lion in his den.*

Which, for some odd reason, reminded me of Magistrate Ridley-Smith and his peculiar lionlike face.

"Dogger," I asked, switching tracks like an emergency on the railway, "what would you say if I asked you about wasted thumb muscles, a drooping hand, and dragging feet?"

"I should say you've been at Bogmore Hall again," Dogger answered, keeping a straight and proper face.

"And if I told you I hadn't?"

"Then I should ask you for more details, miss."

"And I should tell you that I had met someone who had all of those symptoms, as well as wide, round staring eyes, no eyebrows or eyelashes, a crumbled nose, a blotchy, brownish complexion, and the most awful frown."

"And I should say, 'Well done, Miss Flavia. A nicely observed description of *facies leonine*—the so-called 'lion face.'" Would it be out of place for me to ask if this person had spent time in India?"

"Spot on, Dogger!" I crowed. "Spot . . . on! A classic case of lead poisoning, I believe."

"No, miss," Dogger said. "A classic case of Hansen's disease."

"Never heard of it," I said.

"I daresay not," said Dogger. "It is known more commonly as leprosy."

Leprosy! That dread disease we had been warned against in Sunday school—that dread disease which Father Damien had contracted among the lepers of Molokai: the whitened, crusted, peeling skin, the blue ulcers, the rotted noses, the toes and fingers snapping off, and the face falling at the end into a sad and incurable wreckage. The lepers of Molokai to whom the pennies from our Sunday school collection boxes were regularly sent.

Leprosy! The secret fear of every girl and boy in the British Empire.

Surely Dogger must be wrong.

"I thought people died from that," I said.

"They do. Sometimes. But in certain cases it becomes dormant—goes into a state of suspended animation—for years."

"How many years?"

"Ten, twenty, forty, fifty. It varies. There is no hard-and-fast rule."

"Is it contagious?" I asked, wanting suddenly and desperately to wash my hands.

"Not as much as you might think," Dogger said. "Hardly at all, in fact. Most persons have a natural immunity to the organism which causes it—*mycobacterium leprae*."

I had been aching for ages to ask Dogger about his vast storehouse of medical knowledge, an urge I had so far managed to keep in check. It was none of my business. Even the slightest inquiry into his shocked and troubled past would be an unforgivable invasion of trust.

"I have myself known of a case in which the bullae of the prodromal stage—"

His words stopped abruptly.

"Yes?" I prompted.

Dogger's eyes seemed to have packed their bags and fled to some far-off place. A different century, perhaps, a different land, or a different planet. After a long time he said: "It is as if—"

It was as if I wasn't there. Dogger's voice was suddenly the rustle of leaves or the sighing of the wind in a vanished willow.

I held my breath.

"There is a pool," he said slowly, his words strung out like beads on a long cord. "It is in the jungle . . . sometimes, the water is clear and may be drunk . . . other times, it is murky. An arm dipped into it disappears."

Dogger reached out to touch something which I could not see, his hand trembling.

"Is it gone . . . or is it still there, invisible? One fishes in the depths, helpless, hoping to find—something—anything."

"It's all right, Dogger," I said, as I always did, touching his shoulder. "It doesn't matter. It's not important."

"Oh, but it does—and it is, Miss Flavia," he said, startling me with his intense presence. "And perhaps never more than now."

"Yes," I said automatically. "Perhaps never more than now."

I wasn't sure that I knew what we were talking about, but I knew that we had to keep on, no matter what.

Without really changing the subject, I continued as casually as if nothing had happened. "Without giving away any confidences," I said, "I can tell you that the person I am speaking of is Magistrate Ridley-Smith." Dogger, after all, had he been with me in the crypt, might have seen him with his own eyes.

"I have heard him mentioned, nothing more," Dogger said.

"The other, the one I asked you about earlier, is his son Jocelyn."

"Yes, I remember. Lead poisoning."

"Exactly," I said. "You deduced that I had been at Bogmore Hall."

"I have heard the son spoken of," Dogger said. "Servants talk. One hears things at the market."

"But not the father?" I prompted.

"No. Not the father. Not, at least, a physical description."

"Poor Jocelyn!" I said. "If your diagnosis is correct, his mother was lead-poisoned and his father a leper."

Dogger nodded sadly. "Such things happen," he said, "even though we try to pretend they do not."

"Will they live?" I asked.

I had worked my way slowly up to the most important question of all.

"The son, perhaps," Dogger replied. "The father, no."

"Odd, isn't it?" I said. "The leprosy, now that it has come to life again, will kill him."

"Leprosy in itself is rarely fatal," Dogger said. "Its victims are more likely to die from kidney or liver failure. And now if you'll excuse me, miss—"

"Of course, Dogger," I said. "I'm sorry for interrupting. I know you have things to do."

It had been a near thing. Dogger had come within a hairsbreadth of sliding into one of his episodes. I knew that he wanted nothing more than to get to his room and fall quietly to pieces.

The worst was over, at least for now, and he needed to be given the gift of being alone.

"What's up, Daff?" I said, barging into the library as if it were just another jolly day at Buckshaw. My sister was extraordinarily perceptive, even though she pretended she was not. If there had been a crushing call on the telephone, Daffy would by now have ferreted out all the details.

In that way, she was a lot like me.

"Nothing," Daffy said, without looking up from her book-sorting. It seemed as if the warm feeling built up earlier by our sisterly cease-fire had leaked away like the sand in an hourglass.

"Who telephoned?" I asked. "I thought I heard it ring a while ago."

A ringing telephone at Buckshaw was such a rarity that it could be commented upon without suspicion.

Daffy shrugged and opened *The Tenant of Wildfell Hall*.

Whatever it was that had upset Father, he had not shared it.

Which, in a peculiar way was comforting. My sisters shared everything. Whatever Daffy knew, Feely knew. Whatever Feely knew, Daffy knew.

What Flavia knew was, by comparison, like the bump on the log in the hole at the bottom of the sea. Deep, dark, and nobody gave a rat's anatomy.

Trying to cheer things up a bit, I said, "I'm looking for a good book to read. Can you recommend something suitable?"

"Yes," Daffy said. "The Holy Bible."

With that, she slammed shut *Wildfell Hall* and stalked out of the room.

So much for shared blood.

·TWENTY-FIVE·

Supper was a charade.

Father did not put in an appearance.

Feely and Daffy and I sat picking at our food, being horridly decent to one another, passing the salt and pepper and the cold peas with elaborate pleases and thankyous.

It was dreadful.

None of us knew for certain what was happening either with Buckshaw or with Father, and we didn't want to be the first to ask—didn't want to be the one to throw the last pebble: the pebble which would smash, once and for all, our fragile house of glass.

As if words alone could cause its final fall.

"May I be excused?" Daffy asked.

"Of course," Feely and I said too quickly, at the same time.

I wanted to cry.

I also wanted to go to my laboratory and prepare an

enormous batch of nitrogen triiodide with which to blow up, in a spectacular mushroom cloud of purple vapor, the world and everyone in it.

People would think it was the Apocalypse.

The sea of glass like unto crystal . . . the star called Wormwood, the seven lamps of fire, the rainbow round about the throne, and the second angel pouring out his vial upon the sea where it became as the blood of a dead man.

I'd show them!

I'd give them something to think about.

The blood of a dead man.

It had all begun with blood, hadn't it?

That's what was dribbling through my mind as I climbed the stairs.

In the beginning there had been the blood of the flattened frog and the blood of my own family glowing with red iridescence under the microscope. There had been the stained-glass blood of John the Baptist and the blood that dripped from the brow of the wooden Saint Tancred. I had still not had the opportunity to tell the vicar the results of my analysis.

There had been the red stain on the floor of the organ chamber where Mr. Collicutt was murdered, but that, of course, was not blood. It was red-colored alcohol from the organ's broken manometer.

Of Mr. Collicutt's blood, there had been not a trace.

Of course!

Not a single drop.

Not in the chamber where he was killed, not in the tomb where his body ended up, and not, so far as I had seen, anywhere in between.

In the case of Mr. Collicutt, it was not so much a case of bloodstains as the lack of them.

The obvious conclusion was that he had not been stabbed or shot, and poisoning, somewhat to my regret, was out of the question.

In spite of what Wilfred Sowerby, the undertaker, had told Adam about internal explosions, it was obvious that those injuries were inflicted after death.

No blood.

QED.

You didn't need to be a Professor Einstein to see that Mr. Collicutt had most likely died of suffocation. Actually, I should have spotted that as soon as I laid eyes on him.

The gas mask itself told much of the story.

And then, now that I thought about it, there had been that white ruffle at his chin. Like the Highwayman.

A handkerchief. Shoved under the mask.

But why?

The answer hit me like a dropped brick.

Ether! Diethyl ether!

Good old $(C_2H_5)_2O$.

The stuff had been discovered either in the eighth century by the Persian alchemist Abu Abdallah Jaber ben Hayyam ben Abdallah al-Kufi, sometimes called Geber, or in the thirteenth century by Raymond Lully, sometimes called Doctor Illuminatus, and could in a jiff be concocted easily at home from sulfuric acid and heated cream of tartar. It could also be pinched from a hospital, or from a doctor's surgery.

I could all too easily imagine Mr. Collicutt's last moments: the saturated handkerchief clapped to the nose, cold at first, then a fierce burning followed by numbness. The hot sweet taste of it as he gasped for air, the warmth of it in his stomach, the fading of the senses, the swirling darkness, and then—what?

Well, death, of course, if the ether were applied for too long or in too great a quantity. Paralysis of the central nervous system and failure of the respiratory system could possibly result if great care were not taken. I had read the grisly details in Heinrich Braun's classic text *Local Anaesthesia*, a well-thumbed copy of which Uncle Tar had kept on the shelf above his desk. His own experiments with procaine and stovaine (named for the Frenchman Ernest Fourneau, whose name, in French, means "stove") were well documented in Uncle Tar's microscopically inked notes in the margins.

But who, nowadays, in Bishop's Lacey, would be able to obtain ether? Probably very few.

In fact, when you came to think of it, a medical doctor was likely the only person on earth who regularly carried the stuff with him everywhere in his bag.

I needed to speak to Dr. Darby.

Tomorrow was Easter Sunday. He would almost certainly—barring medical emergencies—be at church with the rest of Bishop's Lacey, organizing, as he always did, the pace-egging and the egg hunt. I could catch him at the lych-gate and ask casually if anything had recently gone missing from his bag.

But first I needed to sleep.

Dogger must have brought Esmeralda in from the greenhouse, because I found her roosting contentedly on the iron ring of a laboratory support stand and there was a fresh egg in my bed.

I would save it for the morning, I decided. Tomorrow was going to be a long day.

Father would have us rousted out of our beds by five o'clock so we could have a light breakfast before the three-hour curfew.

As Roman Catholics, we were bound to fast from at least midnight before receiving the Holy Eucharist. Only those who were gravely ill and in danger of death were permitted their toast and marmalade in advance.

Father, however, disagreed.

"A hot breakfast is indispensable, if not mandatory," he used to tell us. "You never know when, or if, you might eat again."

It was a piece of wisdom he had apparently formulated during his military service, but we knew better than to ask questions. In discussion with the vicar, he had settled on a time of three hours as being sufficient to satisfy both tummy and spirit of the law.

Father, I must say, is years ahead of his time. He sees nothing wrong with receiving Holy Communion at the altar of the Church of England rather than driving to Hinley for Holy Eucharist at Our Lady of the Seven Sorrows.

"It is one's bounden duty," he never tires of telling us, "to trade with local firms."

Well, so be it, I suppose.

We would be in our pew for the eight o'clock service, then return for the eleven o'clock service, the one with all the stops pulled out: choir, organ, the Psalms and responses chanted, a bang-up sermon—the whole McGillicuddy.

I dug out from under my bed the set of recordings I had

pinched from Feely's bedroom, Grieg's Piano Concerto in A Minor which, according to Feely, was descriptive of sunlight and shadows on the icy fjords of Norway, with cakes of ice like diamonds the size of Buckshaw breaking away and crashing down into the sea.

I wound up the crank of my gramophone, lowered the needle into the grooves of the spinning disk, dived under the covers, and pulled the quilt up to my ears as the music began.

With the strings of the London Philharmonic singing me asleep, I was dead to the world before the spring ran down.

I dreamt I was in St. Tancred's churchyard where tables—perhaps a dozen of them—had been set up here and there among the tombstones. At the tables were seated the people of Bishop's Lacey and surroundings, dressed all of them alike in harlequin suits of a diamond pattern. The rich colors of their silks made them seem like figures from a stained-glass window.

On the table, in front of each player—or contestant, I wasn't sure which—was an identical jigsaw puzzle, unopened, and behind each player stood a referee with a harlequin flag.

O *what great fun*, I thought, *a jigsaw tournament.*

A whistle was blown, the flags came swishing down, and the players tore open the boxes and began sorting like madmen. Already one or two of them were fitting flat-edged pieces into the border.

A judge in powdered wig and pince-nez strolled among the tables, pausing to watch over the shoulder of each player for a few moments before scribbling notes in a great and ancient ledger.

As I moved in for a closer look at the puzzles themselves (which seemed to depict either a saint with a golden glow around his head or a moonlit rock protruding from a midnight sea) I was warned off by a dark figure in clerical garb (could it be the vicar?) who, by hand gestures, made it quite clear that any interference would be punished at once by the man with the shovel.

I spun round and found myself face-to-face with the punisher—the man with the shovel. Miss Tanty.

I awoke instantly and sat up in bed, my heart pounding.

If I had not known it before, I now knew how Mr. Collicutt had been killed and why.

The clock showed that it was ten minutes to five. Too late to catch another forty winks.

I jumped out of bed onto a cold floor, dashed cold water from the ewer onto my hands and face, and climbed into the starched frilly white frock Mrs. Mullet had laid out for me, like a railway driver climbing onto the footplate of his engine.

Esmeralda's egg, steamed, and a couple of pieces of bread toasted over the Bunsen burner made for a hearty breakfast.

I took a cork from a drawer and charred it in the burner's flame. When it had cooled, I applied it to my eyelids with special attention to the lowers, then rubbed at the soot until it had faded to a realistic purplish gray.

As a finishing touch, I twisted my hair into a tangled rat's nest and sprayed cold water from an atomizer onto my brow.

I looked at myself in the mirror.

With clots of egg still clinging to my lips, the effect was remarkably convincing.

Father, Daffy, and Feely were already at the table as I stumbled into the dining room and looked around dazedly.

I took my seat without a word and sat motionless, my hands folded dismally in my lap.

"Good God!" Feely said. "Look at you!"

Father and Daffy looked up from their dry toast.

"I—I—I'm afraid I'm going to have to be excused," I managed. "I'm sorry. I've hardly slept. I think it must have been something I ate."

I put my cupped hand to my mouth and puffed out my cheeks.

"Have a piece of toast," Father said. "Then go straight back upstairs to bed. I'll look in on you when we get home."

"Thank you," I said. "But I'm not hungry.

"A good long sleep will do me the world of good," I added, echoing Mrs. Mullet.

Back upstairs I changed from Easter frock to skirt and sweater, and from my Goody Two-shoes into plimsolls.

Minutes later I was crawling—quietly, carefully—out the window of the portrait gallery on the ground floor.

It had rained in the night and Gladys was wet. I gave her a good shaking, and the drops of cold condensation flew like a shower of diamonds in the moonlight.

In less than ten minutes we would be at St. Tancred's.

·TWENTY-SIX·

A FRAIL FOG DRIFTED up from the river behind the church, floating like gray smoke among the graves, muffling the sound of the running water.

A churchyard in the March moonlight should be enough to give anyone the ging-gang-goolies, but not this girl.

After all, I had been here before.

I pounded my chest with both fists and breathed deeply of the morning's damp air—a mixture of dank earth, wet grass, and old stone, with a slight aftertaste of fading flowers.

I could see why clergymen loved their jobs.

The ladies from the Altar Guild would soon be here, so I'd have to be quick about what I'd come to do. With any luck, I'd have perhaps an hour, or at most an hour and a half before they arrived with armloads of Easter lilies.

Not that I would need that long. My dream had helped the last bits of the puzzle to fall into place. Before the dream, although I'd had all the facts, I hadn't seen how they fit together.

But now, as sure as shandygaff, I knew what I was going to find, and where I was going to find it.

I stepped into the porch and flicked on the torch, taking care to keep the beam focused on the floor. Seen from outside, the slightest glimmer on the stained-glass windows would make the church glow like a Tiffany lamp in the graveyard.

I opened the inner door and passed from the porch into the main body of the church, or, as Feely would have said, from the narthex into the nave. When it came to ecclesiastical architecture, Feely loved to toss around technical terms as if she were chatting over tea and ladyfingers with the Archbishop of Canterbury, or perhaps even the Pope. Did the Pope drink tea? I didn't know, but I was sure Feely would be able to hold forth upon the subject until the cows came home with the cream.

I stood in the center aisle and listened.

The place was filled with that utter silence which only churches can have—a silence so vast, so timeless, and so loud that it hurts the ears, an echoing vacuum of negative sound.

Could it be the crying-out of the dead who lay stacked within the walls and in the crypt below? Were they lying in wait, as Daffy had once told me, to seize the midnight visitor and drag you down with them into their coffins where they would munch on your bones until the Last Judgment at which time they would spit them out and make haste for Heaven?

Stop it, Flavia! I thought.

Why did I allow my mind to fill with such utter rubbish? I had been here before in the night and had seen
nothing worse than Miss Tanty.

Miss Tanty and Cynthia Richardson.

Now that I stopped to think about it, St. Tancred's in
the wee hours was almost as busy as Victoria Station at
midday.

The boat train to Heaven.

Stop it, Flavia!

I was allowing the place to get on my nerves and I
didn't like it at all.

I moved up the aisle a step at a time—a slow procession of one.

Then suddenly, in my mind, perhaps to keep me company, Daffy was pacing along behind me, chanting in a
solemn, hollow voice, "'Let's talk of graves, of worms and
epitaphs . . .'"

Stop it, Flavia! Stop it at once!

With any luck I was just minutes away from success.
Mere moments away from—

Something creaked.

Something wooden, by the sound of it.

I froze.

Listened . . .

Nothing.

This is ridiculous, I thought. Besides their stones, old
churches are full of oak and elm. The timbers of the roof
which arched above my head, the pews, the pulpit, the
railings were all, once upon a time, trees in an English
forest. They had once been alive—were, perhaps, still
alive, settling, stretching their sinews in their sleep.

I moved up the aisle toward the organ, not daring to

raise the torch's beam to see if Saint Tancred was still dripping.

Splotches of colored moonlight came angling in through the windows, making the shadows all the darker.

Now I had reached the organ, its three keyboards gleaming in the darkness like a triple set of teeth.

Something creaked. Again.

Or was it something else?

I shifted the beam of the torch and the carved wooden imp grinned at me in the gloom.

I pressed my ear to the wooden panel and listened, but there was not the faintest sound from the organ chamber.

A twist of the imp's chubby cheeks and the panel slid open.

I stepped inside.

Here I was again. The spot where Mr. Collicutt died—the spot where, unless I was sadly mistaken, Mr. Collicutt had hidden the Heart of Lucifer.

It was simply a matter of threading the facts together in the right order, like pearls on a string. Once that was done, the solution was not difficult. I could hardly wait to explain it all to Inspector Hewitt—to deliver it up as a goodwill offering with every last bow and every blessed ribbon tied beautifully in place.

He would, of course, share the details with his wife, Antigone, who would ring me up at once and invite me round to tea once again, in spite of my past social blunders.

She would remark on the brilliance of my solution and I would say that it was nothing.

The organ pipes rose all around me—thousands of them, it seemed, rank after rank like mountain peaks of tin and wood.

Each pipe had its mouth, a horizontal slit near the bottom through which it spoke, and I was as sure as I could be that into one of these, Mr. Collicutt had shoved the Heart of Lucifer.

The question had been: *Which one?*

I had spent hours sitting on the organ bench with Feely, watching as she pulled out the stops which gave the organ its voice: the Lieblich Bourdon, the Geigen Principal, the Contra Fagotto, the Gemshorn, the Voix Céleste, the Salicet, the Dulciana, and the Lieblich Gedact.

In which set of pipes would Mr. Collicutt have hidden the Heart of Lucifer?

Oddly enough, it had been the cast-off row of stop knobs in his bedroom that had first put the question into my head.

"Where would an organist hide a diamond?"

It was like a riddle, and like a riddle, the answer, once you saw it, was laughably obvious.

"In the *Gems*horn!"

Feely had explained that the Gemshorn pipes were the ones that were meant to sound like flutes made from animal horns—the ones that looked to me like pygmy blowguns.

There must have been two dozen of the things, ranging in length from several feet to a couple of inches. The smallest ones were too small to conceal anything, their slots too narrow to shove anything inside.

I decided to begin with the largest pipe.

I inserted my first two fingers into its metal mouth and felt both upward and downward—above the slot and below it.

The inside of the pipe was as smooth as a tea canister.

Very well, then—on to the next.

I couldn't hold back a smile as I worked. Feely had complained that the organ had been out of sorts for weeks but she had mistakenly blamed it on the weather.

But I knew otherwise.

Who would have thought that a hidden diamond was giving the poor, tired old instrument a frog in its throat?

Flavia de Luce, that's who!

"Flavia, you rascal, you," I whispered, and shoved my fingers into the mouth of the next pipe.

There's an unwritten law of the universe which assures that the thing you seek will always be found in the last place you look. It applies to everything in life from lost socks to misplaced poisons, and it was certainly at work here.

The only pipe I hadn't yet checked of the Gemshorn rank was the one farthest from the sliding panel through which I had entered the organ chamber.

I made a mighty stretch to reach it—said a silent prayer—and slid my hand into the slot.

My fingers touched something!

There was a lump inside the pipe—a dried lump, like a petrified prune.

I felt the thing, gently outlining its size and shape with my fingertips.

It was, perhaps, the size of a walnut, and about the same texture.

I wiggled it and with a hollow *snap* the thing came free and dropped into my hand.

Careful, I thought. *Don't let it fall down inside the pipe.*

I worked the object slowly, carefully toward the slot

until at last I was able to draw it out into the light of the torch.

What bitter disappointment!

It was nothing but a lump of old putty.

I wedged the torch between two of the organ pipes and, using the thumbs of both hands, dug my nails into the lump and split it open as if cracking an egg.

The Heart of Lucifer!

My heart gave a bound and I'm afraid I said something quite unsaintly which I would not be proud of later.

Brought to life by the torch's beam, the huge diamond lay in my hand, shooting off sparks of light into the surrounding darkness like a new sun hatching.

As I had suspected, Mr. Collicutt had stuck the stone inside an organ pipe.

How clever of him, I thought, *and how much more clever of me to figure out how to find it.*

The Heart of Lucifer! Imagine!

I could hardly wait to tell Father.

I was holding the giant gem between thumb and forefinger, turning it from side to side, sending reflections dancing in their thousands, when a voice behind me said:

"Seize her, Benson!"

And then everything happened at once. Someone grabbed my upper arm and dug powerful fingers into my muscles. My entire arm went weak.

I spun round, kicking out at my attacker even as I twisted away, having the pleasure of feeling my shoe meet shin.

"Damn you!" a pained voice said. "I'll teach you to—"

And then the torch went out.

My elbow had knocked it from between the organ pipes and it hit the wooden floor with a dull thud.

We were now in total darkness and I opened my mouth to scream. But I did not.

Rather, I did something I expect I will never forget.

Hands grabbed at me and slipped off again as I pulled back and banged among the pipes. The wind chest was somewhere in the corner. Perhaps I could scramble up on top of it and hide behind—

Powerful hands had seized one of my ankles and were twisting . . . twisting—

And then the torch came on. Someone had retrieved it from the floor and was shining the beam directly into my eyes.

"Where is it?" thundered a voice from the darkness behind the light.

The voice of Ridley-Smith, the magistrate. I was sure of it.

"Hand it over," another voice demanded, and my arm was wrenched almost out of its socket. I could see strange fingers digging into my whitening wrist.

"Hand it over and be quick about it."

"Hand what over?" I gasped. "Let go of me. I don't know what you're talking about."

"The stone!" a voice rasped, hot in my ear. I could smell the man's breath and it was nothing to write home about.

My first reaction was to stall for time. How long would it be before help could arrive?

An hour? It might as well be an eternity.

Benson (for I could now see with my own eyes that he was my attacker) seized my shoulders and gave me the kind of shake a terrier gives a rat.

I could feel my brain slapping against my brainpan.

"No games," he hissed, his temper short. "Hand it over."

I held out my empty hands in front of me.

"There must be some mistake," I told him, trying my best to stare with open-eyed honesty into the torch's blinding beam. "Honest."

Another shake, more painful than the first.

"You're hurting me," I told him, my head spinning. "Let me go."

Another bone-rattling shake.

I couldn't take much more of this. There was no escape. Both Benson and the magistrate were barring the only way out of this hellish chamber.

I needed to change tactics.

Slightly.

"All right," I said. "I know that the two of you murdered Mr. Collicutt."

The shaking stopped. First point went to me.

"Right here," I added, gesturing with my hand to take in the entire organ chamber, my breath coming in gasps. "I know that—you and your men—have been tunneling in from the churchyard—to steal the stone—for ages—maybe years. I know that you, Magistrate Ridley-Smith—came across the account—of the Heart of Lucifer—in the Public Record Office—the documents held at Chancery Lane. You hid it there in a pile of ancient charters. Who else but someone in the legal professions would have access?"

I was breathing heavily—as overwound as a six-shilling clock.

The Magistrate said nothing. I hadn't been convincing enough.

"Mr. Collicutt was one of your—" (What was the word? Flunkies? Hirelings? Daffy would know.) "Employees," I settled for, aware even as I said it that it was a pretty weak choice of words. "He double-crossed you. You had a falling-out. You murdered him right here in the organ chamber. Method? Diethyl ether. Murder weapon?"

I paused dramatically. *Stretch it as long as you can*, I thought.

"A handkerchief soaked in ether and held in place by a gas mask. And then you dragged him off through the tunnel and dumped his body in the chamber on top of Saint Tancred's tomb."

There was a dead silence during which Benson let go of my shoulders.

"That's why you forced the bishop to withdraw his faculty. You knew what they would find when the tomb was opened, and it was too late to move the body again."

During all of this, Magistrate Ridley-Smith had remained silent. But now he spoke, his words curiously soft in the stone chamber.

"Is that what you think?" he asked. "Is that what you honestly think?"

"Yes!" I shot back, trying to inject a certain tone of accusation into my voice.

"I'm afraid you have sadly misinterpreted the facts, young lady," he said.

Ha, I thought. *I know what he's up to! Young lady, indeed!*

He was going to sneak round the back and try to win me over with fake respect.

"*Have* I?" I asked, as coldly and condescendingly as I could manage given the situation.

"You have indeed," he answered, putting such heart into his words that for a moment I was almost tempted to believe him. Had I detected in his voice a sense of being shaken?

"You have indeed," he repeated. "The truth is quite the contrary."

I let him see me bite my lip. How much longer could I stall?

"*O, blessed ladies of the Altar Guild,*" I prayed. "*Sprout wings! Now! Fly to my defense!*"

"What *is* the truth?" I heard myself blurt, recalling vaguely that Pontius Pilate had once used similar words but in quite different circumstances.

"The truth is that we tried desperately to revive Collicutt. Benson used a length of hose from the tower. Connected it to some sort of valve in the organ here. Tried to give him air. But it was no use."

The air hose? I hadn't thought of that! It would certainly explain the exploded intestines.

"I don't believe you," I said.

Even as I spoke I heard a sudden stirring in the church behind Benson and the magistrate, followed by the hollow banging down of a kneeling bench onto the stone floor.

Rescue was moments away!

"Help!" I shouted in as high-pitched and bloodcurdling a voice as I could manage. "Help me! Please help me!"

There was a shuffle of footsteps.

And then a large face appeared over the magistrate's shoulder—a face with glasses as thick as the Heart of Lucifer.

It was Miss Tanty!

"What's going on here?" she demanded.

·TWENTY·SEVEN·

NEVER—NOT IN MY DOPIEST dreams—would I have believed I'd be so happy to see the woman.

I brushed roughly past Benson and Magistrate Ridley-Smith and took shelter behind Miss Tanty, peering round from behind her ample skirts.

"What's going on here, Quentin?" she repeated, looking accusingly from one of my attackers to the other, and then at me, her thick spectacles focusing that frightful gaze like twin burning-glasses.

"A misunderstanding," the magistrate said, with an apologetic and counterfeit chuckle. "Nothing more."

"Misunderstanding," Benson echoed, as if entering his own plea.

"I see . . ." Miss Tanty said, wavering on the brink of what to do. She seemed to be of two minds, or perhaps even more.

For a long time she stared at them in silence, and they at her.

"Come along, girl," she said suddenly and, whirling round, seized my arm.

I winced. I hadn't realized how much Benson had hurt me.

Without another word, she led me to the center aisle, and down it we marched together, like some nightmare bride and groom, toward the door.

Outside, the fog had lessened, although the air remained cool. The churchyard was empty. It was still too early for the ladies of the Altar Guild. No one was in sight.

Out the door and down the walk we went toward the road, Miss Tanty pulling me along like a toy dog on a string.

I must have hung back.

"Come along, girl," Miss Tanty repeated. "You've had a bad shock. I can see it in your eyes. We need to get you warm. Get something hot and sweet into you."

I couldn't have agreed with her more. My knees were already beginning to tremble as we turned east toward Cater Street and Miss Tanty's house.

I was suddenly exhausted, as if someone had opened a spigot in my ankle and let my energy pour out onto the ground.

The idea of a cup of tea and a fistful of cookies was both oddly comforting and oddly familiar. Like a fairy tale once heard and long forgotten.

We were walking quickly now as we turned into Cater Street.

"I forgot Gladys!" I exclaimed, stopping suddenly. "My bicycle. I left her in the churchyard."

"I'll fetch her while you have your tea," Miss Tanty said. "I shall ring someone up and have them drive you home."

I had a sudden, ridiculous vision of the someone—Miss Gawl, perhaps—herding me along the narrow road to Buckshaw with a shepherd's crook—or a bishop's crosier—as if I were a wayward lamb.

"It's very kind of you," I said.

"Not at all," Miss Tanty replied, with the most awful and comforting grin.

We reached her house so suddenly that we might have been transported there by magic carpet.

Is this what shock does? I wondered. *Warps time?*

Was it possible to be in shock and yet, at the same moment, observe oneself being in shock?

Miss Tanty fished in her pocket for a key and unlocked the door, which was odd, I thought, since nobody in Bishop's Lacey locks their doors.

As we stepped inside and she shot the bolt behind us, the parrot called out from the conservatory, "Hello, Quentin. All hands on deck!" and it whistled four notes which I recognized as the opening of Beethoven's fifth symphony.

"Dah-dah-dah-DUM!"

Hello, Quentin? I thought. That's what the bird had said when I was here before. It was also the name Miss Tanty had called Benson. No, wait—Benson's name was Martin.

She must have been addressing the magistrate?

"Sit down," Miss Tanty commanded. We had now magically arrived in her kitchen. "I'll put the kettle on."

I looked round at my surroundings and they were blue. It's odd but true. That's chiefly what I remember about it: Miss Tanty's kitchen was blue. I hadn't noticed it before.

On the table was a milk pitcher full of decomposing

lilies, a small breadboard and half a loaf of Hovis bread, an electric toaster, a pewter candlestick with a partially melted candle, and a box of matches.

It was obvious that Miss Tanty's meals were lonely ones.

Then there was, in a jiff, a cup of tea steaming in front of me, and I was feeling peculiarly grateful.

"Drink it," Miss Tanty said. "Take these. Eat them."

She shoved a saucer of shortbreads under my nose, then turned away and began fussing with something in a cupboard.

"Those men," she was saying, too casually—too conversationally. "Those men in the church. What were they doing to you?"

"They thought I had found something," I said. "They wanted me to hand it over."

"And did you?"

"No," I said.

The great goggles swung round and fixed me in their gaze.

"No, you didn't find something? Or no, you didn't hand it over?"

I looked into her eyes, mesmerized, and no words came. "Well?"

Too late, the truth came crashing down.

"I have to go home now," I said. "I'm not feeling well."

Miss Tanty's hands appeared suddenly from behind her back. In one was clutched a glass bottle and in the other, a handkerchief.

She sloshed liquid onto the linen and clapped it to my nose.

Aha! I thought—$(C_2H_5)_2O$.

Diethyl ether again.

I'd recognize its sweet, gullet-tickling odor anywhere.

The chemist Henry Watts had once described it as having an exhilarating odor and the *Encyclopaedia Britannica* had called it pleasant, but it was obvious that neither Professor Watts *nor* the *Encyclopaedia Britannica* had ever had the stuff clapped over their noses in a blue-painted kitchen by a hulking and surprisingly powerful madwoman with bottle-bottom spectacles.

It burned.

It seared my nostrils—tore at my brain.

I struggled to get to my feet—but it was no use.

Miss Tanty had crooked an arm around my neck and, from behind, was pulling me down and backward into the chair. Her other hand was holding the handkerchief firmly over my nose.

"Teach you!" she was saying. "Teach *you*!"

I flailed my arms and kicked out, but it was no use.

Less than ten seconds had passed and my brain was spinning like a whirlpool into a sweet, sickening oblivion. All I had to do was give in to it.

To let myself go.

"No!"

Who had shouted that?

Was it me?

Or was it Harriet?

I had heard the voice distinctly.

"No!"

Now she had let go of my neck and was digging with her hand in one of my pockets—then the other.

I lashed out, fingers spread, and knocked Miss Tanty's glasses from her face.

It wasn't much, but it was enough. I turned my head to one side and sucked my lungs full of fresh air—one quick deep breath and then another—and another.

Without her powerful lenses, Miss Tanty looked round the kitchen, her mad eyes huge and weary, weak, watery, and unfocused.

Fighting my way out of the chair, I dodged to the left but she blocked me with her hips like a rugby player.

I dodged to the right, but she was there also.

Even though I could have been no more than a blur to her, the woman managed to throw herself in front of my every move.

There was no way out. No back door.

Now she had her arm around my neck again, tighter than before.

I saw only one chance.

In desperation I reached out and grabbed the match-box. I ripped it open and the wooden matches spilled out onto the tabletop.

As Miss Tanty's massive hand came sweeping round again with the handkerchief, I scraped a match's head on the wooden breadboard and held it awkwardly out behind me.

It went out.

I had moved too quickly.

I seized another—struck it—and slowly, agonizingly slowly, bent my elbow back toward her.

There was a moment's grace, as if nothing had happened, and then a sound as if an exceptionally large Saint Bernard had just said "Woof!"

A great globe of fire rose up like an orange hot-air balloon to the low ceiling, then came roiling down the walls in waves of black greasy smoke only to boil up again around our ankles in a dense, choking cloud.

For a paper-thin slice of time, Miss Tanty was a frozen statue, one arm holding a flaming torch aloft above her head like Demeter searching the underworld for Persephone, her lost daughter.

And then she screamed.

And went on screaming.

She dropped the blazing handkerchief and blundered from wall to wall, beginning now to cough.

Cough . . . scream . . . cough . . . scream.

It was enough to shatter anyone's nerves.

Round and round the room she spun, crashing into the furniture like a monstrous and maddened bluebottle fly, rebounding from one smoking wall to another.

By this time, I was coughing, too, and my face felt as if I had fallen asleep for hours in an August seaside sun.

I stamped out the flames of the burning handkerchief.

Miss Tanty was still screaming.

"Stop it," I told her, throwing open the window, but she paid me no attention, flying round the room with one wrist clasped in her other hand.

"Stop it," I said again. "Let me have a look."

I had already had a look, and could see that her hand was burned.

"Stop it," I told her, but she screamed on and on. "Stop it!"

I slapped her face.

I may not be as nice a person as I like to believe I am, because I have to admit that in rather an unexpected way, it gave me a great deal of pleasure to let her have it. Not because this was a creature who just moments ago had tried to murder me—not because there was any vengeance in the act—but somehow because it was, in the circumstances, the correct thing to do.

She stopped screaming instantly and looked at me as if she had never seen me before in her life.

"Sit down," I ordered, and wonder of wonders, she meekly obeyed. "Now give me your hand."

She stuck out a reddened fist, staring at it as if it belonged to a stranger—anyone but her.

I rummaged through half a dozen kitchen drawers before finding a lint dishcloth, which I draped over her wrist. I reached for the bottle of ether which she had put down on the draining board.

I pulled out the stopper and poured it over the dishcloth, watching the look of cool relief which spread across her face as she looked up at me in dumb adoration or something.

I flung open cupboards beneath the sink and finally, in a swiveled storage bin, found what I was looking for: a potato.

I half peeled it, then cut slices so thin that you could have read the Bible through them. With these, I made a wet poultice with which, having removed the cloth, I dressed her hand and wrist.

"Hurts," Miss Tanty said, staring up into my face with her great moon eyes, her glasses trampled to shards on the floor.

"Hard cheese," I told her.

·TWENTY-EIGHT·

I FLEW OUT OF Miss Tanty's house as if all the hunting hounds of Hell were at my heels, and perhaps they were.

Round the corner and into the high street I ran, and within a minute I was pounding on the door of PC Linnet's cottage, part of which served as Bishop's Lacey's police station.

In a surprisingly short time, the tousle-haired constable was at the door, pulling on his blue uniform jacket, his brow wrinkled, his eyebrows raised into a pair of upward-pointing Vs.

"Miss Tanty's house," I shouted. "Quickly! Attempted murder!" Leaving the astonished constable standing on his doorstep, I dashed off in the opposite direction toward Dr. Darby's surgery.

Would Miss Tanty still be in her kitchen when the police arrived? I had reason to believe she would. In the first place, the woman was in shock, and in the second, she was not constructed with sprinting in mind. And in the third, come to think of it, there was nowhere to hide. Bishop's Lacey was not big enough for bolt-holes.

I was in luck. When I reached the surgery, Dr. Darby was already outside, using a pail and sponge to wash the mud and dust of a country practice from his bull-nosed Morris.

"Miss Tanty's burned her hand," I told him breathlessly. "Ether explosion! I've already applied cold ether and a potato poultice."

Dr. Darby nodded wisely, as if this happened every morning before breakfast. As he ducked into the surgery for his bag, I was off again.

I could be there before him. Or so I thought.

But his Morris passed me even before I reached Cow Lane.

I overtook PC Linnet just as he reached Miss Tanty's gate.

"Stay here," he ordered, holding up a most official hand. "Outside," he added, as if I might not have understood.

"But—"

"No buts," he said. "This is now a crime scene. We have our orders."

What did he mean by that? Had Inspector Hewitt specifically forbidden me access?

After all that I had done for him?

Constable Linnet vanished into the house before I could ask a single question.

A moment later, Miss Tanty began screaming again.

Father, Feely, and Daffy were walking along the road toward me as I came round the corner of the churchyard wall.

The heat from the ether explosion had left my face feeling as if it had been irradiated, but now, at least, I knew firsthand how Madame Curie must have felt.

My skirt and sweater were in ruins, my hair ribbons hanging in scorched remnants.

"Look at you!" Feely said. "Where have you been? You can't possibly go into the church like that, can she, Father?"

Although Father glanced in my direction, I knew he was not really seeing me.

"Flavia," was all he said, before looking sluggishly away and fixing his gaze on some far horizon of his own.

"I thought you were sick," Daffy said.

Daffy was always the one to dredge up the incriminating details.

"I'm feeling much better now," I said, remembering suddenly that I still had burned cork smudged around my eyes.

"Good morning, all," said a voice behind me. It was Adam Sowerby. I hadn't heard him pull up in his silent Rolls-Royce.

"What's happened to you, then?" he asked. "Bit too much sun?"

I nodded. I could have hugged the man.

"I've just come from Dr. Darby's surgery," I said, which was true. "He says it's nothing to worry about." Which was a lie.

"Hmmm," Adam said. "Well, I'm no doctor, I'm afraid, but I do have a few clever tricks up my sleeve from my wanderings up the Limpopo, and so forth. If it's all right with you, Haviland," he said, addressing Father, "I think we—"

Father nodded vaguely, not as if he had really heard, but as if he were trying to keep his head from rolling off his shoulders and into the dirt.

"Let's get on with it," Feely said. "I need to run through the anthem, and I've no time for . . ."

She waved a hand at me as if to add "this sort of thing." She was anxious, I knew, to get at the organ. After all, today was her official debut on the bench.

Father was still staring vaguely off across the fields, but as Feely and Daffy marched off toward the church door, he followed slowly—almost obediently.

Daffy looked back over her shoulder at me as if I were a freak in the peep show.

What on earth, I wondered, *could be happening with the sale of Buckshaw?* I had been so busy with my own concerns I hadn't even thought to ask.

Dared to ask.

But now, seeing Father so like a wraith had moved something somewhere deep inside me.

In a way, I was proud of him. Whatever devils were gnawing at his guts hadn't kept him from his Easter duty. Somewhere inside, my father was a man who still had faith, and I hoped, for his sake, that it would be enough.

"This way," Adam was saying, and he led me round the church, through the churchyard, past the still-slumbering Cassandra Cottlestone to the river bank. I shuddered slightly as I recalled that it was here, on this very spot, that I had once encountered the murderer of Horace Bonepenny. That had been almost a year ago, but it might as well have been in another life.

Adam scrambled down the damp bank and pulled out a cluster of daffodils by their roots.

"You're getting your boots muddy," I told him.

"So I am," he said, glancing down, but he didn't seem to care.

He climbed back up and fished a penknife from the pocket of his vest.

"Do you know what this is?" he asked, cutting a bulb into several slices.

"A daffodil," I said.

"Besides that."

"Narcissine," I said. "In the roots. $C_{16}H_{17}ON$. Deadly poison. If someone crosses you, serve them boiled daffodil bulbs and pretend you thought they were onions."

"Phew!" Adam whistled. "You certainly know *your* onions, don't you?"

"Yes, I do," I told him. "And my daffodils as well."

He separated the cool slices of bulb and rubbed them gently, one at a time, on my face, singing as he worked:

"When daffodils begin to peer,
With, hey! the doxy over the dale,
Why, then comes in the sweet o' the year,
For the red blood reigns in the winter's pale."

He had a pleasant voice, and sang the song with as much confidence as if he were used to performing it on stage.

"What does it mean?" I asked. "*The red blood reigns in the winter's pale?*"

"That blood will out," he said, "even in the coldest surroundings."

In spite of myself, I shivered, and it wasn't just because Adam was rubbing the cooling poison onto my face and neck.

Blood and daffodils. It sounded like the title of a mystery novel by some sweet old lady who dealt in death and crumpets.

This whole business had been blood from beginning to end: my blood, bat's blood, frog's blood, saint's blood, and Mr. Collicutt's lack of.

And daffodils. A fistful of daffodils and crocuses had brought me face-to-face with Miss Tanty. What was it she had said—*Don't waste your crocuses?*

"Do you suppose—" I asked.

"Shhh!" Adam said. "We don't want to get any of this in your mouth, do we?"

With no encouragement on my part, he went on:

"Daffodils,
That come before the swallow dares, and take,
The winds of March with beauty."

His words painted images in my mind, and I thought of Father and of Gladys and of flowers. We would never see another spring at Buckshaw.

"I hate daffodils," I said, and was suddenly in tears.

Adam went on, pretending he hadn't noticed.

" *'Violets . . . pale primroses . . . bold oxlips and the crown imperial . . . lilies of all kinds, the flower-de-luce being one.'* Old Bill Shakespeare was well up on the plant kingdom, you know."

"You're making this up to make me feel better," I said.

"I assure you I'm not," he said. "You'll find it in *The Winter's Tale*. You de Luces have been around for a remarkably long time."

"Ouch!" I said. Adam was now applying the daffodil juice to a particularly tender spot on my nose.

"Yes, they do sting a bit, don't they?" Adam asked. "I expect it's the narcissine. The alkaloids have a tendency to—"

"Oh, shut up," I said, but now I was laughing at him.

How could he ever understand?

It was quite hopeless.

"That's you patched up, then," he said. "Shall we go inside?"

"Inside?" I asked, taking hold of my skirt and spreading it like a fan. "Won't you be ashamed to be seen with me?"

Adam only laughed and, taking my arm, led me upward between the old stones of the churchyard.

Heads turned and bodies swiveled in pews as we made our way up the aisle. No sooner had we squeezed into the front pew beside Father and Daffy than Feely struck up the opening chords of the processional hymn.

Now the choir was coming in procession from the back of the nave, singing their rousing morning song as the organ roared.

As they came abreast of our little party, not one of the singers failed to swivel his or her eyes sideways for a furtive glance at me, although they pretended not to.

There I sat as primly as I could manage, my eyes blackened with burned cork, my face and neck reddened by the blast and shiny with the poisonous juices of the daffodil, my clothing filthy with dust from the organ chamber, scorched and charred with the soot of an ether explosion.

Even the vicar's eyes widened as he went past singing:

"The lamb's high banquet call'd to share,
Array'd in garments white and fair . . ."

The diapason rumbled, shivering the age-stained pews, making the old wood tremble as it shook the fabric of the ancient church.

·TWENTY-NINE·

I DON'T REMEMBER MUCH about the Easter service. To me, it was no more than a blur of singing, standing, kneeling, and parroting responses.

I was told afterward that Feely was brilliant, that the choir sang like angels (even without Miss Tanty), and that the keyboard work set a new standard of musical virtuosity in Bishop's Lacey. Of course, I had only Sheila Foster's word to go on, and since Fossie was Feely's best friend, I wouldn't bet a bundle on her opinion.

The unwritten rule for exiting St. Tancred's was "Front rows first," so that after the benediction, as we bolted for the doors, we always had the opportunity to see who had come in after us.

As we shuffled toward the back of the church, there, completely unexpected, about four rows from the back and seated on the aisle, were Inspector Hewitt and his wife, Antigone. Because I was still suffering some embarrassment over my brash behavior last time we had met, I needed to proceed with caution. Should I look away, perhaps? Give an elaborate greeting to someone on the far aisle and pretend I hadn't seen her? Fake a coughing fit and stumble past with eyes squeezed shut?

I needn't have worried. As I hove alongside, Antigone got to her feet, reached out a slender gloved hand, took my arm, and pulled me to her.

She whispered in my ear.

And when she had finished, I'm afraid I fairly beamed. I even shoved a fist into her seated husband's surprised face and insisted on giving him a hearty shake.

No wonder he adored the woman!

Outside, everyone was gathering in knots in the church-yard to gossip and pretend they were exchanging Easter greetings. Even though the real old chin-wagging wouldn't take place until the later service, the villagers of Bishop's Lacey put on rather a good show for such an ungodly hour—except for Father, who came out the door, gave the vicar a token handshake, and walked slowly off toward home, his eyes fixed firmly on the ground.

I decided definitely in that instant to tackle him. As soon as I got back to Buckshaw I would march straight in and demand to be told what was going on— What was the situation with Buckshaw?

I would demand to hear the gist of his mysterious telephone call and why it had thrown him into such a tizzy.

I had not seen the estate agent since the day he'd pounded in the For Sale sign at the Mulford Gates. Perhaps Dogger would know.

Yes, that was it—I would consult with Dogger before bearding Father in his den.

I was idling beside a gravestone waiting for the Hewitts to emerge when Adam came strolling toward me.

"How's the narcissine holding up?" he asked. "Any pain?"

I shook my head. I wasn't going to share my inner workings with Adam Sowerby, MA., FRHortS, etc., even if we were partners, so to speak, bound together by my most solemn pledge.

Not that that meant anything.

"Wizard stuff," I said in as offhand a manner as I could manage. "A neat trick. Wherever did you learn it?"

"As I told you," he began, "in my wanderings up the Limpopo—"

And then he stopped.

"Actually," he said, "Mad Meg taught me. As a boy, I stayed with an auntie at Malplaquet Farm. One day on my summer rambles I ran across Meg at the old gibbet in Gibbet Wood. She was digging for moss from dead men's skulls."

Even though it hurt, my eyes widened.

"All nonsense, of course. And yet . . ."

"And yet?" I asked.

"When it comes right down to it, she was my first instructor in botany."

"I think she's a witch," I told him. "A Christian witch, but still a witch. Rather like the woman in the story Daffy read to us who could believe in the banshee and also in the Holy Ghost."

Adam laughed. "She's what they used to call a 'simpler.' Someone who gathers herbs in the wild and sells them to the chemists."

"Meg?"

"Yes, Meg. Sells them to the doctors, too, but don't let on I told you."

I must have looked skeptical.

"Where do you suppose the chemists and apothecaries got all their knowledge about plants? Most of those old boys have never set foot in the countryside."

"From the simplers?" I guessed.

"Right. From the simplers, the old women who gather the plants of the woods and hedgerows. Centuries of se-crets handed down in whispers. And where do you think the physicians learn the same secrets?"

"From the chemists and apothecaries."

"Bull's-eye!" Adam said. "It's a pleasure having you as a partner, Flavia de Luce. I predict that we have great things ahead of us.

"Speaking of which," he added, "here comes one of them now.

"Ah, Inspector Hewitt," he said. "I knew it would be only a matter of time."

The Inspector wasn't quite scowling, but he was not the same man I had seen just minutes ago in the pews. Somewhere between church and churchyard he had put on a new face, and an official one at that.

Antigone had been held back at the church door, the vicar clutching her hand and whispering into her ear. Both were blushing.

"Well?" the Inspector said, looking from one of us to the other. He was not tapping his foot, but he might as well have been.

"It was a plot," I said. "Magistrate Ridley-Smith is the ringleader. He's been using local workmen. Mr. Battle, the stonemason, is one—and his helpers, Tommy and Norman. I don't know their surnames. His man, Benson, is another. They've been tunneling into Saint Tancred's crypt for ages—perhaps years.

"Come and I'll show you," I said, waving toward the back of the churchyard. "They tunneled in through the old Cottlestone tomb."

"No need," the Inspector said. "We've already seen it."

At the word "we" he glanced away and I saw Detective Sergeants Woolmer and Graves walking toward us through the churchyard.

"Good work, Inspector!" Adam said. "I've been making a few inquiries on my own and—"

"So I've been told," the Inspector interrupted, rather coldly. "We'd appreciate it if you'd leave the detecting to us."

Adam smiled as if he'd just been given the largest compliment in the world.

"Actually, I can tell you that the magistrate and his associates have been detained. There is no further need for your . . . assistance."

"Splendid!" Adam said. "Then I can assume that you've also recovered the Heart of Lucifer?"

There are blank looks and there are blank looks, but Inspector Hewitt's took the biscuit.

He looked from Sergeant Woolmer to Sergeant Graves as if for assistance, but they were equally baffled.

"Suppose you tell me about it," he said at last, still in command.

"Delighted to," Adam replied, and he began at the beginning.

He told of the person named Jeremy Pole, and of his

discovery at the Public Record Office, of the scribblings of Ralph, the Cellarer at Glastonbury Abbey, and his discovery of the words *adamas* and *"oculi mei conspexi"*—"I have seen it with my own eyes."

I couldn't have given a better description myself.

As Adam spoke, Antigone Hewitt and the vicar stepped from the porch and came strolling across the grass toward us. He was still holding her hand, chatting away in an animated manner, their faces both luminous.

Close behind them came Feely and Daffy trailed by Sheila Foster, with Feely stopping every few feet to receive compliments, curtsies, and kissings-of-her-hand from her admiring subjects.

But soon enough they were all of them surrounding us in a ring, listening intently as Adam finished his tale. It reminded me of a village Maypole dance with the villagers, dressed in their Easter finery, swarming in from every point of the compass for an impromptu gathering upon the green.

"And so the Heart of Lucifer was buried with the saint at Bishop's Lacey," Adam concluded, "where it has lain hidden these five hundred years. Until recently."

He looked round at the gaping faces like a born storyteller.

"And where is it now?" Inspector Hewitt asked. "This stone of Saint Tancred?—this Heart of Lucifer?"

I couldn't resist for a moment longer.

"Here!" I shouted. "In my tummy!" I patted said part of myself proudly. "I swallowed it!"

The crowd fell into an uneasy silence, looked at one another in astonishment, and then broke into an excited babble as at Babylon. I knew, even as I spoke, that until the Heart of Lucifer made its eventual reappearance, Bishop's Lacey would be following my every movement with keen interest.

"I found it in the Gemshorn pipe where Mr. Collicutt had hidden it," I explained. "Magistrate Ridley-Smith and his gang were going to—"

"That's quite enough for now, Flavia," Inspector Hewitt said. "This is neither the time nor the place."

"Quite right, Inspector," I agreed, neatly deflecting his condescending manner. "Especially in view of the fact that there's just been an attempted murder a stone's throw from here in Cater Street. You'll be wanting to get to that, I expect. Constable Linnet's been left alone with a cold-blooded killer."

It was a saucy thing to say, I know, but I was staking everything on my assumption that PC Linnet had been unable to get through by telephone to the Inspector before he left for church. Even if police headquarters in Hinley *had* radioed, the Inspector and his two detective sergeants would not, except for a few minutes, have been in their car to receive the message.

"Attempted murder?" the Inspector asked.

"Cater Street," I said casually. "Miss Tanty's house. The intended victim was me.

"No rush, though," I added. "As I said, Constable Linnet is already on the scene."

I have to give the Inspector full marks, though, for neatly handling a wobbly situation.

"Antigone," he said, turning to his wife, "would you mind running Miss de Luce and her sisters home to Buckshaw in your own car? I'll pop in later for tea and questioning."

Tea and questioning!

I loved the man! Absolutely adored him.

"Thank you, Inspector," I said. "How terribly kind of you."

I'm afraid I pronounced it "teddibly."

"What delicious simnel cake," Antigone Hewitt was saying. "You really must give me your recipe, Mrs. Mullet."

I had tried to warn her off with various signs such as crossed eyes, tongue lolling out, and half an upper lip drawn up like a mad dog as the plate was passed round, but it was no use.

"I always makes it for Easter," Mrs. Mullet said, "but nobody's 'ungry this year. 'Ave an 'ot cross bun else I'll 'ave to toss 'em out."

This was said with a dark look at Feely, Daffy, and me, but it didn't do the slightest bit of good. We sat on our hands as if we had been born that way.

"Thank you, I shall," Antigone said, and she buttered a bun in the way I imagine Moira Shearer should have done if Moira Shearer buttered hot cross buns.

"Mmmm, delicious," she lied through her perfect white teeth.

"You played beautifully this morning," she said, turning to Feely.

Feely blushed prettily.

"Thanks to Flavia," she said. "The organ has been sounding sickly recently because of that stone detuning one of the stops."

Thanks to Flavia? I could hardly believe my ears!

Praise from Feely was as scarce as water on the sun and

yet this was the second time in days she had thrown me a compliment.

I hardly knew what to do with it.

And to refer to the Heart of Lucifer as "that stone"!

I had not yet broken the news of Saint Tancred being a de Luce. It was a thunderbolt I was keeping for Father.

Even if it were a piece of news which meant the saving of Buckshaw, it was crucial that it be broken only when the moment was precisely right. It wasn't that long ago that Father had refused to sell a rare Shakespeare folio which might have secured our family's future. He needed to be tackled tactfully.

"May I be excused?" I asked. "I need to feed my hen."

Daffy snorted, as if I were surreptitiously headed for the WC.

"Perhaps you could bang out some Beethoven for Mrs. Hewitt," I suggested to Feely. "I shall be back in a few minutes."

Without waiting for permission, I made for the foyer, and for the cubicle beneath the stairs in which the forbidden instrument was caged. A quick glance into the Hinley telephone directory gave me the information I needed.

"Hinley 80," I told Miss Goulard at the exchange. It was the perfect number for an eye doctor—a pair of spectacles on edge followed by a monocle.

"Mr. Gideon's surgery," said a gravelish female voice. "Sondra speaking."

It sounded as if she were suppressing a titter.

"Good morning, Sondra," I began, diving in with both feet. "I'm calling for Miss Tanty in Bishop's Lacey. She seems to have mislaid the card for her next appointment. I wonder if you could check your diary?"

"The office is closed. It's Easter Sunday, you know."

Of course it was! How could I have forgotten that.

"Call back next week," she said, and let off a convulsive round of smoker's cough.

"I'm afraid we can't," I improvised. "We shall be in . . . Wales."

I didn't care whether this made sense or not. The great thing was to keep her on the line.

"Sorry—call back Monday."

"Hold on," I said. "What are you doing there if the office is closed?"

"I'm just the char, luv. Eyes are nothing to do with me. Not my department."

"Then why did you pick up the telephone?"

Another ominous cough, and then a strangulated chuckle.

"Truth be told, luv, I thought it was Nigel, my fie-yancey. Nigel always rings me up to see how my sweater's fitting. Always been a card, has Nigel. Call back next week."

"Listen, Sondra," I said. "Just between you and me this is a matter of life and death. Miss Tanty is likely to be charged with attempted murder if she hasn't been already. She needs to prove that she was at Mr. Gideon's surgery on Shrove Tuesday—the sixth of February."

Even over the telephone I could hear Sondra's eyes widen.

"Murder, you say?"

"Murder! Or worse—" I said in a horrible whisper, cupping the speaking part of the instrument in my hands and pressing my lips almost into the thing.

"Hang on," Sondra said, and I could hear a rustling of paper at the other end.

"February sixth?" she asked.

"That's right."

"Yes, here it is. The Tuesday. Your Miss Tanty was down for nine-thirty, but she called to cancel it."

"Do you happen to know the time?"

"Right now?" Sondra asked.

"No! The time it was canceled."

"Nine o'clock. I have it right here: 'Miss T called nine-oh-five A.M. cancellation. Rang D. Robertson to fill vacancy.' Initials LG. That would be Laura Gideon, Mr. Gideon's wife."

"Thank you, Sondra," I said. "You're a brick."

"You won't breathe a word, will you? Nigel would be livid if I got the sack."

"My lips are sealed," I vowed, but I don't think she heard me. A new crackle of coughing fought its way through the telephone wires.

As I was making my way back across the foyer, the doorbell rang. It was Inspector Hewitt.

He took off his hat, which meant he intended to come in.

"We're in the drawing room," I told him. "Would you care to join us?"

As if it were a meeting of the Bell-ringers League.

·THIRTY·

"Right, then," Inspector Hewitt was saying. "Let's have it."

I couldn't help thinking how much progress he had made since we had first met nine months ago, upon which occasion he had sent me to fetch the tea.

There was hope for the man yet.

"I expect you've had this figured out right from the starting gate," he said, with a pleasant enough smile.

His wife, Antigone, touched her hair, and I recognized that a secret signal had flown between them.

"That is, I hope you won't mind filling in a few of the blanks for us."

"Of course not," I said in a sort of humble, jolly-girl-well-met kind of voice. "I should be more than happy to assist. Where shall I begin?"

But don't push your luck, his eyes were saying.

"Let's begin with suspicion," he said, taking out his notebook and opening it flat on his knee.

I saw him write down "Flavia de Luce," and underline it.

He had once, in an earlier investigation, added the letter "P" after my name and had refused to explain its meaning. There was no "P" this time.

"When did you first begin to suspect that something peculiar was going on at St. Tancred's?"

"When the sexton—that's Mr. Haskins—mentioned the mysterious lights in the churchyard during the war. Why would he tell me a thing like that unless he wanted to scare me away?"

"So you think Haskins was in on it?"

"Yes. I can't prove it, but a gang of men could hardly tunnel in his churchyard without his knowing about it, could they?"

"I suppose not," Inspector Hewitt said.

First point to Flavia.

"As Mr. Sowerby has told you," I said, "they were after the Heart of Lucifer. They've been at it for ages—years perhaps. Magistrate Ridley-Smith was paying them off—"

This was the point where he had stopped me before, and I paused to see if he would let me go on.

Feely and Daffy were gaping like a pair of guppies and Antigone smiled upon me like a madonna who had just had a foot massage.

It gave me the boldness I needed. There are times when honesty is not just the best policy, but the only one.

"I have to admit I had just a quick look round Mr. Collicutt's room at Mrs. Battle's boardinghouse."

"Yes, I thought you might," the Inspector said. "Good job we'd been there before you."

"I found six hundred pounds hidden under Mr. Collicutt's bed. It was in a Players tin."

I knew in a flash that I was in official hot water.

Exasperation was written all over the Inspector's face, but to his credit, he did not explode. The presence of his wife might have had something to do with it.

"Six hundred pounds," he said, and the words hissed out of his mouth like hot steam.

I smiled brightly, as if I thought I deserved a pat on the head. "It was in an envelope which had once had Magistrate Ridley-Smith's initials embossed on the flap: QRS—Quentin Ridley-Smith. Hardly likely to have been anyone else's. Not many people have three intials which are consecutive letters of the alphabet."

I have to say that Inspector Hewitt was doing a remarkable job of keeping his temper in check. Only the color of his ears betrayed him.

I decided it was time to provide a diversion.

"I expect you noticed that someone had written 'Deceased' after Mr. Collicutt's name on his manuscript?"

"And if we did?"

The man was giving nothing away.

"It was in a woman's handwriting. There were no women in the Battle house except Mrs. Battle and her niece Florence. Mr. Collicutt was said to—"

"Hold on," the Inspector said. "Are you telling me that one of them—"

"Not at all," I said. "I'm simply pointing out a fact. George Battle's handwriting was all over his account books in his work shed. Large and messy. It wasn't him."

From a distant part of the house came the sound of the doorbell, and before we could get back to our duel of wits, Dogger was at the door.

"Detective Sergeants Woolmer and Graves," he announced. "May I show them in?"

It was Feely's place, as eldest member of the family present, to give her assent, but before she could open her mouth, I beat her to it.

"Thank you, Dogger," I said. "Please do."

Woolmer and Graves came into the drawing room and promptly melted into the Victorian wallpaper.

"Six hundred pounds in a Players tin at the Battle residence," Inspector Hewitt said to Sergeant Graves. "Did we note that? I don't remember seeing it."

Sergeant Graves's blush made words unnecessary but he spoke anyway.

"No, sir."

Inspector Hewitt turned to a new page and made a note that did not promise a happy future for poor Graves.

"Carry on, then," he said after an agonizingly long time.

"Well," I went on, "six hundred pounds seemed like a lot of money for a poor country organist. The fact that it was hidden under his bed, rather than being put safely into the bank, suggested something fishy. It was only when I met Jocelyn Ridley-Smith that I put two and two together."

Inspector Hewitt couldn't conceal his puzzlement. "The magistrate's son?"

"Yes. I believe Magistrate Ridley-Smith was doing research in the Public Record Office in London when he came across the marginal note by Ralph, the cellarer at Glastonbury Abbey.

"*Adamas*, it said. 'Diamond,' in Latin. Ralph had seen it with his own eyes. He also said quite clearly that it was buried with Saint Tancred at Lacey. Which is here."

"Go on," the Inspector said.

"He believed that the stone would cure Jocelyn of his affliction."

Antigone gasped, and I loved her for it.

"Mr. Sowerby says diamonds were once believed to be 'a help to lunaticks and such as are posessed with the Devil.' What else would an elderly magistrate want with a diamond?

"Jocelyn is not a lunatic!" I blurted. "He is lonely, he's a captive, and he's suffering from lead poisoning, which he inherited from his mother.

"It's too late for diamonds," I went on. "Or for anything else. There's nothing I can do about the lead poisoning, but I *can* help him with the loneliness—just as Harriet, my mother, did before she died."

The room filled slowly with silence and suddenly there was a lump in my throat. I covered it up by taking several unnecessary but deep sips of tea and blinking casually out the window.

I pretended to scratch an itch that had suddenly arisen in my eye.

"The magistrate," I continued, "could easily have bought a diamond, of course, but it wouldn't be the same as the Heart of Lucifer. It wouldn't have the power of a stone that had been touched by a saint."

The Inspector was looking at me skeptically.

"He's dying of leprosy, you see. Even if I'm wrong about the magic, I expect he planned on fetching enough for the Heart of Lucifer to care for Jocelyn after he's gone. I'm speculating, of course."

"I see," the Inspector said, but I knew he didn't.

"Mr. Collicutt had been in on it from the beginning.

As organist, he could be in the church in the middle of the night without attracting attention. Miss Tanty told me she sometimes heard him playing at strange hours. He must have been the first to enter the lower tomb when the tunnelers had broken through, and he would have crawled into the tomb alone. Neither the opening nor the tomb itself was big enough for two. He levered the lid off the sarcophagus, pried the diamond from the crosier, and pocketed it. He probably told the others that the tomb had already been vandalized. But as I've said, I'm speculating."

"Interesting," Inspector Hewitt said. "And then he returned to the church on the morning of Shrove Tuesday and concealed it in the organ pipe."

"Exactly!" I said.

"Where Magistrate Ridley-Smith and Benson, or Haskins, or his workers—what were their names?" He flipped back through the pages of his notebook. "Thomas Wolcott and Norman Enderby," he said. "Where Magistrate Ridley-Smith and Benson, or Haskins, or Tommy Wolcott and Norman Enderby, or some combination of the above killed him. Is that what you're saying?"

The Inspector was twitting me, but I no longer cared.

"Yes," I said. "But not intentionally. It was Miss Tanty who was trying to kill him."

I waited for my words to have their expected effect, and I was richly rewarded. You could, as Mrs. Mullet once said, have heard a pan drop.

"Miss Tanty," Inspector Hewitt repeated. "And her motive?"

"Thwarted love," I said. "He had spurned her advances."

SPEAKING FROM AMONG *the* BONES

Daffy and Antigone burst into laughter at precisely the same instant. Antigone had the good grace to stifle it at once and put her hand to her mouth. Daffy did not, and I shot her *such* a glare.

"Even more interesting," Inspector Hewitt said, and because I had trained myself to be so adept at reading upside down, I saw him put down *"thwarted love"* in his notebook.

"Perhaps you'd be so good as to explain."

"It was the handkerchief," I said. "I knew as soon as I saw it sticking out from under the gas mask that Mr. Collicutt had not been murdered by a man. The frilly border gave it away."

"Excellent!" the Inspector said. "We had come to much the same conclusion ourselves."

I ventured a peek at Antigone to see if she was paying attention, and she was. She gave me a radiant smile.

"The vessels of his neck were still darkened, even after six weeks."

"Hold on," Inspector Hewitt said. "You're getting ahead of me."

"It's a well-known fact," I said, "that the administration of ether vapor darkens the blood. The fact that his blood vessels were still black after six weeks shows that Mr. Collicutt died after the ether but before his body could reoxygenate his blood."

"Quite sure of that, are you?" the Inspector asked, not looking at me.

"*Quite* sure," I answered. "You'll find it in *Taylor on Poisons*."

I did not mention that I kept this gripping reference on my bedside table as a midnight comforter.

347

"Let's return to Miss Tanty for a moment," the Inspector said. "I don't think I've quite grasped how she managed it."

I gave him a patient smile. "Miss Tanty had planned on having Mrs. Battle drive her to her ophthalmological appointment in Hinley, but when Florence, the niece, telephoned to say Mrs. B was ill, and that Mr. Collicutt had offered to drive her instead, Miss Tanty saw her opportunity.

"But—Mr. Collicutt, rather than going directly to Miss Tanty's house, went first instead to the church to hide the diamond. She probably watched him drive past and stop at the church. She has quite a good view of both the road and the east end of the churchyard.

"She took the bottle of ether—which I suspect she got from Miss Gawl, although I can't prove it—it has 'D.H.U.,' which means District Health Unit, stamped on the bottom in red ink—I took the precaution of pocketing it for evidence—don't worry, the ether explosion vaporized the fingerprints anyway—it's upstairs in my laboratory. You can have a look at it later, if you like."

"There's our missing bottle, then," Detective Sergeant Woolmer growled.

The Inspector nodded grimly as the sergeant gave me a look that I would not exactly describe as appreciative.

"Go on, then."

"Well," I said, "Miss Tanty cornered him in the organ casing and clapped the ether-soaked handkerchief over his nose. It doesn't require great strength and it doesn't take long. Ten seconds, I believe, may be enough to produce unconsciousness.

"Miss Tanty, being much larger than Mr. Collicutt, would have overpowered him easily. In fact, she gave him such a dose of the stuff that he had convulsions."

"Convulsions?" the Inspector said, startled.

"Yes, you'll find the fresh nicks and gouge marks where his heels kicked the wooden pipe casing. They're quite easy to see if you get down on your hands and knees."

The Inspector did not look up, but made another, and this time quite lengthy, entry in his notebook.

"So," he said. "She killed him by administering ether."

"No," I said. "She didn't kill him."

"What!"

He said it with an exclamation mark and about six question marks, which I have not attempted to reproduce here.

"She etherized him and left him for dead. She intended to kill him, but she probably didn't."

The Inspector wrote that down and paused, his Biro hovering, waiting for me to go on.

"Just after she had gone, you see, Magistrate Ridley-Smith and his henchmen came on the scene. You'll find an interesting mixture of footprints in the corners of the organ chamber—workman's boots, and the sole of an unusually small handmade shoe—the magistrate's. They believed, of course, that Mr. Collicutt was dead, and if that were true, the diamond—if it were not in his pockets—might be lost to them forever. They must have spotted some slight sign of respiration. They had to revive him—and quickly!

"Someone—could it have been Mr. Haskins?—who remembered the old ARP trunk in the ringing chamber went up to the tower and fetched down the gas mask, the stirrup pump, and the spare length of rubber hose.

"But they soon found that the hose fitting on the old pump was rotted almost to crumbs. Actually, I spotted that the first time I saw it.

"There wasn't a second to waste. No time to lose fiddling with the bits and pieces. Someone strapped the mask onto his face. They didn't even bother removing the handkerchief—not completely, anyway. Someone else thought of switching on the organ's blower and connecting the hose to the manometer fitting. We know, of course, that at this particular instant, Mr. Collicutt was still alive."

I paused to let my words sink in.

"Of course!" the Inspector said. He was slightly brighter than I sometimes thought. "The broken glass!"

"Exactly," I said. "He grabbed at the glass manometer tube and it broke off in his hand. He was still clutching it six weeks later in the crypt. It might even be that the hiss of the escaping air was what gave them the idea."

"Hmmm," Inspector Hewitt said.

"It must have been a madhouse in that little chamber," I went on. "All they could think of was that they needed to get him talking. To hand over the Heart of Lucifer, or at least tell them where he'd hidden it. But they underestimated the power of air to kill. It required only a touch of the hose—under that great amount of pressure—to instantly rupture most of his internal organs."

"Hold on," the Inspector said. "Where did you get *that* information?"

"Well, it only stands to reason, doesn't it?" I countered.

"How much air pressure does the blower produce?" I asked, turning to Feely, whose face was growing more ashen by the minute.

"Three to five inches," she whispered, looking up from the floor for the first time.

I stared at the Inspector triumphantly.

"Good lord," he said.

"They probably thought they could pump air into his lungs through the gas mask. A similar thing is done in hospitals and in aircraft every day with oxygen masks. A strange idea, to be sure, but people do peculiar things under pressure. Adam—Mr. Sowerby, I mean—told me what unexpected effects diamonds can have on some people."

I shot another glance at Feely, but she was not looking at me. She was staring blankly once more at the carpet.

"You're telling me that Magistrate Ridley-Smith and company did *not* commit the murder, is that it?"

"Yes," I said. "In fact, quite the contrary—they were trying to save his life by applying artificial respiration—trying to resuscitate him. They knew nothing of Miss Tanty's scheme, and she knew nothing about the Heart of Lucifer."

I could see the Inspector mulling this.

"Resuscitate," he said at last. "Rather a big word, isn't it?"

He did not add "for a little girl," but he might as well have.

"It so happens that we were taught artificial respiration in Girl Guides," I said. I did not feel it necessary to add that I had been sacked from that organization for having an excess of high spirits.

"We were thoroughly instructed in the Silvester, the Schaefer, the Holger-Nielsen, and the Barley-Plowman methods."

The first three were true enough, but the Barley-Plowman

method I had invented on the spot simply to put the man in his place.

"I see," the Inspector said, and I hoped he was humbled.

"At any rate," I continued, "the problem is this: At the time he seized the glass tube, Mr. Collicutt was alive. By the time they finally got him connected to the air blower, he was already dead of suffocation from the mask."

"Was he, indeed?" the Inspector asked.

"He was," I said. "The blower did not reoxygenate his blood."

It was going to require the wisdom of Solomon to decide the precise moment of death, and hence the identity of the killer or killers. Was it the ether and the handkerchief, or the gas mask and the wind chest?

In death, split seconds could make the difference between the gallows and a slap on the hand.

"Still, I hope their lifesaving attempts will be found in their favor," I added. "I'd hate to think I'd helped hang an innocent person."

"I shouldn't worry," the Inspector said. "You can be sure that if there's anyone who knows how to get round the courts, it's a magistrate. What are you grinning about?"

It was true. I couldn't help myself.

"I was just thinking of the look on his face when you ask him how it is that Miss Tanty's parrot calls him by his first name."

"I beg your pardon?"

"Hello, Quentin!" I squawked, in my best parrot voice.

Now it was the Inspector's turn to smile.

"I see what you're getting at," he said, and another note went into his notebook.

"One last question, if you don't mind," he added. "This

business of the bleeding saint. It has nothing to do with the case, of course, but I must admit to having a certain personal curiosity. I understand from Mr. Sowerby that you took a sample of the stuff, and that he assisted you in performing a chemical analysis."

"That is correct," I said, a little peeved at Adam for blabbing.

"And? May we be favored with the results?"

"Quite conclusive," I replied. "CH_4N_2O. I subjected it to the nitric acid test for urea. It's bat's urine."

Everybody in the room except Feely was suddenly nodding wisely, as if they had known it all along.

"Adam had already tasted it and come to the same conclusion."

Where was Adam? I wondered. It would have been ever so lovely if he'd been here to witness my triumph.

"I'd be happy to turn over my notes if they have any relevance in this case."

"Indeed," Inspector Hewitt said, getting up and putting away his notebook. "Well, thank you, Flavia. I believe that will be all, at least for now. I'd appreciate it if you'd take Sergeant Woolmer upstairs to retrieve the bottle in question. Antigone?"

He turned toward his wife and offered his hand as she rose from the chaise longue.

I was stunned! I had presented them the case on a silver platter. Where was the lavish thanks? Where was the praise? Where were the congratulations? The plaudits? The accolades, and so forth?

Where were the trumpets?

But suddenly Antigone was taking my hand, her smile shining like the Mediterranean sun.

"Thank you, Flavia," she told me. "I'm sure you've been of enormous assistance. I'll ring you up next week and we shall go shopping in Hinley. A girls' day out—just the two of us."

It was reward enough. I stood there at the window with a sappy smile on my face, not thinking, until long after I had watched her leave, long after her husband had driven her away down the avenue of chestnuts and out through the Mulford Gates toward Bishop's Lacey, to look down at the wreckage of my skirt and sweater.

There was going to be trouble. I could smell it coming.

Just as fear has the taste of copper, so trouble has the smell of lead.

And then, as my thoughts turned to poor Jocelyn Ridley-Smith, I was seized by a sudden idea.

I would beg Antigone to take him with us! Shopping for dresses in Hinley and lunch afterward at the ABC Tea Shop. The three of us would make a feast of buns and clotted cream!

What an adventure for Jocelyn! I was sure we could arrange it. I'd telephone the vicar or even, if necessary, the bishop, just as soon as Father finished with his announcement, whatever it may be.

Daffy and Feely had left without my noticing, and I found myself alone in the drawing room for the first time in ages.

How much longer, I wondered, before strangers would be looking out of our windows and calling the place their own? How much longer before we were tossed out into a cold, uncaring world?

There was a discreet tap—no more than a fingernail on the woodwork—and Dogger entered.

"Pardon me, Miss Flavia," he said.

"Yes, Dogger? What is it?"

"I wanted to say that I took the liberty of listening at the door. You were superb. Absolutely top-notch."

"Thank you, Dogger," I managed, in spite of my eyes brimming suddenly with tears. "That means a lot."

I could have gone on but I hadn't the words.

"Colonel de Luce," he said, "would like to see you in the drawing room in forty-five minutes."

"Just me?" I asked. I was already dreading another ban on my activities.

"The three of you: Miss Daphne, Miss Ophelia, and yourself."

"Thank you, Dogger," I said. I knew better than to beg for details.

I believed I already knew them. But before the dreaded interview, I had a duty to perform.

In silent procession, I would tour the house, perhaps for the last time. I would bid farewell to the rooms that I had loved, and keep clear of the ones I hadn't. I would begin with Harriet's boudoir, even though it was technically off-limits. I would touch her combs and brushes and inhale her scent. I would sit for a while in silence. From there I would proceed to the greenhouse and the coach house, where I had spent so many happy hours chattering with Dogger about everything under a thousand suns.

I would walk, for one last time, the portrait gallery, saying good-bye to my grim old ancestors who were framed in solemn rows. I would tell them that a portrait of Flavia de Luce was not destined to hang among them.

And then the kitchen: the dear kitchen which overflowed with memories of Mrs. Mullet and pilfered supplies. I would sit at the table where Father had talked to me.

From the kitchen, I would proceed up the east staircase to my bedroom, where I would wind up the crank of the old phonograph and put on the Requiem Mass of Wolfgang Amadeus Mozart. I would hear it through.

And finally, my laboratory.

At this point I must end my description.

It is too unbearably sad to go on.

At the appointed hour the three of us came slowly to the drawing room, Feely and Daffy descending from their bedrooms in the west wing, and me, dawdling down the stairs from the east.

I had changed into a clean frock, pulled on my comfortable old cardigan, then touched up my singed face with the powder I had pinched from Feely's room several weeks ago for an experiment involving poisoned cosmetics. I had painted in new eyebrows and a couple of eyelashes with powdered carbon.

We did not speak, but took up our places in silence, as far as we could get from one another, each in her own far corner of the drawing room, awaiting Father's arrival.

Feely fiddled with sheet music, flattening the pages with her hand as if they needed it. Daffy fished a book from behind the cushions of the sofa and began reading at the point where it fell open.

Father, at last, came into the room. He stood for a few moments with his back to us, his hands flat on the chimneypiece, his head bowed.

His hands trembled as he fiddled with his pocket watch.

It was in that instant that I began to love him completely, and in a new and inexplicable way.

I wanted to rush to him, wrap my arms around him, and tell him about the Heart of Lucifer—tell him that there was a chance, however slight, that the stone of the saint would at last bring happiness upon our house.

But I did not, and the reasons are as countless as the grains of the Sahara sands.

"I must tell you," he said at last, turning round, his voice like the ghost of the March wind, "that I have had a piece of news, and that you must prepare yourselves for a very great shock."

The three of us were rapt—staring at him like so many stone statues.

"I have agonized for several days over whether to tell you, or whether, at least for now, to keep it to myself. Only this morning have I come to a decision."

I swallowed.

Good-bye, Buckshaw, I thought. *The house has been sold. We will soon be driven out—forced to leave its dear old stones and timbers, its dreams and its memories, to the barbarians.*

We had never known any home but Buckshaw. To live anywhere else was simply unthinkable.

What would become of Mrs. Mullet? What would become of Dogger?

And of Feely and of Daffy?

What would become of me?

Father turned and moved slowly to the window. He lifted the curtain and looked out for a moment upon his estate, as if the forces of an overwhelming and invisible army were already gathering in the kitchen garden and advancing across the little lawn.

When he turned again, he looked straight into our eyes, first Feely's . . . then Daffy's . . . and finally mine, and his voice broke as he said:

"Your mother has been found."

ACKNOWLEDGMENTS

EVERY BOOK IS A pilgrimage, made in the company of congenial traveling companions, most of whom must remain forever invisible to the reader.

Along the way, these kindred souls have provided kindness, conversation, inspiration, food, friendship, love, support, and thoughtfulness.

As always, my fellow travelers have included my editors Bill Massey at Orion Books in London, Kate Miciak at Random House in New York, and Kristin Cochrane at Doubleday Canada. Loren Noveck and Randall Klein at Random House, New York; my literary agent, Denise Bukowski; and John Greenwell of the Bukowski Agency in Toronto have been of immense assistance.

Family, too, have been there to wave flags and shout encouragement at every way station, and I'd like to especially acknowledge Garth and Helga Taylor, Jean Bryson, and Bill and Barbara Bryson, and to remember with affection the shared enthusiasms and joy in life of my late cousin John Bryson.

The late Miss Doris Vella will also be sorely missed. Her remarkable ability to enter wholly into Flavia's world is unparalleled. Her love and friendship will never be forgotten.

Dr. John Harland and Janet Harland have again volunteered themselves as sounding boards, and have contributed many excellent ideas, as well as functioning as unpaid medical consultants. Any slipups in such specialized matters are, of course, my own.

Special thanks are due to Xi Xi Tabone, who has taken time out from her own busy career to assist in so many thoughtful ways.

And finally, to my wife, Shirley, who has voyaged with me and cheered me along from the very first steps of this journey. Words can never be enough: Only love can settle such an enormous debt.

ALAN BRADLEY IS THE internationally best-selling author of many short stories, children's stories, newspaper columns, and the memoir *The Shoebox Bible*. His first Flavia de Luce novel, *The Sweetness at the Bottom of the Pie*, received the Crime Writers' Association Debut Dagger Award, the Dilys Winn Award, the Arthur Ellis Award, the Agatha Award, the Macavity Award, and the Barry Award, and was nominated for the Anthony Award. His other Flavia de Luce novels are *The Weed That Strings the Hangman's Bag*, *A Red Herring Without Mustard*, *I Am Half-Sick of Shadows*, and *Speaking from Among the Bones*.

ABOUT THE TYPE

This book was set in Goudy Old Style, a typeface designed by Frederic William Goudy (1865–1947). Goudy began his career as a bookkeeper, but devoted the rest of his life in pursuit of "recognized quality" in a printing type.

Goudy Old Style was produced in 1914 and was an instant bestseller for the foundry. It has generous curves and smooth, even color. It is regarded as one of Goudy's finest achievements.